Under The Red Ribbon

by

KAROLYN MILLER

Under the Red Ribbon

Karolyn Miller

Copyright © 2013 Karolyn Miller
All rights reserved.

ISBN-13: 9781492720836
ISBN-10: 1492720836

We need, in love, to practice only this: letting each other go.
For holding on comes easily; we do not need to learn it."

Translations from the poetry of Rainer Maria Rilke

*For my loving father, Joe Friedman
a free spirit,
who rejoiced in the gift of life.*

Lucille

The year is 1926. The Cardinals defeat the Yankees in the World Series, Marilyn Monroe is born and Rudolph Valentino dies. More speakeasies than coffee shops open in New York City and Iowa farmers live by the motto, "Good Farming, Clear Thinking, Right Living."

The day is June 26th, the day Lucille Kramer is to give her high school valedictorian speech. At four thirty in the morning, unable to sleep any longer because of the heat and excitement, she pushes the door open to let in some fresh air, and then walks out to the porch. She is careful not to slam the screen door because she doesn't want to awaken her father who was up late last night rummaging through the cabinets, getting the candles and dishes ready for her mother's tribute. She heard him call out Evelyn's name and then play his harmonica. He did that when he was melancholy.

Leaning on the porch post of the white clapboard farmhouse, she amuses herself by watching the fireflies light up, their way of attracting a mate. She thinks of Harry who has been courting her for years and now doesn't even bother to slick back his hair when he comes to visit.

The sound of grinding gravel and a cloud of dust disrupt her thoughts. Hurrying off the porch, she peers through the thick cluster of poplar trees that separates the house and expanse of grass from the road. Daddy planted the trees to protect his private domain, and now Lucille can only make out the outline of a car speeding away.

Returning to the porch, she trips on the hem of her nightgown and with the moon lighting her way, she spots a note near the spindle railing. Her name is written across the envelope. Whoever wrote it was in a rush: the *i* is not dotted and the loop of the *e* is closed. The *l* could pass for a *t* if it were crossed.

She holds the screen door steady before tiptoeing into the parlor. Eager to know who left the note, she sinks into her mother's chair, the green velvet one with the crochet doily on the headrest, and tears along the edges of the envelope. She removes a piece of lined paper, the kind she uses at school, and reads the short but surprising message. *Lucille, save a dance at the picnic for me. Nick Martin Jr.* Staring at the page, she remembers the only encounter she ever had with him. It took place just a few weeks before Mama died.

Walking home from school, her arms had given way because her books were too heavy, and they tumbled to the ground. The wind blew her papers over the schoolyard fence. That's when Nick Martin Jr.'s Model T appeared at her side. He bounded from his car, jumped over the fence, and rescued her papers. Then he crouched on the ground beside her and helped her pick up her books. When she tried to flatten the curled edges of the pages he did the same, and their fingers touched. She thanked him, and he said, "My pleasure."

He wore a blue shirt, overalls, and a cap pulled forward, drawing attention to his eyelids that folded slightly over his penetrating blue eyes. When he cupped his hand around his chiseled jaw and studied her face, her knees shook and she felt dizzy. When another car came along, he drove off. Her heart beat so fast that when she got home, she could barely explain to her mother what had happened. With a twinkle in her eye, her mother warned her not to tell her father.

Lucille places the note in the pocket of her robe and walks into the kitchen. She is surprised when she sees her father sitting at the table drinking coffee. He stands up to give her a kiss on the cheek.

"Big day today, honey," he says. "Imagine, my daughter, class valedictorian." Then his demeanor changes. Slamming his coffee cup down on the table, he says, "That kid got me out of bed, making such a racket. He thinks he's king behind the wheel. Looked out the window and I saw him pulling away. Know that car anywhere. Just like his Daddy, cut from the same pattern. Nick Martin Jr. and Nick Martin Sr., one and the same."

Under the Red Ribbon

Lucille pats the outline of the envelope in her pocket and hopes her father doesn't notice any change in her expression. "Mr. Martin is a prestigious attorney," she says, "and if his son is cut from the same pattern, what's wrong with that?"

"What's wrong with that is, I don't want that boy around this house. You are to have nothing to do with him."

Already dressed for the graduation ceremony, Bill looks dapper in his blue plaid jacket, white shirt, and pressed pants. He even has his bushy brown hair parted in the center, the part straight as a ruler.

"You look nice, Daddy," she says, happy to change the subject.

"Do I? I want to look my best today."

The light from the kerosene lamp brings Lucille's attention to the calendar tacked to the wall. It is centered between the icebox and the wood-burning iron stove, so she can reach it readily. She steps over to it and removes the page where June 26 is circled. She tugs open the kitchen drawer to reach the other calendar pages she has collected through the years. Some yellowed, some frayed, each is significant in its own way.

When she places the pile on the table, Bill looks at the stack. "You're still doing that?"

The ritual began on her tenth birthday, when she entered her first regional poetry contest and won. She also came down with the chicken pox and broke out in a rash just as she started reading her poem. Her mother said a day like that needed special remembrance, so she removed the calendar page and wrapped a red ribbon around it. Since then when a memorable day came along, the special calendar page that marked the event went under the red ribbon.

Bill searches through the stack and finds another June 26th: June 26 1925. "Imagine, your mother gone a year now."

Lucille looks at the paper. It is still smudged with her tears.

Bill breaks their silence. "Last night I was preparing the stuff for your mother's tribute, cleaning under the couch, which I haven't done for some time. That was your mother's job, bless her soul, and I found something else quite by accident. Rather strange, really." He guides

Lucille into the parlor and pulls two canvases from under the sofa. "Take a look."

On one canvas, a woman leaps through the forest dressed in a sheer organza dress that barely covers her knees. She runs toward a young man whose face is obscured. The small sculptured face, the short black bob with a spit curl hanging down the center of her forehead and the finely shaped nose can only be Evelyn's. On the other canvas, a dark-haired woman reclines in a high meadow. The same man lies at her side.

Lucille's father holds his hand to his forehead. "What was your mother thinking running toward that man? And then in that other one . . . I mean, that man is so close he could . . . Well, what else can I say? See for yourself. Who the heck is he?"

"Not jealous of a painting, are you?"

"Damn right I am." After hiding the canvases back behind the couch, he says, "Hell or high water, I'll find out who that man is."

Later that day, Lucille Kramer stands at the podium set at the far end of the football field, ready to begin her valedictorian speech. Her preparation for this day started early on, before she was even of school age. It started on the farmhouse porch where her mother recited poetry as they huddled in her rocking chair. With Evelyn Kramer's arm around her, she learned that words had the power to transform. When she sat at the kitchen table with her father, he read articles to her from the Harvest Gazette, articles about President Woodrow Wilson and the tariff issue, a subject children her age typically were not interested in. She learned to appreciate the world beyond the farm. As she grew older, she searched for truths beyond the mundane and became an avid reader. It surprised no one that she would graduate first in her class.

Those steps, large and small, led her to where she stands today. Yet, looking out at all the people who turned out to support the graduates, her eyes focus on the empty chair next to her father. She falters, then finds solace in the words of Ralph Waldo Emerson: *There are degrees of courage, and each step upward makes us acquainted with a higher virtue.*

Under the Red Ribbon

Exactly a year ago on June 26, 1925, Lucille's world, as she knew it, changed. The school day began like any other with her mother standing at the window and waving goodbye. Sunrays spilled through the windowpane and landed on her hair. Her face held a wistful expression, one Lucille had not seen before, that made her look like she was withholding something not quite ready to be said.

Later that day, Lucille was chosen to represent Harvest High in the inter-school oratorical contest. Her principal complemented her, saying that she will make not only Harvest proud, but all of Iowa. Elated, she hurried home to share the news. But when she arrived back at Kramer Farms, her steps slowed. The threshing machine and tractor lay idle, and the animals were already drawn into the barn. Her father was nowhere in sight. Entering the house, she was struck by the bizarre state of the kitchen. The room was dim with the curtains pulled over the window. The breakfast dishes piled in the sink had traces of egg still clinging to them. An apron hung haphazardly on the cabinet doorknob, a shattered cup beneath it.

Placing her books on the counter near a pie tin partially filled with sliced apples, Lucille shut her eyes, hoping that when she opened them the pie tin would be brimming with apples, the top dotted with brown sugar. She hoped her mother's apron would be neatly folded and the broken cup would be whole again. She hoped the curtains would be gathered to each side of the window and the sun would be pouring in. But shutting her eyes didn't change anything.

She heard hushed voices and muffled cries coming from her parents' bedroom. That's where she found her mother slumped in bed. A yellow pallor obscured her normally rosy cheeks and her blue dress with white flowers clung to her body, which was soaked in perspiration. Bill Kramer stood at the bedside with a prayer book in his hand and Doc Greene stood beside him monitoring Evelyn's pulse.

Stunned, Lucille bent over the bed to push away the clump of damp black hair that had shaken loose from the hair comb that had shone so brilliantly that morning. Her voice trembling, Lucille cried, "Mama, what happened? You were fine this morning. You waved to me from the window. I wanted to tell you I'm going to represent our school in the inter-school oratori…" But her voice trailed off. Her mother had stopped breathing.

"Evelyn will be with the Good Lord soon," Doc Green said. Then he muttered something in her father's ear.

Bill's body stiffened and he clenched his fists. He dropped the prayer book. "What are you saying?"

Dr. Greene whispers in his ear again

"No, that can't be true," he said, with fury in his voice.

Lucille couldn't hear what Doc Green said, and when she looked to her father for an explanation, all she saw was grief.

Lucille finishes her speech. The audience stands to applaud. Bill rushes toward Lucille, clutching Evelyn's picture. He wraps his arms around her and says, "You made me so proud."

೧

Hours later, Lucille sits beside Nick in his Model T staring at him, shivering slightly in his presence. As resplendent as the sun itself, his tanned face looks like summer and the emancipation that comes with it. He turns to her and smiles, showing a deep dimple in his left cheek. *Yes,* she thinks, *Nick is like his shiny Model T and I am just like my Daddy's pickup.*

Her zest for life took a turn after her mother died. She cried at the very mention of her mother's name, and she had difficulty concentrating on her schoolwork. She was haunted by flashbacks of the chaotic state of the kitchen on the day of Evelyn's death, by the blue flowered dress drenched in perspiration, and by her father's reply. She is still plagued by the question of why and how her mother died. When she asked Doc Greene to explain, he just shook his head. When she asked her father the same question, he reacted the same way. No wonder she sees a lifeless reflection when she peers into the mirror.

Driving down the gravel road, Nick honks as they pass a farmhouse, and he waves to the men working in the fields. He stops his car to chat with the children on tire swings and winks at their mothers. But when he slows down to tip his hat to a woman hanging clothes out to dry and blows her a kiss, Lucille scowls. The woman has two young children pulling on her skirt. Laughing and blowing a kiss back she calls after him, "See you later, Jr."

"No disrespect, Lucille. That woman is goofy over me."

Pressing on the gas pedal, Nick slides the car into a sharp turn and heads down Pine Street, stirring up a cloud of dust. "Hot dawn!" he howls. The wind tousles Lucille's blonde hair and puffs the sleeves of her white blouse. Losing her balance, she lands on his shoulder.

Nick whirls the steering wheel with one finger, maneuvering his Model T around the potholes. Lucille braces herself, gripping the door handle with one hand and her book of T.S. Elliott with the other. *This is the way the world ends*, she thinks, *not with a bang but a whisper*. But the only whisper she can hear is the one that echoes around Harvest: *Nick Martin Jr.? That kid's got fire in his veins.*

A grin spreads across Nick's face. "More fun than a day at the county fair, huh?"

Still trying to catch her breath, she thinks he might be right.

Nick whistles along to "Bye Bye Blackbird," which blasts from the dashboard radio, swaying his head from side to side to the beat as he drives over the rolling hills.

Spotting the berry bushes along the road, Lucille begs him to stop so she can pick some blueberries. A squirrel scurries across their path, and Nick spins the vehicle to the side of the road. The car plunges into a thicket of brush.

Slouched in his seat, he says, "Damn! What the hell happened? Any driver worth his salt knows better than to do that. I don't want anyone finding out about this, especially my good friend, Arnold Mosley. He thinks I'm the living end when it comes to driving. Embarrassing, really."

"This mishap could happen to anyone."

"Mishap? Is that what you call it? It's bad judgment."

Adamant, he shakes his head. "And I'm not anyone."

Lucille looks down at her hands in her lap. "Ralph De Palma lost the Indianapolis 500 in 1912," she says.

"That's different. He lost the Indianapolis 500 because his car cracked a piston." Nick puffs his cheeks and then exhales. "How do you know about that anyway? Don't tell me you're interested in stuff like that?"

"I also know he remained a good sport when he lost."

"Well, that's where we part ways." Nick grabs hold of the wheel and moves it back and forth. "Maybe I broke a steering knuckle."

He jumps out of the car and lies on the ground so that his head is buried in the brush. He inches his way under the framework. After checking the underside, he circles the vehicle and examines the tires. He pulls the choke lever to prime the engine, and listens for a sound while mumbling something about knowing his car inside out—every spring, every axle, every screw.

"Maybe you…"

"Don't start with excuses. Making excuses is a sure way of becoming mediocre. No, that's not my style." Nick opens the glove compartment and finds the shimmy neatly folded. He reaches up to clean the windshield with his sleeve. "Took hours to polish this baby last night, and now look."

A bee flies through the open window and Lucille waves the buzzing insect out. Her eyes follow it as it lands on a patch of bluebells. She watches a rabbit romp through the thicket of brush. Her eyes follow a chipmunk frolicking in the jack-in-the-pulpits, gooseberries, and hawthorns and then she glances at the birds that flutter from branch to branch and between trees. Her afternoon has come to an abrupt halt.

She and Nick are quiet and then they look at each other and break into laughter. Pleased to have broken the silence, she continues to laugh long after he has composed himself.

"I like seeing you like this," he says. "It doesn't seem like you ever have fun."

Taking the book from her hand, he places it on the seat, and places her arm around his waist. "This is where your hands belong instead of around those books. None of my beeswax, but you've missed out big time."

"Missed out? Why do you say that? I'm going to be a poet, like . . ." She has to stop to think; she reveres so many poets. "Like Edna St. Vincent Millay. If you haven't read her poetry, *you've* missed out." Certainly she's being presumptuous because the author, besides being a Pulitzer Prize winner, is a free spirit, something Lucille is not.

"Well Miss Powers has you up there with the *greats*, so maybe you will be a famous poet someday. That teacher has no use for students like me. Anyway, poetry is crazy. Who can understand it? The author says one thing and means another. Do you understand double talk like that?"

She wants to tell him that cars and poetry have much in common. They both have rhythm, and the parts must fit together just right. And they both transport you to another place. But he wouldn't understand, although he did surprise her on the last day of school. Most of the boys shortened the school year on their own and didn't show up, but Nick did. He sat in his seat drawing an engine on a piece of paper, but his hand shot right up when their teacher discussed "The Road Not Taken." Lucille, aghast to hear him join the discussion for the first time, listened intently.

"Now that's a poem I can understand," he said to Miss Powers. "When a bunch of us jumped into our cars and drove down to the creek, we took one road, but Lucille here took another. She had a load of books in her arms, going home to study. She should have taken the road we took."

The other students laughed but Lucille blushed and hid her face behind her notebook. But on the way home from school that day, her body bubbled with an effervescence that could only be explained by Nick's attention.

Now his arm sweeps across her body. He leans over, pulls on one of her blonde curls, and opens her door. "Always wanted to do that."

"Open my door?"

"No, pull on your curls."

She wonders if her curls remind him of the coils in his car.

"And while we're talk'n, gotta tell ya, that fella Harry you hang out with—what a dud. Too dull for my taste. He can't see two feet in front of himself. I didn't think they made glasses that thick. I'll show you how to have a good time."

Poor Harry. She had left him at the graduation picnic holding two hotdogs, hers with double mustard, his plain. He didn't deserve that kind of treatment. After all, she was his date. After Mama died, he'd made sure that she kept her mind on her schoolwork. "Penny for your thoughts," he'd say, as he opened her books and placed them in her hands. And he put his arms around her shoulders as if she'd collapse if he let go. Yet, they were both vying for first place in their class.

Before slipping out of the car, Lucille has a question for Nick. "Why did you decide to take me for a drive today? We don't exactly run in the same circles."

"Same circles? You and Harry don't make up a circle. I think they call that a twosome. But to answer your question, I asked you out to prove something to myself. That I can have any woman I want—including the class valedictorian."

His arrogance compels her to turn away.

He laughs and pulls on her curls again. "I'm joking. I've always had my eye on you. Didn't you hear me say that in class? I thought you were the only woman who *would* turn me down."

About to step off the Model T running board, she sees him come around from the other side, but she's caught off guard when he lifts her up and carries her to a wide-spreading dogwood. He lowers her to the ground beneath the tree. Sitting down next to her, he brushes aside the stray curls that have fallen on her forehead and with one swoop reaches for a spray of pink blossoms and places them on her head.

"That does it. With this crown, I pronounce you my Fairy Princess.

He tugs on his socks and removes his shoes. Away from all the distractions, his springy movements prove endearing. Barely cognizant of the breeze scattering pink petals on her shoulders or the butterflies pirouetting past, she focuses her eyes on the young man in front of her. If ever she saw a conflicting conglomeration of characteristics rolled into one person, it's now. Nick is playful and serious, blatant and beguiling, almost a man but still a boy. When his eyelids lower ever so slightly, the sun falls out of the sky, sprinkling him with a golden halo.

Straightening her dirndl skirt beneath her and pulling her legs up to her chest, she folds her hands around her knees, appearing unruffled. But his presence has her stomach doing cartwheels.

"Don't get too cozy, Princess. We're about to venture into the creek."

"Thought we'd sit here awhile and watch the birds. Maybe look for some swallow nests, or read poetry."

"We did the poetry thing, remember? We talked about Miss Powers. And now about the birds." He points his finger toward the upper branches of a maple tree. "There's an Eastern Goldfinch. Look, that yellow one there."

She stretches her neck to look. "It's a male. See the black . . ." But the bird takes off before she has time to finish her thought. "I wish he'd stayed longer."

"He can't do that. Even a bird knows staying in one place too long can make you stale. Stale as an old piece of bread. That can happen to you, if you stay in Harvest too long."

"That's not true," she says. "My books take me everywhere."

"Keep telling yourself that and you might actually come to believe it. There's a whole world out there. Gotta see it firsthand."

"Bet anything that bird comes back one day," she says.

"Only if he has something worthwhile to come back to."

"Like what?"

"You know. You've heard of lovebirds, haven't you?"

She laughs. She has a feeling Nick knows more about life than she thought.

As she's about to push up from the ground, he places his hands on hers. Unable to move, she stares into his eyes. He reaches under her skirt and slowly moves his hands toward her thighs. Bit by bit, he rolls down her stockings.

An electrifying chill charges through her body. "I–I could have done that myself."

"Yeah, you could have, but it wouldn't have been as much fun."

He takes her hands in his and pulls her up. After warning her to be careful of the splintering rocks, he leads the way toward the creek. He rolls his pants up and sloshes right in. If the water is cold, he shows no sign of discomfort.

She tests the water with her toes and finds it too cold. She withdraws her foot.

"Hey, Lucille, c'mon in."

If only she had brought her bathing suit.

"Take off those silly clothes."

She giggles, but when he steps toward her close enough for their bodies to touch and starts unbuttoning her blouse and then her skirt, she knows he isn't kidding. Her clothes float in the water. Nick bunches them into a ball and tosses them under the tree, as swiftly as tossing a baseball. Her arms move to cover her chest and she looks away.

"Don't worry, Princess, you still have something on." He cups his hands, fills them with water, and splashes her. "Now you have water on you, too."

A splash of water is enough to ease the heat rising in her flushed cheeks, and she squeals with laughter. Splashing him in return, she understands why all the girls love Nick.

"That's not fair. I'm getting my pants wet." He tugs them down and flings them towards the tree. "Bulls eye," he shouts. His pants fly through space and land on top of her skirt and blouse.

She averts her eyes toward the sky.

Cracking a smile, he pulls her toward him. "Now let me take a really good look at you. Without those books covering your face, you are a real babe."

If only his eyes weren't so blue. She's losing touch with time and place. He outlines her lips with his fingers. "I like those rosebuds, Princess." When he glides his hands over her belly, she surrenders to his touch. He reaches for her soft, rounded buttocks, and in that state that negates all judgment, she is only partially cognizant of what he is doing. With the light touch of a sorcerer, he loosens the hooks of her Maidenform brassiere. The cotton garment falls below her breasts, and her heart falls with it. She'd been saving this new brassiere to wear on a special occasion, never dreaming this would be it.

"Look at me, Princess. Nothing but lots of water in the other direction."

He pulls down on her bloomers. With magical maneuvering, he rubs the nape of her neck, caresses her breasts and belly with soft kisses and whirls his tongue inside her mouth. Nothing like the way Harry kisses her. With Harry, it's merely two lips smacked together.

Nick's hands elude her. He cups her breasts to his mouth, moving from one to the other. The earth spins faster, threatening her equilibrium. Her legs bend, and he raises her toward him. She hears thunder drumming and lightning crackling through the sky. Elizabeth Barrett Browning's words pound in her ear:

"Guess now who holds thee!"—"Death" I said.
But there
The silver answer rang,-- "Not Death, but Love."

Nick presses himself against her. Her heart leans toward him, but her body pushes away. Daddy had warned her: "Don't go give'n your body away like those other girls. Men don't respect that."

"You're going too far," she whispers. "Stop. I want you to stop."

The air is still. The call song of the Eastern Goldfinch subsides, and the leafy images of the trees reflecting in the creek retreat.

"Stop, huh? Just like that." Nick's head tilts to the side, his jaw juts forward. "What do you think I am--a fuck'n machine? You can't do this. You play by the rules."

Rules? What rules is he talking about? Almost inaudibly she manages to say, "Thought we were going for a ride, Nick."

"Going for a ride?" The ridicule in his tone stings.

Thrusting his arms out in front of him, he emphasizes each word with the push of his hands. "Lots-of-hours-in-the-day-to-take-a-ride."

He steps toward her and again draws her against him. With his voice soft he says, "Baby, we're all grown up now. Yeah, we have our high school diplomas to prove it. That's what our graduation was all about. Don't you remember what you said in your speech? 'The class of '26 is ready for takeoff.'"

"But I meant . . ."

"Oh, I want to love you tonight. Please, you're so beautiful. I want to have you. I've been think'n about this for a long time."

Between sobs she utters, "I see my father's face telling me it's wrong."

He nods his head mockingly and his eyes narrow. "Oh, you see your father's face? I get it."

She looks down at a leaf floating by and she wishes she could ride on its back and float away with it.

"What about me? Don't you see my face? That's what you're supposed to be seeing."

"I just can't."

Nick splashes her with water, not playfully this time. He sprints toward the brush. Rummaging through the pile of clothes on the grass, he fumbles until he finds his brown pants, now drenched from the rain shower. He draws them up as far as his thighs, his hands holding them in place as he heads toward the car. A folded piece of paper falls from his pocket.

Opening the door, he climbs in and drops his head on the steering wheel. Before speeding off, he rolls the window down and yells: "Fairy Princess, let your fuck'n father take you home."

Still within earshot of Nick's angry voice, Lucille juxtaposes it with the soothing one he used earlier, trying to create a link between them. It's a problem more difficult than any she confronted in math class. The tears well from deep within, blurring her vision. *How could he use that word?*

Lucille works her way out of the water and toward the dogwood. From the position of the sun, she surmises her mother's memorial tribute has already begun. Approaching her rumpled clothing, she stops to pick up the piece of paper, now sopping wet. Her wet skirt sticks to her body as she pulls it on. Her blouse seems to have lost a button or two. Sliding down under the tree, she leans her back against the trunk and unfolds the paper. A long list covers the page and she recognizes the names of the girls in her class. Jagged lines separate them into categories. She finds her name under, "Girls to Take to the Creek." There is a star next to Sheila's name and two stars next to hers. Three other names are crossed out. She wonders how long she's been on Nick's list, or if he just decided to add her this morning over his breakfast cereal. She stuffs the crumpled paper into her skirt pocket. Wandering over to the creek again, she immerses herself in the ripples.

When Nick stormed away and left her at the creek, Lucille didn't expect him back; she didn't rule out the possibility that he would be, either. But now the sun is setting, and she remembers her father saying that twilight is the master of trickery. She decides that she'd better make her way home.

Taking the shortcut through the woods, she stops and looks around to make sure she's heading in the right direction. A wild turkey rams his long neck through the low branches and with his blackish body she almost misses seeing him. The innocent bird quickly vanishes when a grotesque figure springs out from behind the tree. The foul smell of stale liquor must have scared him off.

It's Madeline. With her bright red lipstick smeared across her mouth, rouge splotched in round circles on her cheeks, and a gash across her forehead, she looks ghastly. As she has so many times before, Lucille asks herself, how could her father have married this woman only months after losing Evelyn? But she knows the answer; he did it for her.

Bill met Madeline at a church function. He came home with a smile on his face and told Lucille that the woman he had danced with made him laugh, and he was in need of that. He continued to meet with her every Sunday, overlooking her excessive drinking. He focused on her attributes, the main one being that she told him she had a daughter Lucille's age attending a school in England. Bill thought that Madeline would know all about raising a daughter. But he didn't know that her own daughter had died years ago and Madeline found her hanging from a tree. Madeline told her that, one-day, when the woman was on a drinking binge.

"Madeline, what have you done to yourself?" asked Lucille. "You are a fright. Where did you get the gash on your head? Oh my, the blood is dripping down your face. Your hair... it's crusted with blood."

"I was over at the house and your Daddy got so carried away preparing for your Mama's tribute he threw a pot at me when I walked through the door. He wouldn't give me a measly drink. By the way, did you miss me at the graduation?"

"I thought you'd show up."

"Your father was glad I didn't. He's ashamed of me, you know. He only married me because, well, I don't need to tell you about men. They need their fix, if you know what I mean."

"Daddy thought I needed a mother. He thought you would be that to me."

"A mother?" Madeline moans. "I can't be anyone's mother. But your daddy won't get rid of me. I know too much."

"About what?"

"Not for your ears. Weren't meant for mine either. But he talks in his sleep. But who wants to talk about him? I want to talk about Nick. He's the fella I want."

"Nick? You're old enough to be his mother."

"Like I told you, I'm no good at being anyone's mother. Your father is a flat tire in bed. I need someone young and exciting. I watched you and that handsome cad at the creek this afternoon."

Lucille, revolted by the woman standing before her, looks up at the sky. "Oh Mama," she cries, "I'm sorry I missed your tribute." She glances around the wooded area and when she spots a small bed of wild roses through the dusk, she picks a bunch of the brightest flowers and holds them close to her heart. Standing amid the greenery, flowers in hand, she visualizes the tribute at the house: Daddy's eyes misting over, the glow of white candles in her mother's memory, and the longing in the notes as Dan plays "Always" on the piano. She recites her poem:

> *I want to see you Mama,*
> *I search for you each day.*
> *I yearn to hear your voice, Mama,*
> *but the sound has gone away.*
>
> *The clothes lined in your closet*
> *await your tender reach,*

Under the Red Ribbon

Your garden lay unattended,
bewildered and beseeched.

Tell me where to find you,
to hold my hand when I'm forlorn
Mama, I want to be with you
when all alone I mourn.

Madeline's eyes grow sad. She extends her arms to Lucille but then quickly drops them. "You're a lost soul," she says in a gravelly voice. "Wanting to hear a dead woman's voice. Your mother is gone. She's dead. No silly poem is going to bring her back."

Lucille walks toward her, urging her to stop talking. When she gets close, Madeline shoves her and she falls on a thorny bush before rolling on the ground. The sky turns green with specks of brown, the ground blue with strands of white. The trees whirl like pinwheels and Madeline's image fades.

Madeline screams. "My God what have I done? Did I kill ya?"

Lucille doesn't answer. Her mind has traveled back to her graduation. The principal calls her name. "Lucille Kramer, Class Valedictorian." She straightens her gown, adjusts her cap, and tucks her long blonde curly hair behind her ears. She walks toward the podium, stops center-stage, and glances at the empty chair reserved for her mother.

"Lucille?"

She looks up. "Mama?

"Look out at the world, my baby. It's all there waiting for you. And the crowd is waiting to hear you speak."

"Fellow students." Lucille pauses to look at her father, leaning forward in his seat. His expression is indescribable. He looks as though he is surrendering to the voice of an angel. She turns to look at her classmates whose lighthearted expressions have turned serious. Dottie and Gil will marry and have four children. Gil will own a dry goods store. Harry will become an eye surgeon; nothing will deter him. His twin, Sheila, will fight the odds and with her keen mind become an attorney. And Arnold, of course, will live out his dream of becoming a veterinarian. Nick Martin Jr.? He'll get a job in Olson's garage. Before long, he'll own the place.

And you, Lucille, and you?

She continues her speech: "Dreams create the fabric of life. Use them, or the threads will shred and the gloss will fade. Put them on a shelf, and they will gather dust. Hold them in your hands, clutch them to your heart, and life will weave them into reality. You may be whisked away by a gale of wind and find yourself traveling in another direction. Hold on tight. The class of 1926 is ready for takeoff."

Her head hurts. More images. She sees the banner at the picnic, with "Class of 1926" scrolled across it. Her favorite literature teacher, Miss Powers, walks toward her, so stylish in a low-waisted dress and a matching cloche. The slope of her hat hinders her vision, so she tilts her head when she speaks. She looks adoringly at her student. "And now, college."

"Not just yet, Miss Powers."

"I won't hear of it. Putting it off can mean not going at all."

Bits and pieces come together in a jumble of words and images. "May I have this dance?" It's Nick. Miss Powers smiles and says, "Be careful, Lucille."

Harry breaks in. "You need someone smart like me."

Lucille opens her eyes. Everything is a blur. Madeline's flabby arms pull her up. Lucille, still groggy, calls out, "I want Nick."

"Well glory be," Madeline cheers. "Don't we all?"

By the time Lucille approaches home, all of the shops in town are closed for the night except for Jerry Sloane's General Store. Lucille sees Jerry sitting on a bench in front of the store with his wife, Lily, beside him. He's wearing a bright yellow shirt with red horizontal stripes, worn overalls, and a black cap. Lily wears a purple flowered housedress. Both are dressed in the same clothes they wore when they posed for a snapshot in the Harvest Gazette, representing the average small-town couple. Except Jerry's not average. His general store is *the* place for news. When Daddy walks in for a bottle of milk, he leaves with a package in his hand and a Harvest news release in his head. And when Jerry puts his hand to his heart and says, *honest,* Daddy is convinced. Jerry saw Lucille leave the picnic with Nick, and he'll wonder what happened. What he doesn't know, he'll make up. As long as it makes a good story.

Her feet throb and her clothes feel damp against her body. She tries to arrange her hair so she can look presentable when she faces her father. She's almost home and the sky is filled with black clouds.

The rain held off for most of the day, but a sudden downpour leaves Lucille running for cover. Finding shelter under the overhang of an old shed on the Kramer property, she watches the rain slice through the trees with vengeance. The leaf-laden branches sweep back and forth almost to a breaking point. Hailstones hit the ground sounding more like rocks, and Lucille thinks she would be safer inside the shed. She tries the door but finds it locked. Peering through the window, she sees her father pacing the floor. His forehead is deeply creased. He drops to the floor in prayer.

Her parents often used this rundown structure as their hideaway. Sometimes when Lucille passed by after school, she found them dancing across the jagged floorboards acting as though they were still courting. Then the three of them held hands and walked home. But now there is no *three of them,* only two. Lucille places her hands over her face and sobs.

Ignoring the gathering storm, she hurries down the road to fetch Dan. She knows that her father's best friend can help her at a time like this. The potholes in her path are flooded with water and so are her shoes, and Hillsdale Farms is still two miles away. Passing the Mosley farm on her left, the pit bulls make their presence known. Running the full length of the fence and growling, they stop intermittently to try to jump over the wire. Lucille picks up her pace, dodging the frogs moving in groups across the road.

Nightfall is setting in and the wooded areas lining both sides of the road darken the path even more. Rounding the bend, Lucille breathes a sigh of relief when she sees the silos in the distance and the sign that reads "Hillsdale Farms."

The crops at Hillsdale Farms are drowning in water. They bow their heads. The ducks have abandoned the pond and huddle in the weeds. Fallen branches, broken and scarred, scatter the gravel path leading up to the Hillsdale farmhouse.

Lucille continues to make her way. A trash can rolls down the hill in front of her; she jumps out of the way. Finally, she sees Dan standing on the porch, studying the sky.

"What are you doing here, and in this weather?" he asks, removing his cap and moving toward her. "Heard the Mosley dogs barking and I knew someone was passing through. Let me get you a towel."

Shaking her head, she says, "Dan, Daddy's not himself. He was having the best time at the graduation picnic, and when he fell over in the potato sack race, he said it felt good to laugh again. But you should see him now. Maybe I should have stayed until the picnic was over. I think I have a real problem, one I have no answer to."

"I've heard it said that rainstorms bring solutions to problems. Maybe the weather is a good omen, after all."

Lucille follows Dan into his truck. She trusts him. She's come to him before; she'll come to him again. Like a magician, he makes a bad situation disappear.

Dan says, "I haven't seen a storm this bad in a long time. Knocked my fence down. And my crops, I wonder if they'll survive the night." But that conversation terminates when they reach Bill's house. Bill hurries from the shed, the rain pounding down on him, and lurches toward the truck before the vehicle stops. Dan rolls down his window and hollers: "Calm down, Bill. Don't you remember back when you were seventeen? Give the kid a break."

"I remember. Only too well. I took Betsy 'Boobs' to the creek after my graduation."

"Every guy in town made out with her. Lucille is a good kid."

"What in hell would my daughter be doing running off with that Martin kid?"

With one hand still on the wheel, Dan moves his head out the window, the rain splashing over his face. He looks directly into Bill's eyes. "Don't be too hard on the girl. Don't forget, she made us all stand taller today."

"I think it's my daughter who forgot a few things. And Dan, we've been lifetime buddies, but you stay out of this. Hear?"

Lucille has never heard her father speak to Dan like that before. She jumps from the truck and with small, quick steps heads toward the house, letting the rare discord between the men continue. But her father turns his back to Dan and lets him drive off without even giving him a *thank you* for driving her home.

"Not so fast," Bill says, following her into the kitchen. With a stern assessment of her wet, wrinkled skirt and soiled blouse, he shakes his head. "If only it stormed earlier there wouldn't have been a picnic and you wouldn't have gone off to the creek with *him*. So, I'll get right to the point. You have disappointed me."

She wonders how he knew she was at the creek. And she disappointed him? She has worked so hard to make him proud. He didn't seem disappointed earlier in the day, when his friends had gathered around him, congratulating him and saying things like, "Wow Bill, imagine you have'n such a smart girl." His face had beamed and the guffaw that burst from his throat could be heard throughout the picnic tent. He had plunged into his story about when his Lucille, only three or four years old, reached up for a pile of farm books. "I tell ya," he'd said, "those books fell out of her arms and then she started reading all of 'em. My Lucille knows how to make a father smile, especially today."

She yearns to hear that again. But her father is looking out in the distance as if remembering something too painful to talk about. "Daddy, Daddy," she says. "You're making too much of this I know you put me on a pedestal, but I'm just like every other girl my age."

"This has nothing to do with pedestals. I don't want you seeing that Martin boy--not ever. Anyway, we went on down to Scoops without you. Imagine, a graduation celebration without the graduation girl. Good thing I had Dan and Paul with me. We were sitting under the green umbrella and saw you speeding through town with *him* in his red breezer. Even Mr. Olson peeked out from his auto shop next door and remarked, 'looks like a tornado take'n hold of that damn car.' Got so mad, I threw my cone at Mr. Martin. He was sitting at the next table over with his wife. I yelled, 'Keep your son away from my daughter. I won't have him wrecking her life.' Then of course Anita came over trying to defend her son, saying how wonderful he is."

Hiding her face behind her hands, Lucille sobs, "Daddy that's embarrassing. How could you?"

"How could you be running with the likes of him?"

Now she raises her voice. "Call *him* by his name. He has a name. Nick Martin Jr.—say it." She squeezes her eyes shut. "Besides, Nick doesn't want to see me again."

He peers over the rims of his glasses. "He doesn't want to see *you?*"

Like a drawer too full, her insides come tumbling out. She drops onto a kitchen chair and flings her head on the table. Her hair, disheveled and damp, tumbles over the hard surface. Between gulps of air, her sniffles break into a full-blown cry. Her friends had their mothers at graduation; they had hugged, chatted, and laughed. But her mother, buried at Cardinal Cemetery, drifted like a phantom over the crowd. When Lucille gave her speech, she had needed to see her mother seated in that empty seat. She needed her at the picnic, and she needs her now.

"And you, missing your mother's memorial tribute. How could you?" Bill says, rocking his chair back and forth.

For months Lucille had watched her father scribble recipes for her mother's tribute dinner. He sought her ideas on the format of the ceremony. Should Paul light the tall white candles or should Dan do it? Should Dan play "Always" on the piano to begin the ceremony or to end it? Her eyes filled with tears when she saw him looking off into space and then begin to softly sing, *I'll be loving you, always. With a love that's true, always. Not for just a while, but always.*

"Wasn't Evelyn a good mother? How could you not be thinking of her today? I thought any minute you'd walk in, at least in time to read your poem."

"You know how I loved Mama. Why are you hurting me so?"

He walks toward her and strokes her matted hair. When she looks at him, her eyes are filled with concern, knowing very well how *he* hurts. But with studying taking up so much of her time and the longing for her mother leaving her solemn, how could she resist driving off with Nick? Any one of the girls at school would have done the same thing. For a few hours, she floated free like a kite roaming the sky.

~~~

Sitting at the small desk in her bedroom, Lucille confesses to herself that Nick is not like other boys. Yet, there is nothing so abhorrent about him to make her father go into such a tizzy. She didn't commit a sin. And saying that if the picnic had been rained out none of this would have happened is silly. Nick had had his mind set on taking her to the creek. A rainstorm would not have deterred him.

Lucille hears Bill start up the truck, and she knows he is heading to Hillsdale Farms. He could never sleep through the night knowing that he'd had words with his best friend. But soon she hears him storm back into the house, mumbling that his truck stalled out on him.

Remembering the damp crumpled paper she found at the creek, she pulls it from her pocket and turns it over to the blank side. She writes: *June 26, 1926* and studies the date. Dates are important to her; they ground her in the present. Trying to jot down a few words to recapture the day, the words surface with difficulty. Her mind and body are too filled with emotion. Even after her mother died, she ran to the willow tree and sat under the weeping limbs and wrote a poem.

Giving up, she jumps into bed. Sinking her head into the pillow, the damp paper drops from her hand. About to doze off, the strong pull of the day draws her back. The walls fade into a thicket of greenery and the beamed ceiling ascends into a clear blue sky. The wooden planked floor breaks into a thousand pieces before unfolding into a gravel road. The afternoon of June 26 reappears.

ℬILL

Bill made a special sojourn to the high school last night to post a sign in the parking lot which read, "First Row Smack Center Reserved for the Father of the Class Valedictorian and Family." Since he woke up early anyway because of the Martin kid skidding his wheels, he'll pick up his buddies and get down to the school early before the other parents arrive. No sense taking chances. Some wise guy just might take those seats.

He sits behind the wheel of his truck for a time, taps tobacco out of his small tin, and rolls a cigarette. "Time to clean out the upstairs," he mutters, pointing to his head. Then he leans back and reviews his plans for the day. The early part of the day would be set-aside for Lucille and her graduation. Only one valedictorian in the class of 1926, and he could take credit for raising her. He doesn't want people thinking Bill Kramer got a swelled head, so he would take his time thanking everyone. And at the graduation picnic, with all the people patting him on the back, he would continue to be gracious. When that was over Lucille, Harry, Dan, Paul, and himself would head on down to Scoops Ice Cream Parlor where Lucille could order anything she desired. Then it would be Evelyn's turn with a memorial service at the house, starting promptly at six. Sure, his eyes would spill over like a water glass turned upside down, but the family would be together.

Now with all that squared away, he has a question for Evelyn. Looking up, he recognizes that fluffy cloud, inching in front of the others and moving toward him. If he stares at it long enough, he can see Evelyn's face. He has seen it many times since she died, and it means that his wife wants to chat. Sometimes it appears when he has something pressing to ask her.

"Evelyn, I found your paintings under the sofa. Who was that man you were running toward?" When she doesn't answer, he softens his voice. "Evelyn my love, who is that man in the painting?"

He sees the cloud fade away, so he starts the truck and heads down the road. His thoughts carry him back to the time when he and Evelyn, newly married, danced together after the church dinner. The attorney, Nick Martin Sr., cut in two or three times. *Was he the man in the painting?* He mulls that over in his mind before switching his thoughts to Jerry Sloane. No, it wasn't him. Jerry isn't into that kind of stuff. Jerry gets a kick out of what other people do, but he's pretty tame himself. It's a sure thing he'll be at the graduation, even though he doesn't have a kid graduating. When his customers come in for groceries, they also want to know what's *really* happening around Harvest. He'll give Jerry some information to pass around. He'll tell him that his Lucille, so young and so competent, balances farm work and schoolwork with clockwork efficiency. She reads from dozens of books and quotes the most celebrated authors. He'll tell him that his daughter writes stories as good as the masters and recites poetry with *exquisite poignancy*. The expression, *exquisite poignancy,* words he copped from Lucille, will surely impress him. Heck if Jerry wants to spread that information around, fine with him. And knowing Jerry, he'll add a gem or two of his own.

Bill looks up at the sky again to see if the cloud has reappeared and if Evelyn is ready to answer his question. It's there all right, and in a faint but firm voice, Evelyn asks a question of her own. "Bill, about college. Which one did Lucille choose? Be sure she has everything she needs."

"Evelyn," he says, "there's no money for college." The words come out so fast that he almost bites his tongue. He tries to explain that after she died, he couldn't work; he just couldn't keep going. "Our daughter, thrown a curve ball, took a swing at it, and came up with a home run. But, Evelyn, I hurt too much to do that. You remember when Lucille, just four or five years old, ran in front of a truck, and I dashed out and saved her life? I put my body out there, right in front of hers. I would always do that for our daughter, no matter how old she gets. And college? You bet I'd send her. But there is just no money."

"Don't put the blame on me. If you were staring out the window when you should have been in the fields, that's your fault."

Evelyn always started acting brash like that when she met up with Pauline Powers, Lucille's teacher at the high school who became a Women's Suffrage leader. Together, they led throngs of women through town, waving signs and flags until their feet bled and women's suffrage was finally realized. When Pauline rallied the women with her call to stand not shoulder-to-shoulder with men but in front of them, Bill almost plummeted to the ground. "Stay away from that woman," he'd yelled at Evelyn. "I don't want you or our daughter hear'n stuff like that."

Even so, she was right. After Evelyn died, he had stood at the window watching the rows of corn and oats go unattended, and he did nothing about it. Something strange came over him, something pushing him from the inside. He couldn't stop sketching. He sketched Evelyn in the garden, Evelyn in the kitchen, Evelyn winning prizes for her tomatoes at the county fair. All that didn't do the farm much good, but he had his mind set on preserving every inch of the woman he loved.

"Damn it, who is that man in the paintings?"

"Knowing all the answers makes life complicated," she says. "Not knowing is the Good Lord's way of being kind."

How can knowing the answers make life more complicated? Seems to him that *knowing* clarifies things.

As a child, he didn't know why he carried the blame for something he had nothing to do with. His twin brothers got caught up in the rapids down at the river, and later some men found them lying face down. Mama, watching them swim in the shallow water, had turned around for just a minute to say hello to a friend, and that minute had wiped out five years of living. Ten, if you added the ages of both boys. But the worst part was that Bill's heart had ached, and his parents wouldn't permit him to speak about it. He heard that they had been "caught up" and then they "were gone." He wondered who had caught them up, and why? That's not knowing, and not knowing hurts. Making matters worse, his daddy had said, "If Bill had gone along like I asked him, the twins would be here today." *If Bill had gone along?* What difference would that have made? Not knowing the answers complicated things.

And because he didn't know the answers, he locked his seven-year-old body in the barn, and placed big cans in front of the door. He hid there and tried to figure things out. He must have stayed too long because he heard his mother screaming that she had lost another son. When they found him, his daddy said that pranks would not be tolerated and made him sleep in the barn for the rest of the week. He didn't like it in there when it got cold, and shortly after that he developed asthma. The damn cough has been with him since. He doesn't like it when these memories surface, but he's stuck with them.

Passing the farms along the road that he has passed hundreds of times, his eyes linger on the pigs and piglets, and the cows and calves, the horses and colts huddled together like little families. But when he notices the younger animals making their own way, he feels a pang in his stomach. Just like his daughter graduating and moving on.

Approaching the sign with the big red letters, the one he made for Paul and Dan announcing Hillsdale Farms, he's still dazzled by the landscape: the sparkling pond with the ducks and Mallards skimming over the top, the endless fertile fields alive with golden corn and oats. From where he is sitting he can see the hogs and they look just about market weight. Yup, his friends know what they're doing. With his exemplary farming skills, he taught Dan and Paul to be the zealous farmers they are today. He passed on what his daddy taught him, "Lose a day and you lose a month." He knows precisely when he did not heed that advice himself, when he lost a day, a month, and a year and now unless he can pull himself out of this hole he's in, he's going to lose his farm.

His buddies, looking swell in their church attire, walk toward the truck as it moves up the drive. They won't have to change clothes for Evelyn's tribute. No, they'll come just the same way. In truth, the only other time he'd seen them dressed like that was at Evelyn's funeral. No movie star had anything on Dan in his navy blue sport jacket and red tie, his blond curls tumbling over his forehead. As for Paul, in his brown jacket, white shirt, and tan-striped tie, he could easily pass for a dentist or a doctor. On occasions like this, Paul dresses for the ladies. Word is out that Pauline Powers is looking for a professional man and might just settle for a farmer.

When all three of them settle in the front seat of Bill's pickup, Bill fiddles with his tie and asks, "Do you think my Lucille won't be my little girl anymore, now that's she's graduating?"

"It would be more of a gradual process," Dan says. "Like holding a rope and then loosening the grip. Would you have wanted your father holding a tight rein on you at seventeen?"

"I always sought his advice."

"There's your answer."

While Lucille depends on her books for answers, he has Paul and Dan.

Pulling into the driveway at Harvest High, Bill notices Howie scurrying about putting up chairs and carrying baskets of flowers, working up a sweat until all the last minute graduation preparations are complete. Howie is a man of courage. Last night his daughter, Rachael, was thrown from her bicycle and knocked to the ground; she won't make it to her own graduation.

Howie owns a small farm beyond Hillsdale Farms, and sometimes they meet at Jerry's to roll some papers with tobacco and enjoy a cigarette. The last time they met, they talked about their daughters. Rachael isn't smart like Lucille, but she always wins first prize in the teenage baking contests. It is a well-known fact that the judges have big smiles on their faces when they announce the winner, and every year she's wearing that white tight sweater. Isn't hard to put two and two together.

Bill gets out of the car with a purpose in mind: to see that people take notice of his sign. He meant it when he said that those seats were reserved for him and his family. Watching the people park their cars and walk towed the football field, he detects Nick Martin Sr. in his navy blue pinstripe walking toward him.

Bill nudges Dan with his elbow. "Look who's come'n."

"I remember when you liked the guy way back in high school. What the hell happened to make you change your mind?"

"Just let's say I can't trust him the way I can trust you."

Nick Martin Sr. thumps Bill's back with one hand and reaches out with the other for a hearty handshake. "Must be the corn and goat milk you're feeding her, making your daughter so smart."

Bill frowns and turns to walk away.

"Hey, I'm just fooling around. No disrespect. You have a beautiful young daughter, and so intelligent. Hats off to you, Bill. Today is a special day for both of us."

"But not for Howie. How could your son plow his car into that girl's bicycle and just leave her on the ground?"

"What in heck are you talking about?"

"Your son is trouble. He loves being in the center of trouble. Trouble is his middle name."

"Don't you go speaking about my Nick like that." Mr. Martin's expression is stern.

Bill doesn't back away. "And besides, your son has no business on my property."

"Well, there I can't blame him . . . not with a beautiful smart girl like your daughter living there."

Bill raises his hand as if he might strike Nick Sr., and Dan pulls him away. "Bill, this isn't a time for a fight."

Bill nods, but his eyes follow the attorney who is now walking toward his seat. He notices that the man still has that slight limp he came away with after competing in the Summer Olympics, and he's wearing his scars the way some men wear their medals. He watches him slide his arm down his leg and hold it there, rubbing his shin. Bill knows why he's doing it, rubbing his shin like that. Nick Sr. wants people to remember that although he didn't win any medals, he did hurt himself in the attempt. He received a hero's welcome when he returned. They rolled out the red carpet with a parade and all, like he was Victor Johnson from Great Britain who won the gold in cycling. Throngs of women waited just to get a glimpse of him. But he ran over to Evelyn and spun her around like she was his girl.

Why worry about people like this guy when he has Dan and Paul, two guys he can trust, Bill asks himself. Yes sir. Those two are like money in the bank.

After the river accident when Bill lost his little brothers, he could touch his chest, close to his heart, and actually feel two holes beneath the skin. His brothers were that dear to him. He'd rub that area, hoping they would fill in. After he met Paul and Dan in third grade, he didn't feel those two holes anymore.

His two buddies know that he never got over the loss of his brothers. They are aware of the dreams that still awaken him in the middle of the night when he finds himself sweating, yanking on his blanket as if he's pulling the boys out of the river. Sometimes he yanks so hard his own arms hurt in the morning.

So now he looks his friends straight in the eye and tells them what he should have told them long ago, and not because Dan bought Lucille a piano and Paul kept her well-stocked with books. "I'm lucky to have hooked up with both you guys."

"Like you always say," Dan answers, "Like money in the bank."

⁓

With the graduation ceremony over and the diplomas dispensed, Bill is ready to enjoy the afternoon picnic. The picnic is held in the area behind the church, where the huge maple trees provide lots of shade. Some of the Harvest women arrived early to set up the long tables and cover them with red and white checkered tablecloths. They were busy all week preparing the bean salads, purchasing the hot dogs, and baking cookies and cakes. The picnic area is festive with balloons tied to trees, big banners welcoming the graduates, and the school band playing the school alma mater. With the crowd singing along, the ambience is one of fun and excitement.

At the beverage table, Bill pours three glasses of lemonade, handing a glass to Dan and one to Paul. "Let's drink to our friendship. It's been quite a day and I couldn't be happier having both of you share it with me."

Just as they are about to sit down and eat, the principal interrupts to announce that Lucille Kramer will play some Gershwin tunes. A hush resonates over the grounds. The guests who are eating put down their utensils and give Lucille their full attention. Those who are standing quickly find seats. Bill looks around to make sure that no one moves or speaks. Feeling a separation from the crowd, his chest expands and he lifts his head. He feels his heart spin toward the sky. As Lucille begins her performance, he watches the cloud descend. "Listen, Evelyn, that's our girl."

When Lucille finishes playing "Rhapsody in Blue," Bill throws his arm around Dan, and they stand together soaking up the applause. "You did a good job with her, Dan, giving her those piano lessons. Like you poured your talent into her. I like the way the principal introduced her: 'The young woman who plays with virtuosity.' Who knows what that means, but it sounds good."

His eyes glued on his daughter, Bill sees Nick Martin Jr. take her hand and lead her to the makeshift dance platform adjacent to the eating area.

Students circle around the young couple, clapping their hands and swinging to the music. Bill has no doubt that his daughter can dance with the best of 'em. How many times has he seen her Charleston in front of the mirror, flapping her arms and kicking her legs? She could teach them all a thing or two. It's her dance partner he's worried about. He cringes when Nick Martin Jr. throws Lucille over his shoulder. Bill has just lost his appetite and is about to throw his dish away when Nick Martin Sr. strolls past him. The attorney nudges Bill and says, "They make quite a couple. Imagine, your daughter and my son."

Bill gives him a look that could scare the cows away, and the attorney returns to his wife, who has found herself a spot under an umbrella. Jerry Sloane joins Bill now, still chewing on his hot dog. They take a stroll around the grounds and stop in front of the dance platform. When he inquires about the farm, Bill doesn't turn to face him; he's staring at the dancing couple.

The farm, together with Evelyn and Lucille, completed Bill's life. Like a chain, each link depended on the other. When Evelyn died, the chain broke. "Good times don't last forever, Jerry, and farmers are beginning to feel the crunch," he says. "We're getting half the price for a bushel of corn that we used to."

"That's what I hear. One sure thing, though: Lucille and Harry. Wouldn't you say?"

"Guess so," Bill says, still glaring at Nick and his daughter holding hands. He glances over at Harry who is standing with his classmates watching the couple dance and wonders why he doesn't cut in. He escorted her here, and now he stands back like a wimp.

Bill ambles over to the dessert table and grabs a slice of blueberry pie. But when his daughter and Nick stroll towards him, he swallows too quickly and coughs. He wipes his mouth using his sleeve, leaving a streak of purple on his shirt.

I'll be darned. The kid is the spitting image of his old man at his age. Nothing like the boys who help their dads on the farms. Seeing his daughter's fingers interlaced with Nick's, Bill slams his eyelids down over his eyes.

"Anything I can do, Mr. Kramer," Nick asks. "Need something for that cough? A glass of water?"

"No," Bill hacks.

"Well then, I'd like to ask your permission to take Lucille for a ride."

No question about it, disrespectful too. Holding his daughter's hand, after one dance. Damn it. Harry should be here fighting for his girl. "I'm afraid I've made other plans for my family. Going down to Scoops for ice cream."

"Lucille thought it would be a fine idea if we both took a drive."

"Then why are you asking me?" Bill sees the blush spread across Lucille's face and a crinkle in her nose, but he doesn't care. A father's duty is to do right for his daughter.

"If you think I won't be careful driving, sir, I promise you, I will be."

"I'm not worried 'cause she's going no place with you."

When Nick turns to Lucille to mutter an apology and then walks toward the road, Bill nods his head. *Guess he got the message.* But then he hears, "I won't let Nick drive fast, Daddy. And I'll be home for Mama's tribute, I promise."

Bill doesn't respond, but Nick does when Lucille calls after him. He turns around and grins. Bill keeps an eye on the two of them as they climb into the shiny red Model T and drive off, leaving a cloud of dust behind them.

⁓

After a hectic day, Bill is glad to be home. The day didn't go as planned. What a disaster going off to Scoops without Lucille. Shameful, too. All the other families sat around the small tables with their graduates and he, father of the class valedictorian, celebrated without his daughter present. Hell, that's not a celebration, that's a kick in the stomach.

But now it's time to focus his attention on Evelyn and get ready for the tribute. He finds the stew recipe in Evelyn's cookbook, that he keeps on the counter near the stove. He knows the recipe by heart, but he wants to be sure he prepares the stew exactly the way his wife did. With an apron tied around his waist, he slices the carrots, potatoes, and bell peppers in precise strips. He arranges them in small bunches on a cutting board, and arranges his thoughts. Lucille promised she wouldn't miss her mother's tribute. She won't let him down.

Paul drapes one of Evelyn's white shawls over a small table, places the white candles and the prayer books on it, and then walks into the kitchen to help Bill.

"Lucille should be walking in any minute. Don't you thinks so, Paul?"

"Someone *is* walking in right now."

Madeline prances into the kitchen. Paul steps into the parlor. The moonshine on Madeline's breath angers Bill. When she puts her arms around his waist, he throws them off. She staggers backwards, her body hitting the wall.

"You're not a bad cook," she says, walking closer to him, wiggling her body and ruffling his hair "That's one good thing I can say about you. When do we eat?" She dips a spoon into the pot for a taste, and bits of meat dribble down her chin. When she sinks her spoon in again, Bill elbows her and the boiling stew spills onto her hand. Her glassy eyes become clear for a moment, and she feigns a smile. Then she breaks into laughter, like she's about to tell a joke. "I saw your little Precious down at the creek," she says. "and let me tell ya, she and Nick were do'n more than spoon'n. Want me to show you what they were doing?"

Bill grits his teeth and clenches his fist.

"Not a stitch of clothes on. Just thought I'd come by and ask, if you become a grandpa, what does that make me?"

"Madeline. Out." Bill's voice booms through the house.

"I deserve a little drink for that information."

Bill has just enough whiskey for the tribute. If he gives her one drink, she'll down the whole bottle.

Madeline cavorts around him, her breasts flopping over the top of her dress, her hands on her hips, puckering her lips. "Not still pining for Evelyn? She wouldn't be pining for you if it were the other way around."

"I didn't think women your age went to the creek."

"Like you would know." She presses her thumb and forefinger close to one another. "One little drink."

"No."

"Don't expect your daughter home. She's not thinking about tributes right now. It looks like she might want to stay the night at the creek. Not that I blame her, hey I think you could learn a few things from young Nick."

Bill grabs her by the arm and leads her to the screen door. Pulling away, she slips on the rug. When she falls, her head hits the corner of the baseboard. Her body lies halfway inside the house and halfway out. Blood wells from a gash on her forehead and spills onto her face. Hearing the sound of her fall from the parlor, Dan and Paul run into the kitchen.

"You're my witnesses," Madeline screams. "You saw him hit me!" She worms her way up to her feet against the wall and shouts, "I'm going right down to the creek again, to find Lucille and tell her what you did to me!"

With Madeline finally out of the house, Bill scrubs the floor clean of Madeline's blood. He walks into the parlor again to look at Evelyn's picture. Staring at it, he acknowledges to himself that a man can only truly love once. After that, the rest is . . . well, why not use Lucille's word. . . superfluous.

The tribute is interrupted by a knock on the door. Bill goes to see who could be visiting at this time, and he is surprised to see Nick Sr. standing at the door. He is still wearing his pinstripe suit and fancy tie, and he's holding a package wrapped in white paper with pink ribbons across the top.

"Anita wanted to make sure I brought over this graduation gift for Lucille." When the attorney reaches to shake his hand, Bill keeps his fist balled at his side. "There's no bigger insult to man than that, Bill." Leaving the gift at the doorstep, Nick Sr. walks towards his car, pausing to rub his shin as he walks.

What does that man know about insults? Bill thinks.

Bill is so mad that he rushes the fellas to finish their dinner, if it could even be called dinner. Paul and Dan shove food directly from the pot into their mouths. Bill doesn't eat at all.

After Paul and Dan leave, Bill dashes over to the shed. Here he can mull things over without interruption. He's worried. A storm is brewing and Lucille still isn't home.

NICK

Nick is angry and befuddled. He wonders why Lucille accepted his invitation to go for a drive with him. Now really, what did she expect? Still, what a coup for him, walking off with the class valedictorian. But he never thought she'd be such a pain. She treated him like a regular guy. Would a regular guy come courting at four-thirty in the morning, dropping a note at her doorstep? That's something a troubadour might do, only a troubadour would sing to his princess as she stood at her window, and not use the language he used at the creek when she said she saw her father's face. But that just gave him the heebie jeebies. Mr. Kramer is not quite right in the head, anyway. Nick had never done anything to hurt him, so why was Bill so upset seeing him with Lucille?

Nick considers the problem at hand. He disconnects the events as though he is dismantling his engine, and then pieces them together bit by bit. No, some things don't jive. Everything was going along just ducky at the creek until the real fun got started. Then Lucille gives him that icy mitt. Just can't figure it out. Hey, wait a minute. Maybe she wanted to be the big cheese, the one in control. But he showed her she wasn't dealing with Milquetoast Harry. She won herself a nice long walk home.

Yeah, it's true. His heart cracked down the middle listening to her speech at graduation. He wanted to scoop up all of her words and carry them home in a little box. What a crazy thing, still throwing his cap up in the air five minutes after everyone had finished applauding. His friend Arnold had to tell him to pipe down.

Nick feels a twinge of remorse. Maybe he moved too fast. But hey, things like that can't wait. Still, he'd better check on her.

When he nears the creek, he sees Madeline lurking behind the tree and he turns back in the opposite direction. *Has she been there all afternoon?*

As Nick drives away from the creek, he lists on his fingers all the crazy things Lucille does. First, she carries those schoolbooks right in front of her bubs. Why would she want to do that? They looked pretty damn good with the rain pouring down on 'em, all shiny. Mighty good. Second, when he'd tried to gain her attention in the library the week before final exams by throwing a spitball her way, she didn't even lift her eyes from her book. Yeah, he'd called her name too, but she remained deaf to all human sound. The librarian heard him, though, and ordered him to leave. Because of that, he didn't have his assignment done for the next day. When he blamed Lucille, his teacher just rolled her eyes. Third, she hangs out with Harry, who is a dud. Fourth—and this is the big one—she doesn't play by the rules. All the girls know you don't lead Nick Martin Jr. on and then start whimpering that you're not going to do it.

Nick searches in his pocket for the paper he wrote on that morning, his list of "Girls to Take to The Creek." He'll cross off Lucille's name.

He searches the seat and the floor of the car: nothing. A honking horn distracts him. He looks up and sees his classmate Gil, with Dottie at his side, pulling up close to the side of the Model T so they can talk. Dottie is a real cuddler who doesn't settle for a little spoon'n. Sharing the creek with them is just not his thing. He'd left at the right time.

"I saw you snag the class valedictorian," Gil says. "Did she dump you after she saw your report card?"

"No one dumps me, Gil. That's like somebody dumping a diamond in the ocean."

Gil laughs. "Speaking of diamond rings. Show him, Dottie."

Dottie leans over Gil and extends her hand out the window, showing Nick her left ring finger.

"Wow. A real sparkler. So you two are go'n for it?"

"Looks like it," Gil says, "and we're not going to waste any time. Dottie wants four babies."

How absurd. Who in the world would want to be married and start having babies right out of high school? There's a whole world out there to be seen, and so many babes. And if and when it ever gets down to marriage, he will choose someone like—oh, what is he thinking? He shakes his head and shrugs his shoulders. *Hope I'm not stuck on that girl.*

"You look shell-shocked, Nick. It's marriage we're talking about, not prison."

"I guess. But you better get started on that dry goods store. You're going to need the money."

"What did you think of Lucille's speech this afternoon?" Gil asks, "By the way you were throwing your cap up in the air, I know you thought it was the bee's knees."

Her words were strung together like pearls and rang clear as crystals. "I guess it was okay. Got me kind a tired. Go'n home for a nap. See ya around."

Driving off with the window rolled down, Nick stops for a red light. He taps his fingers on the steering wheel casing and with his other hand he rubs his chin as he waits for the light to turn. Perspiration is forming around his mouth. Things haven't turned out the way he expected. Glancing at the side of the road he spots a bird with a drooping left wing. Jumping from the car to take a closer look, he sees that the delicate creature needs help. Some of his friend Arnold's love of animals has rubbed off on him and spotting the carton of spark plugs in the back seat of his car, he knows just what to do. He empties the carton, pulls his shirt over his head, and tears it under the sleeve, a good place to start since it had a hole there anyway. He lines the bottom of the carton with his ripped t-shirt.

Nick lifts the bird and places him gently in the box. He has the rest of the shirt to use as a blanket for the bird. Feeling good about giving the little creature a temporary refuge, he sings to him. "Don't worry, little bird. We're going to take good care of you." He drives slowly to the veterinarian's, not wanting to jolt the tiny bird. When he stops in front of the office, Nick realizes that it's late and Dr. Mutsfeld might be closed for the day. Still, he lifts the small box and carries it into the office. He moves to the side of the walk to allow an elderly man carrying a dog in his arms to pass in front of him. The man looks at him strangely. Nick remembers that he isn't wearing a shirt.

He walks into the wooden framed house that has been transformed into a veterinary clinic and steps into the waiting room. He recognizes dogs from the neighborhood and the owners who are trying to keep them calm. He sees the black cat that always ends up in his yard gobbling food meant for his own cat, Engine.

Nick finds a wooden straight-backed chair. He sits and talks to the bird. "Did you smash against a window of a house?" he asks, in a chirping voice. At his own house, he keeps stickers on the windows to prevent just that from happening. When his allowance was suspended he didn't have any money to buy them and had to borrow some change from Arnold. Arnold's father, Hutch, doesn't suspend his son's allowance as readily as Nick's father does.

When the vet technician calls him into his office, Nick follows her in, holding the box as though it's a fishbowl and he's afraid to spill the water.

"Lucky for you, we've extended our hours today," the tech says. "We had so many appointments we couldn't fit them all in. By the way, I think you lost something, like maybe your shirt?" She smiles at him coyly.

"My little bird needs it more than I do," he says.

When the vet enters the exam room, he inquires about Nick's cat. The vet treated him for an upset stomach last week. Nick tells the vet that he followed doctor's orders and that now the little kitty has a new diet and a new place to sleep, even though Engine prefers his old diet better, and still prefers sleeping at the edge of Nick's bed."

"Well how do you know, did he tell you?"

Nick doesn't like the tone in the doctor's voice. When Arnold becomes a vet and takes over that job, he'll be a heck of a lot nicer. Nick thinks that Dr. Mutsfeld looks more like a farmer than a doctor in his plaid shirt and overalls. Arnold won't dress like that, either.

Dr. Mutsfeld pushes his few long strands of gray hair to the side of his head and adjusts his wire-frame glasses. He repeats those gestures several times before looking inside the carton. Two small instruments hang from the doctor's shirt pocket and he uses one to examine the bird. "So, you finally did it. Ran over this little fledgling, did ya?"

"No, Dr. Mutsfeld. I found him on the side of the road."

"What will it take to slow you down?"

Nick takes a deep breath, then puffing his cheeks, prolongs his exhale until he is out of breath.

"I'm not going to get into it with you young man, but let this be a lesson to you."

The doctor handles the bird expertly and makes a small splint to hold the wing in place. Nick watches as the bird tries to flutter his wings.

"I'll take him to the wild bird hospital when I get him all fixed up," he says. "It's a small facility, but they'll rehabilitate him before returning him to his natural habitat. And Nick, get yourself a shirt. That's no way for a young man to walk around."

Nick crosses his arms over his shoulders to cover his bare chest.

"This is what happens when you drive recklessly, but I'm glad you had the good sense to bring the bird in. I have to admit, you seem like the kind of person who might try to care for the bird at home, thinking you know best."

Nick's starts to speak, but then spins around and stomps out the door. The people in the waiting room turn their heads in unison. Exerting extra force, Nick opens the car door, climbs in, and slams his head down on the steering wheel. Funny how Dr. Mutsfeld is so sure about the way the bird got hurt, as though he witnessed the whole thing.

Driving home, Nick zips down the road. When he approaches his house, he parks the Model T with a clean stop. He tears into his bedroom and the door bangs shut behind him. If his mother hears him, she knows better than to bother him when he's in this kind of mood. Good thing his dad isn't home. Letting the door bang is reason for a full interrogation. Last week when Nick had arrived home in the wee hours of the morning, his mother had come to his rescue by shooing him off to bed and pleading with his dad to dismiss the matter.

"Stay out of it, Anita," Nick's dad had shouted. "The men can take care of this without a woman's help." Then the questions began. His dad wasn't only the lawyer, but the jury. Verdict? Guilty. Nick had to be home by seven o'clock for the rest of the week.

Nick feeds Engine and then holds him on his lap, stroking his fur. In the purring voice he reserves for his cat, he says, "I hope Dr. Mutsfeld can fix the little bird's wing. That man is a lot of baloney for saying what he did, but as a veterinarian, he is the best."

⁓

It's seven o'clock. With a long evening in front of him, Nick pulls a blue shirt out of his drawer and slips it over his head. The girls say that they like him in blue. Examining himself in the mirror, he likes what he sees. His mother thinks he's too thin, but what he sees is one heck of a muscle man. His exercises are working, and are worth being late for school now and then. He wouldn't even be late if he didn't add an extra fifty sit-ups and pushups to his daily routine. Being on the wrestling team, he needs to keep in shape. Appraising the certificates on the wall, he remembers the applause and pounds himself on the chest.

What he needs now is a smile and a hug from Mom. Nick walks into the kitchen just so that he can hear Anita say, "Lucille Kramer should thank her lucky stars for snatching a date with my son." Anita Martin isn't home, but she has left a note for him, and that is exactly what she wrote. Yes, his mom is the best. To this very day, she tells anyone who will listen that Nick never needed discipline because he never did anything wrong.

Nick grabs a Mounds bar off the kitchen counter. He scoots back into his car and heads toward town. The fellas are gathered at their usual hangout at Kenny's Drugstore. Tonight, with school out for the summer, they're out in mass. He pulls up in front of the drugstore alongside his classmates' cars. Their car radios are blasting, but he has had enough noise for one day; he turns off his radio. The afternoon encounter with Lucille really shook him up.

He sees Madeline strutting in front of the fellas, who might take her for a roll in the hay and dump her soon after. She is out of place here among his friends, and with that gash on her forehead, she looks pretty bad. One of his classmates takes Madeline by the arm and leads her over to Nick's car. "Want to take her first?" he yells.

Nick waves his hand. "You kid'n me?"

When the girls arrive they hurry toward the Model T, but it's his best friend Arnold Mosley Nick came to see. Nick wants to show Arnold how his enhanced engine works. Nick reluctantly admits that Arnold can sometimes outdo him in driving skills, but he, Nick Martin Jr., is savvier working under the hood.

Arnold is standing against the wall of the drugstore with his two pit bulls at his side. He's still dressed in the brown linen knickers he wore to graduation, but his bowtie is missing. He isn't one for dressing up. His caramel-colored hair, combed back in neat silky waves, is his trademark, but tonight his hair is disheveled.

Nick and Arnold. Their names have been linked together all through high school. He knows his best friend well. It isn't hard, because with Arnold, what you see is what you get. Nick remarks on his disheveled hair. "You okay?" he asks.

Leaning into the car's open window, Arnold whispers, "Got something important to tell ya. They're say'n you rammed your car into Rachael's bicycle yesterday and she's injured. And because of you, she couldn't even go to her own graduation."

"Who's say'n that?"

"Mr. Kramer."

"Mr. Kramer? How the hell is it his business?"

"Guess he just doesn't like you."

Nick knows where he spent last evening and he doesn't have to explain that to Mr. Kramer or anyone else. But now Arnold points to the car in back of Nick's. When Nick turns to look, he sees Sheriff O'Bryan.

The sheriff pushes out of his car, belly first. He spirals upward, his long body stretching toward the sky. He must be six feet five. He moseys along and then beckons to Nick to get out of his car. The sheriff asks him mundane questions, the last one being Nick's whereabouts the night Rachel fell from her bike. After each answer, he scribbles something on his notepad.

"Polishing my car, like usual" Nick says, "and because of my special polish, even though I drove down the back roads today, and you know how dusty those roads are, you would never know my car ever got a speck of dust on it."

"Special polish?"

Nick walks to the back of his car and reaches into the box he keeps in the backseat. He presents the sheriff with the round tin, which he holds in his hand. "Special from Portugal, and it's all yours."

"Looks expensive," the sheriff says.

"Graduation present from my Dad. Want to give it a try?" He sees the glint in the sheriff's eye and hands him the tin. "A man like you needs to be driving in style. You know, sheriff, people say that anybody who keeps his car squeaky clean has the same attitude toward the community."

The sheriff rubs his chin and nods. Nick knows that he won him over. Now he must not be too smug. "Glad to make you happy, Sir."

"About that accident, lucky for you, Nick, you have the Good Lord and old Mrs. Olson to stand behind your story. The old lady says she saw you polishing your car at eight-thirty that night. You have an eyewitness. Your old man must have told you how important it is to have an eyewitness. Mrs. Olson, sharp as a tack even at the age of ninety-three, sat on her porch watching you do the polishing. She's certain it was you because even at her age she knows your body from the rest of 'em. You can be on your way now, Nick. And stay out of trouble."

Nick turns and walks toward Arnold, who is pacing the sidewalk with his two dogs. Nick forms an "o" with his thumb and forefinger. "You can relax. I'm off the hook."

"Who does he think did it then?"

"He doesn't know. They're dropping the case. Rachael wasn't hurt that bad. I don't think she wanted to go to her graduation in the first place. With her parents helping with the graduation preparation, she probably wanted some private time with the farmhand. Probably they were drinking and hit a tree, and she concocted the bicycle story."

"You sure they're dropping the case? You sure the police don't think a car hit her bike?"

"Do you doubt your best friend?"

"Where are you heading now?" Arnold asks.

"The library." The words burst out of Nick's mouth. When he's thinking about Lucille, the word *library* just automatically comes to mind.

"Let me warn you, the junior librarian started her summer job and holy cow can she fill out a sweater. But she's the sheriff's daughter. Keep your distance."

"I always could depend on you for brotherly advice, Arnold. Tell you what. I'll make sure she's yours." Ready to ride off, Nick sticks his hand out the car window and jerks on his friend's hand. "I'll come by tomorrow." From his mirror he sees Madeline get into a car. He thinks she might have ridden off with the new kid who just moved into town.

"Wait, Nick. One more thing. You know I hate being the bearer of bad news, but Dr. Mutsfeld is out to get you."

Nick chuckles. "Guess this is just my day. What's up now?"

"He said he's call'n your Dad to tell him you ran over a fledgling. I was down helping him close up for the night earlier today, and heard him saying all kinds of bad stuff about you. How about I give you some money to contribute to the bird sanctuary? Mr. Mutsfeld would like that, and maybe he'll change his mind about telling your dad. I mean, I'll give you big money."

So what the fellas were telling him is true, Nick realizes. Arnold is going to help his father out on the farm instead of becoming a veterinarian. His college money is the big money he's talking about. Nick shakes his head. "I'm not taking it. I know where that money is coming from. You're not turning your back on your lifelong dream, are you? Didn't you hear Lucille today? 'Follow your dreams or they'll get old and dusty.'"

"But my dad always had dreams of me working side by side with him on the farm."

That's another thing Nick doesn't understand. When do you know that it's time to give up all that you ever wanted for yourself to do something someone else wants? He'd asked his mom about that once and she'd said that if you had to ask, then it probably wasn't the right time.

"Okay, suit yourself."

"Nick. Your taillight is out. Take care."

Nick juts his arm out the window and jerks on his friend's hand again. "See ya, pal."

What a friend Arnold is. But him giving up becoming a veterinarian is like...Nick giving up his car. No wonder Arnold's hair looked disheveled.

The library is located on top of a hill right next to the post office. Nick curves into the parking lot and moves into a space, leaving lots of room on either side. Some lunatic might scratch his fender and drive off. He moves the car back and forth until he's satisfied with his parking job. He examines his taillight, and within a few minutes it's fixed.

Inside the library, the mood is somber. *Why does it have to be so quiet? It's almost like Frederick's Funeral Parlor. Maybe that's why Lucille always has her head "buried" in a book.* The student librarian has indeed started her summer job, and she acknowledges him with her dark green eyes. He quickly looks away. This is not the reason he came to the library. He has more serious intentions. Still, there's no harm in looking at the white sweater with the two rounded cups that are ready to spill over under just the right touch.

Against the back wall of the library, Nick finds the shelves containing poetry books and hauls a pile to a table. He has seen Lucille go to these shelves many times. He flips through the pages of poems. *What are these writers trying to do? Why don't they write in good old plain English? Does Lucille really understand all this?*

At last he finds a poem he can understand and hopes Lucille will appreciate. "I Think I Will Never See a Poem as Lovely as a Tree," by Joyce Kilmer. He memorized it for Miss Powers' class last year and she discussed it many times, so he should understand it. But as he turns the pages, another poem catches his eye. He reads it, and then reads it again. Searching for a pad of paper so he can copy the verses, he walks over to the student librarian sitting at the desk. "I've seen you around school. Nice job you have here. How many of these books have you read?"

When she giggles, she pulls her shoulders back and her sweater down. Nick notices. She leans across her desk, as if to hear him better.

"You may have something I could use," Nick says.

A blush washes over her face. "Heard you were in some trouble—something to do with a bike? Want me to talk to my Daddy?"

"My good name is enough. Well maybe I should rephrase that. My honesty is enough."

She laughs like she knows what he meant, but when she says, "That's the same, isn't it?" he realizes that unlike most Harvest people, she doesn't know much about him.

"What I really need right now is a pad of paper and a pencil."

When she reaches for a shelf below her desk, his eyes follow the outline of her buttocks in her slim skirt. When she hands him the paper and pencil, her hand touches his. "If there is anything, anything else I can help you with, let me know," she says.

Nick doesn't want to get involved. He just barely eked out a win with her dad about the accident. But she'd be a trophy for his friend Arnold. He walks back to the long table and can feel the girl's eyes following him. He can always tell when a babe's eyes are on him. Now he gets down to business. He reads the poem he has chosen one more time, just to be sure. Author Unknown. Why would anyone write such a beautiful poem and not put a name on it? Even Robert Frost knows better.

IF YOU BUT KNEW

How all my days seemed full with dreams of you,
How sometimes in the silent night
Your eyes thrill through me with their tender light,
How oft I hear your voice when others speak,
How you 'mid other forms I seek—
Oh, love more real than though such dreams were true
If you but knew.

Nick jots down the poem and adds the other two stanzas.

When he notices Harry looking through the stacks, he feels sorry for the guy. Sweeping Lucille away from him this afternoon must have slaughtered him. But Harry has to learn to fight for what he wants. Like a beaten man, Harry just stood there with those hotdogs in his hand until he finally put them down to mop his brow.

Harry glances up and their eyes meet. Nick thinks of making it up to him by teaching him a few things about women, trying to level with him. But when Nick approaches Harry and gets close enough to put his hand on his shoulder, Harry adjusts his glasses, slams his book shut, and stomps out of the library.

Nick could mail the poem right then and there at the post office, but something else comes to mind. He returns to his house and pulls a chair up to his desk and stuffs the poem he copied into an envelope. He'll drive by and deliver it himself. He wouldn't mind seeing Lucille again. If Mr. Kramer is home, he'll drop it on the porch and run like a bat out of hell.

When he's done, Nick looks around the room thinking about what to do next. Now that school's out, he'll have time to organize his stuff. His shelves, crammed with miniature cars and magazines, need arranging. He started collecting them as far back as second grade. He eyes the package sitting on the floor, still unopened. The parts for a new engine he's designing.

His father wants him to work in his law office over the summer, but that is not what he wants to do. No need for a law office for him; he has to defend himself all the time, anyway. There's nothing he'd rather do than get a job at Olson's Garage. Still, his father is after him. "Having a hobby is one thing, but no son of mine is going to end up working in a garage," Nick Sr. says.

There's always the recreation center; the manager asked Nick if he wanted to work there. How could he not ask him? One look at his body, and people would hanker to look just like him. Besides, what fun taking the women through all those positions.

Above his mirror, Nick has pictures of iron men like Siegmund Klein and his favorite, Siegmund Breitbart. Breitbart did a stupid thing. While hammering a railroad spike through five one-inch oak boards resting on his knee, he punctured his leg with the nail. Nick can't imagine hammering nails with his bare hands because it would hurt too much. Although it happened last year, Nick still agonizes over it. The day he heard that Siegmund had to have his legs amputated, Nick stayed in bed all day and refused to eat a thing. When blood poisoning killed the man, Nick put a sign on his bedroom door that read, "Nick's Funeral Parlor," and had his own private funeral for him right in this room. He laid Breitbart's picture on his bed and kneeled down and said prayers. Not the church prayers, but prayers he made up. They made a lot more sense to him.

The picture of the matinee idol, Valentino, is tacked on the wall between the two Siegmunds. Nick looks at the actor and then back at his own reflection in the mirror. He takes a comb, wets it, and slicks back his hair. He moves his head in several directions, each pose validating for him his resemblance to the "Latin Lover." Lying down on the floor, he does one hundred sit-ups. He adds another fifty for good luck.

The hot day, the excitement of graduation, and Lucille's rebuff at the creek has left Nick's hormones raging. Lucille got him revved up and ready, and then poof, she starts seeing faces. He shakes his head. That girl tricked him. He feels claustrophobic in his room. He looks at his watch and then leaves the house again. He drives past the library, turns back around, and parks in the same spot he did before. He sees that as a lucky omen.

Still at her desk, the student librarian thrusts her bosom forward when she sees Nick walking toward her. He winks and she smiles back. One time can't get him in trouble, and then she's all Arnold's. "What time do you get off work?"

"About fifteen minutes."

"I'll be waiting for you in the parking lot. Red Model T."

"I know."

"You know what?"

"That you have a red Model T. I've noticed."

Fifteen minutes later, she walks out with a new coat of red paint across her mouth. This is his kind of girl, Nick thinks. Take her for a spin, have some fun, drop her off. What went through his head thinking he could take Lucille to the creek? She might know her onions when it comes to schoolwork, but she's no bearcat to take to the creek. If he can satisfy his urges with this babe, maybe he'll stop thinking about what it would have been like with Lucille.

The student librarian slides into the seat next to him and then moves closer. As a formality, Nick suggests they go for a soda. She agrees. He drives back to the drugstore and they sit down at the counter. Arnold and his other friends are already there, at a far table. Nick tells her to wait at the counter. He has something to tell his friend.

Nick finds Arnold in the group. Knowing that his friend spends most of his spare time with his dogs or working with the Vet and has little left over to scout for girls, he says, "Hey Arnold, like I said, this girl is for you, for being my good buddy."

"You sure, Nick?"

"Have you ever seen me when I wasn't sure?"

Nick returns to the counter. The girl orders a chocolate soda, and Nick orders nothing. He tells her he doesn't drink.

In a few minutes they are back in the car and driving through town. This is the slowest Nick has ever driven, except for when he attended a funeral. He doesn't want to be stopped with the sheriff's daughter in the car. He drives down a gravel road. Not the one going to the creek, but a new one he discovered on his own. Trees line both sides of the road, and Nick has no idea where the nearest house is. When he turns off the car lights, they sit in total darkness.

Consumed with arousal since this afternoon, he gets right to it. The student librarian wants to talk, but that is not on his agenda. He pushes her skirt up and unzips his pants. He pauses for a minute to check out her breasts and then concedes to the moment.

"You're in a hurry," she says, when he reaches his peak in minutes.

"Don't have all night," he says.

The innocence in her voice conflicts with the seductiveness of her body. But he's careful not to create any animosity with the sheriff's daughter. "Look, I'm sorry, I promise to make it up to you."

"When?"

"I have a buddy who has lots of time. He's even going to be around next winter."

He detects the disappointment in her voice, but he's already thinking of dropping the envelope with the poem on Lucille's porch step.

"Don't you like me? You really didn't give me much of a chance."

He hears her sob and he tries to reassure her. "No, don't do that. It has nothing to do with you. You're one choice bit of calico. Very sexy. A real babe. Great gams. Honest. It's me. What's your name?"

"Millie." She spells out her name. "M-i-l-l-i-e."

He wouldn't do her much good anyway. He's leaving town in the morning.

Nick reaches toward the back seat and pulls a crumbled piece of paper off the floor. He straightens it and scribbles Arnold's name, address, and phone number and hands it to her. "Call him, Millie. He will change your life. Introduce you to the whole animal kingdom."

LUCILLE

Staying in one place too long can make you stale, stale as an old piece of bread, Nick had said that afternoon at the creek. Now, three years later, Lucille sits at the kitchen table, sifting through the calendar pages under the red ribbon, and realizes he may have been right. Nothing new, exciting or stimulating has happened to her since he left town.

She didn't believe Nick's words then because Harvest was where she'd always lived and moving away from the familiar wasn't something she ever thought about doing. But in the three years since she last saw Nick, she heard little tidbits about the exciting things he was doing in New York, and his luxurious style of living. She wasn't sure of the work he did, but when she shopped at the General Store, Jerry always had something to say about Nick. Things like, "Your friend Nick has come a long way since you two were dancing at the picnic. He's move'n up. Move'n with the big boys now." Or he'd say, "I hear Nick has a new girlfriend, and he spends money on her like it's water."

She'd leave his store feeling forlorn. Nick probably didn't even remember taking her to the creek, and yet she has never forgotten the effect going there with him had on her. And being truthful with herself, she admits that Nick may have been right: her daily routine has become stale, and she has too. Caring for the pigs and chickens, cooking, cleaning, and working in the garden, and doing the Kramer farm bookkeeping keeps her busy enough, but that is not what she wants to do forever. She ought to be almost through with college by now, but she never even started.

To ward off Nick's prophecy of becoming stale, Lucille spends part of her day writing at her desk. She usually does this after dinner. She realizes that if she can't physically leave Harvest, at least she can imagine what it would be like through her writing. She doesn't know how much paper she uses or how many words she writes, but one day after looking at the handwritten papers piled high in front of her, she realizes she has completed her first novel. The novel takes her to New York City, and she writes of the wild parties held in the clubs and the beautiful women and dashing young men who frequent them. She writes of a handsome young man who has the pick of any woman he wants, but chooses the girl he left behind in a small town in Iowa.

After many rewrites, she can no longer deny that Wade, the romantic figure in her novel, is actually Nick Martin Jr. Angry with herself for letting him consume her time and her life in this way, she takes a match to each page and watches her work go up in flames.

She tries instead to write about something that has nothing to do with romance. She writes about farmers and the new struggles they face in an industrial age, which she sees first-hand from watching Bill. When Jerry Sloane gets wind of Lucille's talents, he implores her to hold readings and discussions at the General Store. He pays her a small stipend, but the farmers are so enthralled with what they hear that they leave her generous tips in the cup Jerry discreetly places on the counter. Lucille hides the money in her bureau drawer, under her socks.

BILL

On the day Lucille graduated from high school, Bill promised himself that he would again be the acclaimed farmer that others looked up to. His father had been right: lose a day, you lose a month, then a year, and then you lose everything. Bill knew he still had it in him to prevent that from happening. If it meant toiling in the fields until sundown and dreaming up a new formula for feeding his livestock, so be it.

Three years later, his work has paid off. Sure, the price of corn has dropped and the falling prices fall lower every day, and he has debts to pay, but at least he saved enough to do what he always intended to do for his daughter. On this warm October morning, Bill is up and out of bed feeling happier than he has felt in a long time. He pulls on the overalls and white short-sleeved shirt that he left on a chair by his bed and walks into the kitchen for a cup of coffee. He changes his mind and foregoes the coffee; today is the day he has been waiting for, and with his excitement mounting, he doesn't need a boost from drinking coffee. He finds his boots at the kitchen door, and with a quick jerk of the hand pulls them on and he's out the door. Walking toward the field, he examines his property. He looks at the cut grass around the freshly painted red barn, the yellow birch and hemlocks that have grown so large they almost cover the hill leading up to the farmhouse, the new roof he put on the house, and of course his new tractor. He considers himself a lucky man. If his goal was to grow more crops per acre than his father did, he accomplished that. He's had his best corn-growing season in years. Lucille warned him about producing more corn than he could sell, but he paid little heed to her words. He's a farmer through and through and seeing his farm flourish once again makes his heart swell. For too long he sat on the sidelines while the other farmers were humming along. They were buying refrigerators and vacuum cleaners while he still used the icebox and a broom. But he has sound credit at the bank and if he needs another loan, he'll get it.

His daughter once again is reaping praises that are music to his ears. Farmers flock to Jerry's to hear her stories about the new machinery that's changing the way farmers work. Once again he hears his friends say, "You sure know how to raise a daughter, Bill. She has a good head on her shoulders." Words like that make his heart swell with pride. Yet, his daughter has been acting strangely. She habitually greets the mailman with a huge smile, as though her smile can magically solicit a letter from his sack. In the early hours of the morning, even before he climbs out of bed, sometimes he sees her on the porch, holding a candle in the darkness. He's heard that some people who start out acting a bit strange can suddenly become downright screwy. No, he won't let that happen to his daughter. Today will change everything.

Looking over the fence that surrounds the Kramer farm, he notices sections that have rotted and decides to take care of that right away. He goes to the barn for his tools. He finds a hammer and saw on the shelf, gathers some nails from a pail on the floor, and with the extra wood planks he stores in the corner of the barn, he's ready to make the repairs. After replacing the rotted segments, he goes back to the barn for a bucket of paint and soon finds himself retouching the entire fence. The time whizzes by because his mind is on the surprise he has for his daughter.

With the sun now pouring over him, he returns to the house and grabs a cold beer from the icebox. Soon he will count the money that he has hidden away in a place no one could possibly find it. He stacked the bills in little bundles and seeing all that money made him dizzy with happiness. He has saved just enough for Lucille's college education, and maybe a little more to pay for a wedding when Lucille and Harry get married. He thinks about finishing work early and cooking a special dinner for this occasion. He'll even place some flowers on the table. Then he will break the good news to his daughter. He'll invite Dan, of course. Paul and Pauline Powers ran off and got married last week; he'll invite them, too. And of course he'll invite Harry. Maybe the young man will make an engagement announcement. It's about time. Then Bill will make his announcement that Lucille will be able to start college next fall. Just to see the look on his daughter's face will give him such pleasure.

Finishing his beer, he reaches for another one and releases a dragged out *ah* after the first swallow. Evelyn never liked when he did that, but today is different. If she were here, his little annoyances would be overlooked. Making himself comfortable, he sits down at the kitchen table and tosses his feet on a chair. Letting his mind drift, he thinks of his daughter finally using her fine mind to do what the Lord had planned for her, and him becoming the farmer the Lord destined him to be. His prayers have been answered.

When he hears something crash to the floor, he gets up and looks around to see what fell. He cocks his head. The noise is coming from his bedroom. He moves out the door to pick up the shovel he left on the porch. Shovel in hand, he kicks open his bedroom door. The room is in disarray: shirts tumble from open drawers, books and papers are scattered on the floor, and the lamp has toppled on its side. Not expecting to see Madeline, Bill drops the shovel and says, "What's going on here?"

"You miser," she says. "You haven't given me any money in months. How do you expect me to live?"

"For crying out loud, I gave you money last week. You probably spent it down at the juice joint. The truck drivers are coming to town next week for their convention, get it from them. I don't have any money for you to piss away."

"Piss? That reminds me, are you still have'n trouble with that?"

"Lay off."

"Well then, if you won't give me money how about you pay'n me for... you know for me do'n what I do best? Only this time, call out my name."

When they were first married and still making love, Bill caught himself calling out Evelyn's name. But he doesn't want Madeline reminding him of that now.

Although she has already done a pretty thorough job, Madeline continues rummaging through the draws. Her blouse catches on the drawer knob, and as she pulls away, so does her top button. Her heavy, large breasts spill over her ribcage. Bill turns away.

"Ignore me, will ya." Madeline tugs on her skirt, ripping the seams as she jerks it over her hips. "Can you ignore this?" In typical Madeline fashion, she places her hands on her hips and parades in front of him. Bill notices that she has given up wearing underwear. Madeline kneels on the floor and extends her arms. "Please, take me."

He'll show her what a little discipline can do. He walks toward the door, her arms pulling on his legs as she pleads, "Please, please take me."

Bill slams the door behind him and walks into the kitchen. He sits down at the table to finish his beer. After not eating all day, his mind clouds over and he hears Evelyn's voice whispering to him. She has a message. "Stay away, Bill. She's trouble."

"Damn it, Evelyn, a man has to do what he has to do." He throws the bottle into the sink and hurries back into the bedroom.

Madeline is lying on the bed with her legs over her head. "I knew you'd be back," she says. "Go on, try something new."

But with more than sexual arousal driving him, his anger blasts into her with each thrust. After an explosive release, he rolls over next to her, one hand still on her belly.

"You are a man after all. I had my doubts about you." She stands and puts out her hand. "How much for that?"

He stares down at his pants and pulls them up.

When he looks up again, she is on all fours pulling the neat bundles of money out from under the bed. Waving the cash at him, she nods in defiance. "This will do."

His anger escalates, but it just isn't in him to physically fight with a woman. He must find another way to get those bills out of her hand. "You know that's the money for Lucille's college tuition. I wouldn't even trust the bank with that money, and then you come along and think you can just grab it away from me. Don't you have a conscience?"

"A conscience? What can you buy with a conscience?" Madeline pulls on her clothes, finds a safety pin in the drawer to replace the missing button on her blouse, and tucks the bills between her breasts. She moves to leave.

Bill beats her to the door and bars it with his body, spreading his arms. "You're not going anywhere with that money. I worked too hard for it. The Good Lord is watching you," he yells, but his voice is overtaken by the sound of pounding on his bedroom window. From where he is standing, he can see Hutch Mosley. Bill waves him around to the front door then goes to meet him there.

"I've been banging on the door with my fist," Hutch Mosley says. "Couldn't you hear me?" He looks over at Madeline, who is now standing next to Bill. "I'm sorry, I didn't know you had company."

Bill shakes his head in disgust. "Not very good company."

Hutch stands at the door, his arms trembling, holding a bunch of newspapers. Hutch rarely comes around at this time of day. Bill wonders what brought him here. "You don't look well, Hutch. Nothing wrong at home, I hope. Arnold? Brenda? Your family okay?"

"It's nothing like that."

Bill walks out of the house. He doesn't want Hutch to come in with Madeline there. The two men walk across the front lawn and stop under the apple tree. Hutch is telling him something about the stock market and Bill can't take it all in. The fracas with Madeline is still on his mind.

"Wait here, Hutch, I have to settle a little matter first." Bill walks back into the house to confront Madeline again, but she's nowhere to be found. He looks around the kitchen and the parlor then runs into the bedroom, but he can't locate her. In the bedroom, he notices the open window. Looking out, he sees Madeline teetering in her high heels toward the road. Bill runs out of the house to stop her, but he is too late. A truck stops at the side of the road and she gets in. Madeline is gone, along with Lucille's college money. The big dinner with his good friends, his announcement that Lucille will indeed be attending college, the look of joy and surprise on her face when she hears the news have all been snatched away by a ruthless woman. He feels an ache in the pit of his stomach. If he wasn't a grown man, he'd throw himself on the ground and kick his feet like a child. Looking up at the sky, he sees the fluffy cloud move toward him.

"I know, Evelyn," he says, staring up at the cloud. "I must deal with this like a man."

When Bill gets back to Hutch, he sees him pacing back and forth and looking down at the ground, as if he were oblivious to the commotion. "Hutch," Bill yells, "stop pacing. What's wrong? Why are you carrying all that stuff?"

Hutch places his armful of newspapers on the bench under the tree. "I'll let you read the headlines for yourself."

The wind picks up, knocking a few apples off the tree, but the papers barely move. The men look at each other in disbelief.

"Yup," Hutch says, "a bad omen." Leaning over the bench, he points to a headline. "Stock Prices Crash in Frantic Selling, Speculation to Blame."

Before Bill has a chance to glance at it, Hutch points to another headline. "Slow down, Hutch. Give me a chance to read something." Bill picks up the paper. Now his hands tremble too. Another headline leaps off the page at him: "Stocks Crash in Heavy Liquidation, Total Drop of Billions."

"We're all going under," says Hutch. "My Arnold says we're going to lose everything."

Bill had heard something about stocks dropping earlier in the week, but he thought that it all got straightened out. Now, reading this, he wants to throw up the beer he drank.

"Investors are going nuts. They overextended themselves buying stocks on credit, and then—boom! Like a balloon, they burst."

"So what are you saying? Stocks fall and people are left flat broke?"

"It's not a fall. It's a crash. October 29, 1929 will be remembered forever."

Bad times. Heck, Bill knows about those. Farmers never had it as easy as those city people. No speakeasies, wild parties, and big spenders around Harvest. Just farmers doing what they always do. Hell, he's not going to let any damn stocks get in his way. Not when he just got rolling again. But remembering the bright new yellow tractor, the addition on the house, and the roof that needed fixing, he feels sick. He makes a quick mental tally of how much he borrowed from the bank to pay for all that.

"Yup, Arnold coaxed me into buy'n all those stocks," Hutch says. "Would've been better off if he'd become a veterinarian and I took care of my own finances."

Bill knew little about stocks, but he'd invested anyway. Down at the General Store all the men were talking about investing. Maybe he'd get lucky yet. Everything he worked for now hangs on a thin branch. One swift wind and down it goes. Bill pushes his hands so far into his pockets that they almost come through the other side.

Bill alerts Harvest residents not to sit back and take it on the chin. Jerry accommodates him and places a sign in his store window announcing a meeting at Kramer Farms. The meeting is scheduled for two days following the stock market crash: October 31, 1929. Eight o'clock sharp.

On Halloween night, farmers and business owners knock on Bill's door. They move into the parlor. Some stand, others sit, but they all agree that they have to do something. "We must get rid of President Hoover—get him impeached," Bill says. "We'll circulate a petition—go door to door. We will let Washington know we have the wrong man in office."

But it's Dan who interrupts him. "Bill, why do you blame everything on President Hoover? People went stock market crazy and then they started pulling all their money out at once. That's what caused it."

Hutch has something to say, too. "This is a worldwide thing, you can't blame our president."

Mr. Olson blames it on prohibition and the wild living in New York City.

Everyone has something to say, but no one says anything that could change the situation. People leave Bill's house more dejected than when they arrived.

In the weeks that follow, crop prices tumble, businesses close, banks fail, and stocks continue to drop.

On a cool afternoon a few days before Thanksgiving, Bill Kramer jumps into his truck and speeds down the road. He wants to be the first one down at the bank to see the loan officer, Mr. Drake. Mr. Drake is an understanding man. He will offer Bill a cup of coffee, and they'll talk business, man to man, just as they did when he applied for the loan. The loan officer will understand that although Bill promised to have the loan paid in full by the end of this month, circumstances have changed for him, and he needs more time.

Bill's foot is heavy on the gas pedal. As he nears the bank, the sheriff pulls him over. "Slow down, Bill. You've already reached your destination. We all have. We've reached bottom."

Besides his daughter, Millie, the sheriff has two sons. Both young men own farms, so Bill knows the sheriff knows what's going on. When they attended the meeting at Kramer Farms, they listened but were too glum to speak. "Tell your boys we're not giving up," Bill says, trying to keep his voice steady.

The sheriff's eyes tell a sad story. They mist over, but he smiles. Bending his lips together, the sheriff looks out into the distance and then with a sigh, he says, "I'll tell them."

When Bill approaches the bank, the number of cars lining both sides of the street over- whelms him. He looks at his watch. With a few minutes to spare before his appointment, Bill visualizes Mr. Drake. The man rarely changes his demeanor. He will sit erect behind his desk wearing his trademark gray suit and decide the future of Kramer Farms. He will appear impeccably neat and organized.

Bill made sure to look businesslike. He slipped on a clean white shirt to go with the pants and jacket he wore for Lucille's graduation. He even wore his Sunday fedora and made sure to dab on some aftershave lotion. He didn't want any fertilizer odor lingering on his skin.

Entering the building, Bill detects the usual professional tone of the tellers as they talk to each other in hushed tones and go about their work. Still, his heart is beating fast. Maybe he's being too optimistic and he won't get the loan extension. He removes his hat and comforts himself by stroking the brim. He glances around at the slew of men standing around. He knows most of the farmers there and has done business with some of the shopkeepers, but he's never encountered any of them looking so overwrought. Some are shuffling their feet and chain-smoking. Others don't move. Howie, Rachael's father, is staring at the floor between his feet.

Spotting Hutch in the far corner of the room, Bill walks up next to him. Hutch nods and goes back to reading the Bible, then begins singing softly from the Book of Psalms. Bill joins him, glancing at his watch from time to time. After an hour, he nudges Hutch. Hutch shakes his head. Several names have already been called and when he hears his name, Bill pulls down on his jacket, straightens his tie, and follows a young woman into Mr. Drake's office.

Bill steps toward the desk, hoping the squeak in his shoes doesn't annoy the loan officer. But Mr. Drake is not behind his desk. He is standing in front of the window, facing it. Bill waits for him to turn around and greet him with a handshake. Bill hums until he reminds himself that it is not good manners. He glances at the watch on his chain. He coughs and clears his throat, and finds himself humming again.

When the loan officer finally turns around, Bill relaxes. But there is no greeting and no handshake. Mr. Drake has a blank look on his face. His eyes stare blindly at the wall. Bill doesn't want to interrupt. He will wait until he is spoken to. Sometimes business people think farmers are around animals too much to learn proper etiquette.

Only Mr. Drake's hand moves, and Bill sees the revolver. Already, he can foresee the morning paper's headlines: "Bill Kramer, Harvest Farmer, Shot in Bank." He thinks of Lucille without a mother or a father.

"Mr. Drake, wait." Bill holds up his hands in front of him. "I will repay the loan as soon as I can. Come out to my farm. It is prospering. Come see my silo. I have more crops than I need." He should have known better than to borrow so much money. Now he will pay with his life. He's heard that expression before, but now he knows what that means. Bill's scalp prickles. Sweat trickles down his face and he feels very hot. He can feel the beat of his heart through his shirt. He closes his eyes and he hears a blast. It's loud. Everything is hazy. He touches his body. He's still standing. The man in the gray suit, who held Bill's future in his hands, no longer has a future of his own. Mr. Drake is lying on the floor.

The bank guards rush through the double doors. Lights, sirens, police cars, and an ambulance, the icons of tragedy, arrive on the scene. Mr. Drake's secretary, no longer composed, speaks in disjointed sentences to a man wearing navy blue suit. Bill catches bits of the conversation. He hears talk about auditors catching Mr. Drake embezzling money from the bank to pay for his investments. "Mr. Drake, he- he intended to give the money back," the secretary says, her voice cracking. "He's honest. The most honest man I've ever known."

Bill, the last person to see Mr. Drake alive, is dragged in for questioning. "I just came in to inquire about my loan," he argues. The inquiry lasts for hours. Soon he can't distinguish between his imagination and reality.

Snippets of gossip circulate about who got shot at the bank. When Bill arrives back at Kramer Farms, he sees Nick Martin Sr.'s car parked in front of his house.

"Came over to see if you are okay, Bill, and if there is anything I can do for you. Want to tell me what happened?"

Bill simply shakes his head and mumbles, "I don't need any help from you. I never have."

With puzzled look on his face, Nick Martin Sr. drives off.

༄

By November o f the following year, Harvest foreclosure signs have popped up everywhere, but when a sign appears at Kramer Farms the other farmers become more concerned. Kramer Farms has been around for as long as anyone can remember. It was passed down from father to son for generations. Hutch arrives at Bill's door almost as soon as he hears the news.

Bill and Hutch take a slow walk around the farm, blaming themselves for not recognizing when trouble was coming. "Guess I'll be next," Hutch says. He insists that they do something, anything. "Years of hard work, for this to happen."

Bill agrees. "Corn has dropped to ten cents per bushel, maybe even eight by now. How can a farmer pay his mortgage and his debts and provide for his family? And to top it off, Hutch, my new tractor cost me a lot of dough."

"You bought it outright?" Hutch asks.

Bill gets a little flustered now and clears his throat. "No, on credit," he answers. "But let's look at the bright side. Lucille is well, and so is your son, Arnold. That's a lot to be grateful for."

Hutch shakes his head and looks down. "I wish I could say my son is doing well. You know they took the pit bulls away from him. Those two dogs found a way to jump the fence and when the sheriff saw them wandering the road, he had no choice; he had the pound pick'm up. Second time he caught them wandering. Arnold loved those dogs. And now with his wife cheating on him, he feels a double loss. I don't think he and Millie share the same bed anymore. People are talking and he's ashamed. I caught him sitting on a bale of hay, the wind blowing dirt all over him. He misses those dogs, he's sick over Millie, and with this financial mess…I tell ya, my kid just can't take much more."

Bill puts his arm around Hutch's shoulders. "Sorry to hear that, Hutch. I thought Millie was a good woman. But one never knows."

The spring and summer months of 1930 are the driest Bill can remember. All summer, the crops at Kramer Farms lay like crumpled brown bags scattered across the fields. Bill tries his best to raise some money, but the mortgage payments are too much for him to handle. Things look grim heading into winter.

LUCILLE

"Guess you can tear this page off your calendar and circle November 27 and put it under the red ribbon, Lucille. Yup, we're move'n," Bill says. He breaks the news to his daughter after Thanksgiving dinner, after Dan, Paul, and Pauline have left. When Lucille gets up from the table to clear the dishes so her father doesn't see her tears, Harry follows and puts his arm around her. "When we're married, we'll have our own place," he whispers in her ear.

Dan arrives early the next morning. He pulls up close to the house to help lug all of Bill's and Lucille's belongings onto his truck. Lucille runs out to meet him. There is a November chill in the air, and Lucille tugs her sweater closer to her body.

"This is the least I can do to help a friend," Dan says. Removing a wooden plaque from the front seat of his truck, he hands it to Lucille. "I made this for you. Hang it where you can see it every day."

She studies the word carved on it. *Trust*. "I love the baroque lettering."

Dan says, "Trust has brought your father and me a long way and trust will help you get through this. I'd be in the same mess as Bill if my father didn't leave me a nice inheritance. First thing I did was pay off the mortgage on the farm. Best thing I ever did."

"That was a good thing to do," she says. "Moving from the farm is so hard. I can barely look at the pain in my father's eyes."

"I know what you mean, honey. It kills me to see this happening too. Go now, and say your own private goodbye to the farm. We'll still be here working when you get back."

Lucille walks back to the house to tell Bill that she'll be gone for a short time. He feels uneasy about moving, and she knows that having her nearby gives him comfort. "I'll just be meandering around the farm," she says, and he nods at her. On her way past the house, she finds an envelope on the porch step addressed to her. She puts it in her pocket to read when her father's eyes are no longer on her back.

She walks toward the barn, committing every detail along her path to memory. Many of the trees have lost their leaves; a few yellow ones still cling to the branches. She stops at the base of the weeping willow beside the barn, the tree that Bill planted in memory of his little brothers. It was the place Lucille went to when her spirits dropped. She started going the day she saw her parents fight for the first time. It was a silly argument over a bottle of lilac and apple blossom perfume. Lucille still remembers the poem she wrote that day:

> *Good morning little piglets, squealing in your space.*
> *Good morning little chickens, and the wind blowing in your face*
> *I heard something this morning, I think that you should know*
> *Don't tell Mother Goose and least of all the crow.*
> *Something about lilac and apple blossoms made my daddy mad,*
> *My mama's eyes turned tearful, and her pretty face so sad.*
> *If you have an answer, ask the birds to sing a tune.*
> *Cause I want Mama and Daddy to kiss and make up soon.*

She laughs at her childish rhyme, but she hadn't laughed the day her parents argued. It had started when Bill found the perfume in their mailbox. He demanded to know who sent it. When Evelyn said she didn't know, he insisted he'd get to the bottom of it. But Lucille knows that her father is no ogre. His heart brims with love and kindness, especially concerning "his Evelyn." Looking out at the pigpens off to the side of the barn, she recalls a time when she was about ten years old and out helping her father feed the pigs. Bill said, "No tail docking for our pigs, just give 'em lots of room and it won't be necessary. There are other ways to keep pigs from running after each other's tails and fighting. I don't care what the other farmers are doing. If cutting pig's tails upsets your mother, I will take no part in it." He was always considerate of Evelyn.

Under the Red Ribbon

೧೨

Lucille removes the envelope she picked up on the porch step from her pocket. The *i* in her name is not dotted, the loop of the *e* is closed, and the *l*'s could pass for *t*'s if they were crossed. She rips open the envelope, removes the note, and reads the one sentence written on the page: *Lucille, I'm in town and want to see you. Nick*

Holding the note to her heart, she stops at what was once her mother's tomato garden and kneels. Touching the soil, she whispers, "Mama, tell me, should I see Nick?" Musing, she pokes around in the sand using a rusty tool that once belonged to her mother. She finds old bottle caps, buckles, stones, and even some slow-moving worms, but no answer. She hears her mother's voice: *Of course you should see him. Why not? Besides, I don't think I could stop you.*

Lucille continues sifting through the soil. She unearths a thin gold chain buried in the dirt. Lucille nods, taking it as an omen that her mother has answered her question. She remembers the locket that once hung from that chain. Wiping her eyes with her sleeve, she catches sight of the glimmering gold heart clinging to the point of the rusty spade. Lucille tucks her newly found treasure into her pocket along with Nick's note. With Dan's plaque in her hand, she walks back to the farmhouse.

Back at the house, Dan drapes a sheet over the piano and hauls it toward the truck along with Evelyn's paintings. Lucille calls out for him to stop. This is the last of her belongings, and it places finality to all the years she lived here.

"Dan, when I was little you came by and twirled me around until I laughed so hard my side hurt and made you stop. After mama died, you sat with me under the willow tree and dried my tears. I could find my way to your house blindfolded. My whole life is in this farm. How can I leave?"

Dan stops pushing the piano and wipes his brow, taking a moment to consider. "We go our merry way," he says, "and hope life stays good, but sometimes there is a roadblock. We take a detour, and then we get back on track."

A car speeds down the road, whipping up a cloud of dust. The driver slams on the breaks, backs up, and brings the vehicle to a screeching halt next to Lucille and Dan.

"Hi, Lucille." Nick leans out of the driver's side window. "See you're move'n. Where to?"

"Oh, not very far from here."

"I saw a pretty woman and knew that it was you. I've been thinking about you. Get my letter?" His voice is low and intimate. It oozes through her body, melting her heart like butter left out in the sun. If she were ever angry with him, that feeling is gone.

He looks so clean in a light blue short-sleeved shirt with the collar open. His face is shiny, as though he just stepped out of the bath. When his eyelids close halfway, Lucille is lost. She's wearing an old brown dress that is torn at the hem, what she put on for cleaning and packing. Her hair is caked with dirt. *Why does she have to run into him when she looks like this?*

"It's been awhile, Nick." Lucille concentrates on keeping her voice even. "I heard you left Harvest right after our graduation. That's about three years ago. Actually, that was the last time I saw you."

'Could it be that long? Time flies when you're busy, I guess. And I've been busy. I don't get back here too often." Nick's elbow hangs out the window. "Princess, you're one heck of a babe. Three years turned you into a real woman. Bet you behave like one, too."

Nick's stopped car is blocking the road, and drivers behind him are lining up and honking their horns. Nick pulls into the driveway. He extends his hand to Dan, who is tossing some cartons of clothes onto the truck. Dan stops what he's doing to shake his hand. Bill continues piling the cartons into the truck and stops only to give Nick a scathing stare.

"Would you care to take my car out for a spin, Mr. Kramer? It's a brand new Model A. I didn't even have to paint it red myself, like I did my Model T. I got it on special order. Or, I could take you and Lucille for a ride and you can see how smooth this baby drives."

Lucille knows that Bill admires those cars. He'd told her so, as he glanced through magazines. She'd also heard him talk to Dan about the new arched fenders, the safety feature of the four-wheel mechanical brakes and hydraulic shock absorbers. But Bill turns away and walks into the house.

"How about you Lucille? Hop in. Nick's eyes gleam and his dimple begins to appear in his left cheek.

"I'd like to. I really would."

Nick opens the door for her.

"But I can't."

"What is it this time, Lucille? Whose face do you see now?"

Embarrassed, Lucille turns and runs into the house.

Nick

After leaving Lucille, Nick drives off in a huff. He can't believe he allowed her to make a fool of him again. He'd planned to ask her to a party, but the heck with that. He has more babes than he can handle anyway.

He sees Madeline wearing a sleeveless blouse and short tight skirt walking up the hill. The wind has picked up and the temperature is dropping. She's struggling in her high heels and the flask in her hand isn't helping her balance. He shudders with disgust, but by the time he reaches her, his empathy wins over. He doesn't think she'll have a long life anyway, but it's cruel to let her suffer out here in the heat. He read that whiskey could damage the liver and the brain. Nick is sure that Madeline's brain has already dissolved in all that moonshine. He slows down and drives alongside her for a while.

Nick stops and opens the passenger's side door. Madeline's expression changes, her eyes suddenly clear. "Oh it's you, Nick," she says. "What a nice surprise. I knew we'd meet up again someday." Madeline lumbers into his car. In no mood for her nonsense, he tries to block her chatter by concentrating on the road. Her eyes cling to him. Her wild hair, painted face, and big tits busting through the top of her blouse make him want to drive into the ditch.

"Where are you going?' he asks. I'll drive you."

"How about the creek, Nick? Doesn't that sound nice?"

"I'm serious Madeline, where shall I drive you?"

"Well then, just drive me into town."

They drive the rest of the way with her chattering about how happy she is to see him. He remains silent.

Closer to town, Nick pulls onto a side road so that Madeline can exit the car without anyone seeing them together. But when he opens her door, she slams it shut. Removing a red hat with a big red flower, Madeline ties her hair into a bun. Her cheeks are now fully exposed, and they droop like two empty pouches. Her body isn't bad, there's just too much of it. Nick moves away from her, lifting his shoulders when she puts one hand on his knee and the other on his crotch. "Madeline what are you doing?"

"Come with me, Nick. I know a place we can go."

Out of curiosity, he gets out of the car behind her and follows. But if she's expecting him to be her lover, he has news for her. His first sexual encounter had been with Lily, Jerry's wife, but that couldn't be helped; her shape put all the young girls to shame. When his daddy got wind of it, he made Nick promise not to do any more married women. "Way too dangerous, son," Nick Sr. had explained, as though he'd had first-hand experience with that kind of thing.

"Wait, Madeline. I have a dentist appointment." Nick trails behind in the brush as Madeline runs ahead.

"The dentist can wait," she says, winking. Moving fast now, she stops when she reaches a hut surrounded by trees. Nick wonders how she ever found it. Madeline pulls open the door and beckons Nick to hurry.

He couldn't walk any slower. When he catches up with her, she has her dress unbuttoned. She asks him to help her untie the laces of her corset.

"You gotta be kidding," he says, lifting his eyebrows.

"Nick, help me. I'm just not good with these strings. Damn it! A knot."

Ignoring her request, Nick lies down on a bed of crunchy leaves. He places his arms under his head. *Might as well see what this old lady looks like under her clothes. No harm in that.*

Madeline finally strips off her corset and she poses in front him with her hands on her hips. Her belly protrudes, round as a beach ball. When she circles around him, her breasts flop like undercooked pancakes and the slabs of flesh on her buttocks bounce. Nick covers his mouth so that Madeline won't see him grinning. But when she plops down on top of him and moves her hand toward his crotch, he jumps to his feet and runs toward his car. He sees her pitiful image in his rearview mirror, and stops. He can't just abandon her. After all, she is Lucille's stepmother. He yells for her to get in the car. She runs for her clothes.

Madeline is out of sight when Nick spots the sheriff combing the area. The sheriff also sees Nick and walks over to his car.

"Well, Nick, what are you doing here?"

"Same thing you are, Sir." He holds his breath, hoping he said the right thing.

"So you heard about the guy who escaped from the county prison? We were about to take him to the big house, but he disappeared. Escaped from right under our noses. Don't look good for us. No, sure don't. Grapevine has it, he travels in a green truck but hides out in the woods whenever he can. Glad to have your help in the search. We have Mr. Olson and Hutch out helping and Jerry said he'd keep an eye out for any strangers, but we need as many eyes as possible."

Madeline runs toward them. "To the creek, chauffeur!"

"Did I hear her call you chauffeur?" asks the sheriff.

"Yes. I take the widows on outings. They don't like being out alone."

"What a nice thing to do." The sheriff looks at Madeline again.

"Nick, is that the woman who..."

Nick cuts him off. He reaches into the backseat where he keeps a jar of the gel for those intimate moments and fills up an empty tin he has there. "It's a little different from the last stuff I gave you, but it's guaranteed to give you an extra glow. Your car, I mean."

Reaching for the tin, the sheriff smiles and pats Nick on the back. "Guess I'll take this woman home now, sheriff, but I'll keep my eye out for a green truck."

Nick and Madeline drive past Jerry Sloane, who is out sweeping the walk in front of his store. Madeline calls to him. Nick surmises what Jerry must be thinking.

Nick knows where Madeline lives, or at least where she spends most of her time. It is well known in Harvest that she hangs out at the

Good Night Motel. He knows he is approaching the rundown structure when he sees, from a distance, the large sign atop the long pole with the *o* missing from the word *Motel*. Making his usual clean stop, he opens the passenger door. When Nick doesn't follow her out of the car, Madeline looks like she might cry again. He reluctantly concedes. He sits on a stone ledge in front of the motel. His hands dangle on his knees and Madeline scoots over to sit on his lap.

"Madeline, this place is a dump," he says, looking at the building with the loose clapboard siding, the roof missing shingles, and the piles of leaves in front of the entrance. Beer cans are strewn all over the place. Staring at the people coming and going, he says, "Look at the creeps that come here." He points to an old man with missing teeth and gray stringy hair walking with a woman who has her arm around his waist to hold herself up. A cigarette dangles from her other hand. With her skirt so tight, he can almost see the crack in her ass, and her blouse doesn't cover her midriff but exposes a roll of fat. "It's enough to make you sick." Nick is disgusted and he takes a deep breath. "Madeline, you can do better than this. Let me ask you something. Do you like me?"

"Oh, Nick, do I."

"Then do something for me."

"You know I will." She wiggles close to him. "Let's go to my room. I'll do anything you want. You won't have to pay. I have enough money."

"Now where did you get money?"

"From Lucille. I swiped it out of her drawer. I sneaked into her room and grabbed it all, and her old man's money."

"Madeline, that was an awful thing to do. They both worked hard to get that money together. And get your hands out of my pants. When I asked you to do something for me, that wasn't what I meant. I want you to turn your life around, just like making a U-turn when you're driving. You can start by giving that money back."

"If I turn my life around, then would you want me?" Her voice sounds like a child's.

"Then you wouldn't want me."

"I will turn my life around. I promise, Nick. Just spend the night with me."

"Sorry Madeline. I would if I could."

Nick gets back into his car. He calls out the window, "Give that money back."

A green truck pulls up to the front of the motel. A hand waves to Madeline. She looks at Nick and shouts, "See he wants me."

ℒUCILLE

The Kramer and Hillsdale Farms trucks move slowly down the road, in no hurry to reach their destination. Holding the plaque Dan gave her, Lucille studies the word again. *Trust*. As they move further away from Kramer Farms, they pass abandoned houses with doors ripped from their hinges and windowpanes cracked or missing. Lucille can hardly believe that families once called them homes. A blanket of dry weeds and brush makes it difficult to distinguish one property from another.

"This is it," Bill says, stopping the truck in front of a rotted wooden structure. A message scribbled on a board tacked to a tree reads, "Yours for the Taking."

"This house looks like it's been vandalized," Lucille says. She climbs out of the truck and examines the paint-splattered porch, the kicked-in front door. One look at her father tells her that he's not happy. Lucille enters the house cautiously, careful not to trip over the pulled-up floorboards. The charred walls are covered with soot and the acrid smell of fire damage fills her nostrils. It appears as if the Morris brothers, who owned the property, started to burn the house down and had a change of heart. Removing her bandanna from her head, she uses it to wipe the perspiration from her face. A parade of rats runs along the woodwork, and Lucille dashes out of the house.

Bill leans against the truck, his shoulders slumped and eyes downcast. Lucille wraps her arm in his and leans her head on his shoulder. "It's not your fault, Daddy."

"What was I thinking? This is no place for you to live."

"I have the perfect solution," Dan says, emerging from the truck he has just parked. "We'll knock the place down and start over again.

We'll build a brand new house. Why not? You didn't have to pay for this one, not that it's worth much. Live at Hillsdale Farms in the meantime. I'll drive Lucille to my place and when I get back here, we'll start making plans."

On the drive over to Hillsdale Farms, Lucille is in a better mood. She's always loved Dan's farm.

"I saw you talking to Nick," Dan says. "I like the kid. I got to know him a little bit. He comes over to my place now and then, when he's in town that is, to work on my truck. I don't know what he did to my engine, but my truck drives smoother than those newer automobiles."

She can't fool Dan; he knows her too well. He's trying to find out why Nick stopped by the house earlier.

"You know, Dan, I wanted to ride away with him and—and, oh, what's the use? Did you see my father glaring at us? Why is he so down on Nick?"

"I know Bill inside and out, but this, I just don't know. We were both friendly with Nick's father in high school. We all got along great. I can't figure out myself what changed. Anyway, aren't you seeing Harry?"

"I guess you can say that. He thinks we'll get married one day."

"And you? Do you think that too?"

When Dan stops in front Hillsdale Farms, Lucille sits in silence for a moment. "Harry and I have a lot in common and he's a good person, yet something is holding me back."

"You mean *someone*, don't you?"

―

It has been a memorable day. If she had her calendar with her she would circle November 28, 1930 and place it under the red ribbon. Getting up early to pack her things, saying goodbye to the farm, seeing Nick again, seeing that dilapidated house she almost had to live in, and then coming here—that's a lot for one day. Now, at three in the afternoon, she still has things to do. But she shouldn't complain because her father, Dan, and Paul will be at the Morrison house ripping it down and won't be home until dark. She has a good feeling here at Dan's house. It feels just like home to her, except that there's music. Dan usually has the radio on in the kitchen, like it is now. She hears the song "Bye Bye Blackbird" playing. Her stomach turns cartwheels. She remembers her first and only date with Nick, when that song blasted from the car radio.

Lucille has been lucky enough to get a part-time job writing articles for the Harvest Gazette, and she decides that it's time to do some work. She fills a glass with cold lemonade and goes into Dan's room to write an article on the topic of transition. After writing for a few minutes, she realizes that she has written a short poem to Nick.

The leaves are turning green again,
I still remember the first time when,
I saw your face, heaven sent.
And fell in love with you.

The thought of him leaves her feverish.

Slipping her hand into her pocket, Lucille removes the necklace she found at the farm. She wipes the grime off the locket to make it glisten like it did when her mother wore it. Turning it over, she sees "Evelyn" carved in baroque lettering, but she is taken aback when she reads below it, "Promise me, Love Dan."

Why would Dan give her mother a locket? Her eyes settle on the floor and she remembers the day Dan and Evelyn made the rug for this room. They sat at a worktable cutting two-inch strips of material. Her mother held the ends of the ties while he began the braiding. The two of them went through the motions intuitive to each other's every move. Neither one of them spoke, but when they were done they embraced.

Walking over to the rocker, Lucille picks up the scrapbook lying on the table next to it. Turning the pages one at a time, she looks at the photos of Bill and Dan as children, then as teenagers, then as adults. Best friends through the years. There are lots of pictures of Paul, and so many of Evelyn. She finds herself in there, too.

Two envelopes fall from between the pages of the scrapbook and land on the floor, both bearing Dan's address. They are written in her mother's handwriting. Curious, Lucille removes the letters from the envelopes and sits down to read them. The first one is yellowed, as though it was written many years ago.

Dear Dan,
I am concerned that Bill will find out. He is a gentle man, but there comes a time when the most gentle among us lose restraint. It is all so complex because we both love him, and what happened between us is magical. I hope you feel the same. Love, Evelyn

Her heart beating rapidly, Lucille reads the letter in the second envelope. The paper is newer, whiter.

Dear Dan,
Come soon. I'm lonely and Lucille hasn't even left for college. Love, Evelyn

Placing the letters back into their envelopes and the envelopes back into the scrapbook, Lucille looks again at the most recent picture of her father and Dan. They have their arms around each other's shoulders. Best friends.

It's easy to see why a woman could fall for Dan. With his gentleness, the way he plays the piano, his muscular body, blonde curls, and blue eyes, he could excite any woman. But her mother? She belongs with Bill.

Lucille decides on a new title for her newspaper article: "Living a Lie." Dan always reads her column. Although she does not mention any names, she hopes he'll make the connection. She was unable to sleep last night. Dan and Bill left Hillsdale early this morning to work on the house, and she spent the rest of the day alone. Now that she has had time to ruminate, she wonders how Dan was able to fool her and her father so thoroughly all these years. She wonders about her mother, too.

Mr. Sherman walks into the house to deliver a chunk of ice. He's been delivering ice to Kramer Farms for years. It was always a treat seeing him because he has a cheerful face and a big smile. His eyes are small and they twinkle. When Lucille was much younger, and he saw her reading at the kitchen table, he pulled out a long string of licorice, and said, "For the little girl who will grow up to be a professor."

Lucille glances up to see him coming through the door.

"Hope I didn't scare you. Dan told me I could come right in." He places the ice into the icebox with large tongs and then reaches for the pan beneath it and empties the water from the pan into the sink. He is so adept at doing this that the three steps seem to be of one motion. "I don't know how much longer I can keep doing this job with people not paying their bills. I hear Dan might be leaving us soon for the big city. Can't blame him. He can't hold on to this farm much longer."

"There's nothing really keeping him here," she answers.

"Oh, sure there is. Paul, Bill, and you." As Mr. Sherman is about to leave, the three men walk into the house and join him in the parlor. "I was just telling Lucille," Mr. Sherman says, "that you're just like one family. The three of you have been friends since you were kids. I remember seeing you horse'n around when you walked home from school. You fellas got a minute?" Mr. Sherman lowers his voice, but from the kitchen Lucille can make out every word.

"It must be about three years now that Arnold and Millie have been married. Ain't that right? Three years?"

When he continues, Paul drops his coke bottle on the parlor table and laughs so hard that liquid explodes from his mouth.

"Not funny at all. So Jerry caught that no-good son of his, Derik, making out with Millie in the back room of the store, and she lay naked as a maple tree in winter," Bill says. "I really don't give a damn what he saw, Millie's tits, nipples or ass. Derik and Arnold were friends. Derik do'n his wife is horseshit. Isn't there such a thing as trust anymore?"

"Cool down, Bill. Don't get so hot under the collar," Mr. Sherman says. "I'm just telling you because, well, I mean gee, Jerry seeing Derik making out with Millie isn't just ordinary stuff. I mean . . . it's Jerry's son and Arnold's wife. That's crazy. Jerry would be blabbering the story to everyone if Derik wasn't his son."

"Good thing Arnold's father wasn't in the store that day. Hutch would have blown a fuse," Bill says.

Without a word to anyone, Lucille leaves the house and walks into town.

Kenny's Drugstore doesn't look the same without all of the high school kids out in front of it. The young girls who crowded the cosmetics aisle and the boys who came out to romance them have more serious things to do now. But Lucille does see familiar faces when she spots Anita Martin standing behind a long table in front of the church handing out free bread to Harvest residents. Lucille is familiar with breadlines. The front pages of the newspapers show long lines of people, from many different states, waiting for bread. Some have their collars up to hide behind—ashamed to be there.

Howie waits his turn, and then looks around before taking his piece. Hutch is staring at the ground as he receives his portion. Bill said that he'd rather chew on the soles of his shoes than beg for food. By the looks of them, he might just be doing that.

The sign in Jerry Sloane's window is huge, and he means every word written on it: "Buy Now, Pay Later." The people in line are his friends, and he won't let them starve. Olson's garage is closed. People aren't driving much anymore, so he's only open during the morning. The liquidation sign in Gil's dry goods store window gives Lucille stomach pangs. Gil's wife, Dottie, is expecting again and this will be a hardship.

"Don't let the sign in the window fool you," Gil says, when Lucille walks through the door of the dry good store. "For all intents and purposes, 'Gil's Dry Goods Store' is already closed. I haven't had any business in here for months. I've applied for some odd jobs, but there are hundreds of applicants ahead of me."

Packing up bolts of fabric and throwing them into cartons as he speaks, Gil's expression tightens. Lucille looks over at the counter and sees a picture of Gil and Dottie at their high school graduation. Gil's face is bonier now and the lines around his mouth are deep. She'd predicted that he'd have his own dry goods store and that he and Dottie would have four children, but she never could have predicted this.

Gil reaches for a bolt of blue satin material. He measures a few yards, folds it, and hands it to Lucille. "Make yourself a dress for Sheila's party."

"Sheila is having a party? I'm not invited."

"Sure you are. Her brother Harry is your boyfriend, isn't he?"

Lucille had never been part of Sheila's group in high school, and she doesn't expect that she will be invited to her party. The doorbell jangles and Sheila bursts through the entrance with all the enthusiasm of a cheerleader.

"We were just talking about you," Gil says.

"Talking about the party, I hope. One, two, three, it's our time to parte-e-e-e."

Gil and Lucille do not return her enthusiasm.

Sheila's mood darkens. "For crying out loud, I'm just trying to keep all of us from falling apart. Harry says he'll be bringing you, Lucille." Lifting her package off the shelf, Sheila places it in a bag. Her voice trails after her as she leaves. "Thanks for the material, Gil. And Lucille, dress to kill."

Lucille hasn't been to a party for a long time. It would be fun to go.

"I don't think Arnold and Millie will be there," Gil says. "Did you hear?"

"I think everyone has. How sad for Arnold."

"He's really not doing well. I contacted Nick. He came into town as soon as I told him. If anyone can help him, he can, don't you think?"

Just hearing Nick's name leaves Lucille trembling. "Well yes, of course."

With the bundle of blue silk tucked in a bag, Lucille strolls into Kenny's Drugstore to browse. She's in no hurry to get back to Hillsdale Farms. The less she sees of Dan the better.

At the perfume counters, she indulges herself. If she did have the money, which perfume would she purchase? The owner used to have some open samples for customers to test, but not anymore. She picks up several bottles and admires their colors and shapes. It would be nice if she could buy some bubble bath, or a bright red lipstick to go with the blue silk.

"Hey, baby, let me buy you something nice." It's Nick, standing right next to her. "Stay here and don't move." He moves off and after a few words with the manager of the store, he returns with a bottle of Evening in Paris. Placing it in Lucille's hand, he says, "Now, tell me why you wouldn't take a drive with me?"

"I was busy, with moving and all."

"Princess, women don't refuse a ride with Nick Martin Jr. for any reason. I told you, you don't play by the rules."

"Who makes these rules, Nick?"

"Who? Now who do you think? The man who rules the road."

She looks directly at him. "You don't rule my road." She doesn't know where those words came from, but she's thankful they were there when she needed them.

Nick pulls on one of her curls. "I make the rules. Always have."

She can hardly compose herself; her heart is pounding so hard. But she can't let him see that she is nervous. She continues in a steady voice. "There's always a first time."

Nick looks as if he's been hit with a rock. "Now wait a minute. You're not talking to Harry, here."

"It's just that you left that beautiful poem for me, and then three years pass before I see you again. I'm confused."

"Let me make it up to you. Come with me to Sheila's party."

"I'm going with Harry."

Nick throws his hands into the air. "You're kid'n me, right?" He makes a quick turn and he's out the door.

"You sure got Nick in a lather," Sheila says, appearing at Lucille's elbow, as if from nowhere. "I saw you two talking. I almost needed smelling salts to believe anyone could get him so mad. You two were *so* engrossed, you didn't even see me standing here. Tell me, does he have a crush on you? That would make my brother *so* mad. Harry would be *so* jealous if he saw you talking to Nick. When you left him for Nick at the graduation picnic, Harry had *so* much trouble dealing with that."

Under the Red Ribbon

Lucille notices that Sheila elongates her *o*'s when she speaks. She didn't notice it when Sheila was speaking to Gil. Maybe something about Nick brought it on. But Lucille isn't surprised. Most girls act like they are on giggle juice when he's around.

When Lucille arrives home, Bill is leaving to go into town to see Jerry and see if he will maybe give him an hour or two of work at his store. At the door, he suddenly keels over. Lucille knows why; he hasn't been eating enough so that he can save his share of food for her. Lucille goes to the icebox and takes out the last small orange, placing it in Bill's hand. She tries to convince him that it isn't shameful to wait in the breadline or visit a soup kitchen, but he won't hear any of it.

When Lucille shows him the beautiful blue satin material and tells Bill that she's going to a party with Harry, the color flows back into his face. "A Christmas party?"

"I don't think so. Just a party."

"That is better news than the orange. I love seeing the two of you going out for a good time."

Tomorrow, she'll buy a pattern for her dress. She'll do it on her way to the church.

༄

Lucille has been working at the church since she moved into Dan's house. Now that it is close to Christmas time, more people will be coming in, needing gifts for their families. At nine o'clock in the morning, Lucille arrives ready to set up tables and fill them with mittens and gloves she has knit for the children. With so many people out of work, funds for the poor are dwindling. Sheila walks in lugging a bag of clothes.

"Donations for the needy," she says. "I just cleaned out my closet. Someone can make good use of this stuff. I even brought in some of my Dad's coats."

The clothes are snatched up almost as quickly as they are put down. When Bill lumbers in through the side door looking like a rag-a-muffin,

Sheila and Lucille turn and look at each other, their faces showing despair. They watch him poke around on the back table before he walks out empty-handed.

"I hear it's going to be this way for a long time," Sheila says. The elongated *o* is gone, along with her liveliness.

BILL

Bill didn't make it to Jerry's store yesterday; he was too weak. But he'll get there today. He peers out the window of his house and sees the black sky. It's morning but it looks like night might be approaching. The dust clouds are heavy and dark, obstructing the light. Referring to the wind gales that are blowing dry soil from miles away, he mumbles, "People need to keep their dust where it belongs. We have our own mess here." His inner chatter creates or perhaps reflects his inner turmoil: *If we had a decent president, he'd do something about this.* He puts on his goggles and coat. "Feels like I'm wearing an old bathrobe," he mumbles. When he opens the door, a heap of sand hits him in the face.

Bill stumbles through the dust and he thinks he sees Howie laboring down the road, but he's not sure. With their handkerchiefs wrapped around their noses and lips to keep the dust at bay, all of the men look pretty much the same. Catching a better glimpse as they near each other, Bill sees that Howie has gotten thinner. Bill inquires about Howie's daughter as usual, and Howie admits that Rachael has been in a lot of accidents since she fell from her bike, and he's running out of people to blame.

"Well, just because the attorney got his son off, that doesn't mean he wasn't to blame."

"Nah, it wasn't Nick. Rachael admitted to that. He even came over a few times to see if she was okay."

Bill waves his hand in disgust and moves on. He only asked out of courtesy. He remembers something Jerry told him: that Rachael, tired of being hungry, dressed up like a boy and started hitching rides on the railroads, going from town to town looking for work. She even fooled one girl into falling in love with her, and now they're a couple.

Bill trails after other men who trudge down the road, a regimented army of desperate farmers looking for work. He licks his cracked lips. His mouth is parched. He should have gone back into the house for his scarf.

He comes side by side with another person on the road. "Is that you, Hutch?" Bill asks skeptically.

"It's me. Though I can't blame you for not knowing that."

"Know what you mean. I'm a mess, too. I've just been staying close to home, seeing no one and hearing nothing. I think I almost like it that way."

"I don't feel right, Bill," Hutch's voice is hoarse. "I don't feel like myself anymore. I'll never be the same old Hutch again. Brenda won't ever be the same either, I guess." His diminutive eyes take on a tortured look. His pores are so clogged with dirt that he looks like someone dotted his face with a pencil. He pulls down on his fedora and pushes the collar of his overcoat up to his chin until his neck is all but lost inside it.

"I've been walking around like this since it happened. Hell has reached down and gathered us all up. A man can no longer feed his family." He muffles his hacking cough with his hand.

Bill takes his goggles off to wipe them. One look at Hutch tells the whole story. Bill feels the horror deepening around him. He hasn't bought soap, tobacco, or a container of milk in weeks. Yesterday he worked all day for Mrs. Olson, cleaning her house for fifteen cents, and he felt bad taking the money from the old lady.

"How about that breadline, Hutch? Doesn't it just make you feel like a beggar? I just won't be a part of that. I'd rather starve to death." Bill fumbles in his pocket, checking for his fifteen cents. "I'm going down to see how Jerry's doing."

"Jerry's a good man. He'd give a man his last penny." As they approach Olson's garage, Hutch pulls down on his hat again. "I have a few coins. I'm buying myself a drink. It's hush-hush, but Jim Olson's got some hard stuff hidden in his garage. To top it all off, that

Prohibition makes you feel like you're doing something wrong when all a man is trying to do is ease the pain."

"You would think coming from Iowa himself, President Hoover would care about farmers. But he doesn't give a hoot. We need direct federal aid, but he's leaving it to the state and local government. What money do they have?"

"Bill, some people are even blaming the president for the dust storms. Hell, I got my own troubles."

"We all do. Guess I'll go and see how Jerry's doing at the store."

⸺

The General Store, with its dirty green awning, looks more like a shutdown theater than a place to shop. The men who used to hang out here drinking coffee, rolling cigarettes and exchanging stories are gone. They are out looking for work, as if there are jobs to be gotten. Still, they have to show their wives they are at least trying. Bill, of course, doesn't have to tell his wife anything; she ran off with his hard earned money.

Jerry is hunched over his elbows at the counter, his face resting in the palms of his hands. He pulls up two chairs when he sees Bill.

"Kinda quiet in here," Bill says.

"No kidding," Jerry answers, standing now to shake Bill's hand. "Good a time as any for us to catch up on things. Nice to see you, Bill."

The candy bins are filled with the same candies as before and the shelves are stacked with the same cereals, soups, and jellies. Bill knows that Jerry isn't doing any business, but he can't help asking, "Got any odd jobs? You know, anything like putting up shelves, sweeping? I'll do anything."

"Take a look around, Bill, there's nothing to do. If you need anything for you and Lucille, just put it on your account."

Bill owes him too much money already, but things like that don't trouble Jerry. Jerry knows the meaning of trouble. When his son, Bobby, died at the age of nine from influenza, Jerry went to pieces. He closed his shop for almost a year. It wasn't until he started working with the kids at the orphanage a year or two later that he snapped out of it.

He wanted to adopt an eleven-year-old with red hair and freckles, but Lily dallied too long before making up her mind and another couple beat them to it. Instead they adopted the Indian boy, Derik. The kid had mischief in his eyes, and Jerry needed that challenge to help him forget his grief.

"How is Derik?" Bill knows the story about him and Millie, but he wants to be polite.

"Best thing I ever did was adopt that kid," Jerry says. "All odds against him and he became a family doctor."

Bill knows that Jerry likes the status that goes along with Derik being a doctor, and so he forgives his adopted son for his other unfavorable traits. But now Jerry looks out onto the street as if he's thinking hard about something. He arranges the lifesavers in their boxes, even though they are already lined up in neat rows. "Did you hear about me having my hands tied, while a—well, a young man snatched a bottle of milk and some cereal from the store and then ran off?"

"Now, what kind of a robber does that?"

"With Hutch as his father, how would he know how to rob anyone?"

Bill scratches his head. "Who are you talking about?"

"Arnold. It happened last week."

Bill sits down on the chair next to the window and grabs a pack of Lifesavers. He pops one of the yellow circles in his mouth. "What are you saying? Arnold robbed you?"

"Poor guy. A wife and kid, no job. Just things on his mind."

"I just saw Hutch. I was worried about him. He was really down. Worse off than I am, that's for sure. Now I know why."

༄

After a meager dinner of a bowl of soup thickened with cubes of hard bread, Bill sits in the parlor talking to Dan about Arnold. Dan looks like he wants to tell Bill something but he can't quite manage to say it. "What's up, Dan?"

"There's something strange about the way he died," Dan says.

"Died? Who died?"

"It just came on the local news. He was come'n out of Apple Grove and he didn't see the car come'n over the hill. Had too much on his mind to pay attention to the road, I guess."

"Dan, who died? I don't know who you're talking about."

"Arnold. Arnold Mosley."

"Venture out, you hear bad news. Come home and hear more bad news. Where can a man go to clear his head?" Bill can't help himself; he bows his head and sobs.

"If we lost Lucille, our lives might well be over," Dan says.

"Maybe Arnold would still be alive if he could afford food for his children. Maybe Millie wouldn't have cheated on him, if her life weren't so bleak. While everyone's struggling to put a meal on the table for their families, the president entertains politicians at big dinner parties. He doesn't go to the church looking for a coat."

"Bill, why does everything have to come down to the president?"

Bill answers with an ache in his voice. "Maybe I'm so angry over Evelyn's death I have to lash out at somebody."

LUCILLE

Lucille had expected Sheila to cancel the party; Arnold had been her good friend, too. But Sheila told her that a time like this was just the time for friends to get together. "We can help each other get through this," she said. "Strength in numbers."

On the night of the party, Harry arrives early to pick up Lucille. Standing at the front door, he shifts his weight from foot to foot and repeatedly pushes back the hair on the front of his head. He wipes the dust off his coat sleeve and hands Lucille one long stem rose. "Oh, Harry, you shouldn't have spent money on that," she says, accepting the gift.

Tripping over the rug as he enters the house, Harry says, "I wish I could afford a whole bouquet. I want to cheer you up. Losing Arnold has put us all in a funk."

"What can I do to cheer *you* up?" she asks, dropping the rose in a jelly jar and filling it with water.

"You can become my wife."

Bill walks in from the yard. "Did I hear you say something about Lucille becoming your wife?"

Lucille blushes. "You are taking words out of context."

"Don't give me this context stuff, I know what I heard."

Lucille ushers Harry out the door, and kisses Bill on the cheek before she leaves. "Daddy, don't worry. When the time is right, you will be the first to know."

Harry rushes around to the passenger's side and opens the car door for her. The maroon mohair seat feels prickly beneath her and she straightens the skirt of her dress. The car sparkles; Lucille thinks that Harry must have spent hours cleaning and polishing this old Buick.

As they drive, Harry comments on how much he admires Bill, and how well the two of them get along. "A man of integrity. That's the kind of man I want to be." Lucille thinks that if her daddy knew of Harry's affiliation with the Republican Party and his admiration for Herbert Hoover, they might not be quite as friendly.

Harry swings his arm around Lucille and nudges her closer to him. He holds one hand on the wheel and one hand on hers. "Tonight is going to be a great night for us. I feel a real turning point in our relationship."

Attempting to steer the conversation in another direction, Lucille asks him about his part-time job at the printing factory. He laughs.

"Does that mean you're having a good time there?"

"No, but some people are. Every time I think about it, I crack up. A certain man and woman at work are having a good ol' time together. Both of them married to other people. You know them, Lucille, but I won't say who. The woman's husband got wind of it, and at noon, when he knew he'd find them in the car, he was there waiting at just the right moment to do something about it." Harry's laugh is out of control. "Lucille, her husband opened the car door, pulled the man out, and twisted his arm like it was made out of clay. Then he dragged his wife into the car and drove off. The man, obviously in pain, stood like a statue in a national park, unable to move, and a bird flew by and perched on his head. And you know what happened next? That's right-- droppings. All over his face!"

"Harry, do you actually think that's funny?"

Harry sinks into his seat. "No, not really. But I'm nervous tonight, very nervous."

When they reach their destination, Harry puts his hand in his pocket and pulls out a rolled tissue paper tied with a string. "I meant what I said in your house. It would make me very happy if you became my wife."

Lucille pauses. She knows that she would be foolish to let Harry go. She's been his girl on and off all through high school and since. He's kind, he loves her, and the phrase *doctor's wife* has a nice ring to it. "Harry," she says, "Let's talk more later."

They step onto the porch of Sheila's house. Looking through the window, Lucille sees a party in high gear. Couples dancing the shimmy move with reckless abandon. The girls wearing skirts hiked up above their knees must have spent hours in front of the mirror getting those finger waves and spit curls just right.

Walking through the entrance, Harry and Lucille are greeted by loud music, laughter, clouds of smoke, and dim lights. Boys who before had paid her little attention now whistle and call out, "Wow, Lucille, you look nifty." Girls rush over to her as though she has always been a part of their clique. Sheila, looking every bit the glamorous, gracious hostess, drifts through the crowd wearing a lavender tiered chiffon dress and a matching headband with a feather.

"Lucille, you took me literally. I said 'dress to kill,' and your dress is dynamite." Sheila whispers something in her brother's ear, and he winks back at her. "Set the date, little brother," she says, with a lilt in her voice.

Dottie and Gil arrive late. "You know Gil," Dottie says to Lucille, when they meet each other near the entrance to the house. "He refused to close the store until after seven." Dottie has that pregnant blush on her cheeks and with her auburn hair hugging her shoulders and her pink lace dress skimming her body, she is radiant. Gil has lost his peaked look and seems ready for a good time.

"You did wonders with that blue silk, Lucille. You look like a deb," he says, and Dottie nods in agreement.

The couches and overstuffed chairs are pushed up against the walls, creating space in the center of the room for dancing. Lucille and Harry sway to a Louis Armstrong recording and Harry tells her how the musician learned to play the cornet while still in reform school.

"How did he end up there?"

"Shot a gun into the air on New Year's Eve. He was only twelve years old."

Harry guides her over to the table for some punch, but suddenly he takes a turn and directs her to a corner of the room hidden from the crowd. He cups her chin in his hand and turns her face towards him. "How about we talk some more, here, right now?" As he bends down to kiss her, Lucille hears Gil yell, "Hey Nick, I knew you wouldn't miss the party."

Over Harry's shoulder, Lucille watches Nick unwrap three bottles of whisky from brown paper bags and place them on the table. "Help yourself," he says. "Mum's the word." He's about to lead the woman he walked in with to the dance floor, the one with the voluptuous body and nude-tinted dress, but stops when he sees Lucille looking at him.

"Hey, what have we here? Is that my Fairy Princess?" He crosses the room to join her.

"Hi, Nick."

Harry's hands shake as he adjusts his tie.

"This dance is mine," Nick says, taking Lucille's hand.

"Lucille is with me," Harry replies, mopping his brow.

Nick and Lucille move across the parlor floor. *Yes sir, she's my baby, no sir don't say maybe,* the song goes. Nick is humming to the music, holding Lucille close, and whispering in her ear. Her flushed cheek presses against his. "How's my Fairy Princess?" he whispers. She presses closer to him. She doesn't want him to disappear again, like the Eastern Goldfinch at the creek.

"Save a drink for Nick," Gil says to the group standing around the table.

"I'm already intoxicated with Lucille," he calls over his shoulder to the guys. But then he abruptly pulls away. "Excuse me, Princess. Wait right here and don't move."

Nick peels out some bills clipped together in his pocket. In the dim light she can see him by the door talking to the woman he came in with. He hands her the money. "Here, this will pay for your train trip back to Minnesota," she hears him say. "Better yet, why don't you leave with Harry?"

Taking another look at the woman Nick arrived with, Lucille knows that plan is sure to backfire. Harry doesn't do well with fast women. He has enough trouble with someone like her.

Harry walks over to the table and drinks directly out of the flask, draining it. The woman in the nude-tinted dress approaches him, but he ignores her. With fury in his step, he leaves the party. Lucille hears his car pull away, and for a moment she has regrets. But only for a moment. The young men and women pair off and move towards the bedrooms. Lucille hears Nick call, "Wait a minute. Stay where you are."

The music and chatter stops. "Anyone here know a prayer?" Nick asks the crowd. When no one responds, he says, "How about you, Gil. You know any?"

"If I knew a prayer that could help, I wouldn't be closing down my dry goods store."

A hush fills the room. Lucille notices tension in Nick's face as he begins to speak. "Our good friend, Arnold, died just two weeks ago driving down Apple Grove," he says, with a quiver in his voice. "He knew that street like the back of his hand. His mind was just somewhere else, I'm guess'n. All the same, I'm going to the Town Hall to see that we get a light or a stop sign put up so something like this doesn't happen again.

"At the private service I saw his little boy Skip holding tight to Grandpa Hutch's hand. His Grandma Brenda was inconsolable. She couldn't stop crying. And Millie, she's way too young to be a widow. You all know Arnold cared about the world. He had true affection and concern for animals and he would have been the best veterinarian in the world. He became a farmer instead. Remember Lucille's speech at our graduation? She said to follow our dreams. Arnold didn't. And now he never will. Let's keep Arnold's dream alive. Lucille, please hand me the jar on the table." When Lucille moves to gather the jar, all eyes remain on Nick Martin Jr. "Pass the jar around the room, Lucille. I'm asking you, my friends, to give what you can toward the Arnold Mosley Bird Sanctuary here in Harvest. I've already set up a special bank account for Arnold's son, Skip."

Arnold's old classmates empty their pockets. The jar fills with coins. Gil's pockets are already empty, but he drops his gold wristband, the one his father gave him for his graduation, into the jar. Nick looks toward him and nods.

Soon, the party guests begin to make their exits. Gil and Dottie head for home first. They have children to care for and Gil's mother will only babysit until eleven. Nick and Lucille stand in the center of a quiet room.

"Nice dress, Lucille." Nick's voice is soft, the way she likes to remember it. "And your hair, smooth as silk. I now have a picture of you in my mind that I will keep right here." He points to his heart. He takes a deep breath. "When I gave that talk about Arnold, I didn't look like I was going to cry, did I?"

"No. Of course not."

"Arnold and I, we were so close. Neither of us had sisters or brothers, but we had each other. Come to think of it, you're an only child, too." Nick's eyes are so penetrating that Lucille is forced to look away. Nick suddenly picks her up and twirls her around in his arms. They both land on the sofa. He lies down and places his head on her lap.

"Nick, I think I feel a tickle in my throat, and I feel cold."

"As long as you don't see your father's face," he says, smiling up at her.

The only face she sees is the face on her lap.

Nick reaches over to the table and pours whiskey into a glass. "A little bit of this hooch might help."

Lucille gulps it down and winces. She takes another gulp, then another. With Nick and awash with a sense of freedom, she couldn't be more content.

"Turn off the lamp, Lucille." He draws her head toward him, stroking the nape of her neck. When he changes her position and leans her body down on the couch, she encourages him to move his hands up towards her breasts. He kisses her, like she dreamed he would. When his hands travel under her skirt, she urges him to continue, but he abruptly stops.

"It's getting late. Time to go," he says. He helps her up from the couch. She needs his help; the liquor has taken effect. "Now you know why I don't drink," he says. "I like to be in control."

Steering her toward the car, he shields her eyes from the wind. He brushes her hair away from her face and wipes her eyes with a handkerchief before helping her into the car. With a burst of urgency, he heads in the direction of Hillsdale Farms.

"How do you know where I'm staying?" Lucille asks.

"I always know where you are. Our bodies are like magnets. You should know that. That's what attraction is all about."

So why is he in such a hurry to take her home, she wonders? When they reach Hillsdale farms, Nick takes Lucille's hand. She thinks he is going to kiss her, but instead he touches her forehead and says, "Baby you are sick. Your head feels hotter than my motor after a race." He leans over her body, opens her door, and says, "Take care, baby. See ya around."

She watches his car race down the road. He didn't even kiss her good night.

The house at Hillsdale Farms is quiet. Bill is in his bedroom. Still bothered about Nick's abrupt departure, Lucille appraises herself in the bathroom mirror. Sheila said she looked dynamite when she saw her at the party and Harry thought she looked good enough to marry. She imagined she looked like one of the those girls she saw in Harper's Bazaar going off to a New York City party with—well, with Nick. But maybe the reason she thought she looked so good was because she hadn't worn a party dress for a long time. She pushes the neckline of her dress down a little lower in the front and then studies her image in the mirror again. Harry found her hard to resist, but evidently Nick didn't.

After changing into her nightgown, she walks into the kitchen for a cup of hot tea. Her throat feels raw and her bones are like icicles rubbing against each other. She might be coming down with something. Her legs are still wobbly from the whisky and she holds onto the wall for balance.

Bill walks into the kitchen with a bounce in his step. "I was just lying in bed, thinking about you and Harry. Bet you had a nice time tonight. Any news for me?"

"No, we didn't talk about that at the party."

"'Cause you were having so much fun? I know you and Harry don't need alcohol to have a good time, but I hear someone's bringing the hard stuff into town. That's what Jerry tells me. No one drinking at Sheila's party, was there? No, your friends wouldn't be into that sort of thing, even if there were booze around. And I know I brought you up right."

Nick

On his way home, Nick evaluates the evening. When he'd strutted into the party, everybody stopped what they were doing and called out to him. Just like when he was in high school. His friends admired him then and they admire him now. Only now, he has become someone who deserves to be admired. In three short years he has become a rich man, and he sure knows how to spend that dough.

Harry, of course, had disappeared like he'd seen a wolf. Poor Harry never did know how to fight for his girl. The only part of the evening that really broke him up was when he talked about Arnold, but he did a great job hiding the choking in his voice. When he'd almost cried, he'd pretended that he needed to swallow. He is still skeptical. Was Arnold's death really an accident? Arnold drove across that road every day. It just didn't add up.

Lucille looked like a doll: like one of the smarties he sees at the club, but with class. Boy, did she want him. But he outsmarted her. He couldn't let her make a fool of him again. He pulled away just when she begged for him. What a move. Another gem he learned from his father: "Just when a woman wants you, check out."

Imagine, turning me down for a date with Harry, Nick thinks. *I can't have my women behaving like that. Then tonight out of the blue, her hand is hot, her head cold, or was it the other way around? Then she couldn't speak. Lucille really is a strange woman.*

Nick notices a car trailing him. With his trained ear, he can tell it's a hay burner from the sound. That car can guzzle gasoline faster than he can guzzle water. Only an arrogant person would drive a car like that. Anyway, someone tailing him this closely bothers the heck out of him. There's no reason for that.

He has a good mind to stop, get out of the car, and throw the driver a punch to the jaw, although he can't remember ever hitting anyone. If that car slams into him and dents his red baby, that palooka better run for his life. He owes it to himself to tell that driver a thing or two. You don't trail Nick Martin Jr. that closely and get away with it.

The driver of the hay burner suddenly turns and heads down Pine Street. *Is he kidding me?* Nick thinks. *I know how to drive that road blindfolded.*

The black car stops, and Nick rides up alongside it. "Hey, what are you so lathered up about?" the driver asks.

Nick recognizes him. He's Derik, Jerry's son, the Drugstore Cowboy. Nick has seen him standing around Kenny's Drugstore picking up women and he's seen him at the local restaurant eyeing them. Being a family doctor and doing that just don't mix. "Stay away from my car. Don't you have enough road to drive on?"

"Nick, bug off," says the woman sitting next to Derik

He leans into the car to gets a good look at the woman. He recognizes her. Looks like she's wearing the same white sweater she wore when he drove her down that dark side street and they had a quickie all those years ago. She's too made-up, he thinks, with a beauty mark penciled in by her eye and that bright red lipstick. Like she's trying to look like the girls in the New York City clubs. But that's the problem. She's trying too hard. She's just a country girl, and makeup can't conceal that. "Millie? What are you do'n here?"

Arnold has been dead for only two weeks. Two damn weeks, and she's already out with someone else. Nick heard that she was cheating on Arnold with this creep, but he didn't believe it until now. He'd even tried to convince Gil that it was just gossip. But now he knows for sure. Jerry sure picked himself a bad apple when he adopted this guy. He tells everyone he's proud of him, but how can he be, when he's been making out with Millie in the back room of the store?

"Why don't you dry up and get lost," Derik says.

Derik should know better than to talk to Nick like that. "What is your name?" Nick of course knows his name and everything else about him, but he won't let on.

"I'm a doctor. What are you, big shot?"

"A doctor? Do you think you can grab business away from Doc Greene? He's idolized around here. And you talk like that to me again and you will need to see *him*. But I'm a nice guy and I'll tell ya what I'm going to do. I'll race you to that bridge up ahead. I'll give you the advantage. I'll drive your jalopy and you drive my baby. Whoever wins, wins a buck and is King of the Road."

"Good deal." Derik gets out of his car and hands his keys to Nick.

Nick gets into the black jalopy. Derik turns to get into Nick's car and pulls on the door handle, but he's been duped. Nick is speeding down the road with Derik's keys in the ignition, his own keys in his pocket, and Millie at his side. Nick looks back to see the chump puffing on a cigarette and lumbering down the rutted road toward town. What the heck is Millie doing, dancing on Arnold's grave with this fella? And while she's still living with Arnold's parents.

The rattle in the engine bugs him. If he had this car for a few days, he'd fix it up sweet as baby corn.

Nick plans to drop off Millie at home and then go back for his own car. When he sees the Mosley house with the curtains pulled over the windows, he stops so abruptly that Millie's head just misses hitting the windshield. He sits looking straight-ahead, thinking about how much he misses his friend. He's been coming over to this house since grade school. He and Arnold would goof around all afternoon while his dogs stayed right at his side. Strange about Arnold, about the way his life turned out. He gave up on becoming a veterinarian, and when Millie gave up wanting to be his wife, he just gave up on life. That's how he died. He just gave up on life.

"How long are you going to sit like that, just staring into space?" Millie asks. "Guess you're not in a hurry tonight, the way you were the last time we were together. Remember that night you picked me up at the library? You were done before I had time to . . . well you know. But you said you'd make it up to me."

He remembers. And he remembers scribbling Arnold's address on the back of a crumpled piece of paper. Maybe Arnold would be alive today if he hadn't done that. Arnold needed a special kind of woman, one who was faithful like his dogs. But there was something about

Millie that he wanted. Maybe it was because she didn't want him so much.

"How long have you been seeing that Drugstore Cowboy?"

"Nick, he's a doctor. And a good one," she says, snuggling up to him. "You were Arnold's best friend. He wouldn't mind if you and I…"

Nick lowers his eyelids and pulls Millie closer to him. He reaches across her body, sliding his hand along her waist. She snuggles closer.

"We have all night," she purrs.

"Yeah." His hand finds the door handle. He pushes her out of the car.

As he rides off, he sees her in his rearview mirror struggling to stand up. But heck if he's going to help her.

Bill

Two weeks have passed since Sheila's party and Lucille has been lethargic ever since. Every afternoon after lunch, she sinks into Evelyn's green velvet chair and falls asleep. Bill is worried. Lucille usually has a lot of pep. Cleaning the house, cooking the meals, working on the farm—she usually did all that with energy to spare. But today and all of last week, the kitchen floor has gone unswept, the beds unmade, and he's even making his own dinners. "A young person shouldn't be sleeping away her days," he mutters. Thinking that maybe some books might perk her up, he heads to the library.

When he enters the building, the door to the meeting room on his right is open. He hears a familiar voice. He peeks in. The room is packed with women. Pauline Powers, Lucille's literature teacher, is speaking in front of the group. Her cheeks are flushed and her eyes blaze with excitement. To make her point, she enunciates each word and pounds her fist on the podium. She's at it again, he thinks, reciting the same old bull.

"Remember the words of Susan B. Anthony," she says, "'Modern invention has banished the spinning wheel. And the same law of progress makes the woman of today a different woman from her grandmother.'" The women applaud.

Bill finds Paul in the audience and decides to take a seat on the folding chair beside him. They are the only two men in the audience. "Give the women an inch, and they want the whole yard," Bill says to Paul. "What is she after this time? Women are voting aren't they?"

Paul laughs. "Yes they are, but you know my wife. As far as she's concerned, women are still not getting what they deserve. She wants better for young women like Lucille."

"Speaking of Lucille, Paul, I'm worried about her. She seems sick. I'm calling Doc Green in the morning."

"T.B. is going around," Paul says. "Maybe she's coming down with it."

Bill doesn't like hearing that, and he jumps out of his seat and walks down the hall to the room where the books are located. He sees Harry sitting at a table, reading. Bill walks up to him.

"Anything been wrong, Harry? You've made yourself scarce."

Harry looks up and nods at Bill. "Don't you know? Your daughter flat out left me for Nick at my own sister's party." Harry turns the pages of his book.

"That's news to me," Bill says. *So that's where she picked up her germs.* He won't tell him Lucille is not feeling well. If word gets around Harvest that Lucille is sick, people will be streaming into Jerry's to find out the details of her condition.

Back at Hillsdale Farms, Bill sits at the kitchen table, thinking. Lucille has been seeing Nick again. If Lucille weren't under the weather, he'd confront her. He turns on the radio and hears the bulletin. Tuberculosis is working its way through Iowa. He turns off the radio in disgust.

Dan is in the parlor, sitting on his overstuffed chair reading the Harvest Gazette. "Lucille wrote a darn good article. Did you read it?"

"Yeah, I read it. It's about a man living a lie. An impostor. I have no use for a person like that. Reminds me of the Martin men."

Dan shakes his head. "Why in the world do you think that? They're not bad people. Nick is a nice kid and his father was our high school buddy. Remember when my fields flooded and I lost most of my crops? Nick Sr. made sure I got compensated and he did it pro bono. He'd do the same for you. He even fixed you up with Evelyn. You have to be grateful for that."

"Dan, the man can't be trusted. Don't you understand?"

"Not really."

"Then who is my daughter writing about? The only other person I can think of is President Hoover, if you can call him a president." Bill is quiet for a few moments. "Who am I fooling? She's referring to me. Why didn't I see it sooner? How can I call myself a father when I'm unable to provide for my daughter? But all that is going to change. I'm going to find a job, hell or high water. I'll leave in the morning. You keep an eye on Lucille while I'm gone."

"Where are you going?"

"There must be work for me out there somewhere. I'll go freight hopping, and jump off at every town and city until I find a job. I really don't know how long I'll be gone. But leaving Lucille isn't going to be easy, so I hope I find something nearby. You're the only one I can depend on to watch over Lucille while I'm away. You can see for yourself, she's not the same and I hate leaving her alone. I trusted you to look in on Evelyn when I was out of town. Please Dan, I need you to help me out."

When Lucille was two or three months old Dan had carried her in his arms. When she was ten or twelve he taught her how to carve ice and she took first prize in the school contest for her ice carving of a swan. Of course, he had taught her everything he knew about playing the piano. Bill wouldn't have to worry with his good buddy watching over her.

"Freight hopping is dangerous," says Dan, getting up from the chair and putting his arm around Bill. People have gotten killed doing that. I'll worry every minute you're away."

"Don't worry about me, I'll be careful. People all over the country are freight hopping looking to find a job."

"You're not made for a hobo's life, Bill. I don't like you doing this. Besides, it's illegal. I have some money left from what my Daddy left me after he was gone, I'll give it to you."

"What are you crazy? What will you live on?"

"Then if I can't convince you not to go, wear a scarf while you hunker down waiting for a train to hitch onto. It could get cold."

Bill throws his arms around Dan. "You *are* a worrier."

The two men walk out and sit on the porch steps, but not before Dan goes to the pantry and pulls out a brown bag to carry out with him.

"Where did you get that, Dan?" Bill asks, when Dan removes a bottle of whisky from the bag.

"Olson's garage. He has a few cartons of these bottles tucked away behind some tires. You know, for himself and his good friends. Prohibition won't separate him from a drink."

"I'll take a swig from that bottle right now. I'm going in to tell Lucille what I'm going to be doing and I know she'll start fuss'n. She'll get all worried. She's like you in that way."

$\mathcal{D}$ A N

The holidays arrived with little celebration. It wasn't a time for festivities. Dan of course went to church with his brother and Pauline, but Bill never made it home in time to go with them. Bill arrived late on Christmas Eve, looked in on Lucille who was sleeping, said a few prayers by his bedside, and hopped right into bed. The poor guy still hasn't found a job.

With Bill still out there looking for work, and Pauline insisting that Paul be in the audience whenever she gives her speeches, it is up to Dan to finish construction on the house he's building on Oak Street for Bill and Lucille. It is part of his routine now. He hops into his truck every morning, drives the fifteen minutes to the house, and works until his bones ache. He doesn't mind. His farm has been destroyed by the drought, and building the house gives him something to do.

Dan set a deadline for himself. He wanted the house finished by March 20, the first day of spring, and he's going to make that deadline. Yes sir, as of March 20, 1931, Bill and Lucille will be the proud owners of the house at 100 Oak Street. It took four months to build, but today he'll finish working on Lucille's bedroom. It's going to look just like the picture he saw in *Better Homes and Gardens*. Lucille has been abrupt with him lately, but he can't blame her for that, she's sick. When he comes down with an ordinary cold, he's grumpy for a week.

The house is nothing more than a bungalow with five steps leading up to the front porch, a low sloping gable roof, and a basic layout. But it's new and clean, and it will keep Bill and Lucille from having to live in that rotted Morrison house.

Dan grabs his tall ladder, some flowered wallpaper, some buckets, a large sponge, and paste from his truck and lugs them into the house.

He places them just outside Lucille's bedroom door. Then he sizes the wallpaper. With each strip of paper that he pastes on the wall, he thinks of Bill and Lucille. After a few hours, he steps outside holding a glass of cold water. Dan sees three young boys in bathing suits heading toward the river as they push and shove each other in jest. The boys are roughly the same age that Paul, Bill, and he were that unforgettable summer, about eleven or twelve. Actually, it was only one day that made that summer unforgettable. It happened over thirty years ago. He never forgot it and never will.

Dan and Paul had their parents' permission to go swimming, but Bill's parents were reluctant to let him go. Since they lost the twins, the river was off limits to Bill. After hours of pleading and promising to be careful, Bill got the okay. The three of them journeyed out on the winding road leading to the river. The sharp curves of the road left them exposed to speeding cars, but they were careful to stay on the shoulder of the road in single file. When they passed the small yellow bungalow surrounded by high grasses and wild day lilies, they knew they were getting close to their destination. They waved to Izzy with the Tin Lizzy, who was polishing his Ford, the first model ever made. "Wish I were going with ya," Izzy shouted. The boys knew it wasn't true. Nothing could separate him from that car.

When they reached the river, the boys saw the warning sign written in big black letters against a yellow background. It read, "Danger. Keep Away From The Rapids." The sky looked like it was about to rain. No sunbathers lay with their towels on the large rocks circling the river.

Yanking at his pants, Dan almost toppled over trying to remove them. When he jumped into the water, Paul and Bill ignored him. They were busy yanking off their own clothes. Challenging himself against the current, he plunged under the bridge and flung himself into the rapids. He raised his hands over his head to Bill and Paul and yelled, "Look, no hands!" Not getting their attention, he dived again into the rapids. When he surfaced, he found that he couldn't get out. Dan yelled out in fear this time. He wasn't hoodwinking the boys when he called out for help. Paul leapt into the water. The rapids devoured him immediately. Then Bill followed, jumping in with all his clothes on to help them both.

The eddy swallowed their bodies, and they were flung up and down with the frantic rise and fall of the water. They strained to reach a rock jutting into their path, and all three were able to hold on. Dan still can't figure out how they got out of the turbulence without drowning, but he knows his friend Bill grabbed his hand and held it until they safely reached the edge of the river.

When they climbed ashore, Bill's wheezing scared Dan. Bill's lungs were closing and he couldn't get any air into them. He took a breath and gasped, releasing a desperate whistling sound. "My asthma," he struggled to say.

Keeping his eyes on Bill, Dan wiped his blonde curls with a towel, realizing how calamitous the whole incident could have been. He remembered Bill's little brothers' funeral. The little boys had looked like they were sound asleep in those wooden boxes, as though nothing could awaken them. And of course, nothing could. Dan's mother made him and Paul stare right into those caskets so they would learn their lesson about the river.

"You're afraid of the dark, Dan, and then you go and do something like this," Paul said. "What are you trying to prove?"

Dan wondered that, too. He wasn't the daring type. He pushed his blonde curls off his forehead, and then lifted one leg and then the other, because the hot rocks were burning the soles of his feet. He coughed and spit. "Guess we did a dumb thing."

"We?" Paul and Bill asked simultaneously.

When Bill calmed down, his breathing improved. Dan placed himself between the other two boys. He rolled his eyes from side to side. Without warning, he bounced upwards and enclosed the two boys in his arms. The three of them, two twelve-year-old boys and one eleven-year-old, looked at each other and roared with laughter. Throwing off their towels, jumping and running in circles, they pushed each other to the ground. They laughed so hard they had to hold onto their bellies.

"It sure was fun," Dan said.

"The most fun of the summer," Paul agreed.

Bill bellowed, "This calls for a special meeting of the Men's Club," referring to the meetings they held in Bill's tree house.

They raced into the wooded area. The thorns and mosquitoes didn't bother them. Nothing could, after what they had been through. Ignoring the thunder and lightning, they ran until they came upon a clearing. Finding a large rock, Bill crawled his way up first, and then extended a hand to Dan and then to Paul. All at once, it began to rain. In their bathing trunks, wet hair dripping down their faces, the three of them held hands. The energy of one flowed into the hand of the other. Dan can still call upon that energy when he's in a tight spot.

"Look at that river. We beat it," Bill said. "It might be tough, but we're tougher. The three of us together. All for one, one for all. Sink or swim." Dan's and Paul's faces drew into serious expressions as they listened to Bill. "We'll always be there for each other," Bill said.

"Forever," Paul agreed.

"Forever and after that," Dan added.

"Forever and after that." Their voices blended into one

Dan closes his eyes as he remembers each of Bill's words. The hold of the rapids had been replaced by a friendship that had lasted all these years, but when Evelyn came along, things changed. Not between Dan and Bill, nothing could change that. Just other things, because, well damn it, they just did.

His friendship with Bill is something he cherishes, and using his own money to purchase so many of the supplies for the house gives him great pleasure. Of course, there were sales all over the place for the supplies he needed. At Bernie's Hardware store, a sign in the window read, "Name Your Own Price." And he used wood he found around the outside of the house to build the furniture. So when he walks back into the house and picks up the last strip of wallpaper and smoothes it in place, he remembers the pledge the three of them made at the river to always be there for each other.

It's impossible to tell how long he's been working on Lucille's bedroom. The walls are finished, now he's ready to arrange the furniture. He places the handmade desk in the corner of the room and the bed near the window. He enjoyed making the furniture. It's something his Dad taught him how to do. He dusts the books and arranges them on the wooden bookcase he finished painting a few days ago. When Jerry's wife, Lily, heard that Bill and Lucille were moving, she made some white crisscross curtains with ruffles for Lucille's room and red and white gingham tie back curtains for the kitchen as a moving in present. As he hangs the curtains, he pauses to turn on the radio. There is a transformation going on in the world of music, and he yearns to be a part of it. Blues is the up-and-coming sound. Catchy tunes like "Ain't We Got Fun" are being replaced by more somber music. He feels his fingers itching to get to the piano.

Dan had never wanted to be a farmer. When his father died the year Dan graduated from high school, he left Dan and Paul a three hundred acre farm and Dan couldn't walk away from that, but his first love was and still is music. As a young boy, whenever he went to play with Hutch, he'd listen to his friend's mother play the piano and he'd forget about playing ball. Seeing his interest, Hutch's mother invited him to sit down at the piano and she gave him a few instructions. He soon could play every song she played. He discovered that once he heard a melody, he could play it. Hutch's mother said that the word for that was talent.

∽

Dan hears the screen door open and Lucille's voice calls to him. He answers, and he hears her moving closer. She eyes the ladder in the hallway, the pails of water, scraps of wallpaper and brushes scattered around the floor. A chill runs up Dan's back. He expects her to be delighted with the room, to hug him and say, *Dan, you are too good to me.*

Lucille pauses as she nears the bedroom. With her face flushed and a kerchief tied around her head, she looks like a character from a children's book. "Dan, what have you done to my room?" she asks.

Her tone pierces through him like glass. Dan turns and scrutinizes the wallpaper. Perhaps the small daisy pattern on the rose-colored background with white scallops circling the ceiling is not the pattern a young woman would choose, though it is exactly like the picture he saw in *Better Homes and Gardens*, which said that it was the latest wallpaper used by the young elite in New York City. Dan examines the handmade desk. Is it too small? Too big? He thought Lucille would love the multicolored hook rug and the crisscross curtains that hang like puffs of clouds. The sheath of paper, the jar of pencils, and the calendar for her wall are there, all things he thought she would appreciate. He'd put all of this together to make her happy, but he feels like he was wrong. A young girl doesn't want her father's friend designing her bedroom. It was foolish of him to think otherwise.

"I was planning on using my old furniture," says Lucille.

But they'd gone over the plans together before he did any of this.

"I changed my mind about you decorating my room," she adds.

Dan realizes that he has overstepped his bounds.

"You're just full of surprises, Dan."

Flustered, he lifts his ladder and carries it outside to his truck. He comes back to pick up the pails and brushes, and hauls the scraps of wallpaper out in a can. He wonders how long he has been overstepping his bounds.

Walking back into the kitchen, he sees Lucille rearranging the ruffles on the kitchen curtains. Trying to ignore her bruising comments, he says with a burst of energy in his voice, "The house is done. You can sleep here tonight. I'll bring your belongings over later."

ℒUCILLE

It feels strange sleeping in the new house. With Bill not there, it feels even stranger. Her room is beautiful, she can't deny that, her bed so pretty with the new white blanket. If circumstances were different she would praise Dan for his talents and generosity. But circumstances aren't different and she can't forgive him for betraying her father.

She has difficulty getting out of bed that morning. She's so tired she feels like she didn't sleep at all. She musters all of her strength and pushes herself out of bed. While brushing her teeth in the bathroom, Lucille notices splatters of blood in the sink. The bright stains alarm her. Keeping her promise to Bill to see Doc Greene that day, she checks out back to see if Dan is still working on the fence, and sees that he is. This would be a good time for her to sneak away without him noticing. She doesn't want Dan driving her to the doctor. She wants to have as little to do with him as possible. She decides to take the main road, because the shortcut has too many inclines and bushes and she wants to walk on steady ground.

Her arms ache as she pulls on her dress, and her head throbs. It is an effort just to move her legs. By the time she puts her shoes on, she's ready to lie down again. She secures a kerchief around her nose and mouth, ready to start her journey.

She opens the door, and a gust of wind slams it shut. Using all of her strength, she pushes again on the door and manages to exit the house. Once on the road, the wind rips at her skirt. She concentrates on keeping herself erect. Feeling lightheaded, she hopes she can make it to the doctor's office.

Lucille puts her hands in her pockets. The feel of the sand repulses her. Her lungs seem like they are packed with the black dust. And each gasp of air is accompanied by a stab in her chest. The usual fifteen-minute walk takes twice as long. By the time she reaches the doctor's office, her body is cold and clammy. She finds the closest seat in the waiting room and sits down, rubbing her lower back.

When she starts to cough, two women seated nearby move to other chairs. She recognizes them as old Mrs. Olson and Nick's mother, Anita. Lucille pulls her scarf over her face so that they don't recognize her. She stumbles into the bathroom to splash cold water on her face. When she looks in the mirror, her swollen eyes and chapped lips frighten her. What happened to her face? She turns to leave, but a wave of nausea seizes her and a shower of black spots appears before her eyes. Her body goes limp.

Lucille awakens to Doc Green's face. Doc Green delivered her into this world and pronounced her mother dead. He is an elderly man wearing a white coat and he has a white mustache and white hair. His deep blue eyes bring Lucille to attention.

"Gave us a little scare," Doc Greene says, putting the stethoscope to Lucille's chest. "But fainting is more common than you think." When he hears her cough, he says, "That cough you have gives me some concern." He takes a swab of saliva and places it on a transparent dish. He asks her to extend her arm so that he can take blood samples. "We'll take an X-ray too, to see if anything unusual shows up."

While the doctor makes notes in his file and talks to the nurse, Lucille enters a state of mind where she is neither asleep nor awake. She overhears the words "sanitarium" and "tuberculosis." She turns her head toward the doctor. "John Keats died of tuberculosis in 1821 and Henry Thoreau at age 45 in 1862. I'm 23. I'm too young to die. I haven't even gone to college yet."

"Things have changed in medicine since then. You can get well."

How long will that take, she wonders? *Months? Years? Will I have to go to a sanitarium?*

"I'm concerned about the dust storms and the lack of fresh fruits and vegetables," Doc Green says. "A sanitarium might be the best place for you. I know of one in Asheville, North Carolina. The temperature and barometric pressure there are ideal for treatment."

Daddy has no money for that, thinks Lucille. *He can hardly afford to put food on the table.* Besides, she doesn't want to go away. Lucille sits up, her feet dangling from the doctor's table. "Doc, I'll get better while staying in Harvest. You'll see."

"With your resistance so low, you've also developed a case of influenza, which accounts for the chills and fever. I'll be over to the house later to check on you." Doc Green opens a drawer and takes out two or three face masks and puts them into a brown bag. "Take these. For anyone who comes in contact with you. You do have someone to drive you home, don't you?"

Lucille nods. She'll make it home on her own, the same way she got there. She thanks the doctor. When he puts his hand on her shoulder, his face grows serious and his gaze tender. She looks into his eyes with understanding. This is going to be a long illness.

Wrapping the scarf around her neck, Lucille slips out of the office. The wind is still raging, making it difficult for her to move forward. The dry, bumpy ground tires her legs. She finds a stick on the ground at the inner edge of the road. She picks it up and leans against it for support. The small brown bag with the face masks drops out of her hand. When she bends to pick it up, her legs collapse and she falls to the ground. She loses consciousness.

NICK

Nick has lived in New York City for several years now, yet Harvest is still the place he calls home. When he first left, just a day or two after graduating high school, he believed this small town would no longer hold any meaning for him. But he has friends here, and since Arnold died, he and Gil have been thick as thieves.

Nick never misses an opportunity to give Gil some business. Even when he has no need for dry goods, he buys some just to keep Gil's store from shutting down. Now that he has a new apartment to move into back in New York, he's preparing a big order for Gil.

He is visiting Harvest for the weekend. After looking at more bolts of material than he can remember, Nick is starving. The men decide to have lunch at the diner. "No speeding, Nick," says Gil. "I have to be careful. Going to be a father again. I'll take my own car and follow you so I can get back right after lunch and start on your order and you can be on your way."

"Suit yourself. Funny, you said you're thinking of being a daddy again, and I'm thinking of adding a Bugatti to my family of cars."

"I could see you in one of those. Why not? You got something in you the rest of us don't have. *Chutzpah*. Even heard Hutch using that word when he talked about you."

Nick slaps Gil on the back and laughs. "If Hutch says it, it must be true."

"And Nick, you've got—well, generosity. If it weren't for you, I'd have been out of business long ago. The last bunch of customers you sent me looked a little tough, but they rolled out the bills like it was play money."

"Here's a way you can pay me back. Keep an eye on Lucille, will ya? I don't want her marrying Harry. I'll be back for her when I'm ready."

"Let me give you her new address. Bill and his buddies tore down the Morrison brothers' dilapidated house and replaced it with a new one. I drove by it the other day. Nothing fancy, but it's nice enough. Anyway, that's where Bill Kramer and Lucille are living now."

"I know where that is. 100 Oak Street. I used to take Jon Morrison's daughter out. You remember Sarah Morrison. She liked to have a good time. Hear she's married now, with four kids."

Nick leads the way to the diner. It's located about a mile from town. Although he is speeding by anyone's standards, he's driving slowly by his own. He has all the time in the world to admire the scenery. He sees a bundle by the side of the road and signals Gil to slow down and stop. He'd better see what it is. It's a distraction and might cause an accident. Like he always says, as a driver he's smart, speedy, and safe. He slams on the breaks and backs up. Gil gets out of his car, too. Taking a closer look, Nick sees that the bundle is actually a body. He takes a closer look. "Holy Cow, it's Lucille," Nick says over his shoulder to Gil.

"Do you think maybe we should drive her to the hospital?" Gil asks.

Lucille's eyes are partially open, and she says, "It's not too comfortable lying on these little stones. I just saw the doctor. Must have gotten dizzy and maybe I passed out. Please drive me home, Nick."

"I'll take it from here, Gil. I'll get in touch with you later." He watches Gil drive off.

Nick lifts Lucille in his arms and holds her body close to his. Her head falls against his chest. He calls her name softly, his lids lowering over his eyes. He places her in the back seat as though she is a bird he has found on the side of the road. He had yearned to see her again, but no, not in this way. With a silken voice, he whispers:

If you but knew
How all my days seemed filled with dreams of you,
How sometimes in the silent night
Thrill through me with their tender light
How oft I hear your voice when others speak . . .

To see Lucille this way disturbs him. By the time he reaches the house on Oak Street she is fast asleep. When he lifts her from the backseat, Lucille opens her eyes and looks surprised. "Did I forget that we had a date?"

Nick laughs. "No, you didn't forget. But I guess we have one now."

He knocks on the door and when no one responds, he fumbles in her jacket pocket, searching for her house keys until he finds them. Lucille closes her eyes again. Nick watches her chest move up and down. The magic of breath. Carrying her into the house, he eyes the filled bookshelves, the piano, the sofa big enough to stretch out on, and a tidy kitchen with a small yellow bowl on the table. He likes the little house with the little porch and handmade furniture. His parents' house is big, and places appearance before comfort.

He searches for her bedroom and finds it right off the kitchen. He can tell it is hers by the books on the shelves, the stack of paper on the small desk, and the pink slippers at the side of the bed. He marvels at it when he enters. Yes, his princess deserves a room as pretty as this one. Seeing her nightgown on the chair, he decides to make her more comfortable. He looks away as he removes her dress. He pulls the nightgown down over her head, and as he smoothes it around her body, he hears the front door open.

Bill's footsteps are loud and quick. He heads straight to Lucille's room and finds Nick beside her. "I thought that was your car in the driveway," Bill shouts, "What are you doing in my daughter's bedroom? Get out of this house! Don't you ever step foot in here again."

"I was . . . you can ask Gil. He was with me when I found Lucille. She was lying on the side of the road. I picked her up and brought her home. I was just putting her nightgown on to make her more comfortable."

Bill looks at his daughter lovingly, now unconscious in bed. "What has he done to you?"

"No, sir. It's not what you think."

"I'm calling the sheriff."

Nick dashes out of the house. He tumbles into his car and lets his head fall into his hands. Whatever Mr. Kramer is accusing him of no longer matters. He's worried. Is Lucille going to die?

Nick puts his hand on his heart and makes a promise to God. "If you get Lucille better, I'll give up . . ." He almost says, *give up driving*, but that's as good as promising that he'll die. Nick decides that he'd better forget about the agreement and go to church on Sunday instead. He drives off.

Bill

Bill is sitting at Lucille's bedside when he hears a knock on the front door. He looks at his sleeping daughter and mumbles as he gets up and walks to the door. "Better not be that boy coming back," he says.

It's Gil. "What is this, social hour? My daughter is sick." Bill slams the door in Gils's face. Immediately, he's sorry. He likes Gil. He gave Lucille that pretty blue material so she could look nice for Harry at the party. He'll apologize the next time he sees him.

Before returning to Lucille's bedside, Bill calls the sheriff. He wants Nick arrested. "And keep him behind bars for a long time," Bill says. He also calls Doc Green. He speaks with cordiality, as though his manner of speaking could somehow change his daughter's diagnosis.

"It's tuberculosis," says the doctor "and there is treatment." He mentions the sanitarium, a vaccine, and a better diet.

Who does Doc Green think he's talking to, a man of wealth? Bill massages the muscles and joints in his leg, both stretched like rubber bands about to break. When Evelyn died, he thought that the worst had happened, but at least he still had Lucille.

As a farmer, he worked through his problems tilling the soil. When the crops were ready for harvest, his anxieties were packaged up along with the corn and soybeans and sent off to town. Now his anxieties are in a tight bundle with nowhere to go.

Lucille calls out. Who is she's calling? He couldn't have heard right. He dips a towel into the ice water from the tray under the icebox and places the towel on Lucille's forehead. He falls to his knees and pleads with God.

$\mathcal{D}$ A N

Dan finds Bill praying on his knees in Lucille's room when he comes over the next morning.

"Thought we'd talk a little before you go looking for work again. You're not a kid anymore. You hopping freight trains and jumping off at the nearest city scares me."

"Hey, I've been pretty lucky so far. Never even got caught by a guard ready to haul me away. Anyway, running like hell to hitch a ride on the freight keeps me in shape. I get to meet interesting people, too. I met a woman at a farmhouse in the city of Coreville, or some such name. Imagine I actually begged her for food. A pretty woman, nice brown hair. And she invited me in for lunch. We had a nice talk. Rose is her name."

"Nice name," Dan says. He walks Bill to the door. Dan watches him walk toward the rail yard, which is at least a half-hour walk.

With the responsibility of watching over Lucille, Dan wonders what he can do to help her get better. Maybe Lucille will perk up if she sees Nick. He grabs the phone and calls the Martin home, but no one answers. He probably shouldn't have called this early. Anita is probably sleeping. He walks into the parlor and sits down at the piano. Giving Lucille this gift as a graduation present was the right thing to do. That girl has real talent. He taught her everything he knew, but she has surpassed him. Now playing "The White Peacock," recently recorded by the outstanding pianist Olga Amaroff, he feels affected, and tears roll down his cheeks. Maybe he's affected because Lucille is sick, or perhaps because Bill is hopping freight trains, or maybe it's because he has stayed in Harvest too long. After playing for an hour or so, he tries to reach Anita again by calling the Olson house. He'd heard that she'd taken a liking to old Mrs. Olson and took it upon herself to care for her. He'd also heard that she'd taken more than a liking to Mrs. Olson's son, who owns the garage.

Anita answers the phone and tells Dan that the sheriff picked up Nick for questioning. She doesn't know what it's about, but she's certain it's something far worse than a speeding ticket. "I'm upset," she says.

What are they accusing Nick of this time? Dan wonders. *He gets blamed for every bad thing that happens in town. Why would he ever want to come back to Harvest?*

The time passes slowly. Dan tends to Lucille, who has not been out of bed, trying to spoon-feed her warm soup. He glances through the newspapers on Bill's kitchen table. He's restless. He looks at his hands, imaging them on a piano. His longing for New York City returns. That's where he belongs, playing at one of those jazz clubs. But he won't go anywhere until Lucille is well.

The sun may as well have not have come up that day, because he wouldn't have noticed. Now, he looks out the window and sees that the day is almost gone. In the twilight, he thinks he sees a figure on the porch. He opens the door and sees Nick.

"My mom told me you called," Nick explains to Dan. "If it weren't for Gil, I'd still be down at the sheriff's." Nick explains about finding Lucille by the side of the road. "Mr. Kramer got it into his head that I was being disrespectful with Lucille. Can you imagine him thinking I'd take advantage of a sick girl? What does he take me for?"

Dan beckons him to come in and they both walk into the kitchen. Nick looks around before throwing Lucille's brown bag containing her face masks onto the table.

"Don't worry," says Dan. "Bill isn't here. I'm not expecting him home tonight, not this early anyway."

"I just want to see Lucille." Nick takes a mask from the bag and covers his nose and mouth. He tiptoes into her room. She's asleep, so he places a note on the nightstand, touches her cheek, and stays only a few moments. Walking out of the bedroom, he thanks Dan for calling his mother. He opens the door to leave and bumps into Bill.

"Why the hell are you here?" Bill yells. His clothes are dirty, as though he jumped off the freight train and landed on a heap of dirt. He throws his hands up in the air and says, "Something told me to come home early."

Dan urges Bill to calm down and come into the house, but he can see that there is no calming Bill. Dan is shocked when Bill says, "Stay away. Lucille is spoken for. She's marrying Harry as soon as she gets on her feet." He never heard anything about that.

"That doesn't change the way I feel about your daughter, Mr. Kramer."

"There's something wrong with you if you can't understand that you don't bother a woman about to be married."

With the front door left ajar and the confrontation going on, no one notices Anita enter the house. "Bill, there's nothing wrong with my boy," she says, pulling down on her black shawl and smoothing her dark blond hair back from her face. She walks toward Bill. "My Nick would never do the things you accuse him of. He's a good boy."

"I'm sorry to distress you Anita, but he's not."

The anguish on Anita Martin's face prompts Dan to speak up. "Bill, Anita has had a hard day too. Let's just all calm down."

Bill ignores him. "Anita, you can't even keep tabs on your husband, much less raise a son right."

Standing squarely in front of him, Anita spits in Bill's face. She places her hands on Nick's back and pushes him toward the door.

"Bitch," Bill mumbles when the door slams. "I think I'll take a walk down to Jerry's to cool down. Please Dan, don't allow Nick in this house again."

Dan walks out of the house behind Bill and sits down on the porch steps. The squabble unnerved him. With Lucille sick, the dust storms, and his farm deteriorating, he just can't deal with arguments. His stomach is beginning to cramp. The wind catches hold of his cap and blows it to the edge of the front lawn near the road. Dan runs after it. A woman walking toward him grabs his arm.

"Can I help you?" he asks.

"Don't you recognize me?"

Her voice is familiar.

"Come stand under the porch light so I can see your face better."

"You don't want to do that."

When Dan gets a closer look at her face, he knows why Madeline doesn't want him to see her. The story had made headlines. Madeline had been found in the woods badly beaten. It was the talk of Harvest. Jerry Sloane's store had never been so busy. Some people said that Madeline had been asking for trouble, and others felt sorry for her. Dan went to the hospital to see her only once, although he doesn't expect her to remember.

She's thinner, and scars cross her face. Her eyes speak of tragedy. One eye pulls to the left and the other barely moves at all. Her voice is the same, but gentler.

"You just caught me by surprise, Madeline."

She follows him to the porch and they sit on the rockers. At first they speak of hard times and Bill losing the farm, but then Madeline explains that she really came by because she heard Lucille had contracted tuberculosis. "Or is it pneumonia? At any rate, I want to help," she says.

"Doc Green and prayer. That's the help Lucille needs. Bill and I will do the rest."

Dan doesn't smell any liquor on Madeline's breath. Her voice stays soft. She's nothing like the woman he remembers. "It looks like you turned your life around," he says.

"Imagine young Nick telling a woman like me that it would be as easy as making a U-turn in a car. I wouldn't say it was that easy. But one ride in a green truck sure taught me something. Reckless behavior begets reckless results. I'm not much of a philosopher, but you see what I mean." Madeline's story soon becomes ghastly. She tells about hitching a ride with a handsome devil, unaware that he just escaped from under the deputy's not-so-watchful eye. "He had a pleasant smile," she says, "one that reminded me of Bill's, actually. And he looked so powerful behind the wheel of that big, green truck. But then he started talking funny. He said something about how all who inhabit our planet are evil, and every last one of us should die. He said he would provide the poison. I said he was talking like an asshole. I guess that wasn't the right word to use. He stopped the truck and started shaking me. He said that I didn't know what it was like to be called an asshole by the kids in school. I told him that kids say things they don't mean. That's when he started up the truck again and drove down to a vacant field. 'Damn right they meant it,' he yelled. He pulled me out of the car and threw me down on the ground on my stomach. He pulled up my dress. He had . . . had a firecracker in his hand." Madeline begins to cry, and Dan puts his arm around her. "He…he…he took that firecracker and Dan, Dan he…he… Oh Dan, I was so frightened I passed out.

"So that's what happened to the woman who flaunted her body, drank with the boys, and lived by her own rules. Nothing used to scare me." She touches the scars covering her face. "Now I'm afraid of everything. I hear an unfamiliar sound and I jump. Every time I see a green truck, I run." Madeline stammers so badly that Dan can barely understand what she's saying. He takes her hand, trying to sooth her. "I prayed for death while I was in the hospital. Lucille came to visit me, you know. It seemed like she really cared about me."

Madeline takes out a stack of bills from her pocketbook and stuffs them in Dan's palm. "This is for Lucille's college. Don't thank me. It was hers to begin with. And tell Bill I'm ready to go through with the divorce. Why would he ever want me when I look like this?"

Dan waits until the following day to tell Bill about his encounter with Madeline. Bill is home for a few days, so right after dinner, Dan walks him out to the front porch and they sit down on the steps. He tells him about Madeline's gruesome ordeal and about her willingness to sever their relationship legally.

"Not the kind of thing you'd wish on anybody," Bill says, after Dan finishes talking. "I'm relieved to hear about her willingness to go through with the divorce. She always said she would fight it. But that news comes at a good time."

"What do you mean?"

Bill stands up and paces the porch. "Got something to tell ya. Remember I told you about the woman I met at the farmhouse?

You know, when I jumped off the freight train in that small town of Coreville? I went back to that farmhouse again, the following day and the day after that. I wanted to see her, I guess. Her last name is Bush. Rose Bush. That's a funny name, isn't it?"

"Not the same Rose Bush we knew in high school? She was kind of fat, wasn't she? Remember when we told Nick Sr. we'd give him a dollar to walk her home? We trailed behind them, snickering and hooting all the way. Then Evelyn and her friends walked by and he was so embarrassed he ran for cover and yelled, 'You can keep your dollar.'"

"That was a cruel thing to do," Bill says. "Nick Sr. was bad, even then."

"Bill, it was your idea."

Bill blushes. "Anyway, like I was saying about Rose. I'm tired of sleeping alone and it's time for me to have a wife to cook my meals. I'm going to marry her."

"That will make it three marriages for you, Bill."

"I know. Three strikes and you're out. But the first time wasn't a strike."

LUCILLE

Lucille feels feverish. All night, her throat was dry and her lips parched. She attempted to walk into the kitchen for a drink of water, but collapsed in the kitchen. When Doc Green brings another doctor along with him to her house that morning, she wonders why. He sits down beside her bed and takes her hand. "I want you to meet Dr. Russman," he says. "He has lots of experience with tuberculosis patients. He knows about the latest treatments."

Dr. Russman, who is standing beside Doc Green, has a deep but gentle voice. "There is a tuberculosis vaccine. Few people take it," he explains, "because there is a chance of a patient getting sicker. But it is available, and could help. Doc Greene suggested I tell you about it, and administer the shot if you decide to take it. And now it is up to you. If you want to wait until your father gets home to talk it over with him, that's okay. We have time."

I took the road less traveled by, and that made all the difference, Lucille thinks. Throughout her life, her books have been her messengers. She has depended on them for her decisions. She extends her arm for the vaccine.

Lucille worries about how Bill will pay Dr. Russman. After all, he is a specialist and must come with a steep price tag. She worries about putting her father deeper in debt. But when Bill gets home that night, he tells her he found a job in the next town over. He will be working on a road project and he'll be home every night. She rips off the calendar page tacked to the kitchen wall. The date is April 1, the year 1931. The day Bill got a job. She puts it under the red ribbon. Even Bill thought it was an April fool's joke.

By the middle of June, Lucille's cough has disappeared. She's able to read without falling asleep and her appetite returns.

"Nothing less than a miracle," Bill says, when he sees the color seep back into her cheeks. "Guess I'll go to church this sunny Sunday morning and thank the Good Lord."

When she thinks that Bill is out of the house, Lucille gets out of bed. She reaches for the blue silk dress she wore to Sheila's party. It is too big for her now, but she pulls it over her body. She brushes her hair. Remembering the last time she wore the dress at Christmas time, she twirls in front of the mirror. The shadow that has engulfed her for five months has lifted. Walking toward the kitchen, she hears Bill speaking to someone at the front door.

"No, she's very ill. Tuberculosis is very contagious, you know. Besides. I told you Lucille and Harry are getting married. Do you want me calling the sheriff again?"

"The sheriff called me a hero, Mr. Kramer," Lucille overhears Nick say. "I wouldn't call myself a hero. I was just doing the right thing. I just came by to sit and chat with Lucille, see for myself how she is. Doc Green says she's not contagious anymore."

"Don't contradict me."

Lucille walks toward her father and Nick. She's confused by the conversation.

"My Fairy Princess," Nick calls out "My golden treasure. You look the way you did when I held you close and we danced together. Am I dreaming?"

Bill is surprised to see his daughter dressed for an evening out, and he says, with love in his eyes, "Yes, you are a beautiful sight." He turns to Nick. "You two will not be dancing together anytime soon or in the distant future."

"Nick just wants to visit with me," says Lucille. "Daddy, you're being silly."

"I won't allow it," Bill answers. "Not now or ever. No more letters, no secret meetings."

"Dammed if I know why you hate me so much," Nick yells.

Lucille's eyes cling to Nick. "You won't forget about me, will you?"

"I'll make sure he does," her father says.

"Don't marry Harry," Lucille hears Nick say, as Bill escorts him out.

⁓

When Doc Green examines Lucille at his office, he tells her he's satisfied with what he hears: the sound of clear, healthy lungs. "Good thing we were able to get Dr. Russman to see you," he says, putting down his stethoscope. "That specialist doesn't come cheap. Some young fella came to my office a week after you received your tuberculosis vaccine and dropped off the money to pay him. Paid my bill, too. He had a cap pulled down low, and with the goggles people are wearing these days, I just couldn't place how I knew him. Not your Prince Charming, is he?"

After being hidden away for so long, it's time for Lucille to reintroduce herself to the outside world, so after leaving the doctor's office, she takes a stroll through downtown Harvest. She notices all the new store closings. The windows at Hunter's Fish Shop and Carrie's Confectionary Store are boarded. Duffy's restaurant is open, but no one seems to be eating there. Harry's old black Buick is parked in front of Kenny's Drugstore. Lucille sees him coming out of the store carrying a small package. He is about to get into his car when he glances up and sees her. Taking his time, he walks in her direction. She hasn't seen him since Sheila's party.

"I'm sorry for the way I treated you," she stammers, when they stand face-to-face.

"You should be."

"Really, I am."

"That's okay. I'm getting on with my life."

They stand in silence for a few moments. Lucille feels uncomfortable and she wishes she hadn't bumped into him.

"I heard you were ill," he says. "I wanted to come by, but I just couldn't bring myself to do it. I didn't think you wanted to see me anyway."

"Harry, don't say that. We had so many good times together."

He reaches out and takes her hand. His hand feels familiar and comfortable. "Lucille, I…"

"Harry, maybe we should start seeing each other again. I'm well now."

He looks into her eyes. "Aren't you seeing Nick? The two of you were so lovey-dovey that night." When she doesn't answer he says, "Well I'm seeing someone. Her name is Jacqueline."

Accustomed to being the only girl Harry ever loved, Lucille feels a pang of jealousy in her stomach. "I always said you'd make some girl really happy. I wish you and Jacqueline well. I'm sure you will be very happy."

"Lucille, I don't kid myself. You will never marry me."

"Well then, that's that. This is my first day out. It's time for me to start life anew."

A chapter of her life is over.

Sheila runs toward her waving two tickets. "I was just going down to your house with these," she says. Sheila shows the tickets to Lucille, and Lucille squeals. This is her first opportunity to see one of the new Talkies with Al Jolson, *The Jazz Singer*. Sheila has another surprise for her: a Hershey bar to share. Lucille hasn't had one in years.

Lucille learned a lot about Sheila while they were working at the mission. After a day's work of sorting and handing out clothes or preparing and serving food at the soup kitchen, they'd take a long walk and talk about things she couldn't speak to her father about. She used to tell Dan her thoughts, but now that isn't something she does or will ever do again. Sheila is someone she can confide in. She even told her about her feelings for Nick. Although Lucille knows Harry realizes this, those words would never come out of Sheila's mouth, even though Harry is her brother.

And Sheila told Lucille about her dream of becoming an attorney and her hope of finding a man she could love and have children with. On those walks they discussed books and poems and laughed at the funny rhymes they composed. On those walks they became close friends.

"You are exactly the medicine I need right now. I just bumped into your brother," says Lucille.

"Did he tell you about his girlfriend? I think he and Jacqueline will be getting married soon. But you two were together for so long, I feel sad in a way."

"Strange, I feel sad too." Lucille says."

The movie theatre is located in town between Hattie's ice cream parlor and a shutdown cafeteria. From a distance Lucille can read the word "Rialto" looming above the theatre and her heart pounds with excitement. Before entering the theatre, she stops to look up at the marquee. She can hardly believe she's going to see this movie. The letters are spelled out in black against a white background: *The Jazz Singer*, starring Al Jolson. July 7 matinee: 2:15." The two women hurry in to get choice seats.

The movie is emotional, and the women leave the theatre wiping tears from their eyes.

"The rabbi overstepped his bounds when he told his son to give up his dream of becoming a singer and become a rabbi instead," Sheila says. "You were so grown-up in your thinking at our high school graduation, telling us all to follow our dreams. Harry and I think alike when it comes to following our dreams. Being twins, although I am a few minutes older, we surely must think alike in some ways. Neither one of us will give up on our passions. He will become doctor, and I know I will be a lawyer, no matter how long it takes. Look what happened to Arnold when he gave in to his father. He had other problems too, but still…and look at us, we need to get on with our lives."

"This movie was about much more than entertainment for us," Lucille says. "It was sending you and me a message."

For a few moments, there is a heavy silence between the two women. Suddenly, and catching Lucille by surprise, Sheila blurts out, "Well, I got the message and I am going to law school. I have someone who wants to finance me. You'll never believe who."

"I am curious, but I won't ask. I'm happy for you, really I am. I've waited long enough too, Sheila. I wish I had someone to finance me."

The women part ways, but Lucille hasn't forgotten what Sheila said about going to law school. She's getting that feeling again of being left behind.

BILL

Not long after Bill told Dan about meeting Rose Bush, he breaks the news to Lucille.

"I guess you'll never stop looking for a woman to replace my mother," she says.

"No one can do that. But yes, I keep trying. Rose cares about me enough to move in with her aunt here in town so we can see each other more often. And the more I see of her, the more I am convinced that she will make a good wife. Another Evelyn? I doubt that. But I hope you two get along."

"So," Lucille laughs, "that's where you were going those nights you said you had a meeting in town. Let's have her over for dinner tomorrow night. I want to meet her."

Bill tells Lucille to go into town and buy what she needs at Jerry's, on credit, of course, so that they can have a decent dinner for their guest. He also tells her to have a clean white shirt and pressed pants ready for him to change into when he comes home from work.

Lucille does exactly that. She knows this is a big night for her father, and for herself. She prepares vegetable soup, macaroni and cheese and bakes an apple pie. With a yellow tablecloth, a pretty green bowl in the center of the table and napkins, the setting appears quite festive.

The meeting between Rose and Lucille is awkward at first. Rose speaks in a soft voice, and Lucille is noticeably polite. But soon Rose and Lucille find things to converse about. Rose tells Lucille about people making jokes about her name, the strange way she met Bill when he came to the door of her farmhouse begging for food, and the fact that she actually knew Bill in high school. She tells Lucille that she knew her mother, too, and how much she liked her. The stories amuse Lucille, who tells Rose about her academic interests and her desire to become a college professor one day. Bill listens to the conversation and is sure that he has made the right choice asking Rose to marry him.

Soon the conversation turns to the upcoming wedding.

"I'll make all the arrangements for our wedding. "We'll have it here, of course," Bill says. "We'll invite a few close friends." After all, having had weddings twice before, he has the experience. He ought to make the decisions. "Rose, you will write the invitations, but keep the list short. I'll ask Brenda and Lily to help with the cooking."

Bill wants this wedding to be more extravagant than his wedding to Madeline. That simple church wedding was almost over before it started. They took their vows and then spent the evening drinking at the Beerkill Tavern. Lucille feigned illness and skipped the ceremony. He didn't blame her. She was still mourning for Evelyn. Dan and Paul made the stew for the wedding dinner, but he and Madeline were too sloshed to eat anything when they returned. With Evelyn gone only a few months, it had been too soon for him to marry. He knows that now. But years have passed since the death of his beloved, and Rose is a good choice. She won't bad-mouth him the way Madeline did.

As Bill goes on and on about the reception, the flowers, and the food, Rose nods her head.

"Are you okay with those plans, Rose?" Lucille asks.

"Of course she's happy with the plans," Bill says.

⁓

On his wedding day, Bill feels claustrophobic. He feels the way he felt just before he married Madeline. He didn't feel that way on his wedding day to Evelyn. Marrying Evelyn felt like every door in his house was opening to a new life. He goes to his bedroom to dress. He sits down on the bed and thinks that if Evelyn hadn't died, he wouldn't be going through this again. Opening the door before walking out, he hears chatter coming from the kitchen, where Brenda and Lily are cooking.

"What do you think of these two getting married?" Bill overhears Brenda ask.

"For being so in love with Evelyn, Bill is going on his third wife," Lily replies. "But you know Evelyn, she was too darn pretty for her own good. Jerry couldn't keep his eyes off her. When he helped her carry her groceries home, he'd be dumbstruck when he got back. He'd mope around the house saying he could still smell her scent. I wouldn't let him carry her groceries after he told me that. And Madeline, you know what kind of woman she was. When she came out to the store, she'd lean over the counter and Jerry's eyes started, you know, look'n where he shouldn't be look'n. But no one is looking at her anymore, poor thing. I like Rose the best. Not too pretty, and she keeps to herself."

Their conversation irritates Bill. *Is this all these women do when they get together, talk about me and my wives?* He didn't know that Jerry couldn't keep his eyes off Evelyn, or that Jerry stared at Madeline's breasts when she came into the store. Nah, that's not Jerry. Lily is just jealous and making up a story about her husband. If Bill wanted to gossip about her, he'd have plenty to say.

The story about Lily and young Nick do'n it in the car was something only he knew, and he didn't get the story from Jerry either. After a parent-student dinner held in the high school cafeteria, Bill helped with the cleanup and that took a while. When Bill went out the back door where the garbage cans were located, he saw Nick Jr.'s car. He wondered why it was parked there. He found out soon enough.

He peeked through the car window and saw Jr. and Lily both in the back seat, whoop'n it up. A story like that would get lots of mileage in a town like Harvest, but it wasn't his nature to spread stories. Still, Lily would be better off learning to shut her mouth. Jerry eyeing Evelyn is just something he doesn't want to hear about.

Bill is wearing the same navy blue suit he wore to marry Evelyn. It doesn't have shoulder padding like newer suits, but he doesn't care. Dan lent him a pair of his shoes and Paul donated a new pair of socks.

"This is it. Last time. Three times is enough," Bill says under his breath. He chuckles when he sees the Hillsdale Farms truck drive up. From his window, Bill watches Dan and Paul carry a huge "Just Married" banner bearing a picture of a clothesline showing three shirts hanging side by side. The space below the clothesline reads, "We've hung together all these years. This weekend you're on your own."

No, he'll never be on his own. Even when he and Rose go fishing this weekend, he'll be thinking of his buddies.

ℒUCILLE

Searching through her mother's trunk in the attic, Lucille found the perfect dress to wear to her father's wedding. On a sunny day the week before the event, she freshened the garment by hanging it on the clothesline in the backyard. As she watched the yellow organdy sway back and forth in the breeze, she remembered how beautiful her mother looked the night she wore it to the church dance. Bill was called away to an out-of-town farm meeting, so Evelyn asked Dan to escort her to the dance. They made a handsome couple. Lucille heard them laughing as they left the house.

The dress fits Lucille, but she thinks her mother looked better in it. Now taking the chain with the locket dangling from it out of her drawer, she holds it in her hand and studies it. The words *Promise me, Love Dan*, jump out at her. She circles it around her neck, making sure the clasp is secure. Her father could have overlooked seeing the necklace around her mother's neck because Evelyn usually wore several strings of beads that concealed the chain and locket

Peering into the mirror, she sees an attractive young woman. In her mind's eye, she sees a yellow streak of boldness. She brushes her long blonde hair and pins it to the top of her head, allowing a small curl to fall onto her forehead. Mirrors don't lie. Even though her features are not Evelyn's, the overall package is: the way she carries herself, the small curl down the center of her forehead, and of course the dress itself. Tonight she will confront Dan.

Her father made sure that the flowers decorating the trellis included an orchid, Evelyn's favorite flower. He and Rose chose for their wedding song, "You Came to Me From Out of Nowhere," but Bill had the singer change the second line: "You took my heart and found it free." He explained that the sentiment wasn't true, and he didn't want to start his marriage off with a lie. He had the singer change the words to, "You took my heart and found me."

At least he's honest. That's more than Lucille can say for Dan.

Dan plays the wedding march. Lucille was pleased that Rose selected her to be the maid of honor, and she wished Rose well before she walked down the aisle seconds before her. She also helped Rose with her makeup and her wedding jitters.

After a brief ceremony, Bill's good friends, Hutch and Brenda, Jerry and Lily, Mr. Olson, Howie and his wife, and a few people Bill barely knows on Rose's side of the family gather in the dining room. Lily stops to admire Lucille's beautiful dress and compliments her on her locket. "I remember your mother wearing that one Sunday night at a church function. Yes, I admired it then, too. It's like having a bit of Evelyn here tonight. Look, Dan, doesn't Lucille look lovely? And look at her locket—so beautiful."

"Yes," Dan says. "Lucille does look lovely."

Lily moves on to find Jerry, who is looking in the opposite direction, one eye on Howie. He never misses a chance to get the latest news about Rachael. Since he heard she was riding the rails, dressed as a boy, she has intrigued him. And the fact that a girl fell in love with her makes the story even more interesting.

Lucille focuses on Dan. She stares squarely into his eyes. "You have exquisite taste in jewelry," she says, fondling the locket.

His face turns ashen.

"My mother must have lost this in her garden. I found it there." Dan closes his eyes. "Have you been lying to us all these years?" Her voice is accusing and sharp.

"I suppose you could say that."

"*Suppose*? Daddy and I loved you. We trusted you!"

Lucille feels a hand on her shoulder. She turns and sees Bill. His face beams as if a light shines directly on it."

"My two favorite people! How lucky can a man get? A beautiful daughter and a friend who will be at my side until my dying day."

𝒟 A N

On Sunday Dan awakens to church bells, but he won't be going to church. He did say his prayers last night, though. He kneeled before his bed, drew his hands together in prayer, and asked God for courage.

He'll wear a red shirt to appear confident, even cheerful. He'll don the cap he bought when he took Lucille to the county fair. She'll remember the fun they had together.

He climbs into his truck and drives past the Kramer house several times before parking. When he walks up to the front porch, he studies the steps leading up to the door. His eyes linger on the posts and the chairs. He straightens his cap. This place once felt like home. Now he feels like a stranger. The door opens. He hesitates before walking in.

Dan doesn't know if he should talk first, or let Lucille start. Standing in the small vestibule, he notices that two new paintings have been hung on the wall. He remembers dragging them out from under the couch when he helped Bill move from Kramer Farms, but he never took a close look. He stares at the man and the woman in the paintings.

"That's you in the painting, isn't it? And that's my mother running into your arms," Lucille says.

Hearing the agitation in Lucille's voice, he knows this conversation will be agonizing. He rehearsed what he wanted to say, but he's nervous. What explanation can he give that won't hurt Lucille to the core? None that he can think of.

Lucille moves to the sink, pushes up the sleeves of her blouse, and fills the teakettle. At the stove, she waits for the steam to coil above the spout. "Would you like me to get cups?" Dan asks.

Lucille stares at the wall and doesn't answer.

"I have something to tell you. I don't know if you'll understand, but I'll give it a shot."

"Well, just get on with it."

Dan places a sugar cube in his tea and watches it dissolve. He clears his throat. "During those years when your father was active in the agricultural meetings out of town, he wanted your mother to be well taken care of when he was away and asked me to stay with her. There was always something to do overseeing the farm. It was maybe December or January and the snow was really coming down that night when Bill and I had dinner together at the tavern. It was just before he left for one of those meetings. We had a little too much to drink and your father was in the mood to talk. But then his voice got shaky and his eyes filled with tears. He told me something that tore at my heart. I got up from my chair and put my arms around him, and we stood that way for some time."

"Well? What did he tell you?"

Dan closes his eyes and appears to ignore the question. But then he says, "Be patient. I'll get to that. Let me tell you what happened after I left Bill."

Lucille swallows hard and nods.

"Later that evening I went over to see your mother. The snow was so deep it almost reached the top of the fence. The farmhands had a heck of a time with the livestock, and I got there just in time to help out. The snow fell in huge chunks, and I cleaned the snow off the outside of my new red truck a couple of times. Had the truck only a couple of weeks, and I pampered it like a baby. I spotted Jerry out there with a horse and buggy delivering food."

Lucille rolls her eyes.

"You must hear me out. If it were easy to say this I would have told you a long time ago. Like I said, the snow didn't look like it was about to stop anytime soon, so staying on with Evelyn was a good idea. But she seemed anxious that night, scrubbing the kitchen counter over and over again. She broke a dish, and cried over it. Then she took out her wedding pictures and we both looked through them. Your mother was such a beautiful bride. And Bill, he bought her such a large bouquet. When she held it, it covered the entire top of her dress."

"Get to the point, Dan. Why did you give my mother an engraved locket? I know something was going on with the two of you. I have proof."

He had it all planned, but now he doesn't think he can explain what happened very well. It's embarrassing. Telling Lucille will almost certainly turn out badly.

"After looking at the pictures, we continued sitting on the couch for a while, just watching the snow fall. But then Evelyn turned to me and told me she and Bill were having problems. 'He doesn't feel like a real man,' she said. 'He blames himself for us not having children. He's seen lots of doctors and they all tell him the same thing—some glandular problem.' I felt awful when she told me that, but I already knew. Bill had told me at the tavern."

Lucille looks at him, aghast. "That couldn't be."

"Hear me out, Lucille." He takes another sip of tea. "Your mother said, 'Dan, you know the baby Bill and I want?' Then she took my hand and led me into the bedroom, and pulled me onto the bed. I felt like it wasn't really happening. She pleaded for me to . . . well, you know, she pleaded for me to give her a baby. She said if I wouldn't do it for her, I should do it for Bill."

The sight of Lucille moving around in her chair, holding onto the button on her sweater, twisting and turning it, upsets him. He wants to stop and throw his arms around her. He's never been in such a tight spot. "When we were kids, Bill and I made a pledge to each other down at the river. We promised to be there for each other, forever. But I never thought that I would ever be asked to do something like this. I kept saying no, but eventually..."

Dan, tell her the whole story. Finish it. It's Evelyn's voice.

How can I, Evelyn? I'm hurting her.

Dan runs his fingers through his hair. Evelyn had unbuttoned his shirt, tugged on his pants, and placed her body on top of his. Too nervous to get aroused, he attempted to leave the room. She whispered in his ear, begging. She took hold of him until he could no longer resist, and then he let it happen.

"I'm your Daddy, Lucille."

"I don't . . . I don't believe you, Dan! Bill is my father."

"Haven't you noticed how much we look alike? Bill went to see another doctor on that trip. The doctor told him not to give up trying. I don't know what he thought when he found out your mother was expecting. But I never saw a prouder man."

"Do you think that maybe he could have . . .?"

"Think what you wish. I gave your mother the locket the night you were born. The engraving on the back, I wrote that to remind her to never tell Bill. I made her promise."

Lucille screams. "Don't say any more! You're talking about my mother!" She runs into her bedroom and slams the door. Dan hears her sobbing through the door.

Dan walks into the parlor. He sits on the bench in front of the piano. He did what he came to do. Now it's time to leave. He'll pack up and head for New York.

Lucille's bedroom door opens. She emerges with her face washed and her hair combed. She even has a smile on her face. "I'm a lucky girl," she says. "I have two fathers I adore and two fathers who adore me.

Bill must never know," Dan says. "It would kill him."

LUCILLE

Now Lucille knows why Dan bought her a piano for a graduation present, why he offered to pay for her college when she sobbed to him that she couldn't afford to go, and why he cried alongside Bill during her long illness. She finally understands why so many times he left Bill scratching his head and saying, "Why are you doing that, Dan? That's a Daddy's job."

She can't get used to the fact that Bill isn't her real father. Exchanging one father for another isn't like exchanging a dress at a department store. In bed that night, Lucille remembers all the wonderful things Dan has done for her. Then she thinks of Bill, bragging about "his Lucille, class valedictorian." God blessed her with two wonderful men to care for her. She'll not turn her back on God's gift.

The next morning, Lucille is surprised to see Rose and Bill sitting at the kitchen table having breakfast. She didn't expect them back for another few days. "I didn't want to leave you alone too long," Bill says, standing to hug her.

Alone too long? So many of her classmates are married with families of their own.

Rose says, "I tell your father you are a grown woman, and that he coddles you too much. I guess he doesn't like when I say that, but it has to be said." She takes a book out of a bag and hands it to Lucille. "Here, I brought a poetry book back for you."

"And I brought the newspaper back for you," Bill says. "I got it free at Pappi's Pancake house in Riverview, Minnesota when we stopped there for breakfast. Free with a stack of pancakes. Thought we could read it together, like when you were a little girl."

"I'd like that, but first I want to read a section of it by myself."

Lucille has been thinking about leaving Harvest for some time now. With Bill married again, she doesn't belong here with the newlyweds. She takes the paper and hurries into her bedroom. She spreads the pages across her desk and searches until she finds the Want Ads. Finding a job out of town would be the best thing to do right now.

There aren't very many jobs. Businesses are cutting back, not many are hiring. One ad catches her eye.

Little River Indian Residential School, Riverview, Minn.
-- Wanted: Assistant to Advisor of the Girls' Division--
Eighteen yrs. or older willing to work long hours.
Address application to Miss Wilson.

Lucille reaches for some paper on the corner of her desk and answers immediately:

Dear Miss Wilson,
In response to your advertisement in the newspaper, I am very interested in the position. Long hours and hard work won't deter me. I don't mean to speak too highly of myself, but I graduated as valedictorian of my high school class on June 26, 1926. Letters of recommendation from my high school principal and teachers will follow.
Eagerly awaiting your reply,
Sincerely,
Lucille Kramer

Hoping for a favorable answer soon, she starts planning her future. She won't tell Daddy and Rose yet, but she'll let Sheila in on her plans.

"I'm so happy for you," Sheila says, when Lucille telephones her about the job. "Working at an Indian boarding school sounds very interesting." Sheila also talks about her brother, Harry, who has postponed his wedding twice. Sheila explains that Jacqueline isn't satisfied just being engaged and wants to get married. "She's getting impatient. Harry asks about you, Lucille. He still has your picture in his wallet."

"I'm ready for my new life," Lucille says.

Weeks pass, and Lucille receives no reply from the reservation. She searches the newspapers for other jobs, but all that's available are teaching or nursing jobs, and she is qualified for neither. People are pinning their hopes on a new president, but Lucille doesn't want to wait that long. Finally, she confides in Rose. Lucille tells her she has her heart set on moving out of Harvest, but things don't look promising. Lucille realizes that Rose is trying to be encouraging, but she seems sad. Lucille asks what is wrong, and Rose explains that Bill has been calling for Evelyn in his sleep. "He's still in love with your mother. Of course I always knew I was going to live in her shadow."

"Maybe, just maybe, Rose, if I move away, the two of you will become closer."

Lucille continues her job search. One afternoon after leaving the soup kitchen, already tired from preparing and serving so many meals, she notices the new restaurant that just opened, even as most of the others were closing. A "Help Wanted" sign is in the window. The owner of the restaurant had converted an old house, thinking it was an unusual idea that would draw people in.

Lucille enters the restaurant, gathering the courage to approach the manager. He tells her, "I'm interested in an experienced dishwasher, and if you're not willing to get your hands red and rough, you need not apply." She doesn't like his attitude, but when he throws her a uniform, an apron, and a hairnet and snaps that the kitchen is in the back, she is relieved.

"Today of all days our dishwasher decides to run off and migrate to California. I sure hope you're quick," he says.

Lucille learns from one of the chefs that this is the worst time of all for the proprietor to lose his favorite dishwasher. The farmers with an entourage of important people are going to hold a meeting at the restaurant. He says, "They are here to organize."

"What do you mean?" Lucille puts on her apron and hairnet. Dipping her hands into the sink water, she starts washing cups and dishes.

"Haven't you heard?" the chef asks. "It's been in the papers. The farmers have become irrational and have been doing irrational things like lifting a judge from the bench and carrying him out of the courthouse because he foreclosed on a farm. The farmers realize now, they can't act like a bunch of nuts but need some good common sense ideas."

From the kitchen, Lucille sees Paul sitting at a long table off to the side of the dining area of the restaurant surrounded by men she doesn't recognize. Dan is standing at the front of the table gesticulating as he speaks.

"It's happening all over the world," he says. "Farmers need new ideas in order to thrive again. Walking into banks with pitchforks isn't going to solve anything, carrying judges out of courtrooms isn't going to do anything. We need government aid in these bad times, and we need to find a way to get it." The farmers who have come out in mass applaud in agreement.

Lucille hears someone close to her say, "Dishwashers don't get the short, cute uniforms the girls in the front wear, do they?" It's Mike, the other dishwasher, who has been working alongside Lucille. His apron is splattered with grease and water. When he smiles, more gums than teeth show. His poor diet has taken its toll.

Lucille catches her reflection in the small mirror above the sink, and she can't help but laugh. She can barely recognize herself in that hairnet.

"You won't be laughing for long when the manager gets on your back," Mike says. "I've been working here for two weeks now, and he's tough. I used to be a farmer like those fellas out there, but I just gave up when the dust storms started head'n this way."

As soon as Mike finishes speaking, the manager hurries into the kitchen. "What's going on back here? What's the hold-up? We're run'n out of dishes!" he yells. "You." He looks at Lucille with venom in his voice. He points his finger at her and shouts, "Aren't you up to the job?"

The cup Lucille is about to wash falls out of her hand and shatters on the ground. She stoops to pick up the pieces and cuts her finger. The manager throws her a cloth. "Here, wrap this around the cut," he says.

It's a deep cut. Embarrassed and frightened, she runs from the kitchen and into the dining area. The room is buzzing with chatter. More and more people are arriving. The residents of Harvest are curious as to what the farmers are up to.

Lucille's eyes dart around the room, and suddenly land on Nick. He shakes hands with the farmers, one by one. He looks important, in control, and so handsome in his brown suede jacket and fedora. His striped tie stands out against his suit, dapper and expensive. *Nick looks like a businessman. But why is he here?*

Lucille rips off her apron and throws it, along with her hairnet, into the sink on her way out the back door. Mike calls after her, but she's dashing down the alley, praying that Nick didn't see her.

When she gets home, she finds a message on the table from Bill saying that he and Rose will be out for the evening. Lucille is relieved; she isn't in the mood for conversation. She retreats to her room where she can cry. She sits down on the bed, dispirited and ashamed. About to put her head on her pillow, she sees a letter waiting there for her. Rose must have left it. The return address reads *Little River Indian Residential School*.

Dear Miss Kramer,

Sorry I have not answered sooner, but we are having considerable difficulty at the school. Problems have become so pervasive that I find myself away from my desk most of the time. From your recommendations it appears that you are indeed an astute individual. However, the position also requires great emotional strength. It is necessary to tell you this, because to be quite truthful we've had many people in the position who don't stay very long. If you are interested and are up to the challenge, I invite you to meet with me on August 15. Pack your clothes and plan to stay.

Sincerely,
Miss Wilson.

In the morning, Lucille can hardly contain herself when she tells Bill and Rose about the job. They react exactly as expected. Bill doesn't want her to leave, and Rose looks ready to go with her.

"Well, if you insist on going, I insist on driving you out to Minnesota myself," Bill says.

Lucille leaps over to her father to give him a huge hug. "Your little girl is move'n on!"

"Don't go rubbing it in."

Lucille rushes down to Hillsdale Farms with the news. It's not as close as it was to Kramer Farms, but it's a warm sunny day and she will have lots of time to think about her move during the long walk.

"This is a good time to make a transition," Dan says, after she tells him about her job. "You won't learn anything about life sticking around here." He digs into his wallet and pulls out some bills. He also hands her a book. "This book will come in handy. I read it a few times myself."

"Thanks, Dan," she says. "It's so nice having two fathers."

Before returning home, Lucille stops at Hutch and Brenda's. She wonders how they are faring since Arnold's death. She imagines her father in the same situation and the grief he would be feeling. She's been saying a prayer for them every night before she goes to sleep.

The kennel door is still ajar, just as Arnold left it. "I'm moving to Minnesota and I didn't want to leave without stopping by," she says, when Brenda meets her at the door.

Brenda's body blocks Lucille's clear view into the kitchen, but behind her, Lucille can see pictures of Arnold littering the dining room table. Hutch, his eyes puffy from crying, sits at the table. When Brenda ushers Lucille into the house, Hutch stands and hands her a group of pictures. "Here's one of you and Nick," he says. "I snapped this at your graduation. You two sure looked like you were having a grand ol' time. Nick had chutzpah grabbing you away from Harry. I wish my Arnold had some of that chutzpah. If he did, he'd still be alive today. He was nothing but a broken man after Millie did a number on him, like a bird with broken wings."

Brenda, listening to the conversation, pulls Lucille aside. "I'd like to talk to you privately in another room."

Huddled in a corner of the sewing room, Brenda looks around before speaking. "It would kill Hutch if he knew I told you this. He feels partly to blame for Arnold's death. He discouraged Arnold from being a veterinarian. Hutch wanted a father and son business, and Arnold wanted something else. He thinks maybe that caused him to become despondent along with the other things. It's just eating at Hutch, you know."

"Brenda, we'll never know what caused Arnold's accident. Hutch shouldn't be too hard on himself."

"I have something else I need to get off my chest. You *must* keep this confidential. Remember the night before your graduation, when a motorist knocked Rachael off her bike? It wasn't Nick. The sheriff cleared him of it, but the suspicion lingered."

"I heard the talk."

"After the sheriff questioned Nick, Arnold finally came out with the truth. He admitted that he'd hit Rachael. I guess he wasn't looking where he was going. He told Nick what had happened, and Nick still didn't mind taking the blame for him. He shrugged it off. 'No skin off my nose,' he said. That's the way the two of them were, just like your daddy, Dan and Paul. But Arnold still carried the weight of what he had done. He fainted one day when the sheriff came by the house. The Sherriff was here to visit Hutch, but Arnold was afraid he was coming for him. You know Arnold, always so very sensitive. I just wanted to be sure you knew that it wasn't Nick."

Back in her room, Lucille studies the picture Hutch gave her and realizes that her time with Nick at the creek and at Sheila's party changed her more than any other time in her life. Before she met him, she'd never felt yearning in her heart, or dreamt about lovemaking, or searched for notes at her doorstep in the middle of the night.

Lucille packs her books, pictures, and stack of calendar pages tied in red ribbon into her valise. She decides to take those pages with her, so that if she ever gets lonely, all she has to do is skim through them and her memories will reappear. Certainly, new pages will be added.

She's expecting Sheila, so when she hears a knock on the door she runs to open it. They sit on the bed talking about Lucille's new adventure and the girls vow to keep in touch. "I hope you won't change your mind about me after what I am about to tell you," Sheila says.

"Oh, I'll never do that. You always cheer me up. Even the room looks brighter with you sitting on the bed in your long green skirt." Sheila's eyes evade her. She's looking down at her hands. "Tell me, Sheila. Good friends tell each other everything."

"Here goes, then. That night after my party, I had an unexpected visitor."

Lucille is not surprised that one of the men would want to come back after the party to be with her.

"Something crazy is going on and I don't know what to do about it," Sheila blurts out.

"What are you talking about?"

"I know I shouldn't be having this relationship, but Nick and I are in love."

Lucille stares at the floor, her body trembling. "I bet you two get along great," she says eventually. Her attempt to keep her composure isn't working. She stands and starts throwing clothes, she wasn't planning to take, into her suitcase. The picture Hutch gave her is on her nightstand and she tosses it into her wastepaper basket. She turns away from Sheila to hide her dismay.

"And Lucille, he's paying my way through law school."

Lucille doesn't doubt that. She never said Nick wasn't generous. For some unknown reason, he has money while everyone else is broke.

"His business is the only kind that's doing well right now," Sheila says. "With people losing their homes and banks failing, it is a good time to be an attorney."

An attorney?

"Have you ever seen Nick Sr. up close? He's older, a little smoother, and a little wiser than most of the younger men I know. He came looking for his son after my party, but he had already left with you. I almost called him Mr. Martin. That's sounds funny to me now. I asked him to stay for a drink and he said, 'Sure.' After that, things were never the same for either one of us."

So relieved that Sheila isn't talking about *her* Nick, Lucille throws herself on the bed and laughs. She falls on top of her friend and hugs her.

"He's old enough to be my father, but I love him. I knew you'd laugh at me."

"I'm laughing because I'm relieved you weren't talking about his son!"

"You are? Now I'm relieved you aren't laughing at me."

"Sheila, I want to hear everything."

"He's so much more than a younger man. He knows just what to do. And not just about sex. He stayed until the wee hours of the morning and he, being an attorney, and me hoping to be one, we had so much to say to each other. Now when we meet, sometimes it isn't physical at all. We talk about trials and cases and he tests my acumen. It's just the living end."

"What about his wife?"

"Anita? Well, she moved out to live with Jim Olson's mother. But speaking of the man *you* can't shake, guess what I found out from his father? Nick sold his car to pay for your doctor bills. And he went to church every Sunday and filled those collection bags with every penny left over, praying that you wouldn't die."

"That's nice to hear, but it's over between us, if there was ever anything there to begin with. I'm venturing out into the world, and I hope to meet lots of men."

Sheila quotes Shakespeare. "Love all, trust a few."

BILL

On a Friday morning in August, Dan and Paul arrive early to say their goodbyes to Lucille, and there are plenty of tears. Bill, Rose, and Lucille squeeze together into the front seat of Bill's truck. Bill tried to convince Rose not to go along, but she insisted. She likes Lucille and will miss her too. Besides, she wants to get out of the house and take a long ride. If Bill was planning on taking the scenic route to Minnesota, he soon discovers it no longer exists. Miles and miles of dry farmland stretch on either side of the road. The dust storms have severely damaged the land.

Bill dispenses more than his usual litany of advice to Lucille, which includes safety tips, professional etiquette, and handling finances. He has been giving advice all week, but if he stops talking, he might fall apart. Running out of things to say, the monotonous ride lulls him into a nostalgic state. What will he and Rose have to say to each other now that it will only be the two of them? He'll have to see more of Dan. Since he got the new job driving a truck he's on the go a lot, so that should help. But who is he fooling? It won't be the same without Lucille.

With the women dozing, he gets a preview of the quiet he will experience very soon. When he lost his pocket watch he almost went crazy, because he got so accustomed to seeing it hanging there. What will happen to him with Lucille gone? Not that he's comparing Lucille to his pocket watch, but he's just so used to having her around.

When the lakes along the road become more prevalent, Bill becomes more attentive. When he sees a sign at an intersection that says, "Riverview, Keep Right," he pushes his shoulders up to his ears and his legs shake. He makes the turn and drives about half a mile before approaching a row of buildings with colored canopies and names of the shops printed across the top. There's a Post Office on the corner, and he realizes that that is how he and his daughter will be communicating from now on. When he sees *The Virginian,* starring John Wayne, advertised on the marquee of the movie house, he says, "I can use a whole lot of that actor's toughness right about now."

Bill pulls up in front of the General Store and tells Lucille to get directions to the school from the proprietor. When he sees three or four young men, about seventeen or eighteen years old, standing out in front of the store looking her over when she passes, Bill follows her out of the truck. "None of that, boys," he says.

The boys snicker and move down the street. Bill and Lucille walk up the three wooden steps and stand on the wooden porch looking through the window of the General Store. A round, short man with a mustache, his body covered by a long white apron, is helping customers. He looks up and smiles when Bill and Lucille enter. The smells of sliced turkey and Gouda cheese have Bill yearning for a sandwich. He watches the man in the apron tally numbers on brown bags, and then open the bags with a flip of his wrist before filling them with groceries. A small sign next to a box holding customer account pads reads: "Do not exceed the five-dollar limit." Jerry allowed a ten-dollar limit and then some before putting a halt on credit, and even then there were always exceptions. He couldn't and wouldn't let anyone walk away hungry. Regardless, there will be no credit for Bill Kramer in this store, not as an absolute stranger.

When the last customer leaves, the owner walks toward Lucille and Bill. He extends his hand to Bill. "My name is Mr. Johnson. You two look like you've come a long ways. Where are you head'n from?"

When Bill tells him they're from Iowa, they discover that they have a mutual connection in Harvest: Jerry Sloane. Mr. Johnson and Jerry Sloane are cousins who opened their stores about the same time. Now Bill can relax; Lucille won't be completely alone.

"Well then, maybe you can keep an eye on my daughter, she being a stranger here."

Lucille grimaces and pulls Bill toward the door.

Mr. Johnson directs them to the stock boy for directions to the Little River Indian Residential School. "He knows how to get there. He knows everything about the place. He went to that school himself."

The young man working with large cartons at the back of the store has a way with his hands. He grips and tosses the merchandise with the precision of a juggler at the County Fair. A leather band circles his forehead and turquoise beads dangle below his chest. He's wearing black pants and a bright red sleeveless shirt, and the muscles in his arms bulge each time he picks up another carton. Bill examines him, fascinated by his high cheekbones and his skin, which is the color of toast. He stares at the long, black, shiny ponytail that swings down his back each time he reaches into a carton. "I'll say one thing for those Indians, they put up a good fight in the Great War," he whispers to Lucille.

"How do we get to the Little River Indian Residential School?" Lucille asks.

The young man stops what he's doing. "Are you a teacher?"

After telling him she'll be the assistant to the advisor at the Girl's Division he says, "So you want to know the way to the Little River Indian Residential School? You sure now? Really sure?"

"Of course I'm sure."

"It's not far from here. Go north for about one quarter of a mile. Turn left when you come to the dairy at the corner. Then all you have to do is drive about another half mile or so and you'll pass a white wooden church. Right past that, you'll see the Tanker. The Tanker is a long wooden building. You can't miss it. Then you'll see a sign for the school on the right. Got all that?"

"The Tanker? What's that supposed to mean?"

"It isn't really called the Tanker. I call it that. And Miss, beware, and take care."

Bill grabs Lucille's arm. "Why did he say, 'Beware, and take care?' He's talking like you're going somewhere dangerous." He grips her hand now as they walk back to the truck.

They follow the directions they were given, and when they pass the old weathered wooden building, Bill says, "That Tanker, or whatever that young man called it, needs to be cleared out. It looks like a fire hazard. I don't like that it's so close to where you'll be staying."

A few yards down the road they see the sign: "Little River Indian Residential School."

Bill stops his truck and the three of them get out. Bill looks at the grounds and seeing all the brick buildings thinks, *this isn't a residential school, but an entire community.* Tears stream down his cheeks. "A big man like me crying. I always thought only ladies did that." He wipes his eyes. "Lucille, no smoking. I've see pictures of women with those long cigarette holders. I don't want you doing that."

Lucille pulls a pencil out of her purse and pretends to puff on it. "You mean like this?

"Be serious now," he says, giving her a hug.

Rose speaks to Lucille in a quiet, gentle voice. "I know that when you lived at home, your father thought he knew best. Maybe he did. But now you must know best. This will be a new landscape with new friends. Make the most of it."

"Rose, don't go filling my daughter's head with that talk." He hands Lucille an envelope. "That booze Madeline liked to drink didn't drown all her brains. She brought back the money she stole from you. I know you can use it now."

LUCILLE

The Advisory Building is two stories high. The front of it is brick and the wood siding is painted white. After Lucille knocks on the door and receives no reply, she turns the knob, takes a deep breath, and enters. The room is quiet. There is no one behind the reception desk and no one occupying the row of seats lining the far wall. The familiar smell of Spic and Span fills her nostrils and the wooden floorboards look like they have just been scrubbed with the cleaner. Looking around the room, she hopes that someone will come out to greet her. When no one appears, she ventures outside again to compare the address on Miss Wilson's letter to the address posted on the tree. Confirming that she is indeed at the right place, she checks her letter again for the date and time of her appointment.

Reentering the building, she hears the sound of voices. She's not sure where the sounds are coming from, but she can detect one is a child's voice and the other an adult's. Now she sees a little girl, no older than eight years old, and a young dark haired woman involved in a bristling conversation. The child chatters while the woman pleads with her to stop talking. Eventually, the child takes a seat on one of the chairs in the long row lining the wall. Lucille sits beside her. The woman, who obviously is the receptionist, reaches for a folder on the shelf. The turquoise bracelets glistening on her wrist catch Lucille's attention. The bracelets match her turquoise blouse and pick up the color in her flowered skirt. She writes something in the folder, all the while grimacing.

"Are you going to be my teacher?" the child asks Lucille, twirling a button on her blue uniform.

"No, I'm not."

"You look nice, I wish you would be. And I like your long blonde hair. I had long hair once," she says, "all the way down to here." She stands up and points to her waist. "But the matron cut it. Now it's up to here." She points to where her hair ends, about an inch below her ears.

"I think you look nice anyway," Lucille says. The child has the same color skin as the young man in the General Store who gave her directions to the school. The same warm brown eyes, too.

"What's your name?" Lucille asks.

The child bends toward her, pushes Lucille's hair away from her ears, and whispers, "Kimimela."

The receptionist finishes writing and looks up at Lucille. Not sure of what to do, Lucille walks to the desk and introduces herself. The woman states that her name is Miss Ellie. Her voice has a stern edge to it as she glances over at the chairs, and says, "Wilma, you can go now."

The child runs toward them, pulling up her sleeve showing a red puffy area on her arm. "This is where Miss Halliday pinched me."

"You already showed me that," Miss Ellie says.

"No, I didn't. And if I did, I'll show you again."

Lucille excludes herself from the controversy by staring at the bulletin board on the nearby wall. She reads the names of upcoming seminars printed on white papers and scattered all over the board: "Assimilation Through Education," "Conformity at the Boarding school," "Instilling Proper Ironing, Sewing, and Cleaning Skills." The bottom of each page reads, "Mandatory attendance for all staff members."

The child skips out of the building, turning her head to look back at Lucille.

"Wilma makes up more stories than there are milk duds in here," the receptionist says, placing her hand on the jar on her desk. "I'm sorry if her poor manners unnerved you. That little girl doesn't know when to stop. She accuses one of our matrons of all sorts of things."

In spite of her bright turquoise blouse and colorful beads, Miss Ellie's smile appears constrained. The smell of her sweet perfume conflicts with the pungent scent of floor cleaner. Lucille senses that this place is nothing like home.

Miss Ellie scans her appointment book for Lucille's meeting with Miss Wilson. "I see nothing here. Sorry," she says.

Lucille, irritated by the woman's nonchalance, shows her letter. Ellie reads it and says, "I'm just telling you that I don't see any appointment in my book for you."

Lucille lifts her bags, straining the muscles in her arms, and lugs them back outside. From where she is standing, she sees an expanse of lawn and a willow tree with a bench underneath it. It reminds her of her willow tree at Kramer Farms, and she considers it a good omen. She crosses the lawn to sit under the weeping branches, opens her valise, and pulls out Rilke's, *Letters to a Young Poet*. The inside cover reads, *To Lucille, Let the words of Rilke help you through. Love, Dan*. She's never noticed before how much *Dan* resembles the word, *Dad*. Changing the last letter in Dan's name changes everything. Lucille looks down at her long thin fingers and sees Dan's. She touches her lips, and feels the rosebud outline, also Dan's. She fingers her curly blonde hair. To think she never noticed the resemblance.

She opens the small book Dan gave her and skims through the pages before she begins to read in earnest. The words Rilke wrote to a young military student, jump out at her . . . *Life has not forgotten you, that it holds you in its hand and will not let you fall.*

Lucille's head is bent over the book, but she is aware that someone is watching her. When she looks up, she sees a young man approximately her age leaning against a tree about two yards in front of her.

"Noticed the book," he comments, pulling his yellow sweater down around his waist. "The same one was required reading for my literature class. Rainer Maria Rilke, what a writer. Makes some great points about life, doesn't he?"

Lucille nods, then goes back to reading.

"Don't you feel like talking?"

She glances at him briefly before her eyes are diverted to a parade of children, marching five abreast past the Advisory Building. The boys and girls are wearing uniforms. She recognizes the blue dress with brass buttons that Kimimela had on.

"They try to get them here as early as six years old," he says, eyeing the children.

Lucille wonders *who* tries to get them here. She never saw so many children marching together like this in perfect unison. "You mean all these children go to this school?"

"Oh, we have more than you see here. We have at least a thousand kids attending the school. They come from different cities, states, different Indian tribes."

He bends to pick up a few small rocks and tosses them from palm to palm, "My name is Charlie. And your name?"

"Lucille, Lucille Kramer." She closes her book and places it on her lap. "Do you work at the school?"

"I'm a teacher."

"What do you teach?"

"All subjects. Reading, spelling, arithmetic and handwriting, but I make sure I teach my favorite subject—science. That's my love. I have to cram all those subjects into the morning schedule, because in the afternoon I take the kids over to the vocational school a few buildings down from here. The kids work the machines, press clothes, sew, and do all the laundry. Our Superintendent makes sure our emphasis is on that training. He thinks the morning subjects won't do these kids any good."

This sounds strange to Lucille, and she winces.

Charlie has an interesting face. Despite his smile and sprinkling of freckles, the brown pupils of his eyes appear shattered, like ancient ruins. When he asks why she is sitting out here with valises, she tells him of her appointment that really wasn't an appointment at all. He throws the small stones to the ground and rubs his palms together to remove any traces of dirt. He pulls his sweater down around his waist again. He nods, like he has heard that before. "Wait here," he says. "I'll be right back."

Minutes later, he's back, "I spoke to Ellie. She was just acting like a high hat. Yeah, you know, a snob, trying to pull rank. Your appointment was cancelled and rescheduled for tomorrow at the same time. She could have told you that. Sometimes I think she wants other people to feel as sad as she is."

Lucille wants to throw her arms around this young man she only met minutes ago.

He picks up her two valises. "Let me show you around the place."

After walking about a quarter of a mile, they stop in front of another two-story building that looks just like the Advisory Building. He explains that this is the male teacher's living quarters. The bags look too heavy for his thin body, but he hauls them up the staircase, two steps at a time. He's back in seconds, and pushes wisps of red curly hair off his forehead.

Lucille can't imagine why he whisked away her suitcases, but then realizes that he had to leave them someplace while he gives her the grand tour.

They pass the Boys' School. The front of the building has too many windows to count. She surmises that there are lots of classrooms in there. Since it's Saturday and classes aren't in session, he takes her into his classroom. The room is large with at least sixty or seventy desks. His science experiments are prepared for Monday morning. Lucille looks at the graphs, weather maps, and drawings pinned to the walls, and thinks that he must be a well-organized teacher. The room has the same household cleaner scent she smelled in the Advisory Building. In the hall, she sees a beefy-looking woman overseeing several children as they scrub the floor.

"Superintendent's orders. Mr. Baran is a stickler for cleanliness," Charlie says.

Lucille pictures little Wilma on her hands and knees. Looking at the narrow halls, she thinks that janitors should do that kind of work. Certainly, enough people are looking for jobs.

Charlie is ready to move on, but Lucille thinks she hears strange noises. She listens intently and realizes that whimpering sounds are coming from behind a closed door. "Don't you hear that?" asks Lucille.

Charlie pauses to listen. "I guess I'm used to those sounds by now."

"I don't understand. It sounds like a child crying."

"You don't want to find out too many things on your first day," he says, with little emotion in his voice.

He walks her out of the building, and she senses that Charlie knows more than he's telling. Pointing out a two-story red brick building with white shutters and white columns at the entrance and the huge maple trees circling the property, he explains that this is The Superintendent Building where the big chief thinks up all the weird stuff that we have to do with the kids. "Mr. Baran's office is downstairs and his living quarters upstairs. He's quite a character. Watch out for him. A real lollygagger."

"Lollygagger?"

"You know, he tries to make it with the women."

Lucille is about to learn a whole new vocabulary. They pass a row of red brick buildings with arrows and signs designating the Girls' School, Girls' Dormitory, Little River Hospital, The Creamery, Dining Hall, and Vocational Building. A little town unto itself. He explains that the staff eats with the children to make sure that Mr. Baran's orders are adhered to.

Children are working in the fields weeding, watering, clipping, and fertilizing. They look up and wave to Charlie. Some children have filled their bushels with corn and diligently carry them to the dining hall. When Lucille was in grade school, she only had to concentrate on her studies and piano lessons.

After completing the tour, they find themselves back at the Advisory Building. When they enter the building, the little girl she met before runs to greet Lucille with open arms.

"I'm glad you're back," the little girl says. "You're pretty, and nice too."

Ellie, the receptionist, frowns and shakes her head. "Wilma, this is the second time you've been here today. You haven't even met your quota of ten bushels."

"My arm hurts," she says. "I don't want to do any more work."

The little girl clings to Charlie's pants until the receptionist pulls her away.

"Well then, you know what happens when you don't do as you are told."

"I know. I'll be disciplined by Miss Halliday."

Ignoring the child, Miss Ellie shows Lucille where she can stay the night. They walk down the hall, descend a few steps, and follow a stone path to a small cottage surrounded by trees. Ellie opens the door to a tiny sitting room. "This is it. This is where the assistant to Miss Wilson lives. So if you're hired, this will be your home."

A loveseat and one chair, both covered in identical turquoise and yellow print fabric, cramp the tiny sitting room. The three of them have difficulty squeezing through to the other rooms. A small icebox and a table in the kitchen are placed close together to make room for one or possibly two chairs. Seeing the bedroom, Lucille wishes she could crawl into bed now, lay her head on the pillow, and hide under the striped blanket.

Ellie draws the curtains and tells her about the steam whistle. "Don't let the sound scare you in the morning. You'll hear the whistle at six o'clock. Time to rise. And then you'll hear it throughout the day. It teaches the children to understand clock time." Ellie explains that she had a hard time getting accustomed to it when she first came here from the reservation. She only knew Indian time, which had more to do with the sun rising and setting.

Lucille is exhausted and as soon as she hears the door close behind Ellie and Charlie, she jumps into bed and falls asleep. She dreams that she is eight years old and wearing a uniform. She marches in line with the other children. She fills bushels of corn until her arms ache. Her knees bleed from scrubbing the floor. When the smell of Spic and Span fills her nostrils, she wakes up, screaming. Where is she? She wants to be in her room, the room that Dan designed for her.

A thin stream of light filters through the window and she hears the steam whistle. She sees the unpacked valises beside the closed door. A scrap of white notebook paper is draped over the top of the larger one. The night went by too fast. She closes her eyes and falls asleep again. When she awakens for the second time, she stretches and dangles her feet over the end of the bed. She reaches for the note on top of her suitcase and reads, *Lucille, you were asleep when I got here with your suitcases. I have a feeling it will be tomorrow before you wake up. If it's okay with you, let's have breakfast. I'll meet you outside your cottage at seven-thirty. Charlie.*

Lucille steps over to the window. Her dreams left her in a sullen mood, but the thought of meeting Charlie lightens her spirits. New landscape and new friends, just like Rose said. She tests the water in the basin and finds it cold, so she warms some in the kettle and washes her body with a washcloth. It's getting close to seven-thirty.

When she opens the door she sees Charlie waiting. He's standing against a maple tree, tossing small stones from palm to palm. She smiles at him, feeling lucky to have made a friend. When he suggests they go for pancakes, she can't wait; it's been a long time since her last meal. They stroll down the stone pathway leading away from the Little River Indian Residential School property. From the greetings he receives from the people they pass on the way, Lucille can tell Charlie is popular at the school. Max, the history teacher, stops to talk, and Charlie introduces Lucille. "He thinks he's a real cake-eater," Charlie says, after walking away from him as quickly as he can. "He thinks women drop at his feet just to be his dancing partner. Wants to be a pro, the next Valentino. Max probably uses an entire jar of pomade at one time to get that Valentino shine in his hair. Too greasy for my taste. I have to admit he does look a lot like him. About the same size as Valentino, five eight or nine, and those eyes. Hard to tell whether they're open or closed or somewhere in the middle."

Lucille finds Charlie's comments amusing. "The girls call those kind of eyes dreamy eyes," Lucille says with a laugh.

"Call them what you like, but he might try to get to know you better. But a little advice, stay clear of him."

Lucille will remember his warning, but right now her stomach is growling.

Approaching the road, the light turns green and Lucille holds onto Charlie's arm as they cross over and walk toward Pappi's Pancake House, which is housed within a red stone building with a yellow awning. It is where Rose and Bill ate breakfast on their honeymoon;

Bill raved about the pancakes. The plaque on the building reads: "Built in 1907. Stone from the quarries of Pipestone." Henry Wadsworth Longfellow's "The Song of Hiawatha" is written beneath it:

> *On the Mountains of the Prairie*
> *On the great Red Pipe-stone Quarry,*
> *Gitche Manito, the mighty,*
> *He the Master of Life descending,*
> *On the red crags of the quarry*
> *Stood erect and called the nations*
> *Called the tribes of men together.*

"Every Indian kid knows this poem by heart by the time they are in second grade," Charlie says.

Lucille can also recite every word by heart, and she often uses the poem's meter as a model for her own poems. But now it brings to mind the little girl she met yesterday. "I made a good friend in Wilma yesterday. Or is her name Kimimela?" Lucille asks.

"A school committee changed her name to Wilma. They throw out all of the Indian names, like they're garbage. Mr. Baran's orders."

"I really like her."

"That's because you have something in common. You both miss your families."

Standing in a line inside the restaurant, constricted on both sides by wooden rails, they wait for a table. Lucille's eyes wander around the room. Noticing that many tables are filled with parents and their children, she's surprised so many can afford to eat out. She's about to comment on that when Charlie says, "Sunday mornings, children get free pancakes. The families come here before church. That's why it is so crowded. Hope you don't mind the wait."

Most of the men are wearing their church attire: jacket, ties, and clean pressed pants. Their wives are in floral or gingham dresses. Lucille spots the young man from the General Store who gave her directions to the school. He's hard to miss. In his bright yellow shirt and turquoise beads with a band around his head, and his ponytail swinging down his back, he stands out in the crowd. He is paying his bill when he looks up and recognizes her. He walks over. When Charlie sees him, he says, "Lucille, this is my best friend, Paco Whitefeather, my guiding light. Everyone calls him Whitefeather."

"We met yesterday," she says.

"You did? Then you didn't waste any time getting to know the most important man in town."

Lucille scrutinizes the young man, who appears to be about her age. She wonders what makes him so important.

Whitefeather asks, "What do you think of Little River Indian Residential School? Did you fall in love with the place?" Sarcasm drips from his voice.

"Whitefeather, give the young lady a chance to find out for herself."

A waitress dressed in the Pappi's uniform, a black dress trimmed with white buttons and round white collar, shows Lucille and Charlie to their table. Whitefeather leaves, saying that it's time for him to get back to the store.

"He's my best friend. We're as close as brothers," Charlie says, when they are seated. "He came my way when I needed a friend most. People in town think he should dress more like a *regular American*, but the more they say that, the more he dresses like his ancestors."

The waitress adjusts the white cap perched on top of her head. She pulls a pencil and pad of paper from her apron pocket, ready to take their order. With her hair pulled back, her ears stick out like the handles of a large cup. Charlie has a disgusted look on his face when he sees her. He looks down and pretends to study his menu.

"Charlie, I thought that was you. Heard you were sick. No girl is worth that."

"See for yourself, Roz. I'm getting along fine."

Roz looks over at Lucille, and then fills her coffee cup. "Don't mean to be meddling, but you know people say things."

Charlie cuts her off. "I don't want to talk about it."

"Suit yourself," she says, rolling her eyes. "What will you have?"

Charlie says, "The usual stack of pancakes." He says it calmly but his face blanches. Lucille says, "Same for me."

"Don't pay attention to Roz," he says. "She lives on the reservation and gets her kicks picking up gossip here on the job and then spreading it around when she goes back."

Lucille surmises that Charlie is still having trouble getting over a former girlfriend. Embarrassed to be aware of this personal matter, she tries to move on to another subject. She asks, "Who has the Pipestone hair in your family?"

"Don't really know. I was adopted." He drums on the menu with his fingers until Lucille puts her hands on his to stop him. "Sorry. Nervous habit."

Silence prevails for the next few minutes until Roz brings the pancakes. Charlie drowns them in syrup.

"So, you're still drowning your sorrows," she says.

Charlie pushes his dish away and throws down his napkin. "Let's get out of here, Lucille. There's another pancake spot just around the corner."

Later that afternoon, Lucille is ready to meet Miss Wilson for her interview. Her office is in the Advisory Building directly in back of the reception desk, and Ellie shows her in.

Miss Wilson is seated at her desk when she arrives and stands briefly to shake Lucille's hand. Lucille is struck by the woman's strong resemblance to her high school Math teacher, Miss Lindsey. Maybe it's the black hair, styled like Miss Lindsey's in a bun and the gray streaks running through it, or the wire glasses, or the face that crinkles with every expression. Or maybe Lucille is looking for someone familiar with whom she can be at ease. But looking into Miss Wilson's eyes, she sees something noticeably different from Miss Lindsey's. Her Math teacher's eyes twinkled when she spoke, like she was smiling even when she wasn't. Miss Wilson's eyes are sad. Lucille doesn't think that they would twinkle even if she did smile. Miss Wilson's lips are drawn down, like there is little to smile about anyway.

"I will be up front with you," the woman says. "Like I mentioned in our correspondence, you will face both physical and mental exhaustion in this position. You will have little time off, an hour here and there during the day. But basically it is a seven days a week job. That's hard, not having much time for yourself. I know. I've been at this job for a few years now."

I can handle it, Lucille thinks. *I survived tuberculosis. My mother died, my friend Arnold died, I have two fathers, and I lost my farm. I can do it.*

Miss Wilson's voice grows raspy as she speaks about the children who were torn from the reservation and forced to leave their families behind when they were practically dragged to the boarding school. "It is our job to retrain these children, to strip them of their language, religion and rituals. Government orders. We're successful with some of the students and unsuccessful with others. Ellie can tell you. She attended our school for a few years. She is one of our success stories, if you want to call it that. But then there are other students who stand firm, and you can't knock the Indian out of them no matter what you try. Some end up running away and some do what the little boy did last week. We found him hanging from a tree."

"Hanging from a tree? I don't understand. What could be that bad to cause him to...?"

"I wish I could tell you that we are doing the right thing for these children here, but I can't. I do what I can here to see that the matrons aren't so hard on the kids when they are disciplined, and I have tried to influence Mr. Baran on this issue. We can't have kids hanging from trees because they can't adapt to our culture."

This is a lot for Lucille to comprehend. She had little information about the school when she applied for this job.

"Now let me tell you about your position, unless I have scared you off. You and I will be working very closely coordinating the various departments to find out what is working and what isn't. You'll be out there doing the footwork and then relaying information back to me. Ellie will teach you the ropes and work with you for a few days. She's more than just a receptionist. She's my personal secretary and that is a full time job. Any questions?"

All Lucille can visualize right now is a child hanging from a tree.

Under the Red Ribbon

The next morning, after hearing the first steam whistle, Lucille meets Ellie at the door of the cottage, ready to guide her through the first day on the job.

Ellie recites a litany of Lucille's duties as they walk along the school grounds. "You will eat with the children and note their eating habits. You will report on the matrons and the cooks and see to it that they carry out the necessary disciplinary measures. You will see to it that Indian food is not served. You will check the laundry to see that the children wear their uniforms for a week before washing them. We are short on water; you know that." Passing the school, she says, "You will visit classrooms during the day to see that the children are not using any language other than English. Teachers should be at their desks by eight o'clock. In other words, you will be the oil that keeps the spokes running smoothly."

Lucille, unaccustomed to being told how to carry out her day, takes a deep breath, determined to do what she is told. She uses a small pad of paper to take notes.

"You'll need a larger pad than that," Ellie says. "The list gets longer."

Ellie escorts Lucille into all of the buildings so that Lucille can familiarize herself with the various aspects of the job. She introduces Lucille to the teachers, the cooks, and the matrons. When they break for lunch, they walk to a bench in back of the school, and Ellie takes out two sandwiches from her tote bag and gives one to Lucille. "Just a jelly sandwich, but it's homemade. The kids make these as part of their vocational training."

Lucille is hungry and eager to bite into her sandwich, but she also knows she should make polite conversation first. "How did you get your job, Ellie?"

Ellie's cordial but businesslike expression suddenly changes. It is as if the question causes a dark shadow to spread across her face. Her voice quivers when she repeats Lucille's question. "How did I get my job?" She pauses for a moment. "Mr. Baran. He gave me the position."

"That was nice of him," Lucille says.

"Oh, don't misunderstand. When Mr. Baran does something nice for someone, there is always a price to pay. And I paid it."

Lucille doesn't know what Ellie means by that comment, but she won't ask. "Miss Wilson told me you used to live on the reservation," Lucille says. "What brought you here?"

Ellie's eyes turn wistful, as though she is thinking back to another time, so long ago. "I don't want to bore you with the details, but I think you will understand me better when you learn something of my background."

Lucille ignores her sandwich and holds it on her lap while she listens to Ellie's story:

"Once proud of my Indian heritage, I did what most of the girls on the reservation did at fifteen. I worked in the field, crafted jewelry, and attended school on the reservation. I never considered shedding my people's traditions. They were a part of me—until I met Hanson. The first time we met, he stood at my door wearing a sleeveless black shirt showing a small heart engraved about two inches above his left elbow. A simple leather belt circled his waist. He was royalty in dungarees. He asked for a glass of water. And when I handed it to him, I was too shy to look at him.

"We went for a walk and he told me he was a writer, and that he burned with a desire to write his first novel about Indian life. He was so unlike the over-muscled men I knew on the reservation, interested only in drink and love-making. We went for many walks together after that and he told me about his travels, shared his knowledge with me. Like an artist, he unveiled his stories with vivid words. Sometimes on those walks, we'd stop and kiss, but nothing more than that." Lowering her voice, Ellie clenches her hands together and sighs before going on.

"One dark night, we strolled along the dirt road not far from my family's house. Hanson's face shone like the moon and his eyes twinkled like the stars. I offered to run away with him, but he said he didn't want to leave. He said that the beat of the drums, the enchantment of the dance, and the warmth of the ovens contained all he needed to exist. While we stood with our arms around each other, a rowdy bunch of Indian boys came up from behind and beat Hanson. They grabbed the coins in his pocket and yelled 'Indian women for Indian men!' Blood gushed around Hanson's eye and he said his leg felt like it was broken. I took him back to my house and my mother helped me clean his wounds. He slept in our house for the night—on a mat on the floor. Word got out on the reservation and the Indian people sided with their own. 'She shouldn't be run'n with a white man who's writing tales about us,' they said. A few days later, Hanson was gone. I looked out the window and saw him limping down the road. The people who blamed him for having to suffer from the white man's wrath scared him off. I searched the woods for him, even the mountains. I asked around if anyone had seen him, and ended up in front of the Little River Indian Residential School. Mr. Baran found me. He fed me and offered to educate me in return for special favors. I was young and didn't know better. He arranged for my job as Miss Wilson's secretary. I avoid him now."

So enthralled with Ellie's story, Lucille forgets to eat her lunch.

In the afternoon, Ellie continues to inform Lucille of her responsibilities as they walk toward the auditorium. The children walk in ruler-straight lines as they enter the one-story brick building for the school concert. The matron pushes Wilma's hand down when she attempts to wave to Lucille.

"Are the parents here?" Lucille asks.

"Parents aren't allowed to visit," Ellie explains. "The children become unruly when they spend time with their parents. They want to go back with them, back to the reservation."

Lucille stares at the back wall of the auditorium where several children, their hands held over their heads, struggle to stand on one leg. Lucille looks away, upset by their pained expressions.

"That's what happens when children break the rules," Ellie says. "Oh, if you had been here when Miss Halliday cut Wilma's braids! That little girl is a toughie, a hard one to break. On the reservation, mourners and cowards wear short-shingled hair. So Wilma couldn't understand why her hair would be cut like that when she was neither. She held a purple stone in her hand, and she screamed, 'Die!' The matron is usually hard as nails, but she was petrified of the stone. Purple represents magic in the Indian culture, and the mystery of magic frightens Miss Halliday. She stopped cutting mid-way through. Wilma stuck with one side of hair long and the other short until she let me even out her hair. Now she sticks out her tongue whenever she sees Miss Halliday."

After a trying first day, Lucille lies on her bed letting her mind wander. She is disturbed by the way the children are treated. In Harvest, she gave very little thought to these matters. She never knew many Indian people, only Derik, and she'd never associated his arrogance with the rest of his culture. The young Indian boys who came to town looking for work were respected for their work ethic. All of this talk about "washing the Indian clean" is new and strange.

Remembering her promise to write home often, she rummages through her desk drawer looking for a pen and paper. She finds an envelope addressed to Maggie, the prior occupant of the cottage. She's about to discard it when she changes her mind. She pulls out the letter with some uneasiness. She might learn something about her predecessor, but she's not sure she wants to. She reads,

Hi Maggie,

I've been away visiting some friends in Wisconsin, that's why I haven't been over to see you. I'm back to waiting tables. The money isn't much to speak of. People don't leave tips anymore. Anyway, when I returned, there was a lot of buzz going on at the reservation. Talk about Ellie's sister, Tara. She and Charlie broke up. Did you hear about that? Charlie called off the wedding when he found out she was doing it with three fellas on the reservation at the same time! He hasn't been taking it well, as you can imagine.

Tara got a new job. She works at the Peek-a-Boo Club dancing on tables. Men drop dollar bills in her panties. She comes back to the reservation now and then, and struts around in those high heels and tight skirts. You can smell her perfume and the booze from yards away. It didn't take her long to find a new boyfriend. I hear he's very rich, strong, and handsome.

I can't blame you for wanting to quit. The poor woman who will have to take your place!

Oh, remember to spit in Mr. Baran's eye before you leave!

Write back,

Roz

Under the Red Ribbon

Mr. Baran has strict orders about staff eating with the children. Charlie told Lucille that, but he hasn't been at the dining hall all week. She hasn't seen him since they had breakfast together at the pancake house. She goes to Ellie's office to see if she knows about Charlie's strange disappearance.

"Charlie must be going through one of his dark moods again," Ellie says, when Lucille inquires about him. "When that happens, he stays to himself. Miss Wilson is away for the day. We can use her office and I'll explain." The two women enter the room and sit on two small wooden chairs facing Miss Wilson's desk. "It must be my sister, Tara, teasing him again," Ellie says, twirling her hair. "She's a wicked one. He falls for her game every time. I guess he can't help himself."

"Game?"

"I know you like him, but there are things about him that will make your hair stand on end. Charlie is…how shall I say this? He's a great guy, but he's got problems. My sister only adds to his problems."

"How's that?"

Ellie shrugs. "Everybody else knows. Why shouldn't you? Besides, then you can decide for yourself if you still want to be his friend."

"Tell me, if you think I should know."

Ellie stands up and looks out the window. When she turns around, she says, "I'll tell you something my sister told me." She walks in front of Miss Wilson's desk and begins orating as if she were a teacher telling a story to her student. "Some days ago, Tara waited outside Charlie's room throwing small stones at his window until he came down. When he did, they walked to the clearing in back of the school and lay down on the grass. He liked to stroke her hair, she said. And then she did what she always does when they are alone. She ran behind a tree and came out from behind it completely bare except for her long black hair hanging over her shoulders. While she said his name, she stood in front of him and she…well, she did to herself what he wanted to do, but couldn't. Then she disappeared into the woods."

"That's the game you were talking about?"

"Yeah, that's the game. But sometimes this game becomes too much for Charlie."

"Why is that?"

Ellie sits down again and turns toward Lucille. "You see, Charlie has a history of what some would call weirdness. He told Tara that sometimes a gesture, a voice, a smell takes him back to the orphanage. Sometimes it's a heavy rain, a snowflake, or the slant of the sun's rays seeping through the window. That's the way he told it to her. I'm just repeating. Beautiful words, but not a beautiful story."

"I'm almost afraid to hear," Lucille says, gripping her hands together.

"Don't be. There are lots of things around here that are strange." She continues on. "Tara's hair, her teeth, her smile, her disappearance, brings it all back. He becomes a child again. His mind goes back to when he was younger, ten or eleven, when on rainy afternoons, after he finished washing his bedroom floor, he stood at the window watching the rain splash into the puddles. He tried to guess how many cars would stop in front of the building before dinner. If he guessed correctly, he rewarded himself with good thoughts that someone would adopt him.

"A young, pretty counselor arrived one afternoon and she immediately took a liking to him. She asked him if he wanted to play checkers. For days after, she took every opportunity to read science books with him and even bought him chemistry set. He loved the attention. After dinner, she brought him candy and a scoop of ice cream. She tucked him into bed. Happier now than he had ever been, he looked forward to the next time she would tuck him in.

"One night, that very same counselor crept into his bed. He stroked her long black hair. When she spoke, her teeth glistened. She took his hands and moved them all over her body, and then she stopped and slipped out of his bed. He didn't see her for more than a week, and when he did, she busied herself with some papers and ignored him.

"But a few weeks later, as he sat in bed reading before going to sleep, he smelled her scent and looked up. She was at his bedside. 'Do you want me to hold you?' she asked. 'Sure you do.' She slid in beside him and cradled him in her arms. Then she said, 'this is what you've been missing,' and she lifted her blouse and nursed him as if he were a baby. When he felt the explosion between his legs, he wanted her to hold him forever. But in seconds, she vanished.

"The next day, the two boys who shared his room attacked him. They came into his bed and imitated what they'd seen him do with the counselor. He screamed and the headmaster locked all three of them in the laundry room. He can't remember for how long, but he remembers his terrible thirst. 'You think drinking all that water will wash away your evil?' That's what the headmaster said, when he begged for water.

"He swore he'd never do anything like that with a woman again. Now, as a grown man, when he is with Tara, he wants her, but he just can't make love to her. My sister learned to play her games with him from that story. I tell her that Charlie is too sweet, and she shouldn't do that. She just laughs and says that she's just having fun."

On Saturday morning, still unable to get the story about Charlie out of her head, Lucille tells Miss Wilson she will be gone for an hour or two; she has to attend to some business in town. Actually, the business pertains to freeing her mind from everything that has bombarded her since she arrived. Just walking around Riverview window-shopping will be enough.

She spots Charlie sprinting down the street. When the wind blows his cap off his head, he turns to catch it and acknowledges her with a wave and a smile. "I'll pick you up at seven and we'll go to the Street Fair," he yells. "Will that be okay with you?"

"Street Fair at seven," she calls back.

Miss Wilson told her the town would be a busy place all day with the storeowners, craftsmen, and food vendors preparing for the Street Fair that night. Lucille sees signs along the road that read, "This way to the Street Fair," and show big red arrows. She's excited to be going. If only she hadn't heard that orphanage story. But then again, maybe Ellie is a storyteller like her old boyfriend, Hanson.

Reaching the center of town, she stops in front of Clara's Dress Shop. With the sun so bright, she wishes she could afford one of those huge hats she sees in the window. She studies the dresses. Styles are changing. She likes the red dress with the shoulder pads. It would make her hips look tiny. Sheila would approve.

The salesgirl, with a pale pink complexion and nail polish to match, is leaning over a counter and flipping through a magazine when Lucille enters the store. She's wearing a large blue hat like the ones displayed in the window and a trailing white chiffon scarf around her neck that covers part of her white cardigan sweater. She looks up when Lucille enters. Lucille points to the manikin in the window. "That's the dress I want. And I like your scarf. Is that one you sell in the store?"

"Sure, all the things I wear we sell in the store. I'm lucky I get to model the clothes." The salesgirl searches through the rack and finds the red dress.

"This dress was made for you," she says, when Lucille looks at herself in the fitting room mirror. "Add the scarf, and you will be a hit at the Street Fair. You are going, aren't you?"

"Oh, yes. I am going. This is my first time."

"Riverview really turns out for this event. Gives us a chance to dress up and feel like we are really going somewhere. Especially this year, you know, with this depression. We women need to add some pizzazz to our lives."

Lucille has some of the money that Dan gave her before she left Harvest with her and she doles out ten dollars from her pocketbook for the dress and three dollars for the scarf. She hurries out the door. Further down the street, she stops in front of a hair salon. The sign in the window says, "Three Dollar Haircuts. Go to the Street Fair in Style. No Appointment Necessary." She walks in and waits her turn.

Obviously, lots of other women in Riverview have read the sign because there is a row of hair dryers against the wall and the chairs under them are all filled with women reading magazines while drying their hair. The stylist, wearing a white dress with a black plastic apron covering most of it, approaches Lucille. She is young and attractive and has her dark hair cut in a bob that ends just below her ears with straight bangs across her forehead. Her eyes are heavily made up, and with her pouty red lips and the beauty mark near her eye, Lucille imagines she is quite something after hours. Three other stylists are working in the shop and they are all busy cutting, pin-curling, and finger-waving their clients' hair.

"You sure you want to cut off all that long beautiful hair? Some girls do end up crying," says the stylist, after Lucille tells her what she wants.

"Actually, I want my hair cut like the woman who just left, in finger waves."

Sitting in the chair, Lucille closes her eyes and vows not to open them until the haircut is complete. When she opens her eyes and looks into the mirror, she screams.

"I warned you," the stylist says. "It's quite a change."

Lucille's eyes look bigger, her cheekbones higher, her lips softer. She stares at the chunks of blonde hair scattered on the floor.

"What do you think? You like it?" The stylist spins Lucille's chair around and holds up a small mirror so that Lucille can see the back of her head.

"Like it? I love it! I feel like a movie star!"

Thrilled with her new appearance, Lucille returns to the cottage in a gleeful mood. She bathes, careful not to wet her hair, then dresses early. When Charlie knocks on the cottage door and Lucille answers it, his eyes widen in surprise. "What did you do to yourself? People in town will wonder how a plain guy like me got a babe like you."

Lucille puts her arms around him and gives him a hug. "I'm ready, let's go."

The town is all lights tonight. This is the gala Fall Festival; stores will remain open until midnight. Throngs of people cram the streets. Crowds line up outside restaurants.

Charlie and Lucille enter "Food Fantasia," the restaurant known for the fun-loving crowd, and stand below the yellow and red balloons floating across the ceiling. "Putting on the Ritz" is blasting from a radio and the crowd sings along, swaying to the music. Boys from the reservation wearing leather boots, leather vests, and bright-colored shirts eye the city girls, who respond now that they are out of their parents' sight. The Indian girls ogle the white guys. Tonight, it seems, anything goes.

Charlie and Lucille follow the thirty-something hostess to a small table near the window. Her eyebrows are shaven and drawn on with a black pencil. In her blue uniform that almost looks like an ordinary dress, her small waist is clearly outlined with a narrow belt. Her smile exposes protruding front teeth, and her voice is cheerful when she asks, "Are these seats alright?"

From these seats, they have a broad view of everything going on outside. They watch people stop and look at the long table displays of hand-painted dishes, colorful pottery, and paper flowers. Lucille admires the long tables that spill over with Indian crafted jewelry. Later, she hopes to wander through the tents; the walls are lined with paintings and drawings.

"Those reservation exhibits attract big crowds year after year," the hostess says, "I'm wild for Indian artwork. Love the brilliant colors. I'm surprised we're having the Street Fair at all, with this brutal economy, but it helps us remember we're still alive."

"Look, Charlie! Look at the Parade of Art," Lucille squeals. Dancers parade in front of the restaurant window spinning in circles while holding art above their heads. With delight, she watches the red and turquoise skirts and wide balloon pants twirl around the dancers' ankles like windmills.

"Yes," he says, "they are something to watch."

When Lucille turns her attention back to the room, she looks at Charlie and observes something strange happening to him. She sees his face turn apple red, then drain to white. Lucille wants to ask what's wrong, but she sees him staring at a woman standing near the entrance to the restaurant waiting to be seated. In her yellow blouse, short red leather skirt, and spike heels, she is a striking figure. The woman abruptly leaves the line and hurries toward their table.

"Hello, Charlie," she says in a low, purring voice. Her hair, parted in the center, falls in silky black strands over her shoulders. She strokes her hair as she speaks.

"Hello, Tara," Charlie says in a monotone.

"With all these people here, I bet you were hoping to see your Tara."

Lucille takes a closer look at the woman. No wonder Charlie was fascinated with her.

"So it is true," Tara says. "You have another woman in your life. Did you tell her about the fun we have together?"

Lucille fixes her eyes on the balloons floating across the ceiling. She wants to be any place but here.

"I'm leaving town in a few weeks, only right we say a real goodbye," Tara says. "I wanted us to do that properly when we were together, but you just wouldn't. Or is it, couldn't?" She laughs. "But it was fun just the same." She leans over him and kisses him on the lips. Her hand slips under the table. Charlie squirms in his seat.

Angered by the smug look on Tara's face, Lucille leaves the table and heads for the bathroom. The long line is a blessing; she's in no hurry to return to the table.

She's been standing in line for a few minutes when the person behind her says, "You look familiar." Lucille turns around to see who it is. She recognizes Roz from the restaurant. "Of course, in my job I see so many people. Oh, now I remember. You're the girl who was with Charlie at Pappi's. Tell me, is he okay?"

"He wouldn't be here tonight if he wasn't."

"Just wondering," Roz says. "You don't have to get mad. But being around Charlie when he's miserable can't help but rub off on you."

Lucille doesn't want to continue the conversation. She leaves the line and returns to the eating area.

"This is my friend, Lucille," Charlie says, still blushing, when she sits down at their table. "Sorry about not introducing you before. Lucille, meet Tara."

"Lucille? That's odd. My boyfriend calls me that sometimes. My on-and-off boyfriend, that is. He says he just likes saying the name."

Lucille turns toward the window. When she turns back around, Tara is gone. Lucille is ready to go home.

They shoulder their way through the crowd and when they get outside, Charlie stops at one of the long tables on the sidewalk and sifts through the crafts while Lucille stands beside him watching Tara leaving the Street Fair with a tall, dark-haired man at her side.

At the jewelry table, Charlie buys a sterling silver necklace with a white buffalo stone in the center. He fastens it around Lucille's neck. Her intuition tells her he bought the necklace to make up for ruining her evening. The night that started out with lights and bright colors has turned dim. They walk the rest of the way back home saying little.

"I guess this is goodbye," he says, as they approach the cottage.

"Goodbye until tomorrow?" she asks.

"No, for longer than that."

"You don't want to be friends anymore?"

"It has nothing to do with us being friends. Whitefeather has arranged for me to go to the Purification Ceremony, and then on a Vision Quest."

Lucille knows a little about those ceremonies, but she thought only Indian people attended them.

Taking her hand, Charlie says, "You don't want to be around me when I'm like this."

Lucille liked having Charlie around. She wonders if she'll ever see him again. When she meets Ellie in her office the following morning, she asks her about the Vision Quests and Purification Ceremonies.

"Oh, so Charlie has decided to do something about his problem?" says Ellie. "He's tried that before. But I guess it's time to dip into it again. These quests and ceremonies are sacred, and quite beneficial. Of course it depends on the person. On a personal Vision Quest, he'll feel crazier before he feels better...grand visions, hallucinations, fasting in the wilderness. All those kind of things. Or, he could be secluded in a small room. But he'll come out better for it. He'll come out transformed and you know, get all that weird stuff resolved."

"How long will he have to stay there?"

"Like I said, depends on the person."

"And the Purification Ceremony?"

"The Purification Ceremony, the Oenikika, is uniting the physical body with the spiritual world. Lots of prayer, singing, soul-searching, and breathing in new life. Charlie can ask for specific healing. He'll be staying at a circular lodge, shaped like a womb and made of branches. When he leaves he will be reborn with the richness of the blessings bestowed upon him."

Ellie's eyes seem distant now. Lucille wonders if she is remembering the culture she gave up.

"Maybe one day you will be reunited with Hanson and receive the richness of those blessings." At that moment, she sees a quality in Ellie that she genuinely likes: the way her face lights up at just the mention of his name.

Making her usual evening rounds, Lucille stops by the girl's dormitory. In the dark, she remains unnoticed. From the doorway she has a view of the sleeping quarters. The room is dimly lit, and the girls are all sitting up in their cots except for Wilma, who Lucille spots crouched in the center of the room. Miss Halliday looms behind her. The matron raises a switch in her hand and slaps it across the child's buttocks. The little girl shows her mettle. She elicits no tears, no screams. That comes from the other little girls watching.

Their cries only strengthen the matron's resolve, and she hits Wilma with the switch again. Lucille calls out, demanding that she stop, and Miss Halliday drops the switch.

"Miss Halliday thinks I'm stubborn," Wilma says, running toward Lucille. "I told her it isn't stubborn to be Indian. I like my own language and I like stories about the sun and the rain, and the clouds and the buffalo. I like the drums because they make the earth dance." Her black hair is matted and she gasps when she speaks.

Wilma's wet underwear still hangs over her head like a hat. "She made me stand in a tiny corner with this on," she says, pointing to her head. "She wants me to promise I won't wet my pants again, but I scared her with my stone." Wilma extends her hand and shows Lucille the dark purple object the size of a grape.

Lucille ushers Miss Halliday into the narrow hallway. The matron pushes the stray hairs of her bun into place and says, "How could I allow an eight-year-old to make a fool of me, taunting me with that stone? She wants bad luck to come upon me. Growing up on the reservation, I had many experiences with objects that are purple. It represents magic and I want no part of that."

Lucille knows that rumors always circulate about Miss Halliday, coming mostly from the teachers. Charlie told her that Miss Halliday's parents were illiterate people who did only enough farming to feed themselves. Her father, rarely sober, took liberties with his daughter. Miss Halliday never married. During one of her courtships, an Indian man in a drunken rampage beat her so badly that she ended up with a broken arm and leg. From then on, she swore off Indian men. She had no qualms about trading her Indian culture to live among white people. She thought that if she could assimilate, she could train the children at the school to do the same.

Lucille is straightforward with the matron. "Miss Wilson will hear about this."

The following morning, Lucille is tired before she even starts her day. She splashes her face with cold water, waves her hair with her fingertips, and powders her nose. She decides on red lipstick to brighten her pale face and makes her way to the dining hall. On her way, she passes a young Indian girl walking out of Mr. Baran's office. The girl appears sullen and hangs her head when Lucille passes.

Max, the history teacher, is sitting in Charlie's usual seat munching on a roll. Lucille hasn't spoken to him since Charlie introduced them on the day she arrived and told her to stay clear of him.

Max pulls on her arm as she passes. "So, your friend Charlie left school again. Too bad. It's happened before." He points to his head. "Something wrong upstairs."

With an appalled look, she turns and walks away.

"Wait up, Lucille. Didn't think you'd get so lathered up over that. Actually, I'd like to take you out for a nice dinner and then to the Town Hall for some dancing. Do you Tango?" When she doesn't answer, he says, "Okay, I'm sorry. Maybe I am being too tough on your friend. Just trying to be suave."

"Suave? You're being stupid."

"So it's a date?"

He's wearing a puffy-sleeved shirt cuffed around the wrists and a black vest. On Friday afternoons, after classes let out, she's seen him in the gymnasium practicing the Tango with an imaginary partner, wearing these clothes.

"So is it a date?" he asks again. "Then you can tell your friends you went out with the next Rudolph Valentino."

When Lucille gives him an odd look, Max says, "You know Valentino started out as a gardener before he got the job at Maxim's in Manhattan. I don't know a spade from a rake, but I can Tango better than the man himself."

Lucille has never heard of Maxim's, but assumes it's a fashionable nightclub in New York City. To be truthful, she's never seen Valentino dance in the movies.

"We're both Italian, you know, Valentino and me."

Lucille wants to tell him that the resemblance ends there, but decides against it.

"So how about dinner? I'm pick'n you up at six. C'mon Lucille, get with it."

"Okay, but I want to come home early."

Max must have thought Lucille said to pick her up early, because at 5:30 he's knocking on her door.

When she opens her door, he has an expression on his face that seems to say, *aren't I something?* Looking at her gray pencil skirt and gray sweater, he says, "I thought you might be wearing a get-up like that. You're my dancing partner tonight. I brought you this silk blouse and lace skirt. My other dancing partner wore them. We'll drop over at the diner for a bite to eat first, but we'll keep it light."

Knowing little about what dancing partners wear, she agrees to change her clothes and she returns to her room. She emerges wearing an extremely tight blouse and a much too large skirt. Max tucks her blouse into her skirt and then pulls the material around the waist of the skirt and asks for a pin. He's more obnoxious than she thought.

"Max, I won't wear this. If I can't wear my own clothes, I'm not going."

"Not to worry baby. Suit yourself."

She goes back to her room and changes again.

"Hey, don't you have some beads? We're going dancing, not to a . . . what the hell. Let's go."

Max talks about his dancing all the way to the diner: his grace, his style, and his precision. He's so engrossed in what he's saying that they walk right past the small restaurant. When they finally arrive, her head aches.

The red plastic seats in the diner are cold, and when Lucille shivers Max pulls her close to him. The thought of going to the Town Hall and dancing with him is revolting, but leaving Max at the table and running off might cause a scene.

A man with a round cherub face approaches the table. "Max, glad I ran into you. I'm waiting for a friend, but I'm a little early. I wanted to tell you, the Community Dance Guild is having try-outs for a group dance exhibition. Thought you might be interested."

"You kid'n, Hal? I'm too good for those amateurs."

"Okay, just thought I'd mention it."

The music from the radio, the men and woman laughing, and the hot coffee should make Lucille feel better, but they don't. A long night lies ahead. Max holds Lucille so close to him now that she feels squashed. She pulls away.

Max ignores Hal. He whispers coyly in Lucille's ear, "I can turn you into the next Bonnie Glass." She wishes he'd stop name-dropping. She isn't familiar with any of the names. His remarks about Charlie still disturb her.

"Max, what did you mean when you insinuated that Charlie had a mental problem?"

"Simple question, simple answer. That Indian girl from the reservation, Tara, came around and gave me the scoop. Do you know her by any chance? No, you wouldn't be welcome in her crowd. I gave her a whirl once. She's not bad."

"I didn't ask you about Tara. I asked you about Charlie. Why did you say he had mental problems?"

"You know, he can't...he can't *do it*." Max laughs so loudly that the people at the next table turn to look at him. "Do I have to spell it out? Crazy, isn't it?"

"I'll tell you what's crazy. Me sitting here with you. What kind of a woman is this Tara to spread stories like that?"

"Not stories at all. They're true."

Lucille glances up at Hal, who is keeping an eye on the door. When it opens, his face blasts into pure happiness. His friend has arrived.

Max's eye falls on the man heading toward Hal. "Still catering to his every whim? He's not aristocracy, you know," Max says to Hal. "I would never succumb to that sort of nonsense."

"Hush, he might hear you."

"Lucille, Hal is completely obsequious when it comes to this guy."

"Obsequious? What the hell does that mean?" Hal asks.

"It's you, Hal. You. You drool at the mouth when he's around." Max puts his arm around Lucille again. "You can leave now. Lucille and I are getting to know each other."

"Hi, buddy," Hal's friend says, slapping him on the back. "Let's get seated, I can eat a bear."

It's illusory to think this could be...but his eyelids bend slightly over his eyes, and with that dimple in his left cheek, it must be him. He looks more muscular than she remembered, and his eyes are a deeper blue.

Nick's expression changes, his face crinkling into a huge smile. He moves closer to the table. "Fairy Princess, what are you doing here? Out of Iowa? This just knocks me out. Wow, you're one gorgeous woman. You cut your hair. You're beautiful. Tell me I'm not dreaming. C'mon tell me. You're not with this fella, are you?" Nick says, pointing to Max.

"Hey stupid, what does it look like?" Max pulls Lucille closer.

If Nick hears him, he shows no indication. He's busy making eye contact with Lucille.

"Go chase yourself, Nick. The young lady and I are together. We're going over to the Dance Hall soon. I'll show those buffoons down there how to dance."

Lucille sips her coffee and lifts her eyes from behind the rim of the cup.

Nick extends his hand to her. "Forget the *we*, Max. She's coming with me. Hal, keep this fella from flip'n his lid. I'll be back for you."

Leaving the diner, they are greeted with large, heavy snowflakes. The ground is already covered with snow and a storm appears to be starting. Nick runs around to the passenger side of his car to open the door and help her in. Both finally secluded from the storm, Lucille feels the sparks she has always felt in Nick's presence. "I won't be able to face Max at school tomorrow," she says. "Not very nice to just run off and leave him sitting there. And we were supposed to go dancing."

"Reminds me of when I snatched you away from Harry at Sheila's party. I guess I have a knack for doing that. Harry is nice enough, I grant you that. But this Max is a noth'n who just fools himself into thinking he can dance. Besides, I have to think about myself. I've been deprived of your presence for too long."

"My father really scared you off when he said you shouldn't contact me. I didn't think you'd listen."

"Oh, I've seen you since then. I got a glimpse of you in a white apron at the restaurant when I came home to help the farmers organize. Heck, my forte isn't farming, but I wanted to help out my good friends back home. You know, help out people like Paul and Dan and even your Dad, though he'd be the last person to help me. The farmers could use my business expertise. Dan thought so anyway, so he invited me. I'm glad he did, because I got a good look at you wearing that hairnet. It made your eyes and those rosebuds look even better."

"Oh, Nick, the manager made me wear that hairnet for my dish-washing job. I looked awful."

"You didn't look awful to me. I dreamed of you that night. Yeah, we were making love in the bathtub and you were wearing only that hairnet. The soap bubbles from the dishes were floating all around us. Just visualizing it again gives me the strongest urge to make love to you here and now. And if they find us frozen in the morning, at least we'd be together," he says, squeezing her hand.

Sheila told her that guys go crazy when girls play hard to get. She gathers all the self-control she can muster. "Sounds good, but I have to get up very early tomorrow morning. Please take me home."

He turns to her with a frown. "Lucille, it's me. Nick Martin Jr. You are not talking to Max. No one turns me down."

"I guess you're learning that's not true."

He laughs. "You are funny. Really funny."

Lucille directs him to the Little River Indian Residential School and he drives over the mounds of snow as if he were riding on a smooth, dry road on a sunny afternoon. Cars are stalled along the road, and Nick whizzes passed them. Lucille holds onto the door handle with one hand and her other hand grips his.

"So I'll see you tomorrow night," he says, when they reach the cottage. "I'm throwing a party and I want you to be my date. It's at my place. The place I stay at when I'm not working out of New York. Tell your boss you'll be sleeping in the next day. Get something sharp to wear." He presses a hundred dollar bill into her hand. "I'll pick you up at eight."

Nick

When Nick returns to the diner, Hal is seated at the counter sipping coffee, tapping his fingers and looking at the clock on the wall. In his red sweater, he looks cute enough to be a Christmas tree ornament. But Nick knows his friend has everyone fooled. What he doesn't have in height, he makes up for in strength. With his strong biceps, he can be wicked in a fight and a treasure when there is heavy lifting to be done. Hal is a devoted friend who would give his life for Nick. When his heart palpitations went haywire because he had one too many women, Hal drove him to the clinic. Then he removed his shirt, pointed to his heart and said, "Doc, give him mine."

Nick places his hand on Hal's shoulder. "Have business I want to discuss with you. Serious business."

Hal straightens and places his coffee cup on the counter. He folds his hands and looks directly at Nick.

"Just thinking, Hal. We met two years ago when we had that parking lot accident. I still don't know who backed into whom. But either way, good thing it happened. We've been tight ever since. I trust you."

"What is it, Nick? Ask me to do anything, and I'll do it."

"How well do you know the roads of Minnesota?"

"I have a road map carved in my brain. I could find my way around New York City if I had to."

Nick weighs Hal's words. "I'll make you a proposition. You drive me around like you're my chauffeur while I make out with the hostess in the backseat of my car. If you pass the test, you have the job."

Nick winks at the woman holding the menus. The hostess grabs her coat, puts it over her black uniform, and the three of them leave.

In less than thirty minutes, the hostess is back at work in the diner. Hal is in the driver's seat of Nick's car, and Nick is lying down in the backseat.

"Hal, about that job," says Nick. "You know what driving means to me. It's my passion. Still, I have this reputation at the clubs as someone important and I have to play the role. I'm getting a white limousine, and I want you to be my driver. But remember, your time will be my time. I snap my fingers and you jump."

Hal grins. "You mean the way it is now?"

"Do you want the job or not?"

"Yippee," Hal howls out the window. Nick shakes his head. "I know we are good friends, and this seems like a good way for us to spend more time together, but be serious now. It's a serious job."

"Okay boss, no howling." Hal asks Nick about Max. "You got him mad as hell. Does that bother you?"

"Who gives a damn about Max? Lucille's the love of my life."

"I've heard you say lots of things about women, never heard you say that."

"Never had to. You know how some women can cause a man to drink? This woman got me hooked on poetry."

LUCILLE

The morning after her meeting with Nick, Lucille tells Miss Wilson she has to attend to some very important business and needs to take an hour or two off from work. The woman nods. "With that blush on your cheeks I can see that the business must be quite pleasant."

This is the first time Miss Wilson has said anything that even remotely refers to Lucille's personal life, and it occurs to her that Miss Wilson never refers to anything personal in her own life, either. She ponders whether she should tell her about her big date tonight, but then decides it might be better not to mix business with the personal.

Lucille returns to Claire's dress shop. Today, the saleswoman is modeling a feather shawl. When Lucille explains why she needs a special dress, the woman does not have to think very long. She has the perfect dress for Lucille.

Taking her to the back room where the attire is more elegant and also more expensive, the salesgirl uncovers a royal blue sequined dress with a plunging neckline. Thinking the dress too revealing Lucille hesitates, but the image in the mirror tells her that Nick will go wild. Lucille has more than enough money for a matching bag and dangling earrings.

Leaving the store feeling ecstatic with her purchases, she stops at the beauty parlor and has her hair coiffed in finger waves and has her nails polished in a pretty rose pink. The stylist suggests she buy a new light pink foundation and blue eye shadow, and that she outline her lips in that new raspberry tone. Lucille, seeing the women in the fashion magazines doing just that, agrees to go along with the suggestion. The stylist wraps the cosmetics in lavender tissue paper and places them in a shiny lavender bag. Lucille couldn't be happier. Returning home, she finds a small white box at her door with a note from Nick.

Promptly at eight, Lucille walks to the window and pushes her lace curtains aside. She is happy to see that the snow that started last night and continued to fall until this morning has not started up again. She sees a white limousine parked in front of the cottage. She hopes the driver will move it to make room for Nick's car, but then she sees Nick hop out of the backseat of the limo, his legs wired with energy, carrying a large box in his hands. He springs over the piles of snow and soon he is rapping at the door. Lucille takes a few moments to spray *Evening in Paris* behind her ears and dab some on her wrists. She touches the clasp of the diamond barrette Nick sent her to be sure it is firmly set in her hair. She takes another look at herself in the oval mirror over the couch, grateful to the stylist who gave her the makeup suggestions. Her heart pounding, she goes to the door.

Nick is wearing a raccoon coat, brown leather gloves, and a brown plaid woolen scarf. She reaches to take his hand tugging at it for him to step inside. Placing his gloves and the box on the table in the small sitting room, Nick then reaches for her. He moves his hands over her body and kisses the top of her head. "How about we just stay here all night," he says.

At that moment, she realizes that it isn't just his smile, his handsome face, or his attractive body that she adores, but his affirmation of life. A man of surprises, he pops up when she least expects him, sends her poetry instead of flowers, accelerates instead of slowing down, and buys her a barrette rather than pearls.

"You are something in that blue sequined dress," he says. He touches her neckline with his fingertips. "This shows more of you. I like that. Open up your present."

"Another present?"

She removes the bow on the box Nick placed on the table and arranges it near his gloves. She wishes she could take a picture of the bow, but instead commits it to memory. She lifts the lid of the box and then unfolds the white tissue paper. Inside she finds a silver fox stole.

Stroking the fur, Lucille's eyes fill with tears. She almost says, "Nick, I love you." Instead, she says, "Thank you."

He helps her on with the wrap, and they walk out into the blowing snow, their hands intertwined.

"Hey, move over baby," Nick says, pulling Lucille toward him in the backseat of the limousine. "Before we go to the party, we have to make one stop. We're going to a place a few miles out of Riverview where they play jazz. The guy down there plays like Count Basie. Place is jump'n night after night."

They travel about ten miles before they reach their destination. They park under a sign with flashing white lights, and Lucille holds onto Nick's arm. She's never been to a nightclub. A gentleman in a dark blue overcoat stands at the door. He addresses Nick with a tip of his hat, "Good Evening, Mr. Martin. I see the brutal weather hasn't kept you at home."

Nick nods, and they move indoors. Another gentleman wearing a black tuxedo escorts them to a table. Dim light filters through the fringed lampshade on the table. She and Nick sit close together, and she wonders if this is really happening.

"Please excuse me," Nick says. "I'll be back soon. I have to see someone for a few minutes." He walks into a room just behind where she is sitting. Lucille's eyes drift around the nightclub. The whole room seems to be swaying with so many people gyrating and kicking up their feet. Young women in short, drop-waist evening dresses dance with older, bleary-eyed men. The dozen or more chairs around the bar are filled with people who have already had too much to drink. The air is clouded with smoke. A balding man smoking a cigar sits down beside her, and she shoots him a glance that says he's not welcome.

"Playing hard to get, honey?"

"I'm waiting for someone."

"That's what they all say," he mutters, slurring his words. "He won't show up. Let me show you a good time." He puts his arm around her and snuggles closer to her. She pushes him away.

She hears Nick's voice echoing from the room close by. She turns and sees the door open and Nick start to leave. Then he goes back inside. She hears him say in a stern tone, "I don't care if you have to transport the stuff in garden hoses."

"Calm down, Nick. We'll do it your way. We'll get it done."

"By tomorrow."

Lucille listens in. She hears a woman's voice say, "Nick, can I come with you?"

"No," he says, "You stay here with Joey and take care of things. I'm with a high school friend."

Lucille watches a woman on the dance floor with bright red lipstick, bobbed hair and bare arms and legs remove a flask from her rolled stocking. The gray-haired man sitting close to Lucille notices her and walks toward her.

Suddenly, the tone in the room in the room changes. "Police! Police! This is a raid!" The lights go off. Lucille hears shrieking. The people in the club are running and pushing each other. Lucille stumbles into the chaotic crowd. The man who sat at her table appears at her elbow and grabs hold of her arm. "Let's you and I get out of here. You can pay me later for saving your life." He pulls her toward the back of the building. "Not too many people know about this bookcase," he says.

Lucille hears a creaking sound, and then feels the man dragging her through a long, narrow passageway. Finally, she feels cold air on her face. She looks down and sees that she lost one of her shoes.

The man drops Lucille's arm when the police arrive to cuff him and throw him into the paddy wagon. The policeman turns his head to address Lucille. "This isn't a place for a nice woman like you. Better get yourself home."

"Princess, have you lost your slipper?" Lucille turns to see Nick, laughing and holding up her shoe.

"Nick, that was scary."

"Don't worry baby, I squared it all away with the police."

Lucille has had enough intrigue for one day. Back in the limousine, Nick tells her that he owns the place. He'll show her what a really swanky club looks like when he takes her to New York City.

Under the Red Ribbon

About two miles from the club, Hal makes a right turn onto a secluded street and drives almost to the end before moving up a hill leading to Nick's house. It's a two-story house made of stone and is hidden behind a forest of trees. All the lights in the house are on. Hal helps Lucille out, opening the door and then giving a hand to Nick. The three of them make their way to the entrance. When Hal turns the knob on the heavy wooden door, the first thing Lucille sees is the chandelier hanging from the ceiling of the foyer. The lighting fixture reminds Lucille of one she saw in her art history books. Her eyes take in everything at once: the wallpaper with pale pink roses on a subdued green background, the vases overflowing with flowers, the men and women holding drinks sitting on rose-colored velvet chairs, their feet resting on the plush white carpet. Young waitresses in short black skirts and fishnet stocking are offering small canapés of food to the guests.

"Pretty classy, huh?" Nick says. "But wait till I show you something you will really love." Nick leads Lucille into his library. "You turned me on to books and I read all the time now. You are one bad influence on me."

Lucille's eyes scan the bookshelves. She sees collections of work by Charles Dickens, Edger Alan Poe, Mark Twain, and Herman Melville, all bearing expensive bindings. "Now tell me," she says, "where you're hiding the books on automobiles?"

"I have them, too. In my bedroom, within reach."

The party has spread to all of the rooms except the bedrooms. Nick's guests are jovial. Carrying drinks and cigarettes and dancing to the music, they seem untouched by the hard economic times. They chat about the latest movies, impressed with the likes of Norma Shearer, and inquire as to who saw *The Divorcee*. The men bet on whether or not she'll win the academy award.

As Lucille and Nick make their way their way through the throng of guests, the men pat Nick on the back and the women's eyes linger on him. Hal is busy refilling cocktail glasses. Lucille and Nick stop in front of a window and watch the snow pelt the cars. "Looks pretty bad out there, Princess."

Snowstorms aren't new to her, but Lucille has never liked driving through them.

"You might have to stay here for the night. But for now, honor us with a performance." Nick raises his hand and signals Hal to turn off the Victrola. He leads Lucille toward the piano.

As the guests gather around her, Lucille feels like a real princess. She remembers what Dan said: *playing the piano is sixty percent talent, thirty percent training, and one hundred percent confidence.* She adjusts her seat and places her hands on the keyboard. She plays boogie-woogie with such gusto, the people gasp. She finishes her performance with "Glad Rag Doll" and "Honey Suckle Rose."

"Nice woman you have there, Nick," an older gentleman in a navy blue suit and gray hair says, flicking the ashes of his cigar into a small glass ashtray he carries. "Your taste in women is improving. With that hair, she could pass for Norma Shearer. Let me know if you ever tire of her."

"Tire of her? She hasn't yet given me a chance to really know her."

"Young lady, with your talent I might have a place for you."

Before Lucille has time to reply, Nick does. "Sam, she won't be interested. She's interested in poetry, writes darn good poems herself. She wants to teach at a college. Become an English professor. She's not interested in what you have to offer, but thanks anyway."

"Here's my card just in case, Lucille. Call me anytime." He drops the card in her hand.

At three o'clock in the morning, the guests are beginning to leave. Lucille has never been exposed to so many furs, diamonds, and exquisite dresses. The tuxedos are a far cry from the dungarees and shirts she's accustomed to seeing. She's sorry to see the party come to a close.

Hal carries the used glasses to the sink, careful not to break them. He empties the ashtrays into a garbage bag, then picks up some scraps of paper and rearranges the chairs.

"Guess you're going to stay the night, Lucille. Use my shower. No hanky-panky, I promise," Nick says.

"Where will I sleep?"

"You have a choice. With me or with Hal." He winks. "You know I'm just kidding. Take my bed. I like sleeping on the couch anyway."

Nick leads her into a dressing room with a dressing table and a three-way etched mirror. She notices a bottle of *Evening in Paris* resting on a mirrored tray. "Help yourself to the perfume," he says. "I bought it special for you."

Lucille can't believe her eyes. Nick is from Harvest and she is from Harvest. There are no homes even close to this elegance where they come from, but Nick moves around his home as if he has always been accustomed to such luxury. This is another part of Nick she still doesn't know.

Lucille showers, slips into a pink chenille robe she finds hanging in the dressing room, and walks into Nick's bedroom. She admires the Venetian table lamps on the nightstands. When she rolls down the bedspread and slides between the silk sheets, she savors the softness. It would be easy to fall asleep in such comfort, but she is distracted by Nick's proximity in the adjacent room. About to doze off, she senses someone at the bedside.

"Don't know how it could have happened, but I forgot to kiss you good night," Nick says, leaning over to kiss her. Lucille pulls him toward her. "I said no hanky-panky, but I guess you have other ideas." He lies down beside her and she is hypnotized by the touch of his hands. His voice is soft, his body strong. "I've never asked a girl before, it's always just happened," he says. "But with you, it's different. Can we make love? I mean really make love?"

All she knows about love is right here beside her. In the quiet of the night, she looks at the huge snowflakes covering the window. "Last night you said we could make love in the snow and if they found us frozen in the morning, at least we would be together. But what happens after the snow melts?"

"Lucille, you think too much." Nick takes her hand and places his other hand over it so that their hands rest on his chest. "Princess, what am I going to do about you? I love you too much to marry you. Can you understand that?"

"No, I can't."

"Lucille, I know who I am. I've always known. Like I told you years ago, I'm like that Eastern Goldfinch at the creek, I perch awhile and then I have to move on."

"I know. But you also said that you'd come back if you had a darn good reason too."

"That's true, and I have. I just can't stay."

"But tell me, what do I do in the meantime?"

"I love you. I know that. Let's enjoy the time we have together." He outlines her lips with his finger. "God, how I love those rosebuds."

"I'm afraid you'll go away again and lose track of me."

"Never. I'll always find you. I promise you that."

His voice is honest, genuine. She moves closer to him and touches his eyelids. She helps him slip off her robe. Her breasts tingle under his hands, her body quivers against his skin, and when he bends over her and lifts her hips against his, all her inhibitions recede and fade into the darkness.

. . . the new presence inside us, has entered our hearts. . . is already in our bloodstream. We could easily be made to think nothing happened, and yet we have changed.

How did Rainer Maria Rilke know all that?

The following morning, Lucille sits at the kitchen table near the window, feeling quite different than she felt yesterday morning or any morning before that. The window is open, and she watches the silk pleated curtains change form as they billow in the morning breeze. Before the wind caught hold of them, they had hung undisturbed, each pleat in place. Although her heart swells with the closeness she felt when she and Nick made love, she wonders, if like those curtains, the act has changed her very structure. She and Sheila often talked about the wild girls in Harvest who gave in to boys, and how those girls weren't the ones the boys ended up marrying. Most of those girls lived on the edge of town near the railroad tracks. They came from homes where the fathers drank too much and the mothers were hassled with too many kids. And of course there was also Rachael, Howie's daughter, who spent most nights in the barn with the handyman, until he ran off and married a God-fearing woman. Lucille wonders if she has lost all chance of Nick ever marrying her

Hal brews coffee and places a cup in front of her. The cup glistens. It is made of expensive china. She places an embroidered linen napkin on her lap. Each time Nick passes, he touches her hair and kisses the top of her head. "You're still wearing the barrette. I'm glad you like it."

She catches a glimpse of his cuff links, gold with dark ruby centers. She asks about his work. He spreads his arms, showing off the extravagance of his apartment. "A gift from prohibition. But the Prohibition Act won't be in existence much longer. I see the tide changing. If I'm going to make a killing, I've got to do it now." He looks at his watch. "I start work early and I finish late. And I love every minute of it."

Later that evening, while driving back to her cottage, he says. "Let's make a promise to each other. We'll never give our hearts to anyone else. Let me hear you say it, Princess."

⁓

The melting ice along the side of the road has formed miniature waterfalls over the rocks: a sign of spring. With gray days and hard work ahead, Lucille isn't in the happiest of moods. But what really bothers her is that she hasn't heard from Nick since the party at his apartment, about three months ago. The letters that she receives from Bill and Rose and her correspondence with Sheila help ease her melancholy and distract her from what has become grueling and painful work at the school.

The government recently invested millions in the transformation of the Indian culture and the pressure on the residential Indian schools to conform is enormous. This means more work for her and Ellie. Searching through students' records and noting changes in attitudes, language, and work ethics is a tedious job.

After a long afternoon of sifting through files and analyzing and documenting, Lucille sees a new photograph on Ellie's desk. Ellie notices her looking at it.

"So, you noticed my new snapshot?" Ellie says. "My sister looks smashing. Tara always looks better when she has a rich boyfriend at her side. Take a look at her man; he looks like a movie star."

Lucille stares at the picture. Nick has a big grin on his face. His arm is around Tara's waist, and he's holding her close. She remembers his last words to her: *"We'll never give our hearts to anyone else."* She feels like she has been slapped across the face.

After seeing the photograph, the challenging work at the school becomes a blessing. Lucille takes on new projects and tucks her hurt away. The idea of transforming the Indian child and the methods used to achieve that goal are offensive to her. She decides to do something about it.

Organizing meetings with the parents on the reservation, she listens to their concerns. She lists them on a sheet of paper and expects to take the long list to Mr. Baran. If that doesn't work, she'll write to the state representative, Victor Christgua, and urge him to pass new legislation in defense of Indian children. When the parents ask her why a white woman would take their side, she tells them that there is only one side: the side of the children.

At the end of a day, she yearns for sleep. She attributes that to working long hours and the change in seasons. On the eve of an important meeting on the reservation, she falls asleep on the couch and arrives late.

The meeting is held in a long building made of logs. It used to be the school where the younger children attended, but now of course the children are gone. The walls are bare except for a long list of Indian Chiefs who have carried forth the Indian message. The message of Chief Crazy Horse is printed in large black letters on white paper and tacked to the front wall: "The Red Nation shall rise again and it shall be a blessing for a sick world; a world filled with broken promises, selfishness and separations; a world longing for light again."

Each chair is handmade by the men on the reservation with carvings representing the circle of life, peace, unity, and light. All the seats are occupied except for the front row of chairs reserved for the teachers. Lucille was hoping they would attend, but understands why they wouldn't want to face the wrath of Mr. Baran. Lucille's only experience with him occurred when he came to speak to Miss Wilson when she was leaving her office. Mr. Baran turned to look at Lucille and said, "You and I should get to know each other." His eyes lingered on her long enough to make her feel uncomfortable.

She's surprised when Max strolls in and takes a seat upfront. He has his history books with him, no doubt to impress the parents with his intelligence.

One by one, the parents stand to express their grievances. A broad-shouldered man, his black hair neatly combed back off his forehead, is the first to speak. Lucille recognizes him from the week before, when he arrived at the school and one of the matrons escorted him out of the building. That didn't deter him from returning. He was determined to find out why the matron had locked his son in the hall closet just because he forgot his homework. "I had to wait hours just to speak to Mr. Baran's secretary," he says. Another father stands and speaks. "My daughter was ordered to hold her hands over her head for hours because the matron caught her talking in our native tongue." The parents continue, protesting the tongue piercings, mouth washings, beatings, and hard physical work their children are forced to do.

When Paco Whitefeather stands to speak, the room grows silent. He's dressed in Indian attire, feathered headgear and all. "My friends, my family. We know our plight. This is the time to warn the school. We will not put up with these atrocities any longer."

Mothers in the back row stand in unison. They hold a banner that spreads the width of the room. In bold black letters it reads, "Education not Assimilation."

One of the elders moves to the forefront of the room. "But we ask you, Whitefeather, our young and competent leader, we the children of the Great Spirit have always given assistance. Should we not assist the white man in teaching them how to respect our ways?"

"Now is the time for resistance, not assistance," Whitefeather says. "The school does not want to hear what we have to say. Have you not seen the signs around the school? 'The White Man's Way is the only way.' They want our colors to fade."

"As you say, Whitefeather," the group says in unison. "As you say."

After the meeting, the parents linger, talking amongst themselves. Max, the only teacher in attendance, walks to his car without saying a word to anyone.

The next morning, as Lucille makes her rounds through the classrooms, she comes upon the room where children are sent when they aren't following the rules. She hears a familiar whimper. Opening the door, she finds Wilma curled up in a corner with her hands tied behind her back, her bloomers pulled over her head. Lucille rushes to her and unties the knots.

"Miss Halliday did it, because I couldn't control myself. I had a stomachache and I couldn't make it to the bathroom. She pushed my face into the toilet bowl and said, 'Eat the brown mush for dinner.' I called her a fat pig, and she called me a savage who needed to be tied up."

Miss Wilson had given Lucille full reign over the matrons. It happened at their last meeting a week ago. It was early morning, and the Advisor looked tired, overworked, and as though there weren't enough hours in the day to do all she had to do. The Federal Government wanted to eradicate the Indian in every child, and they wanted quick results. "I'll give them the proof that Little River Indian Residential School is fulfilling their obligations," she said, "but I'll recommend a gentler way to accomplish that. Not that I expect them to take my advice. But you have frequent contact with the matrons. Do whatever you have to do to keep them in line. Don't let them hurt our children, even if it means firing one or two. Imagine, all Indian themselves, doing this to their own. I just don't understand it."

Lucille doesn't understand it either. She sees the beefy figure of Miss Halliday standing in the hallway, pulling on the hand of another child. "Wilma, get cleaned up and return to class." Lucille hurries into the hallway to confront Miss Halliday. "Follow me," she says.

Miss Halliday gives Lucille a scalding glare beneath her sparse eyelashes, but does as she is told and follows Lucille to her office. Standing behind her desk, Lucille reminds the matron of the last time they discussed discipline. "How can you be so cruel to a child?" she asks. Her breath is uneven as she speaks. When Miss Halliday does not respond, she picks up a stack of papers, clips them together, and throws them back on her desk. "Start packing your bags," she orders.

"Miss Kramer, you don't understand! I'm trying to help. Wilma's father is in prison. Her mother gets money to feed the family by pleasuring the councilmen. I am the only one the child has to teach her the ways of the white woman. An Indian woman has no chance in this world. I know. Please, let me help her."

"Let me assure you, cruelty has never taught anyone anything except cruelty."

Miss Halliday composes herself. Indignant, she stomps out of the room.

Days later, Lucille finds a letter in her mailbox. Mr. Baran wants to see her. She thinks that if she plays her cards right, perhaps she can change Mr. Baran's mind about the school's harsh methods of discipline. She dresses in businesslike attire for the meeting, in a white blouse and black skirt. She has a hole in the sole of one of her worn pumps, so she outlines her foot on a piece of cardboard, cuts around it, and stuffs it into her shoe.

When she enters Mr. Baran's reception room, a woman behind a desk is clicking on her typewriter. She glances at her watch and continues clicking. The pungent smell of Spic and Span almost makes Lucille gag. Knowing that the superintendent is a frugal man, she is not surprised to see only two chairs and no magazines on the tables. She's heard him say many times that there was no need for frivolities and he never keeps the people he wants to see waiting. Yet, when a group of parents went to see him, they had to stand all day in that room only to be turned away.

At ten o'clock sharp, the receptionist stops clicking on her Remington and escorts Lucille into her boss's office. The superintendent's desk is freshly polished and slick. Mr. Baran appears freshly scrubbed, his hair still wet from a recent shower. He pushes the handles of his glasses back and down on his ears and looks down at the papers on his desk. Lucille sits down in a chair facing him.

When the receptionist exits, he says, "I understand you had a run-in with one of our matrons." He doesn't look up when he speaks to her. "Miss Halliday is one of our best instructors. Well educated, speaks English perfectly, and an Indian woman herself. She knows these little injuns inside and out. Fine woman. So, let me be clear. Do not interfere with her job."

Rising from behind his desk, he straightens his tie, pulls down on his jacket, and walks to where Lucille is sitting. He places his arm on her shoulder. Her muscles tighten.

"Our students will make fine handymen, mechanics, seamstresses and housekeepers." He points to the three children in the corner of the room, scrubbing the floor. "Most importantly, these children will walk out of here learning the language the way it should be spoken, not that gibberish they learn at home." He espouses his disdain for powwows and ghost ceremonies. He confesses, with a tremor in his voice, that they "scare the dickens" out of him.

"Don't tell me how Miss Halliday persecutes Wilma. I've heard about that. Hogwash. That child comes from a family of pigs. The matron is the best friend she has, trying to teach her the white people's way."

Pushing up from her chair in anger, Lucille's hand hits the drinking glass on his desk and water spills over his stacks of paper. Mr. Baran's eyes squeeze together into angry slits. He orders the two young boys who are on their hands and knees cleaning the tile grout to mop up the desk. He jerks one little boy up by the arm and tells him to hurry.

Lucille heads for the door, but Mr. Baran grabs her arm to stop her. In a voice that is mockingly sweet, he says, "We are both being silly. We can turn this around. You know, we can have a little arrangement. You come here, after hours of course. It would be very nice, the two of us. I'll even forgive you for picking on the matron and organizing those meetings on the reservation. I have a way of finding out those things, you know."

Lucille pulls away from him, but he seizes her by the waist and swings her around.

"Not so fast, little farm girl." He pushes her against the wall. One hand creeps under her blouse, the other down her body. She kicks and scratches, but she can't get free.

The boys stumble out the door, overturning the pail of water they were using. Seeing the floor flooded with dirty water, Mr. Baran grows angry and punches Lucille in the belly. She falls to the ground and into the puddle. He flops on top of her and unbuttons his pants. With her nails, she tears at his face until blood drips onto his white shirt. Raging, he reaches for a vase on his desk.

The boys return with Miss Wilson, who throws up her hands to shield her eyes when she sees Mr. Baran's pants gathered around his ankles.

"Imagine, Miss Wilson, this farm girl trying to seduce me. She thinks having an affair with me will give her special privileges. So young, this hussy doesn't know the ways of the world."

After the incident with Mr. Baran, Lucille bathes several times a day, rubbing her skin until it's raw. She throws her clothes from that day into the garbage. To make matters worse, she doesn't have anyone to turn to. Miss Wilson is still too embarrassed to talk about the incident. If she wrote to Bill and Rose and told them what happened, they would make her come home immediately. Sheila is going to Law School, and Lucille doesn't want her to miss classes.

In the evenings, she looks through newspapers and magazines with blind eyes unable to focus on the words. But a picture of the governor catches her attention. Beneath his picture, she reads that he will be coming through Riverview to meet with the school superintendent, directors, and some of the staff. Lucille wonders if that includes Miss Wilson. She looks out the window and into the darkness. Her father told her that young women should never go out alone at night, but she decides to do just that.

She heads in the direction of the library. She wants to learn as much about Indian history as she can. If she can arrange to see the governor along with Miss Wilson, she can speak to him not only from emotion, but also from knowledge. Astute at finding exactly what she is looking for in a library, she has no trouble gathering the books she needs.

She hurries home to start reading. Returning to the cottage, she hears the sound of rustling. Is Mr. Baran hiding in the bushes, waiting to pounce on her? She reaches for the doorknob and feels a hand slide on top of hers. She screams.

"Can I sleep here tonight?" It's Wilma's voice. "If I can't sleep here, I'm running away."

Lucille catches her breath and calms herself. Convincing the little girl that she'll be in more trouble than she can ever realize if she does that, Lucille walks her back to the dormitory. Fortunately, Miss Halliday is sound asleep. Lucille tucks Wilma into bed. "Don't do this again," she whispers in the child's ear. "It won't end well."

Lucille reads her library books until the steam whistle blows in the morning. She's deeply affected by the words of Duncan Campbell Scott, former Head of Indian Affairs. A decade ago, he wrote: "I want to get rid of the Indian problem. Our object is to continue until there is not a single Indian in Canada that has not been absorbed. They are a weird and waning race, ready to break out at any moment in savage dances."

"Kill the Indian and Save the Man" was the slogan of Captain Richard Pratt, who founded the first Native American Boarding School in Pennsylvania. Things haven't changed much for the Indians. Their suffering continues.

Miss Wilson is standing at the window in her office when Lucille sees her the next morning. "I'm watching the students in the fields," Miss Wilson says. "I'm rooting for them, hoping each one meets their quota of five bushels of vegetables before class. The matrons are getting stricter about that. The punishments for falling short are getting more severe." The deep lines across Miss Wilson's forehead and the large crevices around her mouth are telling. "I'm leaving this place. I made up my mind."

Lucille can't imagine the school without Miss Wilson. She is as much a part of this room as the desk and chair.

"Enough of this. I've become little more than a spectator. I watch what's going on and I don't like it, and I can't do anything about it. You give it a try, Lucille. Take my place."

"I doubt that Mr. Baran wants me to continue working here in any capacity after what happened in his office."

"Ellie has a way with him. She will convince him. She knows your capabilities."

Lucille visualizes herself in Miss Wilson's place. Acting as the arbiter between the matrons and the children, between the Superintendent and the teachers, and carrying out orders from the government will be a real challenge. But if she can change small things, they could add up to big things, and without Mr. Baran knowing. Then it would all be worth it. It would make attending college even more unlikely, but reminding herself of her own words from her graduation speech, she thinks, *you may be whisked away by a gale of wind and find yourself traveling in another direction*. She acknowledges that that time has arrived.

But Lucille is running out of energy. The episode with Mr. Baran, the picture of Nick with his arm around Tara, and the prospect of taking over Miss Wilson's job are catching up with her. She decides that it's time to get a physical exam. A tonic might be just the thing to boost her energy. Besides, something else has changed. She has missed two menstrual periods.

After a short wait at the doctor's office located just three buildings down from Claire's dress shop, the nurse goes through the preliminaries: urine sample, blood pressure, height and weight. Lucille is led into to a small room, given a paper wrap to change into, and told that the doctor will be in momentarily. Cold and shivering, she waits for what seems like hours.

Dr. Richmond is friendly when he enters the room, smiling and shaking her hand. He is short and stout and actually looks like Mr. Johnson, the storekeeper. He has a mustache, jovial eyes, and a bald spot the size of a half dollar on the back of his head. After a set of questions, he says, "Let's see what's going on, young lady."

"Stress, I guess."

With his stethoscope, he listens to her heart and lungs. He feels her glands, pokes her belly, and finally says, "Have you ever had an internal examination?"

She shakes her head.

"Time you did. Now just lie down and relax."

She finds her body tightening.

"Think of something nice that has happened to you."

When he is through with his exam, she sits up.

"About three months, I'd say."

Not wanting to understand, she asks, "Until what?"

"You're pregnant."

She tries to argue his confirmation away. "No. You see, I'm not married, and I'm not about to be. And I have this job, it's a difficult one."

"All that doesn't change what's going on in your body."

"I know. I thought that maybe it was just the stress, but deep down I knew."

"By the way, I see that there are some bruises on your belly. Are you safe at home?"

"Yes. I walked into something. I fell."

"Don't be afraid to tell me the truth. And don't let him just apologize. They do it once, they do it again."

She remembers Mr. Baran's punch to her belly. When she lifts her gown, she sees that the bruise has turned dark purple.

Lucille does not remember her walk home. Her mind is filled with many questions, and few answers. She can't call Nick; she doesn't know where he is. Besides, the picture she saw on Ellie's desk with his arm around Tara proves that he's not interested in her anymore. She evaluates her other options. If she has the baby without being married, the birth certificate will be stamped, "Illegitimate." She can't do that to her child. With poverty rampant, so many pregnant women are opting to give up their babies. She read about women who advertise their babies in newspapers, actually selling them. That's out. So far, she hasn't come up with any acceptable solution.

When she gets back to the cottage, she calls Sheila. Her friend knows more about things like this than she does. Sheila's response is unflinching and direct. She tells Lucille to go to Kansas City, where she can stay at the Maternity Sanitarium, give birth to her baby, and then put the child up for adoption. No one will ever know.

"That's so callus, Sheila."

"Then contact Nick. I can get his number from his father."

"I don't think he's interested in me anymore."

"He'll be interested when you tell him the news. Call him."

It takes a few hours for Lucille to gather the courage to call Nick. When she does, her voice is barely audible.

"Speak up, lady. Who is this?" says the voice that answers. Whoever it belongs to is yelling at someone in the background. She hears a blustery voice giving orders, "Bring down the trucks and load 'm up. People clamoring for that Canadian stuff. What the hell are you doing? Where's the Shore man?" *Is that Nick speaking like that,* she wonders? She hangs up and calls again. "Sorry lady, we're running a business here, no time for chatting."

She probably called the wrong number. She'll try again later.

Lucille almost forgot about the staff meeting that's starting in a few minutes. She hurries over to the school. When she sees Max, she tries to sit as far away from him as possible. She has managed to avoid him since the incident at the diner, when she ran off with Nick. But he stops her before she finds a seat.

"What taste you have in men," he says. "First you go out with that mental Charlie and then Nick, a bootlegger. A member of the mob. Nothing more than a gangster. You couldn't recognize a decent fellow if he danced right in front of you. You know, I won the Tango contest without you that night. Got Mr. Baran to let me borrow his little injun and boy does she know how to groove. I'm working as his assistant now, did you hear?"

"I shouldn't be surprised about that, but I am surprised that you won the dance contest."

"You know, Lucille, I don't find you very attractive anymore. You look rather frumpy."

She doesn't care that Max called her frumpy, but she is concerned about what he called Nick. She's heard the words "bootlegger," "rum-runner," and "land sharks." *Is Nick someone like that? A gangster? Is that what her baby's father is?*

Max served a purpose after all. His information about Nick helped her make up her mind about the baby. She puts on her most comfortable shoes, the ones she usually wears as slippers, and pulls a homemade, shapeless green dress over her head. She did her research. There's a maternity house right outside of Riverview, and she decided to check it out for herself. No gangster is going to be her baby's father.

The walk to Maternity Serenity is a long way from the school. Her feet throb by the time she finally sees it in the distance. Approaching the two-story brick building, she hesitates, and stands looking at the structure. She's afraid. She finds herself trembling, but then Max's words come back to her and encourage her to continue: *Nick, the bootlegger, a member of the mob, a gangster.* She proceeds up the steps and rings the doorbell.

A woman with cropped gray hair greets her with a smile and an embrace. Lucille can tell that's part of her job, to appear friendly and family-like. But instead of seeing a family-like member, she sees a total stranger. What does the woman see? Or is she so accustomed to faces like Lucille's that she no longer cares? The gray-haired woman asks her to come in and sit by the window and wait for the nurse.

"A nurse?"

"Yes, you will be given a complete physical."

A young girl, no older than fifteen, enters the building. Her hair is in disarray and she is sobbing. The gray-haired woman takes the girl aside and says, "I knew you would be back, dear. Go and join the other girls in the sewing room."

The nurse, her short brown hair in tight ringlets, that she tries to tame with her hand, is carrying a file in her other hand and introduces herself as Sadie. "Come with me, dear," she says sweetly, as if Lucille were a child. She leads her down a long hallway with bedrooms lining both sides. "The girls' sleeping quarters," Sadie says. But one room has been transformed into a medical office with a desk, scale, and a long table, which Lucille and Sadie enter. Lucille closes her eyes while the woman continues her chatter about how this facility is run like a hotel with nutritious meals for the women and areas for reading, recreation, and crafts. "Now lets get some information on you," she says. "We'll set up a new file and of course everything will be confidential."

Lucille interrupts her. "Can I name my baby? Can I meet the people who will adopt my child?"

"Don't worry your little head about any of those things. That's what we're here for. Now as I was saying . . ."

The doctor arrives wearing a white coat and Lucille feels her heart beating faster. He's skinny and tall and he doesn't appear very jovial. He says he's had a stressful day. "Have you met any of the other girls?" he asks. He smiles, showing a gap between his two front teeth. "Nice young things, like yourself."

Nice young things?

The doctor continues talking. Lucille hears nothing. She feels thumping inside her head.

"Sadie, tell her about the last day," says the doctor.

"Oh, yes, your last day here is the best. You will see our hair stylist, and you'll get to choose one or two dresses from our collection to take home with you. We make our own clothes. Sized to fit," she chuckles. "After a few months here, you'll be tired of wearing the blue-and-white striped smocks. And about your finances . . ."

The doctor gestures for Lucille to lie down on the long table. "The examination will be over in minutes," he says.

"I'm sorry. I'm sorry, so sorry to have bothered you," Lucille stammers. I need more time to think about this. I want to leave now. Really, I must leave. I don't want the examination." She jumps off the table and heads toward the door.

"Take it from me, this is your best option," he yells after her. "Get your finances in order, and we'll be waiting for your return."

Lucille hurries out of the building out of breath and trembling. She walks towards the bus. She's too exhausted to walk back to the school.

Taking her place in line, she feels light-headed. Her body sways. A woman standing close by, dressed in a simple blue suit takes some smelling salts from a lace pouch she carries and revives Lucille. She lays her hands on Lucille's shoulders and moves her away from the bus stop.

"I know the feeling," the woman says, "The morning sickness is terrible. Let me give you some crackers. They're the only thing that works. Since I had my children, I'm in the habit of carrying some around in my pocketbook."

Lucille takes one and thanks her, and together they walk toward the bench at the bus stop. "I saw you leaving that brick building. It looks so solid and strong, doesn't it?"

"You mean to say that it isn't?"

"You have to be stronger."

Lucille looks at the woman's face. Her eyes are earnest, her expression angelic.

"Don't do it," the woman says. "Giving away your child will torment you for the rest of your life. Every child you see will make you wonder, 'is that my child?' You'll never stop searching. You will never forget." Taking Lucille's hand, she asks, "Where's the father?"

"He's too busy for me."

"You don't mean *me*, you mean *us*. It's not just you anymore; it's you and the baby. It's wonderful to be a mother, I know. Don't miss out."

"Thank you so much. I needed someone to talk to, and suddenly you appeared. Who are you?"

"I do God's work. Here's my bus. I still have some stops to make. Good Luck."

Unmarried mothers aren't big news around Riverview. With families trying to survive the harsh economic times, many young girls run off trying to find a better life, and often find trouble instead. Is that what she did?

The woman doing God's work told her to keep her baby and reminded her that the baby was Nick's, too. Oh, how did she ever think even for a moment that she could give up their child?

When she thinks about her future now, she feels light-hearted. When Nick finds out that he's going to be a father, he'll give up his line of work and start an honest business. Maybe open a garage like Olson's garage in Harvest. And she'll give up her job here, because Nick will have enough money. Yes, they will be a real family.

This time when she calls Nick, her voice is stronger and more confident. But the answer she receives makes her legs so weak that she has to hold onto the wall to keep from falling. The man on the other end says, "Nick? I think he's in Europe. I hear he ran off and got married."

Lucille decides that it's time to tell Miss Wilson about her predicament. The woman has already given notice about leaving, and she has consented to stay on the job for another two weeks. When Miss Wilson told Mr. Baran that she wanted Lucille as her replacement, he agreed. "Miss Kramer will come to her senses soon and see things my way," he'd said, which Miss Wilson related to Lucille. As revolted as Lucille was to hear that, she remembered Dan's words when he said good-bye to her in Harvest: "There is a cruel world out there and I know you are strong enough to handle what ever comes along."

Sitting in Miss Wilson's office waiting for her to arrive, Lucille hears the matrons gathered in small groups outside the office talking in lowered voices. Miss Wilson walks in and slams the door. "Wilma is missing, along with Miss Halliday. I've put in a call to the sheriff," she tells Lucille.

"I found her in front of my cottage one night, hiding," Lucille volunteers. She told me she was going to run away. I warned her not to do it."

Miss Wilson shakes her head. "No, I think it's far more serious than that."

Just minutes after hearing the news of Wilma's disappearance, Lucille walks down to see Whitefeather. He leans his broom against the wall and walks toward her when she enters the store. "With news that the governor will be passing through," he says, "all the shop owners are busy tidying up their stores. Look at the ship shape condition this place is in. Every box on the shelf in place, the floor squeaky clean.

I just have to get rid of this garbage. I'll be right back." Holding some empty boxes, he heads toward the door.

Lucille stops him. "Whitefeather," Lucille says, "I have something important to talk to you about. At the reservation meeting when you spoke before the group I got the feeling that Wilma is your sister."

He laughs. "So you came to tell me that you found us out? But don't let that get around. The matrons will really have it in for her at the school. They hate me. Anyway, have you seen my Kimimela lately? I only get a glimpse of her when she's out in the field working. It amazes me to see her lift those bushels of corn. She's strong like me."

Lucille interrupts. "Your sister is missing."

He goes on talking. "Mr. Johnson wants to repaint the store inside and out. He thinks the governor might walk right in here for a sandwich. But I tell him--" he stops. "What did you say?"

"I said that your sister, is missing."

"Are you sure? Maybe she's trying to trick Miss Halliday and get her in trouble. It's the matron's responsibility to know the whereabouts of the kids at all times."

"Miss Halliday is missing too."

"Hey, Mr. Johnson," Whitefeather yells toward the back room. "I have to leave." He runs outside, gesturing for Lucille to follow him and jumps into his truck. He pushes a banana peel and a Snicker's wrapper off the passenger's side seat, clearing it for Lucille. They drive toward the reservation.

Parking in front of a small, wooden, single-floor house, Lucille stays in the truck while Whitefeather sprints toward a man and a woman sitting on a large rock beside the house. They have pipes in their mouths, and their eyes follow the clouds of smoke that spiral up towards the sky. Whitefeather's mother almost trips over her long green dress when she stands to embrace him. His father pushes his wide-brimmed straw hat back from his face and waits his turn.

After a brief and animated conversation, Whitefeather jumps back into the truck. "They don't seem too worried," he says. "Both of them are of the same mind. They think Kimimela ran away, just as I thought. They expect her to walk through the door any minute. When I went to that school, I ran away all the time. My Mama is a wise woman, that's why her name is Nadie. She knows her kids. And my Papa, Elu, man of grace, is taking it in stride. You should see him when he's in full dress during our festivals. A true warrior," he says, proudly."

Whitefeather starts the truck and they take off down the dirt road, hitting all the potholes. Lucille holds her hands over her belly. She's wearing an oversized dress that she made for herself, sewing into the night so she could have something to wear that fits. It disguises her small bump.

"My parents must be pretty tired to be sitting down. Relaxing like that is not something they do very often," Whitefeather says. "Always puttering around doing something. They built their own little house, just the two of them. They raise all of their own food and make their own clothes."

"That's not the story Miss Halliday and Mr. Baran tell."

"You mean you heard that my father served time and my mother is a loose woman? Mr. Baran and his cronies churn out that same story about all the families on the reservation."

Whitefeather's upbeat attitude is reassuring. Still, she watches him drive slowly, studying the sides of the road. Passing some young men working on their cars, he slows down and speaks in his native tongue. They drop their tools and knock on doors, rounding up other men who are working on their small farms. They make their way through the woods.

"I'm not taking any chances," he says. "We'll start searching."

Heavy black clouds appear ready to burst. "Wilma may be out in the woods, and a storm is brewing," Lucille says.

"Let me drive you back," says Whitefeather. "You look tired."

Arriving at the Advisory Building, Lucille spots the deputy leaning against his car and talking to Miss Wilson. Lucille walks over to join the conversation.

Snuffing out one cigarette and lighting another, the deputy says, "We did a final search through the woods. No sign of her." His jowls bounce as he speaks. "Guess it's time to wrap it up. Superintendent said one injun more or less makes no difference. I won't argue the point."

Lucille looks at him with a stony glare. "You mean you're through with the search?"

"Just about. I'll just make up a report." Ready to take off in his car, he leans out the window and says, "I learned a long time ago that little injuns just grow up to be big ones, and that's not say'n much for them."

The police station, located down the road, isn't far. It's an easy walk. Lucille's anxiety has made her feisty. She can't allow the deputy to get away with ending the search so soon. She'll talk to the Sheriff.

The Sheriff has a cordial smile on his face when he greets her. He's tall and muscular in his blue uniform and badge. He looks like a man to be reckoned with. After she relates her dealings with Deputy Williams, he changes his expression. "I have warned this deputy before about making racial slurs," he says. "But going back to the missing little girl, check around the school. Sometimes those kids run off, but they don't go too far. They rarely make it home. I'll see if I have a file on her. What's her last name?"

"Her brother goes by Whitefeather."

"Paco Whitefeather? His sister is missing? We better get on it. We don't want to hassle with that guy. He's tough." He pulls out a file from the cabinet at the side of his desk. "Mmmm. One page on her. She's done it before. Ran away because she didn't like the matron."

"We already checked her home. I'm worried. The matron's gone, too."

Max is standing in front of the Superintendent Building with a smug look on his face. Now that he is an assistant to Mr. Baran and wears a suit every day, he has taken on his boss's mannerisms. He's even started to part his hair in the center. Lucille approaches him anyway. He's been at the school longer than most of the teachers and he knows the surroundings well.

"Max, I want to apologize. I shouldn't have left you at the diner and gone off with Nick. And don't believe the lies Mr. Baran is saying about me."

He shrugs his shoulders. "Not a problem for me. I'll never ask you out again. No one will."

"Max, I said I'm sorry and I truly am. Maybe we can work together now, and you can help in the search for Wilma."

Max looks at his watch. "It's five o'clock. I'm trying out for a musical tonight, and I need time to get ready. Besides, Wilma has been asking for trouble. That kid is a brat. Why don't you come to the audition and watch me win a trophy? And you know what? My partner might give you an incentive to get back into shape."

Parents from the reservation gather around the Advisory Building, ready to take part in the search. They have been asking around, spying at the school. Now carrying megaphones, shovels and lanterns, they have gathered in the same place, ready to walk every inch of the woods. Ellie is there with her own megaphone urging them all to go home.

With everyone speaking at once, the cacophony is deafening. But when Whitefeather walks through the crowd, the people are silenced. The young man's voice resonates with strength and decisiveness. He gesticulates in all four directions and the people immediately disperse. "Don't forget the rivers," he yells after them.

"Where were my people when I needed them?" Ellie asks, looking directly at Whitefeather. "When those men beat my lover, the Indian people turned their backs. Our old life is dead. Indian life is dead. We need to join the white world. Good to wash our bodies of our own stench. The old ways of our ancestors?" She laughs a wild laugh now. "Folly."

"Did you say, wash our bodies of our own stench?" Paco asks in disgust. "Ellie, how can you say that about your own people? The Creator—have you forgotten him?"

Whitefeather is familiar with every passage and path in the forest. If Kimimela is in there, he'll find her. He and Lucille follow the others and head into the woods. Soon darkness settles in and the crowd thins. Whitefeather takes Lucille's hand and leads her in another direction. "I hope you're up to this," he says.

"Where are we going?"

"The Tanker."

"The Tanker? I've never been inside that building. Why are we going there?"

"When Ellie said that we must wash ourselves of our own stench, shivers ran through my spine. She may have given me a clue."

When they reach the rotted building, they find the door obstructed by two large rusty barrels. Lucille steps away and stands on a mound of dirt watching as Paco struggles to push the barrels out of the way. It's then that he sees the wooden bolt on the door. He uses all of his strength to loosen it, but the bolt remains intact. "Superintendent must have ordered this lock put on to deter people like me." He returns to the truck, pulls out a thick rope, and wraps one end around the bolt. He anchors the other end to his bumper. He puts the truck in reverse and drives backwards. The bolt falls to the ground. He gets out of the truck and pushes on the door until it opens. The musty odor overwhelms Lucille and her feet buckle. She has been carrying crackers in her pocket regularly, and she unwraps one and chews it slowly.

"Don't scare me like that," Whitefeather says, holding her steady. "Are you okay now?"

Once inside the Tanker, Lucille's eyes try to adjust in the fog-like haze. Eventually she can make out wall hooks and the long leather straps hanging from them. Ropes and hickory switches are piled on boxes near metal tubs filled with liquid.

Whitefeather warns her to watch her step. "I used to walk over these planks barefoot."

Lucille grimaces. "Over these nails?"

"That's exactly right. But that was the least of it. The matron used full strength kerosene to 'wash the Indian out of my body.' The skin peeled from my arms and legs in red sheets and while I screamed, the matron pleasured herself."

Lucille hears a soft cry. "Listen."

Whitefeather walks toward the sound. "It's a cat," he says. "Let's set him free." He opens the door, and the cat scampers out.

With the light coming in through the open door, the contents of the tubs are visible. Lucille sees something partially immersed in a tub near the wall and leads Paco to it. Walking closer, they see that it is a small body. The little hands are tied with rope, and her bloomers hang over her head. Blood is dripping from her mouth. Whitefeather unties the rope and lifts his sister in his arms. Kimimela's eyes are empty, her body limp. She looks like a doll someone tired of and left out to mold.

"Paco," she whispers. "Paco, Paco."

"Kimimela, my butterfly. What has she done to you, my little sister?" He gathers her in his arms and carries her from the Tanker. He walks across the school grounds. Lucille walks behind him, carrying Kimimela's blue uniform.

Whitefeather doesn't try to hold back his tears, sobbing openly. He walks beyond Mr. Baran's office. His body is cloaked in shadow as the sun descends. He passes the matrons, who look away. He passes the teachers, who bow their heads. He passes Little River Indian Residential School and the children who stand in ruler-straight lines. "Come see what has been done to my Kimimela," he cries to anyone who will listen.

Paco constructs a coffin no larger than a suitcase for Kimimela. Her body, badly beaten by the matron, bears the scars: the blotches around her neck, the bruised eye and face, and the skin that peeled off her arms and legs from the water filled with kerosene. She will lie on the scaffold in the small backyard of Paco's parents' home for four days with family members taking turns guarding her body. He places a daisy motif of Manidoominens, the spirit seeds, on one side of the coffin; on the other, a book of Hiawatha.

Whitefeather's mother's high-pitched wail sets off the beat of the drums, and his father stands bent over with his hat on his heart. The elder statesman leads them in prayer: "Our Great Spirit, for whom we pay homage, we pray. As our Kimimela journeys closer to you, lead us in our own journey of transformation, to work with honor to find the truth. Our Kimimela's body has been ravaged, but *You* lovingly molded her strong will to make her whole again. For this, we will show goodness toward the earth, and kindness and forgiveness to all people."

In the midst of such sadness, the women wind around in a circle, revering the earth beneath them, raising their arms to the Creator. Lucille joins them. The people bow their heads and once more the drums rock the earth. The sound resonates east, west, north, and south. It echoes through the blue sky beyond the sun.

"Lucille, you are my new sister here on earth," Whitefeather says, putting his arm around her shoulder.

"And you, Paco, the brother I never had."

Mr. Johnson drives his truck up the path and stops in front of the house. He reaches into his vehicle and pulls out trays of food. "I am here in your time of need. I am also responsible for Kimimela's death."

"How so?" Whitefeather asks.

"I did not join your fight openly. Only in my heart."

"You gave me shelter when I needed a place to sleep, you gave me work when my pockets were empty. And you gave me food to share with my family."

"Yes," the elder statesman says. He's a robust man in spite of his years, and in his blue jacket trimmed with a beaded shawl collar, it is easy to spot the elder statesman among the other men. His face is taught and serious, and when he speaks in his deep voice, he gains the attention of everyone around him. "You are good to Whitefeather, Mr. Johnson, and for that we praise you. Welcome, welcome. May we become a nation of goodwill. Let Kimimela's angelic wings deliver our message."

"Kimimela was a lot like you, Whitefeather," says his friend Dakota. "She kicked and screamed the day the bus came to take her away to that school."

Whitefeather puts his arms around his friend's shoulders. They are the same height and with the same coloring, they could be mistaken for brothers. "Embracing a good friend is like embracing the moonlight. It brightens your path. Am I right, Dakota?"

"You are right, even when you are wrong. That's how it is with good friends."

"Enough talk," Whitefeather says. "We must find Kimimela's murderer."

With no one to urge them on the way Miss Halliday did, the matrons begin to lose their zest for cruelty. Lucille notices a change in the women. They no longer turn their backs when she passes. Last night when the children were asleep, they huddled in the corner of the hall outside the girl's dormitory, in conversation. Wishing to find redemption and to once again live in the realm of the Great Creator, the matrons confide in Lucille; they want to help find Kimimela's murderer. They would go to Whitefeather, but they are not sure he trusts them yet.

They think they know where Miss Halliday could be hiding and tell Lucille that the matron has a sister who lives on the far end of the reservation. They think that she might have gone there thinking that no one would expect her to be residing so close to the school. If she is there, they can coax her out of the house, pretending to be allied with her. Then Whitefeather, waiting in the woods, can tackle her.

Breaking away from work, Lucille rushes into town to tell Whitefeather the news.

"I must not jump the minute the matrons decide to change their minds," he says, when Lucille finds him at the General Store. "I will test them first. Ask them if they are willing to let the children recite prayers to the Creator before they go to bed tonight. If they say yes, go there tonight and listen. See if they have kept their promise."

Lucille agrees.

"Let me give you some good news, Whitefeather says. "Charlie is back. He came in on the morning train. He even has a job at The Bureau of Indian Affairs. That's good for us. What happened to Kimimela is sure to come up."

"Where is he staying?" Lucille tries to hide her excitement.

"With me. Mr. Johnson is a generous man. He doesn't mind me sharing my room with him. He owes me."

"How so," she asks.

"A young boy from the reservation held a phony knife up to his neck, a silver rubber one. But Mr. Johnson didn't know that. Fifteen years old, but the boy behaved like he was six. I ran after him and brought him back to apologize. Mr. Johnson thought I saved his life. Now he treats me like his own."

Later that evening, Lucille joins the Indian men, women, and small children from the reservation in the building made of logs. It has become their official meeting room. Charlie finds her in the crowd and sits down beside her. Neither one of them says anything until Lucille breaks the silence. "I'm glad you're back, Charlie."

"I'm glad to be back," he says, his cheeks filling with color. "And I'm glad that you'll finally get to see my true self. Those Indian ceremonies really do a good job on me. Beats any medical doctor I've ever been to. And you know, Lucille, I missed you."

She looks away for a moment, looking at the throngs of people who united for this meeting. "I missed you, too," she says, turning to him. They both hold their eye contact a bit longer and then give their attention to the meeting that is now in progress.

First, the people connect with Mother Earth and Father Sky. As the circles of smoke from their pipes curl toward the heavens, they unite in prayer. The news of Kimimela's death has touched them deeply. They are committed to making sure that no other child will fall prey to the cruelty of Little River Indian Residential School.

Before Whitefeather begins his speech, the men applaud. The women hold signs bearing wolf tracks, their clan symbol for power and authority. Lucille is impressed with their sense of unity.

"Let Kimimela's resolve be permanently implanted in all of us," Whitefeather says. "At the school they scoff at our warrior spirit, our ceremonies, our powwows, our language. Our young ones have been taken from us for years at a time. Some, through no fault of their own, are broken of their resolve and return home also scoffing at our traditions. We are the vessels of stories, legends, and triumphs. We cannot allow these vessels to shatter." Whitefeather lays the groundwork for the protest he's planning. He already discussed the details with Lucille when she came into the store that afternoon, and even asked her for suggestions. "Adrien, man of skill, has the responsibility of gathering the people for the rallies. Odin, fast as the wind, named after his Papa, will see to it that pamphlets go out to other tribes and tribal leaders. Nantan's job is to visit the leaders and get them on board. Lucille, their eyes and ears at the school, will serve as the Meda Minda, priestess of intelligence. She will work with Charlie, the coordinator, to get information back to Whitefeather."

Under the Red Ribbon

He urges the men to arrange transportation for Charlie. Soon, a motor from one car and wheels from another are brought forth to renovate an old truck. Charlie invites Lucille to ride back to the school with him. Ignoring the rattle in the doors of the truck and the bent running board, they make their way back to Lucille's cottage.

Their conversation is awkward at first. Lucille does not want to ask him about his health, but Charlie makes no bones about asking her how it feels to be expecting a child. She didn't think it was obvious.

"Who's the father?"

"Nick Martin Jr."

"Doesn't ring a bell. Are you two getting married? Are you already married?"

"I'm not married but he might be—to someone else. I'm thinking about giving up the baby for adoption."

"Just like that," he snaps. "Just give the baby away, like giving clothes to a church sale? This is a real little human being you're carrying. You can't do that. Most of the kids end up in an orphanage and no one wants them. Just ask me, I'll tell you. A child needs a father as well as a mother living together under one roof. A child needs to be part of a family."

"Where is my child supposed to get that?" she asks.

They sit in silence until they reach the cottage. As Lucille is about to get out of the truck, Charlie pulls her toward him. "Your child can get that right here," he says. "I'll marry you."

"Just like that? You'll marry me? We barely know each other."

"I know one thing. You are not giving away your baby."

As soon as she enters her house she goes to the calendar hanging on the kitchen wall and circles the date, May 16, 1932. Lucille rips off the page and places it under the red ribbon. Tonight she will write Bill and Rose a letter and tell them she is bringing her future husband home to meet them.

Bill

Bill gave the house a fresh coat of paint and replaced the old shutters. He and Dan worked on building a new fence just like the one he saw encircling one of the more expensive homes in town. He saw the same fence going up at the Martins, but he thinks they paid top dollar to have someone else do the work for them.

On the day of Lucille's arrival, Bill stands on the porch steps, his eyes on the road, ready to jump as soon as the truck pulls up. Dan arranges a bouquet of roses in a vase and sets it on the porch table, his ears perked for the sound of wheels. Rose places a pitcher of lemonade and two drinking glasses near the flowers, certain that Lucille and her beau will be thirsty after the trip. Paul and Pauline position themselves in front of the house, holding a "welcome home" sign.

When the truck drives into the yard, they leap from their places. There is chatter, hugging, laughing, and a few tears. When Dan puts his arms around Lucille, he touches the locket and whispers, "My Lucille."

"Excuse me, Dan," Bill says. "I think a father should get to kiss his daughter first." He kisses and hugs Lucille and then, eyeing her stomach, says, "Lucille, the food at the residential school must be mighty good."

Pauline Powers, overhearing this, looks down at Lucille's belly and says, "Bill, it's just the new style of the dresses the women are wearing, to give them a full figure." She congratulates Lucille on her new job, pulls her to the corner of the room, and whispers something in her ear. Lucille blushes and nods.

"Everybody, I want you to meet Charlie," Lucille says, when everyone has calmed down.

Bill asks him, "Where did you get that red hair? In Pipestone?"

LUCILLE

Inside the house, Sheila, Gil, Jerry and Lily Sloane, and even Jim Olson, who has taken time off from the garage, greet Lucille. Sheila not only extends her hand to Charlie, but her arms, too.

"Lucille is my best friend," Sheila says, "so if you're with her, you're okay with me." But to Lucille, her expression says, *you're no Nick*.

Bill hurries to the kitchen carrying a platter of fried chicken. His face is perspiring and he lets the women take over in the kitchen so that he can offer Charlie a beer. "You two going to make the announcement tonight?"

Jerry interrupts, "I'd like to talk to the young man, too." He leads Charlie out to the porch. After several minutes, Lucille joins them.

"We're going over to say hello to Hutch," Lucille says, interrupting their conversation. She knows that Jerry is trying to corner Charlie because people will be dropping into his store to find out all about the man she's going to marry. Jerry doesn't want to disappoint them.

"Thanks for saving me," Charlie says, when they have walked far enough away to be out of Jerry's earshot. "Jerry said that I have a familiar face, and asked me what my interests are, and where I'm from. I wasn't going to get into my personal history with a total stranger."

"Let me introduce you to some people you'll really like."

When she lived on the farm, Hutch's farm seemed like a hop skip and a jump away. Now, it seems they have quite a distance to walk.

Some time passes before Hutch comes to the door. When he does, she notices that his movements are slow and his is hair gray, even though he's just Bill's age. Once inside, Lucille inquires about Millie and his grandson, Skip.

Hutch shakes his head. "They don't live here anymore. She ran off with that Indian fella, Derik, and took Skip with her. Can you imagine? The man comes over to pay his condolences and tell me he's so sorry to hear about Arnold's death, and before you know it, he runs off with Millie. Mind you, I have nothing against Indians, but I don't know about Derik bringing up my grandson." He looks over at Charlie. "This your boyfriend?"

"I guess you could say that."

"Good for you. Sorry you won't get to see Brenda. She works at the bird sanctuary. She's doing a heck of a lot better than me. I'm not do'n well, Lucille. I miss Arnie too much."

"Sorry about that, Hutch. It's a tough go. We're also going through a grieving period right now."

Hutch shakes his head. "Don't like to hear that."

Charlie elaborates, filling him in on Kimimela and Whitefeather.

"That Whitefeather fella sounds larger than life. From what you tell me, he hasn't lost his will to fight. He's found a larger cause. Wish I could do that." Hutch goes to the stove to boil some water. "I'd like to sit with you both and have a cup of tea. Oh, I hope I didn't give the wrong message about Indians. I guess I just don't know many except for Derik, and what I know about him don't seem too good. But I didn't mean to insult your friend Whitefeather, Charlie."

"Doesn't matter, Hutch. Your daughter-in-law running off with anyone so soon after your son died should bother you. But getting back to what you said about a larger cause, I don't suppose you know the Shoshone legend. It's about two caterpillars, a husband and wife, but it also could apply to a father and son. When the husband died, the woman grieved for over a year until Great Mystery told her she'd grieved enough. Then she turned into a butterfly and gave much beauty and color to the world."

"I'm not sure I get ya, Charlie."

"That's because you are still a caterpillar. When you become a butterfly, you will continue on with your son's dreams, and bring beauty to the world."

"I wish I could do that, Charlie. I sure wish I could."

"I know it's hard. I have lots of demons, too."

"You do?"

"Sure. I fight them every day. They're tough to beat, I know that much. You can only beat them by being strong. Otherwise, they win and you're a captive."

"But see, that's the thing. How do I get strong like that?"

Charlie puts his hand on Hutch's and walks with him to the window. He draws the curtain back to let the light in. "Your wife has already blazed the path for you. Let her lead you."

"I suppose you're right. Actually, I stood in Arnold's way. Stopped him from becoming a veterinarian so he could work alongside me on the farm. I'm so sorry for that now. I guess I owe it to him to at least work with Brenda at the bird sanctuary. Some good-natured fella keeps the place going. Sends in a lot of money. I hear he wants to have the name changed to Arnold Moseley's Bird Sanctuary."

Lucille stands back, letting the men continue their conversation. She looks over at the toys in the corner, and her heart sinks, realizing that Skip is not there to play with them.

"Nick Jr. bought Skip all those toys," Hutch says. "Such a nice fella and so generous. He was furious when he found out about Millie. I asked him how long he would mourn his wife if she had died. 'For my wife, for the mother of my child, I would mourn for all eternity,' he said."

'For my wife, for the mother of my child, I would mourn for all eternity.' Maybe if he knew about the baby, things would be different and Charlie wouldn't have to be so noble, Lucille thinks.

They sit with Hutch awhile longer and enjoy a cup of tea. When they arrive back at the party, Jerry and Lily are waiting. "Glad you came back so soon, Charlie. Lily and I will show you around town," Jerry says.

When Charlie leaves, Lucille is grateful for some time alone with Sheila. The two of them fill their dishes with salad and chicken and venture out to the porch. They settle into chairs and place their plates on the small table in front of them.

"So good to see Gil. Does he still have the dry goods store? Where's Dottie?" Lucille asks.

Sheila looks down. She opens her purse and takes out a tissue. "Here, you're going to need this. Gil said they couldn't afford another baby, so when Doctor Derik came along and said it didn't have to be that way, Dottie took him up on his offer. He performed the abortion right in the back room of Gil's dry goods store. A few days later, Dottie came down with a fever. An infection, I guess, and then she slipped away.

"Derik and Millie left town in a hurry. I'm trying to be a good friend to Gil. I help him out with the kids whenever I get a chance." Sheila puts her arm around Lucille. "Lots has happened since we left school. The stock market crashed and we all crashed along with it. Now you have Charlie trying to do the right thing. Do you even love him?"

"Love? Let me see, what is that? Nick getting me pregnant and vanishing? You waiting for Nick Sr. to keep good on his promise to marry you? Maybe Charlie is the only one who knows about love, because he never had it. At least he didn't think he did." She pushes her food around her plate. "Paco Whitefeather would say, 'Those who lie down with dogs get up with fleas,' so we have no one to blame but ourselves."

"Who is Paco Whitefeather? Some Indian Chief?"

"He's my dear friend. You'll have to meet him."

Sheila looks at her with one eyebrow raised. "Being pregnant has definitely put you in another state of mind."

Mr. Olson walks out on the porch and tips his hat to the ladies before leaving. "Nice seeing you again, Lucille. I remember the time you rode through town with Nick and it seemed like a tornado roaring down the road. Got yourself a tamer fella this time. Good luck to you."

Gil opens the screen door leaving with some cookies Rose gave him to bring home to his kids. "Time to go, Sheila." He hugs Lucille and reminds her of the silk material he gave her to make her blue dress. "You know, when Nick comes into town, he still tells me how beautiful you looked in that dress. He had me cut a piece of that material for him to keep. And Lucille, congratulations. Charlie looks like a level-headed guy, the kind that will make a good husband."

"Nick is married now too, isn't he?" Lucille asks.

"Nick? Married? Are you kidding me? Not a woman around who could tame him. That story went around like lots of stories people make up about him. You want to know the truth, you ask me."

Sheila gives Lucille a hug. "I'll write you a letter. Things will work out, you'll see."

It is a warm day with a gentle breeze, but the sun will be going down soon, and a walk by herself may do Lucille some good. She needs solitude after this social afternoon. The road in front of her house is still unpaved and there is little traffic. She hopes to get back in time to take a little nap before Charlie returns.

Walking a few feet down the road, a black car with a curved fender that glides into a deep running board pulls up alongside the road. The man inside looks exactly like a man who should own such a car. He has a perfectly carved nose, large blue eyes, and full lips and with his woven straw hat with a red-and-black band above the brim, Lucille thinks he looks snazzy.

"You're Lucille, Bill's daughter, aren't you?" asks the driver. "I still can picture you and my son dancing at the high school graduation. You made a smashing couple. Nick's in town for the weekend. Came in to say a quick hello to his mother and me. I'll tell him I saw you."

This man has caught her by surprise, but seeing him tells her so much about what Nick will look like when he is his age. He is so handsome and charming. She finds her heart fluttering just talking to him. No wonder Sheila finds him so captivating. "How is Nick?" Lucille asks, trying to sound casual.

"He's still running. Can't get him to stay in one place for too long. But he still enjoys coming home. Where do you live now and what are you doing?"

She talks briefly about her work in Minnesota.

"I'd like to sit down with you and have a talk about your experiences at that school. I'm doing some pro bono work out there, helping some of those Indian people get what is rightfully theirs. Too many of them live wretched lives. But you already know that."

"I'd like that...I mean, I'd like to sit down and talk with you. I'd find that interesting."

"And I find you interesting. I like intelligent women," he says. "Your daddy and I go back a long way. We were once tight as this." He crosses one finger over the other. "But you know how it is, people change. You're still as pretty as a spring blossom. I'll tell Nick I met up with you."

It has been a full day. Lucille finds a leafy tree and sits under it.

Lucille was planning on taking a nap when she returned home, but she suddenly feels energized. She sifts through her closet and finds a dress she began sewing years ago, but never finished. She always loved the dress. It was made of beautiful white lace, with a dropped waist and plenty of room around the middle. Gil brought the material over one day during her bout with tuberculosis. When she started to get well, she started making it. She never did take it in on the sides, now she doesn't have to.

She takes a quick bath, washes her hair, and slips on the dress. She looks in the mirror and she's pleased with the healthy glow on her cheeks and the glossy shine to her hair. She often heard people mention that "pregnant glow," but feeling so awful those first few months, she didn't think she'd ever get it. She's restless and walks out on the porch with some magazines.

A red car pulls up in front of the house. "Hop in Princess, we're going for a ride."

The sooner Nick's car disappears, the better. Bill would be furious if he saw him. Lucille looks around to make sure that no one can see her, and climbs into the car. Nick leans over and kisses her on the cheek, but not before taking a long look at her. "You are beautiful," he says.

"How did you know I was here?"

"You and I are like magnets. We attract. I'll always find you. Haven't I told you that before?" He drives a mile down the road, turns down a side road, and parks the car. "Now where did we leave off? Ah, yes. The night I had that bash at my house. Oh, what a night that was. Now where shall we spend tonight? We'll have candlelight dinner, and I know this beautiful hotel, about twenty miles out of Harvest."

"I'm spending the night at my house. I brought a friend home with me."

"Another blonde?"

"Redhead, actually. He's a very fine person."

"He? You brought a *he* home? You're not serious about this fella, are you?"

"Maybe." She twirls her handkerchief in her hand and looks straight ahead.

"What's bothering you, Princess?"

"You're bothering me. You pop in and out of my life and expect me to welcome you, no questions asked."

"You can ask me any question you want. Spill it, baby. I haven't done or said anything to hurt you, have I? I would never do that."

So much new has happened in her life since she left Harvest, yet here she is years later still entangled with Nick. Still, the transformation within her is suddenly apparent. Nick is still the same old Nick in so many ways, and she has undergone a change. Maybe becoming pregnant, and becoming a mother soon is responsible for that change. *He wants her to spill it? Hold on Nick, here it comes.* "I'm pregnant."

The color drains from his face. He hangs his head over the steering wheel. Then he turns to her, taking her hands in his. "Lucille, what did you do that for? I thought you were different from the other women. I thought you were my Fairy Princess. I can't believe you would let this happen to you. That fella with the red hair, I'll snuff him out."

That fella with the red hair? Doesn't he realize that their lovemaking might have had consequences? "I thought I could wait for you to grow up," Lucille says. "But I can't wait that long."

"Grow up? I'm wheel'n and deal'n with the big shots. Just got back from Europe. You saw those people at my party. They're in the big time. You told me that night that you accepted me the way I am. What changed? C'mon, tell me what's go'n on."

"What's going on is, it's *our* baby I'm carrying."

"Lucille, what are you saying?"

"I'm saying that snowy night at your apartment, when we slept together in your bed, that's when it happened."

"You mean we were making our own little snowman?" He apologizes. "I'm sorry. I shouldn't have said that. Forgive me. Poor joke. Why didn't you tell me sooner? No tears, baby, I could have made it right if I knew. I still can."

She can't believe what she's hearing. He'll make it right? "Nick, I underestimated you."

"Never do that baby. Never."

Lucille is relieved. Charlie will be able to go on with his life, without the added responsibility of caring for another man's child, and her baby will have a real father.

"I know this doctor," says Nick. I think the whole thing takes a half hour at most. I'm not sure. Then you'll be your old self again, the same Lucille."

His words hit her as hard as if he'd driven into her with his car. "The *whole thing*? Dottie died from the *whole thing*. Forget it, Nick. I'll handle this on my own." Lucille looks through the window. Convinced that there is only one way to handle this, she moves toward him, letting her eyes and heart fill with his face. She kisses his lips with the longing of all the years she has wanted him. With her arms around him, she holds him close, listening to his heart beat against hers. Her hands move over his body. "I want to feel all of you for the last time. Goodbye, Nick."

"No, Lucille, there is no goodbye for us. There is no last time. We promised each other. We said we'd never give our hearts to anyone else."

They sit with their arms locked around each other. He slides one hand over her belly and holds it there. When the baby moves she thinks he might cry, but with urgency she has seen before, he starts the car and drives away, leaving a cloud of dust behind.

When they return home, Charlie is standing on the porch talking to Jerry. Nick follows Lucille out of the car and interrupts them. "You must be the red-haired prince Lucille told me about. Don't get any big ideas about you and my Fairy Princess. Don't get too cozy."

Jerry Sloane has heard it all.

Lucille whisks Charlie away from Jerry and takes him into her room so they can talk privately.

"Who is that guy?" Charlie raises his voice now. "Why were you with him?"

"He's the father of my baby."

"What a creep!" Charlie puts his hand in his jacket pocket and removes a little box that he hands to Lucille. Now his voice becomes soft and gentle. "Where I come from," he says, "when you meet a girl's parents, it means something."

She opens the box and sees the ring. Its sparkle matches the sparkle in Charlie's eyes. She gives it back to him.

"What does that mean?" he asks.

"It means, I want you to put it on my finger."

The following morning, they are set to leave before sunrise so that they can reach Riverview during the coolest part of the day. Placing the lunch Rose prepared for them in the truck, Charlie and Lucille see Hutch walking toward them. He's wearing a short-sleeved yellow polo shirt, overalls, and a straw hat.

"Just had to come by and thank you again, son. You gave an old man like me some sound advice. Brenda and I talked in bed last night, for a long time. I'm going to help down at the bird sanctuary along with her. Brenda and I thought maybe we'd even go down to the dog shelter and adopt a dog or two. We still have all the stuff Arnold had for his dogs. He taught us how to give animals a darn good home. And Charlie, one day I'd like to meet that Indian friend of yours. I need to thank him, too."

"The name is Paco Whitefeather. Remember it. You'll be hearing a lot about him."

"And will I be hearing news about the two of you soon?" Hutch asks.

Lucille shows him the ring.

"You got a good guy there, Lucille. And Charlie, take good care of her. Lot of fellas around here have had their eye on her." He winks at Lucille, and she smiles at him.

BILL

Bill's joy at seeing Lucille again is shattered when Dan tells him that he's gotten a job in New York City and will be leaving in a few days. The night after Lucille and Charlie leave for Minnesota, Dan and Bill sit on the porch steps of his house and Dan breaks the news. Bill's stomach sinks down to his knees. If it weren't for the beer he's gulped down, he knows he'd never sleep through the night.

It's a load too heavy for him to carry. First his daughter moves away and then his best friend tells him that he's moving, too. If Rose leaves him he might miss her, but not nearly as much as he'll miss Dan. He and his buddy could live in the same house and never argue. Never had a quarrel in all these years. Got hot under the collar a few times, but no big arguments. He snuffs out a cigarette and lights another.

They planned an evening out together before Dan leaves for New York City and tonight is that farewell evening. It's overcast and heavy showers are predicted. Some newscasters predicted a heavy hailstorm and severe winds, but Bill would never put off this night with Dan, whatever weather comes their way. He stands on his porch waiting for his friend. When he sees Dan's truck drive up, he knows it's the last time they'll be heading out to Beerkill Tavern--for a long time, anyway.

As they drive, Dan talks about Lucille and Charlie, but Bill knows Dan is trying to avoid talking about his big move. Imagine, his friend getting a job at a highbrow jazz club in New York City. And he just won't say how he got it.

"Well wouldn't you know, Charlie was the kid Jerry almost adopted years ago," Dan says.

Bill chokes as he inhales on his cigarette. "Hogwash. Do you think Charlie looks the same as he did when he was a kid? That's like me meeting my grade school teacher now, and her recognizing me."

"Jerry and Lily have proof. They have pictures. Pictures they took of him at the orphanage when he was eleven years old. Same freckles and red hair. Interested in science even back then."

"Leave it to Jerry to give him a tour around town just to get him to talk. Poor Charlie, it must have been like getting stuck in a bowl of taffy on a hot day. What else you know, Dan?"

"Well, Jerry said he found out, and he wouldn't tell me how, that Charlie's real mother grew up living with her grandmother, because *her* mother ran off with a transient worker. But then Charlie's mother was only thirteen when she had a one-night tryst with a farmhand and ended up pregnant with Charlie. She treated him like a doll while the grandmother took care of the important stuff. When the grandmother died, there was only one place for Charlie to go. His mother didn't want him. She couldn't handle the responsibility."

"Sounds complicated."

"You know how badly Jerry and Lily wanted to adopt another child after they lost their own boy. They visited the orphanage almost every Sunday. Jerry took a liking to Charlie, but Lily wasn't sure. She had her heart set on a girl. Then this couple from Brooklyn, the Rosens, adopted him. Charlie's last name is Rosen, so two plus two equals four. The Rosens are Jewish, so I guess he's Jewish."

"Jewish? What the hell do I care? As long as he's not the Martin kid. I have nothing against Jewish. How could I? I don't know anyone Jewish. The main thing is, do you think he'll make a good husband? From what you tell me, his background is a little strange."

"Don't worry about that. He wants to be a scientist. He might be famous one day."

When they're seated at the Beerkill Tavern, Bill becomes grim. He looks around the dim room that smells a little musty. He studies the seats of the booths lined with yellow oilcloth and the tables scattered around the room covered with red oilcloth. Red and yellow is the décor, and that's the way it's been all these years. Bill studies the signs plastered over the walls advertising Beerkill's oversized hamburgers and golden French fries. Those signs haven't changed much either. But what has changed is not being able to come here with Dan.

"I don't know how I can get used to not seeing you all the time. I'm going to be a lost soul."

"I feel the same way, but sometimes we gotta do what we gotta do," Dan says. "I'll come back from time to time, and you'll come and visit me. You'll get to see the big city, and I'll come home to see my big-hearted friend."

"That's a deal." The men shake on that. Bill remembers the time they got lost on a hunting trip. They were so cold they had to rub each other's hands and shoulders to keep warm. When that didn't work, they leaned against a tree with their arms wrapped around each other. That's what he calls being good friends. Not many people appreciate a friendship like that. In the morning, a deputy from the Sheriff's department found them, asleep in each other's arms. "Well, I'll be," he said, "two queers."

"You know Bill, that night after Lucille's graduation and that fierce storm, I was heading out to see you so we could make amends. But damn it, I couldn't get my truck started."

"You're kidding, Dan. I wanted to drive down to see you, but my truck was standing in a pool of water, and it kept stalling out on me. It took all the stuffing out of me, having words with you. I couldn't sleep that night."

"Me, neither," Dan says. "The two of us, one mind, one heart."

Bill explains to Alice, the waitress, that this is a special occasion and prohibition or no prohibition, they are here to drink. It doesn't take long for her to return with two coffee cups filled with whiskey. He slips a few coins into her palm before his eyes travel over to a dimly lit corner. What the heck, she can use the money. Alice has been working here for as long as Bill can remember. She still has that crooked smile and a touch of toughness in her talk. Her husband ran off and left her over twenty years ago and she's supported her kids for all that time. It's taking its toll on her now, Bill can see. Harsh lines poke out like spokes on a bicycle around her eyes, and what were once dimples are deep crevices in her cheeks. But she still fits into her black uniform, filling it out where it should be filled out and she's a heck of a good waitress.

"What's up Bill? What are you thinking about?"

"I don't know, just thinking."

Bill takes a gulp from his cup. Now there is excitement in his voice when he looks across the room. "Look, over there, Dan. Nick Sr. and Sheila. Now wouldn't you know, she's the same age as my Lucille." He takes another gulp and then asks Alice for a refill. With his eyes glazed over, he's up and out of his chair and walking over to the attorney's table. "You're with a woman the age of my daughter," Bill says in a loud voice. "Have you no shame?"

"We'd better go outside and talk." Nick Martin Sr. rises from the table and maneuvers Bill out the door.

"I really bug you, Bill, and I don't know why," Nick Sr. says, when they stand facing each other outside. "What have I ever done to get you mad at me? Hey, when I was a kid I picked apples at your Daddy's house and gave them to the poor old woman who lived in that shack."

"Like hell you did. You were sell'n 'em on the street and pocketing the money."

"I'm a lawyer, but you make a darn good judge," he retorts with a laugh. "Let's forget all about this. I'll buy you a drink. Who knows, maybe our kids will end up together and we'll be family."

Bill feels triumphant when he says, "Didn't you hear, Lucille is getting married to a scientist?

Mr. Martin pulls out a cigarette without offering one to Bill. "Married? Really?"

"Pass the news on to your son," Bill says, walking back to his table.

Dan is finishing his drink too, and acting a bit tipsy. "Bill, what's with you and Nick Sr.? I'm leaving town, you can tell me. We don't have secrets from each other. Well maybe I have *one*."

"You tell me and I'll tell you," Bill says.

Dan begins to speak, but stops himself. "Aw shucks, we are each entitled to one secret. Let's drink to that."

Under the Red Ribbon

The men leave with their arms around each other's shoulders, barely managing to hold each other up. "If ever you meet up with a fella who loves you more than I do," Dan says, "run for the hills. It just wouldn't be healthy."

LUCILLE

Back in Riverview, the words explode on large cardboard signs: No Excuse for the Abuse; Education not Assimilation; Kimimela's Murderer will Pay. Lucille and Charlie have been working all day on the signs and instructing protesters on where to stand. Lucille realizes she has only eaten a few crackers since the morning, and now it's almost dinnertime. She tells Charlie that she feels dizzy. He takes her hand and leads her to his truck. He drops her off at the General Store so that she can get something to eat, saying that he'll meet up with her later.

Mr. Johnson, who is preparing trays of turkey sandwiches to send over to the protesters, hands her a sandwich and a coke. She didn't realize how hungry she was. When Whitefeather joins her at the table, she can't stop eating long enough to converse.

He gets right to the point. "Apparently the matrons were genuinely interested in carrying out their plan to catch Miss Halliday. They went over to her sister's house to convince her to hide out in the woods, telling her it was safer. But she got wise to what they were doing and ran off."

"On to the next strategy," Lucille says. "Funny thing, I had a dream last night that a white deer tugged at me, urging me to follow him so that he could lead me to a woman hiding out in a dark room."

"And you followed him?"

"Yes, and I woke up and smelled something so foul I almost heaved."

"Too much on your mind," Whitefeather says. "And in your condition, you are doing too much. Let's take the trays over to the demonstrators and see how things are going."

Hundreds of Indians are gathered close to the school. Whitefeather takes charge, giving commands and lining the crowd up in an orderly fashion. He pauses suddenly and turns to Lucille. "The white deer told you something in your dream: the darkness, the woman, the foul odor. Lucille, let's go."

Whitefeather helps her into his truck and they reach the Tanker in record time. Surprised to find the door ajar, Lucille says, "Strange, we had so much trouble opening the door the last time. She sniffs the air and makes a bitter expression. That was the odor I told you about."

"Dreams tell us things we wouldn't otherwise realize."

Inside, the Tanker is dim, almost dark. Whitefeather grips Lucille's hand, and she feels comfort in his touch. When they reach the center of the room, he tells her to close her eyes and follow his lead. "Soon Kimimela's spirit will appear," he says. Standing motionless for a few moments, she then imitates him as he begins to sway from side to side. He chants Kimimela's name, and she does the same. They sway faster. Lucille and Whitefeather voices grow louder. "Kimimela, our butterfly," they chant. "Do you see the Ghost dancers, Lucille?" he asks." They are joining us. See the circles and circles of dancers?"

They are interrupted by an unexpected voice. "Superstition, Whitefeather. Lucille, you are too smart for this. The Ghost Dance won't bring Kimimela back. Look around you. Where are the dancers? They're in Whitefeather's head. Don't get caught up in the Indian web." Ellie's eyes are cold, her clothes torn. Her hair falls over her face.

"Ellie, what are you doing here?" Lucille asks.

"Surprised to see me?"

Whitefeather's disbelief is obvious when he speaks. "After all I did for you," he yells. "I hunted through the rough mountains, the dusty roads and the twisted forests and wouldn't stop until I brought Hanson back. Is this the way you repay me? Did you help Miss Halliday murder my Kimimela? Certainly you're not here because you like the smell of kerosene or the view of this dark, damp hell hole."

Ellie walks toward him "Do you speak the truth? Whitefeather, you brought Hanson back? Tell me, are you saying the truth?"

Whitefeather turns his back on her. "I found him wandering in the woods, but when I brought him back to the reservation, you were not there."

Ellie clings to Whitefeather's arm. She falls on her knees and kisses his hands. "Bring him back to me again."

"Why should I help you?" Whitefeather says.

"Because my heart is sewn with Indian thread. So I searched for her. I searched until I found her."

"Found who?"

"I waited for her in the woods. I found her kneeling near the bones of her own dead child. The bones were hidden behind trees and brush and her words spilled like milk out of a mother's breast, glorifying her story with sweetness. When she saw me, she used the force of her huge body and hauled me here like I was garbage. She ripped my shirt, showing me how she ripped Kimimela's dress, trying to pull it over her head. I thought she would kill me, too. She dragged me to a basin of water and threw me in. She poured disinfectant into the water. I yelled for her to stop. I screamed, 'It's me, Ellie,' but she called me Suna, her dead daughter's name."

"Who are you talking about?"

Ellie points to the woman crawling on the floor: Miss Halliday. The matron rips at her buttocks as she crawls. She curses her mother for watching in silence as her father inflicted atrocities upon her young body.

Whitefeather reaches for a rope hanging on the wall. In a quick gesture, he grabs both of the matron's hands and ties them behind her back "Kimimela did not have to die for your father's sins or for your mother's silence." He drags Miss Halliday to the corner where he found his sister, and rips the clothes from her body. Removing her bloomers, now soiled with fear, he stretches them over her head. He tumbles her into a basin of water. He lifts the whip and cracks it against the floor. Miss Halliday flinches and jerks her head back. He cracks the whip against the floor again, and she screams. Her eyes crazed, her mouth distorted, she pleads with Whitefeather.

"I wanted to make Wilma clean and pure. She wouldn't let me. She taunted me with that purple stone."

Whitefeather walks away.

Lucille wipes the sweat from her face with her hands. "Ellie, welcome back to your people."

Whitefeather calls the sheriff. Within the hour, all of Riverview knows that Miss Halliday, the matron at Little River Indian Residential School, has hung herself.

The protestors move down Main Street. The men play drums and flutes while the women carry banners and signs, chanting and singing Indian songs. In cars and on foot, the sheriff and his force stand by waiting for chaos to take hold, ready to haul the Indians off to jail on the slightest provocation. But Whitefeather has warned his people. "We'll show them our hearts are heavy, our will is strong, and the voice of Kimimela will be our only weapon."

Lucille and Whitefeather merge with the parade. When they reach the school, the superintendent, Mr. Baran, shoves his way through the crowd. He stops in front of Lucille.

"You have joined the hoodlums, have you, little farm girl?" He presses against her, and she looks at him with disgust. He pushes her the way he did in his office, and she falls to the ground. Her belly is cramping and she feels pain in her back. She feels liquid soaking her bloomers.

"Holy Smokes," Whitefeather says, "You're dripping blood. I better get you to the doctor fast."

Some of the protestors crowd around her. They ask what they can do to help. Whitefeather spots his good friend Dakota in the crowd and waves him over. Together, they lift Lucille into the truck.

"Whitefeather," Lucille whimpers, "I don't feel well." And then she loses consciousness.

Lucille lies in her hospital bed, her head propped up against two pillows, her eyes staring straight ahead.

Under the Red Ribbon

"I rushed over as soon as I heard." Charlie bends over to kiss her on her cheek. He touches her forehead. "I love you," he says. "Mr. Baran's girlfriend told me she no longer wants to be the superintendent's play toy. She is one of the protesters now," he says, nervously.

Lucille ignores him. "The doctor said it was a boy," she says.

"Soon you will be my wife, and we'll have our own babies. Boys, girls and as many as you like," Charlie says. He sits beside her and holds her hand.

"I want my baby with Nick, I want Nick." The words fly out of her mouth before Lucille can stop them.

Charlie blinks. "So you do still love him."

"It's like he's a ball of yarn, and I'm searching for the end." She extends her left hand. "Take the ring. Maybe we're not right for each other. Maybe we're not the right fit."

Charlie

Maybe we're not the right fit. Words from Charlie's past. He remembers the couples that walked through the orphanage, selecting children like they were choosing furniture for their houses. Once after inspecting him, a woman whispered to her husband that she didn't like red hair. Another had said, "definitely no freckles." Yet another announced that he would not be the right fit for their lifestyle—too many problems.

Although the ring is light and the diamond small, he feels the weight of it in his pocket. He wanders down the familiar back road leading to the reservation, searching for comfort. It's almost dark now, and the tall dark trees lining the road enclose him like a soft blanket. He loves the scent of the trees, the way the branches sway in the wind, their deep color against a blue sky. He was raised in New York City; he doesn't take this beauty for granted. He hears a voice calling him and he spins around and sees Dakota.

"I'll walk down the road with you," Dakota says. "The protest is doing fine without me. Up all night getting ready for it. I'm going home to sleep. How is Lucille? I helped Whitefeather get her to the hospital. She's a terrific woman. I hope it's nothing serious. I heard Mr. Baran pushed her. I shouldn't be surprised by anything he does. But the tables are turning and his time is running out. By the way, did I ever tell you that you and Lucille make a great couple?"

"Dakota, a heck of thing happened. Lucille and I broke up." Charlie flicks his red curls off his forehead and with his sleeve wipes the perspiration from his upper lip. "I'm thinking of leaving Riverview."

"You broke up? I don't believe it. And now you want to leave Riverview? Don't do that. You're one of us," he says, putting his arm around Charlie's shoulders.

Charlie looks down at the ground. He has mixed feelings about leaving. He will miss people like Dakota who care about him. He doesn't know him well, only sees him from time to time when he visits the reservation but even now, in his misery, Dakota cares. He will miss so much about Riverview: this back road, the trees, the gravel under his feet, and the brilliant burst of orange painting the sky when the sun sets. But he knows he can't stay. Walking side by side with Dakota, he feels camaraderie. His thoughts become clearer. After Lucille handed back the ring, he was too shocked to think. He was numb. But now, his mind is alert. Of course, he will go back to New York City. His parents live there and this just might be the right time to enroll at a university and pursue a career in science—and not on a sixth grade level. And he won't have to worry about bumping into Lucille. He really thought he could make her forget about Nick, but he was wrong.

When they reach the reservation, Charlie stops to embrace Dakota. "Thank you, Dakota. Although my heart is heavy, you have uncluttered my road ahead, just with your presence."

Whitefeather is busy filling the bins at the General Store with candy when Charlie approaches him the following day. It's mid-morning and the sky is gray, just like his mood. Gray from the top of his head to the tips of his toes. Mr. Johnson is standing behind the counter waiting on a woman who appears eager to leave because her baby is crying in her arms. She drops a few coins on the floor and Charlie picks them up and hands them to her. He recognizes her as one of the women from the reservation. They nod to each other.

"Nice to see you again," she says.

"Same here," he replies.

The woman smiles and leaves. That's the thing about Riverview. It's small enough for people to recognize you and big enough so they don't know too much about you. Except of course, at the Residential School where the teachers need something to distract them from their own shame. They know they're just helping to keep those Indian children down.

Satisfied that the store is devoid of customers now, Charlie walks over to Whitefeather and blurts out, "Lucille and I broke up. We're going our separate ways."

Whitefeather says a few words to Mr. Johnson who is standing behind the counter and then walks Charlie out the door. "Come, let's walk and talk about this," he says.

They walk up the street to the corner and back several times. It's more like pacing than walking. "I want to ask you what happened," Whitefeather says, "but it must be too painful to talk about just yet." He puts his arms around his friend. "But separate ways?" he asks. "Not possible. As long as we all share the same earth and the same sky, we share a life together. What has existed still exists, only the winds have changed."

"Yes, Whitefeather, the winds have changed, alright."

"But I have some good news that will cheer you up. Our protest had a profound effect on the governor. Heard it from one of my sources that he came to see Miss Wilson first thing this morning. She goes to her office, and he's waiting at the door." Charlie knows who his sources are: one is Dakota's sister, who helps out in the office. "The governor and Miss Wilson had a long conversation. Mr. Baran might, and I say might and I'm holding my breath, *might* get fired. Miss Wilson has been keeping a long list of his atrocities and she said the governor was appalled when she rattled them off to him."

"Well, I guess not everything is bleak. A rainbow does come out after the rain, when the conditions are right. And we made the conditions right with our protest. It was clear to the governor, the Indians aren't going away. But I am."

"You are what?"

"I'm going away, to New York City."

"I thought you'd stay on the job here with the Bureau of Indian Affairs. They like you. You did a good job for them and helped us at the same time. But when it's time to move on, it's like a mammoth wind pushing you. So go, if you must." The look on Whitefeather's face matches Charlie's. A sadness around the eyes and mouth, and the catch in his voice, trying to keep it steady. Whitefeather says no more.

A special ceremony is planned for later that week. It is held on the reservation where Charlie's many friends wish him well. They arrive in force, just after sunset, to shake his hand, pat him on the back, and embrace him. The tribesmen express regret about his leaving. A white man taking the side of Indians is not something they take for granted. They tell him that they enjoyed seeing the young man with the bright red hair and freckles walk among them.

The children present him with gifts: miniature drums, canoes, and cloth woven with Indian symbols. They gather around him as he admires each token of love and hugs each child. The women offer him fruit from hand-woven baskets, and the men sit with him as they smoke a peace pipe. They smile when Charlie joins them in the prayer to the four directions.

The festivities continue, but the heavy toll of Wilma's murder still lingers. Charlie can feel what they feel: anger, pain, and disgust.

With the start of the ceremony, Charlie is called to come before the group. Making his way through the crowd, he sees Ellie with a young man's arm around her waist—Hanson's arm. He sees the young Indian girl, who worked for Mr. Baran, laughing with Dakota. Whitefeather's parents, Elu and Nadie, stand together, holding hands. He sees Lucille sitting alone in the crowd. Her face is thin and wan, and still so beautiful. He yearns to gather her in his arms and keep her safe forever.

Whitefeather extends his hand to Charlie and embraces him. "You are family," he says. He recites the words of another Whitefeather, a Navajo medicine man. "To be Indian isn't to have the blood, it is to have the heart."

The Elder who stands beside Whitefeather says, "All of our tribes are united by a single breath. People in New York City are too busy to think of the Indian. You must remember for all of them."

When the Elder invites Lucille to stand beside Charlie, the crowd explodes in applause. The drummers go wild. They have become accustomed to seeing the young couple together. The Elder takes Charlie's hand and places it on Lucille's.

"Ask her now," he says, "to be your wife. Let us all witness your commitment to each other."

Charlie looks down at his shoes.

The Elder says, "Go on. Don't be shy. Ask her."

Charlie closes his eyes. "Lucille, will you marry me?"

"Yes," she says, just loud enough to make him smile.

When the hoopla quiets down and the crowd has dispersed, Whitefeather tells Charlie and Lucille that he would like to help them plan a wedding in the Indian tradition, if that is their wish. He mentions several types of ceremonies: The Fire Ceremony, The Blanket Ceremony, The Wedding Vase Ceremony, and The Rite of the Seven Steps.

"Can we include a little of each?" Lucille asks.

"I don't see any rule against that," he laughs. "And if you marry while it is still warm, the service and celebration can be held outdoors."

If sorrow has touched Charlie, he has moved beyond it. He and Lucille take a walk around the reservation, holding hands and planning their wedding vows:

> *When our love came, too scared were we to seize it*
> *When our hearts met, too proud were we to feel it*
> *For each of us had to learn anew*
> *To distinguish fantasy from what was true.*
> *Now we lock hands and move forward*
> *Together we walk into the night,*
> *We make these vows to each other*
> *To be each other's endless light.*
> *Trust will be our shelter, loyalty our abode.*
> *We know not what comes before us*
> *But that you and I will share one road.*

ℒUCILLE

Just two weeks later Lucille spends the pre-wedding night at Whitefeather's parents' home. Lucille wishes Bill and Rose could be at the ceremony, or Charlie's parents, but once they made up their mind to get married they set the date quickly with little fuss. They discussed it and they both decided they'd have a nice party with their families when they got settled in New York.

After a dinner of fish, rice, and vegetables, Elu walks with Lucille around the small garden and recites a Cherokee blessing. He speaks in a deep but gentle voice, and she finds solace in his wisdom:

She has so much to think about. Later that night, lying under the multi-colored quilt, she studies the hand-carved eagle on the wall, and the skins of bears, wolves, and buffalo. When she asked Elu what it was like to kill an animal, he explained prayers and ceremonies preceded hunts. His people did not take lightly the act of taking lives.

Taking lives. She thinks of Kimimela. There were no prayers or ceremonies before her life was cut short. She lived believing in herself, and no one could change that.

The moon is waning when Lucille gives up trying to sleep. She rises from her bed and finds Nadie in the sewing room, finishing her wedding gown. Lucille asks if she can try it on again, and Nadie is quick to oblige. Standing in front of the mirror wearing the traditional Indian wedding gown, it feels natural for her to wear such a garment. The dress is red with colorful beads around the neckline. She asks Nadie why red, and she explains that the color signifies good luck, good health, and good fortune. Lucille bows her head and weeps.

You're so beautiful, Fairy Princess. The voice she hears is barely audible, but resounding just the same. She sees his face, his blue eyes, and the dimple in his left cheek. She shakes her head to bring herself back to the present. "You must have been beautiful when you were a bride, Nadie. Elu loves you very much," she says.

"Elu still tells me I'm the most beautiful woman in the world. But Lucille, you know the Elder's younger brother? I gave him my heart first. But he was too busy for me. Whenever we set a date for the wedding, he went off to a tribal meeting. But Elu is a kind man. When he went to a tribal meeting he took me with him. After our children were born, we all piled in the truck and went along. Each day I love Elu more."

"And the Elder's younger brother?"

"I only see him now when I dream."

For seven days prior to the wedding, Elu and Nadie have recited prayers and blessed the earth. On the wedding day, the last blessing is said. On this warm July evening with the sun just beginning to set, Nadie rolls a bright yellow and turquoise rug down the center of their yard. Elu beckons Mr. Johnson, Whitefeather, the Elder, and Hanson to form an aisle on either side of the carpet, and then signals Miss Wilson and Ellie to follow. Clutching small bouquets of white daisies, the women take their places on either side of the wedding canopy. With the bridal party intact, Elu walks the bride toward her soon-to-be-husband.

Choosing a variety of ceremonies, Lucille decides to begin with the very traditional Blanket Ceremony. She stands in awe when a slender young woman, face veiled and wearing a gauzy dress drifts like an apparition down the aisle and wraps the couple in individual blue blankets. Then the Elder ignites two fires on the sandy ground in front of the couple, small fires made of sticks and paper, and pokes a long pole into them. He pushes the embers of both fires together as a symbol of oneness. It is now time for the couple to be wrapped in one blanket. The veiled woman lifts her veil and hands it to Charlie. Allowing her hair to fall over her shoulders, she dances around the couple, winding the blanket around them. Then she disappears from the yard. With the

Elders' blessings, Lucille and Charlie drink from the two-spout wedding vase. The promise of love and eternal happiness is sealed.

Leaving for a small cottage in the woods to begin their honeymoon, Lucille and Charlie travel along a narrow path, driving away from Elu's house and deeper into the woods. They hear the howls of coyotes and the cries of wolves. When they reach the cottage, the moonlight brightens the gravel walkway.

"Lucille, there she is again, fleeing from the house. The woman with the long black hair. The woman who wrapped us in the blanket. Her face, I know it well."

Thinking Charlie has a case of wedding jitters, Lucille takes his hand and steers him into the cottage. The kitchen has an intoxicating scent, strange and different. In the candlelight she sees a coffee pot atop the black stove and a straw basket of biscuits in the center of the table. Maybe Whitefeather sent the woman ahead to prepare the house for them.

Charlie inspects the rest of the cottage while Lucille pours herself some coffee. Following the long colorful rug leading to the bedroom, she stops to touch the beads of the dream catcher hanging over the bed. Charlie climbs into bed. Lying beneath the dream catcher, he is relaxed and at peace. With his arms outstretched, he pulls her toward him and slowly unfastens the buttons that run down the front of her dress.

He breathes into her curly blonde hair, her loving face, and slowly removes her wedding gown. When Lucille starts to speak, he places two fingers over her lips. The scent of sage fills the air, and he pushes back the blanket. A soft warm light washes over them as the dream catcher sways above their heads, the knot in the center ready to catch all bad dreams. The house is still, and they hear only each other's breath. Soon the sky and the earth come together, leaving them both gasping. "My lovely wife Lucille," Charlie says. "You have taken away my sadness."

Dan sent her a letter when he heard she was moving. He wrote, "New York City is an artist's paradise. You know, Scott Fitzgerald was born in Minnesota and shaped his first novel here. This is the place where creativity flourishes." Still, when Lucille gets her first glimpse of the city, she's frightened. All of it is so new for her: people on street corners hailing cabs, tall buildings, dazzling lights, and everyone in a hurry. She feels invisible. No one knows her or her name. No one would miss her if she went back to Minnesota.

After a few weeks living in the lower east side of Manhattan, she wonders what's in store for her next. She wishes she had her high school literature teacher's courage to stand up to Charlie and tell him she doesn't want to be there. On the day when she reaches into her little pouch that she keeps in the drawer beside her bed and hands Charlie the money she saved for her own college tuition so that he can use it for his, she realizes that her life has really changed.

But so much has changed for her. Walking up three flights of stairs before opening the door to her apartment is not anything she's used to doing. In Harvest she flung open the front door and she was outside in seconds. Even living in her small cottage in Riverview she could do the same. And the noise outside her apartment from the traffic, sirens, and people calling out the window keeps her up at night. Even with the windows closed, she can hear them. But she needs the windows open. It is late July and it is hot in Manhattan. She needs to find work, and that is a job in itself. A huge number of people are still unemployed, and a job is hard to come by. When she is offered work in a shop re-hanging dresses left in the fitting room, she swallows her pride and accepts it. Her walk home from work becomes the best part of her day. She passes the small bookstore she always stops in.

Combing through the shelves, she finds a few books she'd like to buy. She can't afford to buy any of them, but she is happy enough just to hold and skim through them. The scent of the pages brings her to another state of mind. She is oblivious to the man standing next to her. When she turns her head, she faces Harry, and his thick glasses and broad smile. She couldn't be happier to see a familiar face. By the looks of him, he feels the same.

He wraps his arms around her. "I just had to do that," he says, when he lets go.

"I'm glad you did," she says.

He tells her that he's married, and she says she is, too. He tells her he has just started medical school and is working at the same time. "Could you believe I pave roads as a side job?"

"I won't even tell you the work I do."

"How about school? You of all people should have a college education. You can contribute great things with your brains."

"Maybe someday," she says with a sigh. "Oh, Harry, I can't tell you how happy I am to see you again. Our minds just seem to click when we talk. We understand each other. It's like we're back in high school, trying to beat each other out for the top grade."

An awkward moment follows and Harry looks directly into her eyes. "Funny," he says, "I knew we would be married someday, but honestly Lucille, I thought we'd be married to each other."

"For a long time I did, too. I'm married now to a man I met in Minnesota. I'll let you meet him sometime."

After a long pause, they promise to keep in touch and attend each other's college graduations.

Seeing Harry leaves Lucille thinking about the past. He was always so nice, so kind. Still, she chose Nick. And now she's married to Charlie. Life has no clear path.

After dinner, Charlie helps her with the dishes. The kitchen is narrow, and it's tight with the two of them standing side by side. They almost touch as she washes the dishes and he dries them. She doesn't tell him about Harry, because she worries that he might be jealous, but seeing Harry reminded her of her own lifelong goal: to go to college. They made an agreement to attend each other's graduations, but she wonders if that is only a fantasy.

Charlie breaks into her thoughts when he announces that he'd like to have another wedding here in New York so that their parents can come. Lucille agrees.

Still unfamiliar with the ins and outs of the city, Lucille calls on Dan to help her shop for a wedding dress. She's had his phone number for a while, but they haven't yet been able to find a time to get together. When Dan exits a cab on Fifth Avenue, Lucille can't believe the change in his appearance. In his light blue silk shirt, navy blue gabardine pants, and ascot tied loosely around his neck, all she can say is, "Clarke Gable, move over."

"You think so, Lucille? I look as good as that actor, even with my blonde hair?"

"With the breeze ruffling your hair, and the sprinkling of those sunrays, you look even better. It's been too long since we saw each other. A few years is way too long. I like your new style. Where did you buy those clothes?"

"A friend introduced me to a magnificent men's clothing shop on Madison, *Taylor and Taylor*. The younger man who works there, Richard, usually helps me with my selections. Charlie may want to buy his suit there." Dan opens his wallet and pulls out a white card and hands it to Lucille. "His business card might come in handy one day."

"Charlie has one suit. He won't buy another."

"Don't blame him. People are holding onto the little money they have. My boss pays for all of my clothes. It's all part of my salary."

Fifth Avenue is lined with expensive shops. The lace and satin gowns in the windows make Lucille feel uneasy. The dress she is wearing looks cheap and is not the least bit stylish. "These stores look too expensive, Dan. Besides, I think I want to wear a dress rather than a gown."

"Then a bridal dress it is. Anything my daughter wants."

It sounds strange to hear Dan refer to her as his daughter. He takes her arm and they walk to the boutique named *Silk and Chiffon*.

"No, I won't feel comfortable shopping here, Dan. It looks too expensive," Lucille argues. But Dan assures her not to worry about money. "The owner will help you, and she's quite amusing."

Dan is right. Doris Lamar has charm and immediately makes Lucille feels at ease and also regal. The smooth silk dresses slide over her lithe body and although she loves all them all, she chooses a white embroidered lace dress with a matching jacket. Being practical, she

Under the Red Ribbon

figures she can remove the jacket for the reception and wear the dress with the neckline slightly draped off one shoulder.

Doris places her between the double mirrors so that she can admire the back of her dress. She places a knit cloche hat on her head. "My dear, notice the satin roses and the pearl so delicately sewn into the center of each. What can I say? Elegant, simply elegant."

When Dan sees the tulle veil attached to the cloche, he turns his head to blow his nose and wipe his eyes.

"You look exquisite," Doris says. "You have an uncanny resemblance to another woman who was in this afternoon. For a moment, I thought she had come back. She was here with a very close friend of mine. He has a patient chauffeur; I will say that. Sat out in that white limousine for over an hour waiting while they shopped."

A white limousine? Lucille only knows one person who has a white limousine and a very patient chauffeur. But this is New York City, and there are probably millions of people who fit that description.

"I'm surprised you're letting your fiancé see your wedding dress," Doris says, "or aren't you superstitious?"

"This is Dan, my dad."

"Did you say, Dad? Oh no, you could have fooled me."

Dan blushes. "We'll take that dress and everything that goes with it. Wrap it up."

"I'll have it delivered to your daughter's home," Doris says.

They walk down the street to the corner, where Dan hails a cab. When they get in, Lucille takes Dan's hand and squeezes it. "Dan, Doris Lamar said you looked young enough to be my fiancé. Little does she know I have two fathers I adore, and one man I love."

"And two men you love."

Lucille looks at Dan sheepishly.

"Lucille, I know you very well. I guess you can say since your conception. You should have seen your face when Doris mentioned the white limousine."

"Dan, pray for me."

"I don't have to. You're married to a fine man. This second ceremony just reinforces it."

ℬILL

The wedding takes place the last week of October, in a small synagogue on Orchard Street at four o'clock. It's raining and many of the guests huddle under their umbrellas as they arrive. This is the first time Bill has been in a synagogue and he arrives early to be sure he doesn't miss anything. Dan arranged for his hotel and even paid the tab; he wonders where he got the money to do all that. He looks around the place and finds it simple enough with wooden benches, beige carpeting, and no stained glass windows.

Yes, his little girl is getting married. Or, isn't she already married? Well, it doesn't matter; the first one really doesn't count without him being there. Who gets married without her father attending the wedding? Unless of course he's is dead, and Bill sure ain't that.

His daughter is breathtaking when he walks her down the aisle. Her blonde hair all wavy, her white dress as white as the white of her eyes. And she's a good girl. First thing she did when she came home from work was run over to the hotel to spend time with him, and the hotel is a good ten blocks away. They talked for hours about Harvest, and he was surprised at how much she recalled from when she was such a little girl. What she remembered most was the times he read the newspaper to her at the kitchen table. He doesn't know how she understood any of it. He started reading the paper to her when she was only three years old. But then, with her intelligence, there is little she doesn't remember, and there is little she wouldn't understand at any age.

Now standing under the small canopy, the "chupah," watching Lucille get married, he is struck by the strangeness of the ceremony. When the rabbi asks Charlie to repeat after him, "ha-rei aht mekudeshet li, be-tahba at zoh, k'dat Moshe v'Yisrael," Bill is perplexed. *What is he saying?* When it's Lucille's turn, he prays to the Lord that his daughter is not getting herself involved with some cult. But then the Hebrew words are translated into English. "With this ring, you are consecrated to me, as my wife according to the traditions of Moses and Israel." *Why didn't he say that in the first place,* Bill wonders. Then at the end of the ceremony, Charlie stomps on a perfectly good glass. He's thankful to the rabbi for explaining the significance of the glass-breaking ritual. "Even in joy there exists a shattering or a loss," the rabbi said. This religion finally makes sense to him; that is just what he was thinking. At this joyous moment, he feels the loss of his lovely wife, Evelyn.

The reception takes place at The Jazz Club, a spot famous for its entertainment and especially for Dan the Piano Man. Not only did Dan insist on hosting the reception in his place of work, he also insisted on paying for the entire wedding. Having a friend like Dan is a blessing, and the fact that his friend was able to come to New York and grab a job at a place like that makes Bill even prouder to know him.

The club dazzles Bill when he enters. He is welcomed into a mirrored room where a waiter offers him a goblet of wine. The walls are lined with tables bearing canopies filled with anchovies, caviar, smoked salmon, and miniature hot dogs wrapped in dough blankets. Bill is confused when another uniformed waiter asks him if he would like a knish.

"Do I want a what?" he asks, but then remembering his manners, he accepts and bites into a crusty dumpling with a peppery potato inside. He reaches for another. When he hears the announcement that dinner is being served, he is surprised. He thought he'd already had it.

At the reception, Bill takes a liking to Mr. Rosen. He may not be Charlie's real father, but he behaves real enough. Bill gets a kick out of his New York accent, especially when he says *umbellar* instead of *umbrella.*

"You know, a *shiksa* marrying a *Yid* is fine with us," Mr. Rosen says, and Bill is lost. His hearing is going, so he surmises that he just misheard. "But I guess Lucille isn't a *shiksa* anymore," Mr. Rosen continues.

Mr. Rosen said to call him Eli. So from then on, Bill did. He couldn't be happier with his newly formed relationship. He likes when Eli, who works in the garment district, compliments him on his style of living. "You are a lucky man," he says, "living out in the country with all that fresh air. It's stifling here in the summer." Bill mentions something about Charlie and Lucille's future children being baptized, and expects a huge smile from Eli but instead the man starts coughing.

When Eli raises an eyebrow, Bill assumes he is admiring his clothing. He straightens the lapel of his jacket and sits taller. Tom, the owner of the only men's shop in Harvest, convinced him to buy this suit and he's confident that he's elegantly dressed. Dan bought him the striped tie he's wearing, worried that Bill might still be wearing the one with the little red apples.

They both stroll around the room admiring the ice carvings, the ten-layer cake with thirty-six pink frosted flowers. "I wanted to pay for this shindig," Eli says, but someone close to Lucille said that was something he wanted to do. Was it you?"

"Why look a gift horse in the mouth," Bill replies, slapping him on the back.

Before dinner, the fathers take turns giving a toast. Bill simply says, "May our children long be committed to each other and to God." He wanted to say, 'committed to Jesus Christ,' but Lucille told him Jewish people don't worship Jesus Christ and to stay clear of any mention of his name. Eli merely picked up his wine glass and said, "Amen."

After dinner there's lots of dancing. "People don't have much to smile about, so many of the guests here are unemployed, so when they get the chance to dance, boy do they dance," Eli tells Bill. "Some out there think they look like Fred Astaire and Ginger Rodgers gliding along the dance floor. Doesn't seem to matter to them if he carries a potbelly or she wears a size sixteen dress. The Foxtrot is the rage, and they're doing it."

"Hey, I think I'll grab Rose and try that Foxtrot myself."

When Lucille and Charlie take to the floor, the guests back away. "Our kids come the closest to looking like Ginger Rodgers and Fred Astaire, don't you think Eli?"

"No question about it," Eli says.

Bill breaks in to dance with his daughter. If looks could talk, Bill's expression says what no words could ever say: he is one lucky man.

Later that evening, Bill is exhausted and ready for bed. He is so accustomed to going to bed early. Dan insists that he keep his suit on, "I'm taking you out on the town," he says.

"I've already been to Chinatown," answers Bill. "And thanks to you, Times Square, and the Statue of Liberty." Bill won't tell Dan that he has cramps in his legs and Band-Aids on his feet.

"Tonight will be different," says Dan. "Tonight is the night for eye-popping fun. We're going to The Stork Club."

When he hears the name "Stork Club," Bill assumes that it is like one of those agricultural clubs back home where farmers meet to iron out their problems. Dan directs the cab driver to 53rd Street and Fifth Avenue. Bill is in for a big surprise. When he and Dan arrive at the club, he sees the name of it written on the long canopy leading to the entrance. He wants to stop and look at the place, especially the two huge potted plants on either side of the entrance, but a gentleman in a dark suit and bowtie escorts them into a world Bill has never even imagined. Black tie waiters dash around filling and refilling drinks, and men and women linger around an oval bar drinking, laughing, and making conversation. And all those balloons on the ceiling! Dan nudges him and says, "I hear there are hundred dollars bills in each balloon."

"You're joking." He realizes that he's in for an education. After being greeted by the host, whose mannerisms are so cordial and polite, he credits the host's parents for raising him so well. When he overhears an attendant say, "Good evening, Miss Merman," he knows he has been transported into a different world. "That woman sings *I Got Rhythm* over the radio," he says to Dan.

His eyes linger on the hatcheck girls, the cigarette girls, and the young women standing around the bar, all too beautiful to be real. Wearing beaded dresses, they shimmer like jewels as their fingers grip tapered cigarette holders. Bill thinks, *before a man dies, especially a respectable man, he is entitled to one night with one of these ladies.* He closes his eyes for a few seconds and thinks, *nah, that's crazy.* When he opens his eyes again, he still can't keep his eyes off of the curves of their slender bodies, their long eyelashes, the penciled beauty marks beside their eyes, and the bright red lipstick outlining their lips. If this was the look Madeline had strived for, she'd really missed the mark. Rose would look downright foolish in this getup. Evelyn would have been able to carry it off, but he liked her the way she was.

A cigarette girl approaches Dan and Bill and asks if they'd like anything to drink. Bill contemplates trying to place an order for one of the girls. He looks down at her short skirt, and then up at her barely covered chest. Rose is well stacked too, but does she throw him into a spin like this woman? Hell no.

"Dan, is this your new way of life?" Bill asks. He can't believe what a long way his friend has come from the farm in Harvest.

"When I'm at the Jazz Club, I'm there to work. This is a special night for me, too." Dan waves to a couple coming through the door, and Bill has trouble breathing. *Who is he going to introduce me to now,* he wonders? *Clark Gable?*

The gentleman comes right up to their table. He's wearing a black suit, white shirt, and black tie with a white handkerchief tucked into his jacket pocket. And his face is so shockingly handsome. Bill barely looks at the woman he is with. He not only has a striking smile with that dimple in his left cheek and the bluest eyes Bill has ever seen, but he has something else about him that grabs Bill's attention. He's heard the word charisma. That's it. This man has charisma.

"Have any difficulty getting in, Dan?" the gentleman asks. "I phoned ahead and spoke to the boss himself. What brings you into town, Mr. Kramer?"

He knows my name? He's too shocked to answer.

When the gentleman moves away from the table, Bill asks, "Who is he? Dan, did you hear him? He knows my name."

Dan laughs, "He hasn't changed that much. He's the same kid you've always known, just grown up. That's Nick Martin Jr."

"You must be hopped up."

"No, I'm not. Nick and the owner of this place have business dealings. Not just anyone can get through that solid gold chain at the door. Nick told the boss that we're big shots in the financial world." He points to a man talking to Ethel Merman at the bar. "Look Bill. Walter

Winchell. He's not very tall in stature, but he is a person feared by some and adored by others."

"You're kidding. The radio commentator and news writer? I wondered what he looked like."

"That's him. Watch yourself now," Dan says, with a huge smile, "You might find yourself in one of his gossip columns."

They find a table and order steaks with all the trimmings and several drinks. Bill can't imagine paying for this dinner. The prices aren't even listed on the menu.

"I have a running charge account here," Dan says. "Nick made sure of that."

"Good thing, or I'd have to make a run for it."

Flash bulbs are going off all over the place. The movie stars pose for photographs, hoping to see their pictures in the morning papers. Other patrons want to have their pictures taken to show their friends, or to hang on their office walls. Bill feels an arm around his shoulder.

"Let them snap one of us together," he hears Nick say. "Our friends in Iowa will get a kick out of seeing our picture in the Celebrity Column."

⁓

It's raining when Bill's train arrives in Harvest. Same as when he left New York. It's Monday afternoon, and he had a week in New York City that is imprinted on his brain, just like a carving on wood. When it rained in New York, Dan told him to hail a cab. In Harvest there are no cabs; he'll have to walk home. He doesn't really mind the walk. He only has a small valise and the rain leaves the air smelling fresh. The leaves covering the ground are wet and slippery and he holds Rose's hand so she doesn't fall. She had a good time on the trip, too. Mrs. Rosen, who said to call her Edith, took her shopping. They went to a museum or two. And when he went to the Stork Club, Rose went to the movies with Charlie's cousin to see "Me and My Gal." She saw Spencer Tracy in the lead role, and she hasn't stopped talking about him since.

Everything here is in close proximity. That's what he likes about this town. The entire town of Harvest would fill only one tiny corner of New York City. But this is home, and he wouldn't trade it for the world.

On his way home, Bill ruminates about his trip. Dan hasn't changed, but the type of people he chums around with have. They seem to know so much about everything. But he and Dan will never grow apart. New York or Iowa, friends are friends. He'll do his part to see that they stay friends. He'll have to change, so Dan doesn't start thinking of him as a country bumpkin. New Yorkers speak and move faster than he does. He could try doing that. He still has some of Lucille's books at home. He could spend more time reading. He could also learn to speak better. Here and there, he drops the ends of some of his words. They don't do that in New York City. Maybe Jerry will already think he's snootier. After all, he's been to the Stork Club. But about Dan hobnobbing with all those big shots, and so chummy with Nick Martin Jr.! If he were being honest with himself, he'd admit he's worried.

⸺

Leaving the valise in the bedroom for Rose to unpack, Bill heads down to Jerry's. He has so much to tell him, especially about the women at the club. He'll brag a little, without sounding too smug, about Lucille's wedding: the ice carvings, the ten-layer cake with thirty-six pink frosted flowers. A father has the right to be proud of his daughter and the wonderful young man she married.

Bill bumps right into Nick Sr. as he's walking into Jerry's. Bill ignores him. Finding Jerry in his usual place behind the counter, he bends toward him, about to tell him about his fabulous time in the city. Nick Sr. interrupts him just as he is about to speak.

"Bill, I saw the morning papers. Great picture of you and my kid." He pats Bill on the back. "The article says some really nice things about you. They interviewed Nick and wanted to know who you were. You know how quick he can be with an answer. He said you were the father of the most beautiful woman in the world."

Bill retorts, "Did he say she's married?"

The attorney pats Bill on the back again and leaves.

"Leave him be, Bill," says Jerry. "That man's got his own troubles now. Tables have turned on him. Anita wants out, for good. Yup, Jim Olson. Some hanky-panky must have been going on while she was caring for his mother. Him being an attorney, you would think he'd be on to such things."

"A man only gets what he deserves. Well, good for her," Bill says. Then he begins to talk about his trip. He is especially enthusiastic about the Stork Club and how only people who know the owner can get in.

"Did you say Stork Club? The owner of that joint served time, you know. He got caught bootlegging."

"I should have known. After all, he is a friend of Nick's."

LUCILLE

After two years in New York, Lucille gives birth to a baby boy. She worked until a week before, until her boss, Mr. Abraham said, "Enough is enough, we don't want you giving birth in the store." So she had a week to fuss with the baby's bedroom, buying new curtains and hanging pictures on the wall. The Rosens bought the crib, and that saved them some money. With money tight, she watches every penny. Charlie takes jelly sandwiches for his lunch so he doesn't have to eat at the Columbia cafeteria. Actually, the two of them haven't spent much time together recently. After he's through with classes, he goes straight to the library.

Charlie was eager to start a family. He said, "I want to take fatherhood by storm and be the best."

This morning, they took turns feeding six-month-old Paco, because Charlie said that he wanted the child to feel the presence of both parents.

Bill wanted to name the baby Franklin, after Franklin D. Roosevelt. He wrote Lucille a letter listing good things President Roosevelt has done, like asking congress to pass the Agricultural Adjustment. "Imagine President Roosevelt doing that. Paying farmers *not* to grow products, raise pigs, and produce dairy products. Lucille, I tell ya, name that little boy Franklin."

Eli expressed his concern to Lucille about the baby's name when he learned that they wanted to name the boy Paco after their very best friend, Paco Whitefeather. "Lucille," he said, "you may not know this, but in the Jewish religion we name a baby after some relative or good friend who is no longer with us. Someone who is dead."

"I say this with a heavy heart," she explained, "but we're saving that name for our next baby."

Charlie is working day and night tutoring students in Chemistry and maintaining his part-time job at the corner drugstore. His full time job is attending classes. He still has two years to go before he gets his master's degree. When Lucille asks him if he's pushing himself too hard to make extra money, he snaps back, "Why shouldn't I provide my child with the things I didn't have? I'd work around the clock if I had to, to keep Paco and his mother and father living together in one happy home. And one day, Lucille, we're going to move from here. I have friends at the university who live on Riverside. Real nice apartments there, where there are no pushcarts on the sidewalks, no children playing right out on the street, and no young kids smoking on the corner. We won't have to worry about our kids meeting nice friends at school, either."

Being a full-time mother is a new experience for Lucille, and she never realized just how time consuming it is. Between diaper changing, feedings, and house cleaning, there is little time left for anything else. When Charlie asks her what books she's been reading, Lucille looks at him like he is delirious. Her life has become all about Paco.

She's discovered a new self emerging, one she doesn't like. Charlie notices the irritation in her voice and her impatience. "I'm beginning to think that all is not well in motherland," he says. "What is it, Lucille? What's bothering you?" She knows what's bothering her. The desire for more intellectual pursuits is gnawing at her. One night after giving Paco his bath in the kitchen sink, she runs from the room in tears. She collapses, sobbing, onto her bed. Charlie follows her into their bedroom and sits next to her. When Lucille sits up, she says, "I thought I'd be through college by now, but I haven't even started."

"You're getting a different kind of education, that's all."

"It gets so boring."

Charlie puts his arms around her. "I understand that. But it's just until our children are grown. Then you'll have plenty of time for college."

Lucille counts the years in her head. *At least eighteen.*

"Lucille, you are a wonderful mother. You know what that means to me. Having my son living with two loving parents is not something I take for granted. What I wouldn't have done for that."

She's heard the orphanage story too many times. She loses her temper. "Charlie," she screams. "Stop living in the past!"

He puts his hand on her shoulder. "Call it what you like. But my son is going to have the kind of home I didn't have. It was eleven years before the Rosens adopted me. And that's not the same as living with real parents."

Lucille wants to shout at him for being ungrateful. But she tries to calm herself and quietly says, "The Rosens are as good, even better, than real parents." Then she throws her head onto the pillow. "Charlie, I need more than this," she screams. "But you can't understand that. You are only thinking of what you want." She stands up now and points a finger at him. "Look," she says, "I lost my mother when I was sixteen years old. Do you know how much I loved her? How much I missed her and still miss her? Do you even want to know? I don't keep throwing that in your face like you do that orphanage story. I'm sick of listening to it."

He leaves the room and she hears the front door slam. Baby Paco is crying. Lucille sighs and goes to his room to feed him.

"I love you, little Paco," she says, cradling him in her arms. "I do. But I need more." Now that he has stopped crying, she starts. She kisses him on his cheek and rocks him in her arms. He looks up at her and coos. How is it that she wants to live two different lives at the same time? Is it possible for her to have both?

The doorbell rings. Charlie probably forgot his keys. He hurt her by walking out on her. Surely he's returned to apologize. When Lucille opens the door, she is shocked to see Sheila standing there, looking as beautiful as ever. Her black curls frame her face, and she wears a brown tweed belted suit that shows off her small waist. Time has not aged her. Lucille is caught by surprise in her housedress. She doesn't even know what her hair looks like. She tries to compose herself, breathing slowly like Whitefeather taught her to do. She doesn't want Sheila to notice how upset she is.

Sheila insists on seeing the baby. She cuddles him and kisses him, and then hands him back to Lucille. "I'm almost through law school," she says.

Lucille has just had her wounds ripped open. She pulls Sheila over to the couch to speak honestly. "I know I'm fortunate to have what I have, and I love being a mother, but I miss… Sheila, I want to go to college. My mind is turning to mush. I need mental stimulation." Lucille takes out her handkerchief and blows her nose, but the tears keep coming.

"You can have motherhood and still go to college at the same time. Why not?"

"Charlie won't hear of it."

"With your brains, how does he have the nerve to stop you? I'm sure you can win a merit scholarship, if you're short on money. You could probably take two courses to everybody else's one, and finish in no time."

"But who will take care of Paco while I'm away?"

"Your mother-in-law, silly." Sheila is quick. She maps out a plan. "Charlie's mother comes over in the morning after your husband leaves. Edith never had a little baby to care for since they adopted Charlie when he was eleven. She'll love it. And Charlie would never know."

"You are a genius, Sheila, but do you think she would do it? She won't want to deceive her son. No, that won't work."

"Never know unless you ask. What mother-in-law doesn't want to brag to her friends that she and her daughter-in-law are great friends? Edith might find being complicit with her daughter-in-law intriguing. I've heard of stranger things. Listen to this: I suppose I could have told you sooner, but it doesn't make any difference, really. It's over with. Your father messed things up between Nick Sr. and me. Bill told him he shouldn't be running around with a woman half his age, and after that, I think Nick started having second thoughts about us."

"Oh, I'm so sorry. I could talk to my father about it."

"What's done is done," Sheila says.

Although her high school records are at least ten years old, Lucille is able to recover them and mail them to the Office of Admissions at

Columbia University. She feels as if Sheila has given her the validation she needs to forge ahead. That day in the bookstore, she and Harry promised to attend each other's graduations. Now she can keep her end of the bargain.

Lucille doesn't tell Edith of the plan yet, but she does ask her to watch Paco while she attends to some business. That business is taking her college entrance exam. Edith is more than happy to help out. Afterwards, Lucille worries about the test results. Three weeks later, when she receives them in the mail and learns that she has been accepted. She's energized and ready to be an even better wife and mother. That evening she prepares a brisket, bathes her son, and tells him she's going to go to the university, just like daddy. Paco waves his hands in the air, and Lucille imagines that he's clapping. Content, she dries the baby and dresses him for bed. She combs her hair, applies a new coat of lipstick, and relaxes for a few minutes before Charlie gets home.

"What are we celebrating?" Charlie asks when he sees her. "And I smell something delicious in the oven." He sits down at the table, ready to eat. "What have you done to yourself? You look absolutely radiant."

"I'll tell you. Let's eat."

"Tell me."

"I'm going back to school," she says, and then wipes her mouth with a napkin.

Charlie puts down his fork. "When did you arrange all that? You have a fine mind, sure, but school can wait until Paco is grown."

Lucille's face flushes with anger. "I spoke to your mother. She said she would be thrilled to watch her grandson while I attend classes."

"I want *you* to watch our son."

"I'll schedule my classes in the morning. I'll be home all afternoon."

"You know that's not how it works. There will be homework, term papers, and lots of reading. It will take up more than your mornings."

She clears the table and places the dishes in the sink, watching the water slip down the drain.

Lucille discards her plans. Too much of a hassle. She continues on with her daily chores and on Paco's first birthday, Lucille has a small party for him. She plans the party for a Saturday afternoon so Charlie can be home, and the Rosens and Dan will be available.

Eli and Edith arrive first with a rocking horse for their grandson. Dan brings a toy piano. Charlie bought him blocks, a teddy bear, a sailboat for his bath, a red sweater, and a chemistry set.

"A chemistry set?" Lucille asks, with a puzzled look on her face, when Charlie lifts the box out of the bag. "Paco is one year old."

"I know, honey. I'm putting it away for when he's six or seven. We'll do the experiments together."

Lucille shakes her head.

Eli is waving a rattle in Paco's face and Edith joins in with another rattle when the doorbell rings. Lucille goes to answer it. She finds a box stamped "fragile" on her doorstep. The handwriting makes her heart beat faster. She takes the box to her room and opens it. Under the tissue paper she finds a miniature replica of Nick's Model T. The message on the card gives her good reason to hide the gift behind her clothes in the closet. It says, "Happy Birthday, Paco. You are a lucky little boy. She's your Mom, but she's my Fairy Princess."

Lucille remains quiet throughout the remainder of the celebration. She cuts and serves the birthday cake to her guests, but when they start eating, she reaches for a dry cracker. Charlie doesn't know yet, but soon Paco will have a sister or brother.

Charlie couldn't be happier to hear the news. He has enough love to go around for both children.

On September 7, 1936, Kimimela Rosen is born. Just as she and Charlie agreed, they named the baby after Whitefeather's sister.

But for Lucille, the nagging feeling returns. Why can't she have her children and return to school? But she won't start that conversation again. It takes too much out of her. The evenings are all the same. She puts the children to bed and she and Charlie sit on the sofa. She breathes a sigh of relief to have some time to herself. He wants to hear every detail of their children's day. Sometimes he fills her in on his work, and then she spends what is left of the evening reading the newspaper. Her favorite column is the one written by Eleanor Roosevelt entitled, "My Day." Lucille respects this intelligent woman who is involved with politics and champions Native American rights. When Lucille reads about President Roosevelt appointing Francis Perkins Secretary of Labor and making her the first woman to hold a Cabinet Post, she realizes that she is not the one who is stuck in the past: Charlie is. Women everywhere are stepping out in the world: into the arts, into the workforce. Charlie is behind the times. When Pauline Powers tried to enlighten him during their visit to Harvest, he walked away in a huff. "That woman thinks she's holding a rally," he'd told Lucille. "I merely said you were going to make a fine wife and mother one day, and she lectured me on a woman's role in society."

Lucille makes another attempt to persuade Charlie that going back to school would eventually enable her to get a good job so that he wouldn't have to work so hard to get food on the table, but he remains steadfast. He wants his children's mother at home.

Finally, Lucille decides *she'll* determine the direction of her life. She's been thinking of her teacher a lot more lately. This morning as she was washing the dishes, she pictured Miss Powers standing on street corners in Harvest or in the library or in Jerry's General Store, espousing the women's creed: "We can do what men can do and more." She's heard her say that many times. While she stands up for women, Lucille realizes she never had the courage to stand up for herself. She approaches her mother-in-law.

"When do I start my job as a nanny?" Mrs. Rosen asks. "If my son can't come to his senses, then we women will do what we must do. Lucille, you're like the daughter I never had."

She feels lucky to have Edith in her life. If she can't have Evelyn, Edith is the next best thing.

Lucille schedules her classes for the morning and she's home at one every day. On the days she spends in the library, she keeps her eye on the clock, making sure to beat Charlie home. Mrs. Rosen is the happiest Lucille has ever seen her; like Sheila said, she never had the chance to care for a baby, and now she has two.

Lucille and Charlie go to bed at ten, but as soon as Lucille hears him start to snore she tiptoes into the kitchen and spreads her books on the table. In the dim, light she attacks her work. She has her children, her studies, and Charlie all under control; the household is running smoothly.

At the start of their marriage, Lucille and Charlie went out almost every Saturday night. It was their date time. Since the children were born, not so much. Persuading him to go to the movies this Saturday night, he reluctantly concedes and calls his mother to babysit. They enjoy the film, "Anything Goes" starring Ethel Merman, and talk about it all the way home. Going to bed, the magic of romance overcomes them. Charlie expresses his love for her with such sincerity when he says, "Lucille, you've done what no other woman could do. You have taken my sadness away." Temporarily forgetting his shortcoming that has divided them, and so touched by his need for her, she responds with a deep and vast surge of emotion, surrendering to him with her body, mind, and her own yearnings. "Don't let anything destroy what we have together," she says.

As soon as she's sure Charlie is asleep, Lucille drags her books from her closet and piles them on the kitchen table. She looks up at the clock, and notices that it's past midnight. She plans to continue on for at least two more hours.

Engaged in her work, she feels breath tickling her neck. Startled, she jumps up from her chair. Charlie stands in front of her, staring at her. He says nothing. He turns, walks back into the bedroom, and slams the door. The next morning, he showers and leaves for the university before the children and Lucille are out of bed.

Charlie doesn't come home for dinner and doesn't call. After the children are tucked in for the night, Lucille pours over her books again. It's long past midnight by the time she gets into the empty bed. She has no idea when Charlie comes home. When she wakes up in the morning, he's gone.

Weeks pass and neither Charlie nor Lucille attempt to make any meaningful conversation. They behave like strangers in their home. Edith and Eli invite them to the house for a Shabbat dinner, a Friday night ritual, and while she and Edith clean the dishes off the dining room table, Edith asks her if she and Charlie are having problems. Lucille just shakes her head. Edith notes that neither one of them made an effort to speak to each other all through dinner, and that Charlie seems to have his mind elsewhere.

One morning, after a long night of studying, Lucille stops for a cup of coffee at the University cafeteria. Glancing around the room for a place to sit, she sees Charlie and a young dark-haired woman sitting at a small round table in the corner of the room.

Lucille sits down at a table that offers her a clear view of her husband. Charlie nods every time the woman speaks. The woman pushes her long black hair off her shoulders and leans in when he speaks. When he replies, the woman stares into his eyes and mimics his every gesture. Their eye contact is so strong, Lucille thinks that the ceiling could cave in and they'd still be looking at each other like that. When their conversation comes to an end and they stand up to leave, Lucille notices the woman's long, lithe body. She moves with the grace of a ballerina. Her legs are never ending. Lucille continues to stare at the woman. Jealousy and anger arise simultaneously within her. Her eyes fill with tears. Charlie helps the woman on with her coat. *So this is the way he's providing a happy home for his children, giving them the security he never had*, Lucille thinks. Now she knows what Edith meant when she said at the Friday night dinner, that Charlie seems to have his mind elsewhere."

Lucille ducks out of the cafeteria before Charlie can spot her. She wanders out onto campus, evaluating the quandary in which she now finds herself. If she and Charlie call it quits, she will need enough money to live on her own. She can tutor or give piano lessons, but who is she fooling? Taking care of the kids, studying, and working will deplete her energy, and she won't be able to do anything well. And she can't expect Edith to continue to help with the children indefinitely. After all, she has her own life to live. She hopes that this is all a bad dream.

Walking home from the grocery store after class, Lucille turns her head and sees Charlie and the same woman seated near the window at a neighborhood coffee shop. This is the second time she catches them together in less than a week. "That takes a lot of gall on his part to choose a restaurant so close to home," she mutters to herself. And then sadness overcomes her. The reality is setting in. Her marriage is about to fall apart. She also feels deceived, like the time she found her mother's necklace, inscribed in baroque lettering with the words, "Promise me, Love Dan," and she thought that Dan and her mother were having an affair. That same sick feeling seeps back into her. With so many emotions spinning within her, she feels dizzy. But when the time is right, she will confront him.

When Lucille arrives home, she and her mother-in-law put away the groceries and talk. They've had many talks since Lucille started school and Edith started watching Paco and Kimimela. After coming home from school, they'd sit around the kitchen table, sip a cup of tea, and talk. Lucille finds it relaxing, and now they are close friends. Not having her own mother to talk to, she feels lucky to have Edith.

During these times, Edith tells her how she'd always wished she had a daughter like Lucille. She opens up to her about her life, revealing how she met Eli on a blind date. She says that she didn't expect to like him at first, but that changed when she realized how much he cared about her. "To this day, he puts my wishes above his own. He says it's easier that way." Edith also tells her about her two miscarriages and her sadness about not being able to give birth to a child.

Today, it is Lucille's turn to open up. Edith shows no surprise, but lots of concern, when Lucille tells her that Charlie is involved with another woman.

"Did the woman have long black hair?" she asks. "That's his weakness, you know."

"Come to think of it, she did. Why do you ask?"

Edith bites her lips and appears to have difficulty speaking. She starts and stops herself twice before she finds the right words. "After we adopted him, Charlie had a hard time adapting to parents who were attentive. He was accustomed to people treating him with indifference. It took him a long time to trust us. When he started dating, he had even more problems. He always chose to go out with women with long black hair, and his relationships always ended abruptly. The aftermath was always a long-lasting, somber mood. His last relationship, with someone called Tara, had terrible repercussions. When I met you, I was surprised and happy to see your blonde hair. I thought maybe he was making progress."

Tara. After all these years, Lucille didn't think she'd still be talking about her.

"Be easy on him, Lucille. He's been through so much. He's so likeable in spite of it."

"Well, he hasn't been too likeable lately. I'll do my best to keep our marriage together, but not if he's seeing another woman, and not if he insists on deciding how I should live my life."

At 6:30 that evening, Charlie arrives home. His brow is furrowed and although he presents Paco with a new ball and Kimimela with a doll, he does not look happy. He looks over at Lucille, nods, and then washes up for dinner.

Lucille removes the roast from the oven, slices it, and puts the platter on the table. She has little appetite and Charlie, who is usually a hearty eater, picks at his food. They eat in silence. She's relieved when the meal is over and jumps up to wash the dishes. Charlie follows her to the sink. He clears his throat and says, "Lucille, I need to have a talk with you."

Lucille doesn't even know where to find a divorce lawyer. She guesses she'll know soon.

"Lucille, why did I have to find out that you were going to college by sneaking up on you in the middle of the night? You know what that reminded me of?"

She looks at him. How is she supposed to know what that reminded him of? The question is ridiculous.

"Do you?" he asks again.

"Charlie, don't play games. No, I don't. "

He picks up a dish and starts drying it. "You told me that your mother hid her paintings under the couch so your father wouldn't find them."

"Of course she did that. She had her reasons, and they were different from mine. My father wouldn't deny her anything. She did as she pleased. She hid those paintings because she didn't want him to find out that..." *Oh, he would never understand.* "Forget it."

After a brief silence, Charlie says, "I've become very friendly with a woman."

"And?"

"She's very smart, very competent."

"Oh, so it's okay for this woman to be smart, but your wife is to stay at home and wait eighteen years before getting herself educated?"

Drying her hands, she pulls on her coat and storms out of the house. She walks sixteen blocks to the Jazz Club.

Dan is on stage, playing the piano alongside the drummer and the Sax player. When Dan sees Lucille enter the club, he beckons a member of the trio to take over for him. He meets her on the dance floor and offers her a drink. She refuses. "Charlie is seeing another woman," she says.

"Calm down, I'd bet my last penny that Charlie would never do that. But then again, one never knows. What makes you say that?"

"I saw them sitting so lovey-dovey at the Columbia cafeteria and then at a restaurant right in our neighborhood. They were so engrossed with each other's conversation, they couldn't get their eyes off each other."

"Confront him. See what happens. Let me call you a cab. You shouldn't be walking alone at night. Ask him right out. Ask him tonight."

The ride home is fast-- too fast. She doesn't want to see Charlie tonight or ever. How could he do this?

The three flight climb up to the apartment is especially tiring tonight and when she opens the door, she plans to go directly to her room. She wishes Charlie wouldn't be there, but of course he'd never leave the children alone. She turns the knob of the front door and it opens much too easily. Charlie is opening it from the inside. He stands at the door with a worried look on his face.

"Where did you run off to? I was going to follow you out, but I couldn't leave the kids."

"Did you think I'd stick around and listen to you tell me about this other woman you're seeing?"

"Other woman I'm seeing? Are you crazy? The woman I was telling you about is a psychologist. She works at the school."

"A psychologist?"

"I'm taking psychology as an elective and she's my instructor. Dr Goldberg is her name. Not a medical doctor, a PhD. She's great with all of her students. Easy to talk to. One day after class, I told her I had some problems and asked if she could possibly help me. She said as long as the problems were not too deep she might be able to help me out. So we met a few times. And she told me that among other things, I was letting my childhood influence the way I raised my own children, and I was carrying it to an extreme. Honey, I behaved like an ass."

"I think you behaved like an ass, too."

He laughs and puts his arms around her. "Do you still love me?"

"I married you twice, didn't I?"

But the days forward are difficult ones. When Lucille and Charlie try to be on their best behavior, they often end up showing their least favorable characteristics.

When Charlie offers to help her with her term papers, she finds that condescending. When she tells him not to work so hard, he thinks she doesn't understand how much time his work requires.

Days turn into months and their relationship shows little improvement. Lucille tells Charlie that she's going to Harry's graduation and asks him to stay home with the children. "Either we both go, or neither of us goes. I don't care if you want to be away from me for the evening," he snaps. "The children must see us as a team."

Lucille realizes that Charlie's problems with parenting won't disappear anytime soon. When she confronts him with the prospect of a separation, he becomes frantic. He vows to do everything in his power to be a better husband.

Lucille recognizes the desperation in Charlie's efforts to save their marriage. He enters therapy at a family counseling service, a suggestion offered by Dr. Goldberg, who told him that he needed deeper therapy than she was prepared to give him. Twice a week he walks ten blocks to the Counseling Center. Lucille wants to see results quickly, but they are slow to come. After six or seven months, she's about to give up. But one evening she senses something different in her husband's demeanor. There is a gleam in his eyes, and he is beaming. In the last year, she's rarely seen him smile.

"The head of the Literature Department, Dr. Beamer, stopped me in the hall today," Charlie tells Lucille over dinner. "He told me that you were a breath of fresh air and we needed more people like you at Columbia. He is hoping you join the staff when you graduate. Honey, I'm proud of you. I am. Good thing you didn't listen to me."

Charlie agrees to have the sixteen-year-old girl in the apartment building babysit while they take walks together after dinner. It gives them a chance to talk about their life together. Brought up so differently, there are bound to be disagreements. Tonight on their walk they hold hands and stop now and then to kiss, and Lucille feels that her life is full of promise. When Lucille sees two familiar faces walking toward them, she looks at Charlie in amazement. "Charlie, I think talking about Riverview brought back some people from our past. Could that possibly be Hanson and Ellie walking toward us?"

"Sure looks like them. They sure haven't changed much."

"Ellie! Hanson!" Lucille calls out, louder than she should. The people around them turn their heads. When she gets the attention of the couple, she asks, "What are you doing here?"

Ellie and Hanson are just as surprised and excited to see them. The women embrace and when they have calmed themselves, the four of them move off the sidewalk closer to the buildings to let the people pass. They huddle in a small circle as Ellie tells Charlie and Lucille that they live in the city now, and Hanson has a great job as a journalist for the New York Times. "Remember, way back when, when I told you Hanson was a great writer?"

"I remember," Lucille says. "I was a kid then, fascinated with your story."

"Did you hear?" Ellie adds. "The matrons at the school left as a group shortly after you moved. Before they did, they trashed Mr. Baran's office."

"Wish I were there to help them," Charlie says.

"And Charlie, it should give you some satisfaction to know that Tara spent some time in jail. Her rich boyfriend dumped her, and after that she got into all sorts of trouble with drugs. I think that boyfriend of hers got her into that mess, and then he ran off and got married to someone else."

Charlie's face flushes at the mention of Tara's name.

"Who did he marry? I mean. . . Is that for sure?" Lucille asks.

"I don't know anything more about him, Ellie says. "It doesn't matter."

"Of course not, just asking."

ℒUCILLE

The year is 1945. The Second World War ends, the Nuremberg trials begin, and actor Steve Martin is born. President Franklin D. Roosevelt dies of a cerebral hemorrhage and Eli and Edith Rosen die in an automobile accident on the New Jersey turnpike.

The day is June 26, exactly nineteen years after Lucille graduated from high school, and Lucille is ready to give another valedictorian speech.

Looking out at the packed auditorium, she spots Bill and Rose. Bill's expression is one of deep respect for his daughter. She looks at the empty seat next to him and knows who that seat is reserved for. Miss Powers wouldn't miss the occasion, and she's there with an expression of admiration. Lucille represents another win for women. Dan is proud of her, too.

To celebrate the occasion, Dan arranges a private party at a new club that just opened on the Upper West Side. He booked the jazz singer, Cab Calloway, to entertain. Lucille wonders how he managed it. Before they leave for the party, Charlie slips a diamond bracelet around her wrist, and her smile turns into a howl of joy. The diamonds are small, but she couldn't be happier even if they were ten times as large.

When Lucille arrives at the club with Charlie, she spots Harry with his wife, Jacqueline, at his side. Harry kisses her on the cheek. "Bad enough losing out to you as valedictorian, but losing *you* was far worse."

Jacqueline, an attractive violinist with the New York Philharmonic, amuses Lucille with her good sense of humor. "He's speaking the truth. I told him that I'm coming along to see who this Lucille is. I can't tell you how often he speaks of you. Charlie, we better not let them spend too much time together. But honestly Lucille, my husband thinks the world of you."

Lucille wants to change the subject. She jokes, "So you are now Dr. Harry. How can I not know that, with that instrument around your neck?"

Harry looks down at his chest and laughs, "Lucille, I do miss you."

Lucille feels a tap on her arm. She turns to find Sheila walking arm-in-arm with Gil.

"Be the first to congratulate us," Sheila says. "We ran off and got married over the weekend!"

Lucille's head is spinning with exhilaration.

"Harvest has turned out quite a few professionals," Gil says. "Let's see, you're going to be a professor. Sheila is an attorney. Harry's a doctor, and although I'm not a professional, I have two fabric factories in Chicago. Not bad for a man who owned a small dry goods store on Main Street. Oh, and Nick…"

"How is he?" Lucille asks.

"You might ask him yourself. He owns this club and you never know when he might drop in. He owns a slew of these places."

Drop in? Nick? Lucille gulps. Why did her heart skip a few beats when Gil mentioned his name? "Growing up in a small town has kept us close," she says. "If it weren't for Harry, I don't think I would have strived so hard."

"And if it weren't for Nick, I wouldn't be where I am today," Harry says.

"Strange to hear you say that," says Lucille.

"I know. But there is so much people don't know about him."

Before Harry can explain his meaning, Lucille spots Nick at the bar, handing Dan an envelope. She excuses herself and runs to the ladies room. "Dear God, let me not faint," she says out loud. Fortunately, no one is in the ladies room to hear her. When she returns to the party, her friends are standing right where she left them, chatting to one another. Dan is standing by himself. Gil's eyes are on the buffet table, where huge trays of roast beef, creamed potatoes, asparagus, and greens are waiting. "One thing bad times taught me," he says to Lucille. "Eat when you see food."

Bill, listening to the conversation agrees.

"Especially when you're not paying for it," Lucille says jokingly.

Charlie stands at Lucille's side, his arm around her shoulder. He pulls her closer and drags her away from the crowd. He kisses her in the dim, narrow hallway leading to the lounge. A song is dedicated to her from the stage: "Is You Is, or Is You Ain't My Baby." Charlie laughs. Lucille doesn't. She knows of only one person who would dedicate that song to her. From the large window facing the street, she sees a white limousine drive away.

When Lucille and Charlie arrive home, a small white box tied with a bow is resting on their doorstep. "Another gift, honey. Open it up, see who it's from," says Charlie.

"I'll open it later after I get out of these clothes." Lucille takes the box from Charlie and heads for the bedroom. She places the box on the night table. She twirls around in front of the mirror for one last look at her beautiful lavender dress. She'd like to stay in it longer. Dan insisted on buying it for her at *Silk and Chiffon*. She feels a bit ashamed when she wonders if Nick saw her, and liked what he saw.

Changing into her lounging pajamas, a gift from the children, she lies down on the bed and reaches for the box. Peeking under the lid, she sees a gold bracelet with three large diamonds across the top. She reads the card: "I saw you from across the room. You are more beautiful than I remember. Best wishes, my Fairy Princess. Nick." Trying on the bracelet, she hears Charlie's footsteps in the room.

"What was in the box?" he asks, entering the room.

She lifts her hand.

"Wow, what a gift! Makes my bracelet look like nothing. Must be from Harry and his wife. Who else but a doctor could afford something like that?"

Lucille sends her resume to N.Y.U and Columbia applying for jobs, but she has her heart set on working at Columbia. On a Saturday afternoon, the house is quiet with the children and Charlie out riding their bikes. She calls Ellie to come over. They sit around her kitchen table nibbling on cookies and drinking tea and reminiscing about old times and how lucky they are to have met up with each other some years back. Then Lucille tells her what she'd like to do in the interim: set up a free tutorial service for children of non-English speaking parents living in poor New York City neighborhoods. With her special love for Indian children, she hopes to attract them in droves. Ellie thinks it's a great idea and says she knows of a small store going out of business that would serve as a wonderful classroom. "The hard part is, alerting the kids to where we are and getting them to turn out," she says.

Ellie designs the fliers, and the two women walk the streets of Manhattan neighborhoods, leaving their advertisements in drugstores, grocery stores, and on doorsteps of apartments.

On the first day of class, only two Indian students attend. Lucille and Ellie keep their spirits up by reminding each other that those two children will tell others to come. But the next week proves equally disappointing; those two students don't show up and the women are left with an empty classroom. Charlie offers a suggestion. "Go through the proper channels: the schools," he says. "Speak to the principals. With your background, they will be delighted to have your assistance. They will notify parents about your service and before long, you'll have more kids than you'll know what to do with."

Charlie's idea works. In the third week, the two boys who showed up the first week show up again, and this time they bring their friends. Whether it is the hot chocolate and cookies that lured them or the principal's message Lucille isn't sure, but each week the group grows larger. The children have heartwarming stories to tell, funny stories and scary stories. Lucille enjoys them all, but tells them that they need to learn basic writing skills so that other people can enjoy them, too. With a combination of patience, perseverance, and diligence on all their parts, the enchanting stories become legible and coherent.

Their project is turning out to be a success, but one Friday afternoon when Lucille and Ellie arrive at the school, they find their classroom in turmoil. The desks and wastebaskets are tipped over and their books are scattered on the floor. The words on the blackboard are glaring: "Injuns go back to the reservation."

"What on earth is going on here?" Ellie asks. She and Lucille hurry to clean up the mess before the kids show up.

The following week, the damage is more severe. They find the children's work crumpled and lumped in a heap. The desks are broken beyond repair. When they hear a knock on the door, they look at each other, fearing the worst.

"Private Security," says the voice behind the door, and Lucille ventures to open it. A man in uniform stands behind it. "Rest assured," he says, "there will be no gangs tampering with this place anymore."

"Private security?" asks Ellie, aghast. "Who decided on that? And who's footing the bill?"

Classes continue, and they open another tutorial center closer to where most of the children live. Lucille works single-handedly at the original school, while Ellie works in the new one with the help of Hanson. When Columbia University offers Lucille a teaching job in the Literature Department, she turns the tutorial work over to her dear friends.

To celebrate Lucille's new job, she and Charlie attend the New York Philharmonics Symphony where Harry's wife, Jacqueline, is a member of the orchestra. After the show, she introduces Lucille and Charlie to the performers backstage. Jacqueline tells the conductor that Lucille is a talented pianist, and he insists she play a piece for him. Blushing, she does so, and is invited to meet with him again and audition as a guest performer.

Lucille and Charlie walk home from the performance hall content with their lives. She talks about their upcoming anniversary, and Charlie says, "Let's have a candlelight dinner at home. I will be the chef and the dishwasher. You just have to bring your beautiful self."

Lucille and Charlie spend their anniversary at home. After dinner, they cuddle on the couch under the yellow and turquoise blanket from Whitefeather. Frank Sinatra is crooning on the radio, "Saturday Night is the Loneliest Night of the Week." They both laugh.

"Not for us," Lucille says.

"That's for sure, honey," he answers. Charlie places the book he's reading on the end table and moves closer to Lucille. She sighs, thinking of their wedding on the reservation, the struggles they endured, the good times, and the unusual times. They survived it all, together, and with love and respect for each other.

Lucille looks at her husband. His red hair is now speckled with brown. The pupils of his eyes that once reminded her of broken shale have taken on a smoother edge. With her encouragement, he has switched to wearing tortoise frame glasses. His freckles have faded and she realizes that in his maturity, he has become quite handsome. "I love you, Charlie. You make me so happy. It took all this time to realize what love is all about. You know what Nadie once told me? She said she loves Elu more every day. That's the way I feel about you."

"Not me. I loved you with all my heart yesterday and I love you with all my heart today, so my love has remained the same."

They both have a good laugh at that. Lucille tells Charlie that she's planning on meeting with Mr. Taylor, the father of young Paco's best friend. Charlie's face becomes serious as she explains. "Another act of anti-Semitism. I have to hand it to his son, Joel. He really stood up to those bullies. Who knows what would have happened to Paco if he wasn't there."

Paco had told them that coming out of Hebrew school on Canal Street one late afternoon, he was ridiculed by some bullies for wearing a yarmulke. One of them walked up to him and tapped him on the head. "Hey, what's that round saucer on your head? You forgot the cup," he'd said. Paco was just going to keep on walking, but another boy pushed him. "You're a bad dream," Paco yelled back. "Guess my dream catcher didn't work very well last night."

That got the bullies real mad and they grabbed him and wedged his leg between the broken bars of a sewer drain. Joel Taylor, a tall, muscular boy for his age and Paco's best friend, saw the whole thing as he was walking out of school and he pounded the bullies with his fists. Lucille wants to meet with Mr. Taylor and tell him of his son's gallantry.

Joel's father owns a men's clothing store on Madison. The name somehow rings a bell. She thinks for a minute and then it comes to her.

She remembers now, *Taylor and Taylor*. That's where Dan does his shopping. He even gave her the proprietor's card. *That is quite a coincidence,* she thinks. While she's there, she'll start looking for a suit for Paco and maybe a shirt for Charlie. Paco's Bar Mitzvah is coming up soon. Hard to believe he's turning thirteen.

On a Saturday morning after Paco, Kimimela and Charlie leave for Yankee stadium, Lucille turns on the radio and hums along to the music. She straightens up the kitchen, and then attempts to arrange the clutter in Charlie's home office. She knows better than to throw away any papers on his desk; in the disarray, he has a knack for finding just what he's looking for. She picks up the coke bottles off of the floor and straightens his stack of magazines.

The monthly magazine, *The Columbia Chronicle,* is turned to the page entitled "Upcoming Events." She sees an asterisk near one of the lectures, and assumes that Charlie wants to attend. She searches for the keynote speaker. It's Nick Martin Jr. PhD. The topic is *Aeronautics in Today's World*. She laughs. A coincidence, but all the same, amusing. The Nick Martin Jr. she remembers is probably still riding around in his chauffeur driven limousine, having himself a good ol' time.

Taking a leisurely shower, she dresses with care, wanting to make a good impression when she meets Joel's father. She wears her new blue suit and matching cloche.

A gold plaque hangs above the door of the men's clothing store with the name *Taylor and Taylor* engraved in black letters. Lucille is fascinated with the window display. The expensive shirts and ties are scattered with deliberate casualness, and the cufflinks shine like beacons of light in their small, open coffers.

She enters the store with slight trepidation, but she's met with a warm smile, a cheerful hello, and a firm handshake.

"Special occasion?" Mr. Taylor's voice is melodic.

When she introduces herself, he gives her a big grin. "Oh, Paco's mother. What a fine boy you have. And Joel tells me you are a professor at Columbia. I am impressed. And if you are going to tell me how courageous my son is, I've heard about that from the cops. He did take a chance pounding those boys. I'm not a fan of violence, but I think he was just defending his friend. My son also has an ulterior motive, though," he says, laughing. "Your Paco tutors him in Hebrew. Joel is having a heck of a time with it. With your son, it seems to come naturally. I understand they will be Bar Mitzvah boys during the same month. I think we'll both sleep easier if my wife starts picking the boys up after Hebrew school. Less to worry about. Now, anything I can help you with? A shirt? A tie? A suit?"

He already has helped her. One less thing to worry about. "My husband owns a navy blue suit, and he wears it with the same shirt and tie to every occasion. Maybe we—"

"I understand." Mr. Taylor reaches for a white silk shirt on a shelf surrounded by glass, and then selects a navy tie with sky-blue stripes to go with it. He gathers several small boxes holding cufflinks, and chooses one pair. "Here. These will give his suit the punch it needs."

Lucille knows that small touches can make an entire outfit, but she also knows that they come with a price tag.

Mr. Taylor looks at her face, and then proceeds to arrange the items on the glass counter top. "You're in luck. We're having a sale on these shirts and ties today. And the cufflinks have been marked down."

Lucille smiles and thanks him. She didn't see any sign announcing a sale. She likes Mr. Taylor for his competence and his generosity. She likes his suggestion that his wife walk the boys home from Hebrew school. While wrapping the items, he makes light conversation about the aeronautics convention in town, but she's concentrating on the artistic knack he has for wrapping the package.

"I know the gentleman who is going to be the keynote speaker at Columbia," he says. "Last name is Martin. He was a young fella when I first met him. Maybe twenty-three or four. Fast kind of guy and smart. Real smart. Not surprised he'd end up in aviation. Shops here every time he comes to New York. I even have things sent out to him. He's living in San Diego now."

Lucille asks Mr. Taylor to remove the price tags before he places her purchases in the gold and black striped box. The man gives an understanding laugh. "Women always hide the price tags from their husbands. But like I was saying about that keynote speaker, anything to do with engines, motors, and speed, wow, you can't stop him from expounding on it. Sometimes he'll get an idea just as I'm showing him a new suit, and wham, he starts jotting notes. How about you and your husband joining us for the convention? Our boys would like us to be friends."

Before she leaves, she looks at the long wall of celebrity portraits and one portrait grabs her attention. Thinking her mind is playing tricks on her, she simply shrugs and is on her way.

Shopping at *Taylor and Taylor* turned out to be a very pleasant experience. Lucille found Mr. Taylor charming, but it is more than that that has her hopping into a cab and returning the next day. She can't get that one portrait on that wall of celebrity portraits out of her mind. She wants to go back and take a closer look.

Busy with a customer, Richard Taylor doesn't notice her when she walks into the store. She mulls around looking at the sweaters in an array of colors and picks up a yellow one. The first time she met Charlie, he was wearing a yellow sweater. She studies the celebrity photographs on the wall. She recognizes most of them: Rudolph Valentino, Fred Astaire, William Powell, Clark Gable, George Burns, and Eddie Cantor. And then she sees Nick Martin Jr. smiling; he shows his left dimple.

Mr. Taylor walks up behind her. "That's the gentleman I spoke to you about," he says, pointing to the photograph.

"I know this man. He grew up in Harvest, Iowa. That's where I'm from."

Mr. Taylor shakes his head. "Not this fella. He's no country boy. Not that I'm knocking Iowa, but you know what I mean." He leans against the wall and dangles his hands in his pockets. "I'll never forget the day I met him. It was some years back. A young couple walked through the entrance, and I thought, *two movie stars*. As you can see, many of my clients are celebrities. Anyway, this fella in his light gray fedora, dark gray overcoat, and checkered pants had real style. And the woman appeared very young, but impeccably dressed. Straight out of *Silk and Chiffon*.

"He chose a dozen suits and shirts in a hurry. After that, he sent his girlfriend here to order his clothes. What can I say? We spent time together. When Nick found out, he was happy for us. He said he could only love one woman, and he hadn't seen her for way too long." Mr. Taylor chuckles. "Lucky for me, I ended up marrying her. Anyway, maybe we can meet at the convention and I'll introduce you to my wife and Nick Martin. Do you want that sweater you're holding?"

Lucille had forgotten she was holding anything. "I need some time to think about it."

"Hope to see you and your husband soon," he says, as she heads toward the door.

When Lucille tells Charlie about Mr. Taylor's suggestion that they meet at the convention, Charlie tells her that he'll be out of town working on his research project that weekend. "Did you get the keynote speaker's name?" he asks. "How can this man have the same name as the jerk we know?"

"Wouldn't be surprised if there are a lot of Lucille and Charlie Rosens out there," she says. "It would be fun to meet them." They're still talking about that when they get into bed, but the name Nick Martin Jr. and the image of that dimple in his left cheek are stuck in her head long after Charlie falls asleep.

NICK

Nick leaves Minnesota for New York City in the fall of 1932 and takes exotic Tara with him. Although the Great Depression hit people hard, The National Prohibition Act inadvertently hands him a lucrative business. With people clamoring to have the Act repealed, he moves quickly. Unsatisfied with being just a bootlegger, he aspires to a higher position. His bosses recognize him as a real mover and he is promoted to King Pin of the New York City territory. And they recognize that he has that certain something that clicks with people. He can kiss their cheeks, but still be tough.

Nick is a detail man, and oversees what others consider minutia. He checks the bars and backrooms of night clubs, meets with other bootleggers, and meticulously examines the crates of liquor imported from Canada for authenticity. Once he found himself with crates of whiskey bottles filled with ginger ale. He took care of that distributor in a hurry and it never happened again.

Despite his busy schedule, Nick is loyal to his hometown. He has to be, or Harvest might fold up like it never existed. Considering himself a philanthropist of sorts, he donates to the Harvest library and the Arnold Moseley Bird Sanctuary. He gives Gil some cash to keep his business afloat, and makes sure that Hutch, Brenda, and Skip are well taken care of. As far as Millie is concerned, he wouldn't throw her a breadcrumb unless he thought she might choke on it. And Harry turned out to be a one-of-a-kind guy. Smart and dedicated. He doesn't regret snatching Lucille away from him though; she was meant to be Nick Martin Jr.'s girl, not Harry's. But he made it up to him in another way. That counts for something.

Nick lives by his own code of law "Honor what God has given you." God has given him the confidence to take on the world and for that he is grateful. Hey, if he can help his friends and fill up on that good feeling along the way, why not? When he really wants a laugh, all he has to do is picture Bill Kramer trying to figure out who's paying his bills at Jerry's General Store.

Nick is an ardent fundraiser for tuberculosis, and he and Tara make an electrifying entrance at the Waldorf Astoria annual fundraiser. With Tara in a silver beaded gown with her black hair tucked under a shimmering cloche, and him in a *Taylor and Taylor* black silk suit, all eyes are on them. At the podium, he tells the story of a young girl in Harvest, Iowa who lay near death at the side of the road, and the cost of her recovery. The tears flow, along with the contributions.

Still, he must take care of his own business. After the ball, and after taking Tara home to her apartment, he makes the rounds at his nightclubs. Leaving the Baker Jazz Lounge much too late, even for him, in the wee hours of the morning when most people are getting up, he's in a somber mood. There is something bothering him. Lucille left Minnesota, and he can't locate her. He asked Hal to find every Lucille Kramer in the phonebook, and he hasn't come up with anything.

Standing under the outdoor canopy of the Lounge, he pulls a pack of Lucky Strikes from the upper right hand pocket of his black overcoat and tips out his last cigarette. Cupping one hand around one side of his mouth to light it, he mutters, "Damn this wind."

A young woman, pulling her raincoat around her body, turns in his direction. "Having trouble?"

"I shouldn't be smoking in the first place. It's giving me a hacking cough," he answers. He takes one puff, then tosses the cigarette to the ground and snuffs it out with his shoe. "There. That's the last of this habit. Do you smoke?"

"No, can't afford it."

"Good. I mean, good that you don't smoke. Kind of late for you to be out by yourself."

"I'm waiting for a cab."

"You won't get one at this hour. How about I give you a ride?"

The woman shakes her head.

"Now, that's using your head." He read about Madeline going off with that truck driver, and that firecracker up her butt. What a ghoulish thing to happen. "Not a good idea going off with a stranger. But I own this place, everyone around here knows me. My name is Nick. And your name?"

"Lola." Her voice is barely audible.

"But you know, Lucille, it's dangerous for you to be standing out alone at this time of night. How old are you?"

"Eighteen."

He graduated high school at eighteen. He's lived a lifetime since then.

"You called me Lucille. My name is Lola."

"I'm sorry." The sound of wheels turns his attention toward the street. He takes Lola's arm and helps her into the backseat of the white limousine. "You're safe with me." He tries to guess what this girl does to make money, and why she is standing outside the club by herself. He won't ask. Maybe she had a fight with a boyfriend and she left him sitting at the table. Instead he asks something that surprises her: "Do you read?"

"Read? She has a quizzical look on her face. "I don't have time to read. I work for Cody Cosmetics on the Plaza. Takes up all of my time."

"Go get yourself a library card first thing tomorrow. A good-looking girl like you should be reading. Are you a model with Cody? You know, walk around looking pretty, all made up? Other women trying to look just like you?"

She shakes her head. "No, I work behind the counter in the makeup department. Nine to five every day but Sunday."

"You need to have a goal, be ambitious. Put some zip into your life. People who settle for mediocrity bore me. I could help you find that zip."

"You'd help an absolute stranger?"

"If you had a little scar by your left eye, you would look just like someone I've known all my life." He thinks he may be moving too fast.

Does she live alone, or with her parents? If she lives alone, he wouldn't mind coming up. She's no bug-eyed Betty by any means. When his car stops at a storefront brick apartment building, he finds himself sitting in total darkness. Maybe he can get some street lights installed on this street. But that's for another time. "I'll tell you what. Here's my card and phone number. Call me if you want to see me again. But give me a chance to get home," he says with a wink. "Don't forget the library card."

The next morning, Nick sends two dozen long-stemmed roses to Lola at Cody Cosmetics. *Why does her name have to begin with L*, he wonders, *and she even has those rosebud lips*. At the end of the day, he slumps in the backseat of the white limousine parked along Union Square with Hal behind the wheel. He waits for Lola who said she works until five.

Union Square is a frenzy of activity. People bustle out of department stores with bargains stuffed into *Orhbach and Klein* bags. Hotdog stands and craft displays line the street. People everywhere: eating, buying and on the move. Men and women rushing home from work heading for the subway. At a time like this, Nick longs for the quiet of Harvest.

When he sees Lola walk out of the building, he calls out to her. She doesn't smile or wave, but she turns toward him and walks toward the car. "Why so glum?" he asks, as she gets into the seat next to him. "Didn't you like the flowers?"

"It's not that at all."

"Then what's wrong? Any woman in this city would gladly change places with you. Hey, you're with *the* Nick Martin Jr."

"Nick, I lost my job," she says.

"Of course you did, and you just got another. You have become the face of Cody. You'll have your picture on magazine covers and on all of the Cody advertisements. I called your boss. I thought he'd like to meet his new boss. I just bought the place. He works for me now. I guess you do, too. Oh, by the way, I have a little present for you." He hands her a copy of *The Great Gatsby*. "I know someone who really enjoyed that book. Now, don't read between the lines. I'm like none of those characters. I'm Nick Martin Jr., only one like me." He motions to Hal to start driving. They pass the Lombard Hotel, a dump to begin with, Nick thinks, with a sign posted on the door, which reads, "Absolutely No Filipinos Allowed."

"Hal, stop the car. How many times have we ripped that sign down?"

"At least ten times, Boss."

"Tear it down for the eleventh time. If they need a sign to put on the door, I'll give them one: 'Keep Prohibition Going.'"

Hal does as he is told. When he gets back into the car, he switches on the radio. They hear the usual news commentary. The economic outlook is grim, bread lines are long, and people are pushing for a new president. Then he hears that a police crackdown on speakeasies is in progress. Racketeers are being thrown in jail.

Hal says, "Maybe we need to do what Al Capone did and open a soup kitchen. You know, get the heat off our real job, and us."

"What, are you crazy? We're not anywhere near being an Al Capone."

"Al Capone? Isn't he a gangster?" Lola asks. She appears bewildered, even frightened, because her eyes are fluttering and her face is flushed.

"Now how would I know about gangsters? He swings his arm around her shoulders to comfort her and says, "Let's drive to your place so you can change your clothes. We're spending the evening at one of my clubs."

Soon after reaching her apartment, and Lola exits the car, he gets right down to business. "Hal," he says, "we don't need soup kitchens to make us look good. We have the police on our side and people situated right where we need 'em. So forget that idea. Now hand me a pen." He writes a note for Hal to give to Tara: *"Can't see you this week. Going out of town."*

"Got some news, boss," says Hal. "I located the love of your life. She's Lucille Rosen now. Yup, married. A student at Columbia University. Far cry from your line of work. And get this, boss, your Fairy Princess was pregnant before she got married, but she lost the baby. Someone pushed her at some Indian rally and that's how it happened."

Nick sits up and leans in closer to Hal. "Someone pushed Lucille? Hal, who pushed her? Why would anyone push her? Find the guy. Find out his name, where he lives, and his phone number. Find out which hand he used when he pushed her and then break it. Break it in so many pieces he won't ever be able to use it again." He then becomes very quiet. "Where is the baby? I mean, where is the baby buried?"

"On an Indian reservation."

He throws down the pen." Find out which one."

"Calm down, Nick. Noth'n we can do about the baby. Lucille is married to a science professor. She's his business now."

"Find out who pushed her and then we'll go from there."

"Got it, Boss."

"Now give me a swig of what you've got up there." Hal hands over the flask. Nick drinks enough to light a fire in his belly. He doesn't know what burns more, his anger or his innards.

When Lola gets back into the limo, Nick glances at her low-heeled shoes and dark green suit. He'll have to teach her a thing or two about dressing. "Hal, drive over to *Silk and Chiffon*. Doris will outfit you, Lola. She knows what I like my woman to wear." He's blunt, but he's in no mood for sweet talk.

Silk and Chiffon is *the* place to shop for his women. Once Nick takes a babe there, she becomes putty in his hands. Doris is especially attentive to him because he does so much for her. When she split with Anna he found her someone new. Of course, she meets lots of women in her line of work, but she separates business and pleasure.

When Nick and Lola arrive at the store, Doris smiles, showing big white teeth. She reaches out to shake Nick's hand. She swings her arm around Lola's waist and leads her to the dressing area.

"When Nick brings a woman here, I know she's special," Doris whispers in Lola's ear. "Going to one of his clubs tonight?" Stepping out of the dressing room without waiting for an answer, Doris returns with a royal blue silk strapless dress. She helps Lola fasten the buttons and then hangs a string of pearls around her neck.

Nick greets Lola with an enthusiastic whistle. "Now that's more like it! But go on back in and try something else." He watches the smile vanish from Lola's face, but a blue satin dress like that belongs on only one person.

"The dress is smashing, Nick. Lola looks like a princess." Doris says.

"That's exactly the point."

They finally decide on a pale green chiffon dress. When Doris shows him a silver fox wrap, he nixes that, too. He closes his eyes, remembering when he surprised Lucille with the fur. He remembers the snowstorm and the night he made love to his Fairy Princess. "Get Lucille a boa. It goes better with that dress."

"Nick," Says Lola.

"I know. I know. I called you Lucille again. I'm sorry."

They drive to the West side of Harlem and stop at Sax, Drums and Trumpets, Nick's most lucrative club. It's next door to the Cotton Club, but that doesn't scare him. Competition is the energy surge that keeps his heart pumping. The Cotton club may have Billy Holiday singing the blues but at his club he has three black men and two white women, known as the Jump'n Five. They sing, dance, and play instruments with music that could blast folks out of the gates of heaven just to listen to them. The new male vocalist who will be joining their group tonight can only expand the crowds they're having. Only eighteen and as good as Calloway. But he better remember to take a peek backstage; he doesn't want anyone snorting back there or coming on stage fumbling or mumbling.

He stops to shake hands with Sal, who is greeting the patrons. He nods, and Nick nods in return. Nick appreciates Sal. He's a nice fella, like family, and he really takes care of things at the door. He's worth the money Nick pays him.

He waits at the door with Lola at his side, admiring the club. His eyes move to the mahogany walls, the round circular bar, the tables effectively spaced so that every patron can have a clear view of the stage. The pure silk sea green lampshades on the table lamps diffuse the light just so. But he wants to make the place grandiose to make room for the likes of Duke Ellington and his orchestra. Or even Cab Calloway and his band.

"Mr. Martin, your table is ready," the maitre d' says, with a touch of aloofness that comes with training. Nick is in a happier mood now, and he winks and blows kisses to the ladies at the bar as they extend their hands to him. They stare at Lola with envy. The men have a glint in their eyes when they look at her, and Nick quickly leads her to a table.

Their waiter fills two crystal goblets with whisky. Nick assures Lola that she can drink it; they are well protected here. Looking over at her, he can see her possibilities, but he's beginning to tire of his rotation of women. He doesn't touch his drink and excuses himself.

He walks over to the bar and engages in conversation with a heavy-set man in a dark suit. The man's hair is loaded with grease and slicked back off his forehead. His face is sallow with pockmarks, more like crevices, covering most of it. When he smiles, his rubbery lips slide back to his ears.

When Nick returns to the table, he's in a jovial mood. "That fella I was talking to, Lola, doesn't look like someone you'd want to come across in a dark alley, but you know he's a loyal fella. His name is Joey. I'd like you to meet him some time. Just like family. And with this deal I just closed, I can buy you a diamond that can cover your entire finger."

The entertainment is about to begin, and Lola smoothes her dress under her and leans in.

"We're going," Nick says.

"But the show! Can't we stay to see it?"

"I have better things in store for us," he says.

As they are leaving, he takes a wad of bills from his jacket pocket and places it in Sal's palm. The men give each other a knowing nod. Sal stuffs the bundle of bills in his pocket as casually as if it were a handkerchief.

Hal is waiting outside in the limousine. "Where to?"

"My place."

A doorman, flashing white-gloved hands, welcomes Nick by name and escorts them through a green marbled lobby. The walls are covered with art deco mirrors. Lola's eyes widen as she passes the stylish men and women dressed for an evening out.

"Don't let this place scare you. All you need is money, and of course, to know the right people."

They enter the mahogany paneled elevator, where the operator automatically presses the button to the penthouse. Upon leaving, Nick gives him a twenty-dollar tip and a cheerful "thank you." He drops the key in Lola's hand. "Here, open the door." He can anticipate her reaction when she catches sight of his apartment.

"Gee," she mutters, out of breath, when the door opens. He watches her eyes take in the white plush carpet in the living room, the glass vases overflowing with white lilies set on top of marble tables, and the crystal chandelier overhead. He puts his arm around her waist. "The music room is down the hall. I don't play the piano myself, but I know someone who plays pretty darn well. I keep it here to remember."

"You live here?" she asks. "I thought places like this only existed in the movies."

"Not only do I live here, but I also own the apartment next door for visitors." He takes Lola's boa and throws it on a chair. He leads her to the oval glass bar, and gestures for her to sit on the stool beneath it. She touches the white leather seat and stares at the glass that looks like it is suspended in air.

"I know what you're thinking. So many people forced out of their homes, farmers losing their land and livelihood, businesses shut down. I'm sorry for them, real sorry. But God didn't intend for me to be like other people."

"He must have made you smarter," she says.

Remarks like that alert him to her innocence, nothing he's accustomed to anymore. In his world the men are tough, even crude, and the women are cunning. He hands her a drink.

"Aren't you drinking?" she asks, looking into his eyes.

"I had one drink tonight. My first and last," he says, moving her closer to him. He kisses her lips and she responds placing her hands on his face, eager for more of his kisses. This woman would do anything he wanted her to do. But he wants nothing from her.

His reason for bringing her here is falling apart. He walks her into the bedroom, regardless, but he's in a bind. He doesn't want to be here with her, and she is expecting him to make the next move. Since Hal told him that Lucille lost their baby, he hasn't been himself. He stares out the window and remembers that special night when he and Lucille made love. He made a promise to her: never to give his heart to anyone else. If he could only relive that night again.

The moonlight slips through the window, casting a glow on Lola's face. He looks at her and wonders if his mind is playing tricks. Her strong likeness to Lucille overwhelms him. His passion surges, putting him into frenzy. He grabs her, throws her down on the bed, and rips off her dress. He forces himself inside her. In moments it is over. It happened so fast that even he is stunned. Sitting at the edge of the bed, his head hanging toward his lap, his hands on his forehead, he is ashamed, ashamed that he lost all control. This cannot happen again.

"I'm sorry," he mumbles. "I can't tell you how sorry I am. No man should ever be that inconsiderate of you. I'm just upset tonight. I heard some pretty bad news."

Her face becomes sorrowful. "Bad news?"

"Very bad. I love my Fairy Princess so much that sometimes I don't know how to handle my feelings. It all started on June 26, 1926. Our high school graduation day. Three o'clock in the afternoon. I remember everything about that day because I took the most beautiful girl in the world to the creek. She had long blonde hair and a pretty face like yours and she had those long thin fingers. And when I kissed her, something happened. I fell in love."

"And you still love her?"

"Always will."

"Could you ever love me like that?"

"I could never love anyone else like that."

Nick takes a break from his usual carousing with women. The incident with Lola has taken its toll on him. Ashamed is an understatement. He's humiliated. Putting all his energy into his work, he calls Tara and tells her he's got a big job and she'll be working tonight.

His affection for her faded a long time ago. Now their relationship is strictly business—on his part anyway. "Sax, Drums, and Trumpets," he tells her. "I'll pick you up at eight. Wear the white lace halter dress with the white sequined cloche. The way the light hits that cloche and diffuses over your black hair might just clinch the deal."

When Joey called from the club, he said he had good news for Nick and reminded him to bring Tara. She has a way of turning the man on. She'll have a few drinks with him and promise him a good time. She always carries through with her promise, so that's no lie.

When they arrive at the club, Sal is at the door. He greets Nick with his usual nod. Joey runs toward him like a rolling boulder. *He's eating too much spaghetti*, Nick thinks, and *getting too fat*. Yet, he moves with alacrity. Nick is certain there is a big-time deal in the making.

"Big news, real big news," Joey says. He walks them to their usual table and Joey bends down to kiss Tara on the cheek. "Tara, you look ravishing tonight. Nick is a lucky man. Maybe lover boy will let you stick around a while after we're done with our business."

"I think that can be arranged," Nick says.

"You look swell tonight, Nick," Joey says, directing him down a flight of stairs leading to the cellar. "But then, with your looks you can dress in rags and have the women swooning."

"Thanks Joey. I buy everything at Richard Taylor's store on Madison."

"You gotta be kid'n. I almost bashed his old man's face in when he was still down on the lower east side. You gotta hear this story. His old man, a bohunk, had a dump of a storefront where he sold shirts. I heard about the place and I went in to pick up some things. Came all the way from Houston. I get there and the shirts don't have all their buttons, the seams look like someone drive'n with an edge. They curve all over the place. Then to top it off, his son spilled shaving lotion all over the dump so I couldn't smell the stink. They bought the stuff from the fire sale down the street. I said to the old man, 'Mister, don't play tricks with me.' I took out my shiv and held it to his neck. And then the kid throws a box at me. Good thing Marcello drove down with me and held me back, or I would have wiped 'em out, the both of 'em. Came back a few weeks later, scared the shit out of the old man. This time I came back in the morning, when the kid was in school. I walked out with piles of shirts and sold 'em on the corner of Delancey near the hotdog stand for two dollars apiece. The money came roll'n in. Get it? Near the hotdog stand. With the smell of hotdogs, who could smell the stink from the shirts?"

Nick doesn't appreciate the humor. He likes Richard Taylor, and he doesn't like the idea of anybody treating him and his father like that. "Mr. Taylor could have had a heart attack, the way you scared him."

"Well he didn't."

"And that kid had the last laugh. He dresses some very important people. You're a big cheese now, you can afford his clothes. Go in and get outfitted. He won't remember you, but you could still say you're sorry."

Joey bends down and pulls two big bags out of a carton. "Maybe after we unload some of this I'll buy myself a whole new wardrobe and even take that Taylor kid out for dinner. We'll talk about old times. I don't hold no grudges."

"What do you got there, Joey?"

"Great price, mixed it myself to add a little heft, but who knows the difference? Lot of Cadillac here, and easier to get than booze. We gotta move on. What do you say, baby, what do you say?"

"Let me think about it, Joey." Nick, who gave up smoking, is chewing gum instead.

"You'll see more mazuma than you can find in the bank vaults. I'd tell you to give it a try, but I know how you are. No booze, no dope, no married women. What the hell do you do for fun? Just hold the bags, Nick."

"Heavy," he says, balancing them in his hands.

"We gotta go for it. Coppers are cracking down. Give prohibition another few months and we're out of business. We gotta change direction."

"Joey, you're talking to me, Nick Martin Jr. Don't you think I know that? I've been contacted."

"Well then, did you think about it long enough? What's your answer?"

"Yes, I . . ." Nick begins, when Sal walks into the cellar with two men flanked at his side. Sal takes out his badge. He's an undercover agent. The men have guns drawn. "We're taking you in for bootlegging, possession of dope and bribing the authorities," the agent says. "Sorry, you're one hell of a guy, Nick, but the law is the law. That doll you got out there and Joey, they set you up. They've been working with us for a while now. And they were skim'n your profits right off the top and you never knew it. Nick, if you don't want to end up in a Chicago overcoat, stay clear of these guys. Get yourself a good mouthpiece. Someone who really knows what he's doing in the courtroom."

The cops lead Nick out of the club in handcuffs. They pass the table where Tara sits, tapping her fingers. "No wrath greater than a woman scorned, huh, Tara?"

"That's right, Nick. All those nights you left me at home gave me time to think. I can wheel and deal, too. Joey and I, we'll take care of things from now on."

News of Nick being hauled away in handcuffs hits the morning papers. Although he hoped it wouldn't make such a splash, he's more concerned about his mental state. He can't be cooped up like this in a holding cell. He needs to move. Running a major part of the organization, he was even scheduled to meet with the commission, the heads of all the organizations. The Don would be there. Things were looking up, way high up. Making so much money he could support charities, needy families, his friends, and still have the money to spend on cars, limousines, fancy suits, and women. All of that is gone now, like shutting off his breathing valve, and he's waiting to die. He prays Lucille never hears about this. She's married to that straight-laced science professor; a much better life for her. He always knew that.

He's not locked up for very long. The mob puts up the money. In a few days he's out on bail, but he doesn't feel like the King Pin anymore. He feels like a scared kid. He receives a phone call from Dan on his first day home. "I read the news in the morning papers," Dan says. "I haven't forgotten about all you did for me. Getting me this job at the club, paying me more than I'm worth, letting me run up a charge at

Taylor and Taylor. I'm standing by you. Meet me at the club tomorrow morning. We'll think of something."

After a restless night's sleep, Nick treks into the club, his face drawn and his eyes puffy. He is startled to see who is sitting at a table with Dan, drinking a cup of coffee.

"Need the best attorney, you call Nick Martin Sr.," Dan says.

Nick throws his arms around his Dad. "Dad, the mob won't let me go. I know what they do to you if you don't play ball. How can I get out of this?"

"Calm down, son. They won't have you rubbed out. You're not that important to them. Unless you're involved in the big stuff. Gambling? Narcotics? Prostitution?"

The sweat is beginning to pour down Nick's face. He looks away. He can't look his father straight in the eye. "No, Dad. I'd never be involved in that."

His father's voice is firm. "Look at me, son."

"They want to send me to Chicago or San Francisco."

"Sit down, tell me everything. Dan, get him a cup of coffee, black. You don't want any part of Al Capone territory. Get out of the business and get out fast."

"I don't know how."

"I know you don't. Sell off some of the clubs and get out of town."

"I'll do it, Dad. And I'll be swift about it. But they'll be looking for me."

"That's what you have me for. I'll get it all worked out. It will kill your mother if I don't get you through this. And Nick, it will kill me, too."

∽

"Hal, we're moving to the Catskills."

Hal and Nick sit at the kitchen table having breakfast. Hal put down his cup, and says, "Okay, Boss."

They buy a used truck from a friend of Hal's and after two hours of driving, Nick is back into small town living.

Under the Red Ribbon

He opens a combination car repair shop and gas station, similar to Mr. Olson's arrangement in Harvest. He calls it by the same name, Olson's Garage. Customers refer to him as Mr. Olson, but he doesn't care. He is tired of being Nick Martin Jr., the man who took too many chances and hung out with people who were nothing but trouble. He keeps his prices low because he already has enough money. Customers flock to his shop because he adds interest to their mundane life; the men are awed by the sense of urgency behind his quiet demeanor, and want to know more about this newcomer. The women, aroused by the longing behind those dreamy eyes, create their own car problems and stand close by as he works on tires that don't need patching and engines that already run smoothly. When a young woman, cute as a bug's ear, tells him of her fantasy of luring him into the woods, he tells her to keep her fantasies in her head, because he isn't going to do anything about them.

In the evening, he enjoys a cup of coffee at the small coffee shop in town. At village meetings, he sits in the back row listening to the people discuss the upcoming rummage sale, the scholarship fund, the road that needs fixing, and the Labor Day parade. These things matter to the residents. Really matter. Hands shoot up to join committees as if lives depend on it. Nick listens, watches, and smiles. Nick is content to be a spectator.

He starts taking classes two and three nights a week at a community college, then at Highland University, sixty miles from his residence in Wood Hill. He enjoys the intellectual stimulation more than he realized. He's studying now, repairing cars, and forgetting the life he once knew. After four years at this routine, he receives a degree in mechanical engineering.

He's living a quiet life, until his small business gets a write up in *The Catskill News*, and his quiet life takes a turn. Business increases. He extends his hours and no longer has time for his evening stop at the coffee shop. Seeing one of his old cronies from the city drive up with a malfunctioning steering wheel is all the excuse he needs to close up shop and leave town. The man looked at his face and said, "Hey, for a minute I thought you were someone I knew, but no, the fella I was thinking of wouldn't be caught dead in overalls and with dirt on his shirt." When the car drives off, Nick puts a "Closed" sign on the door of his shop and he and Hal jump into his used truck and drive back to New York City. They find a used car lot, dump the old truck, and take a cab to the Carlton Hotel. No doorman to recognize him, and no slipping the elevator man a twenty just to press a button.

After checking in, Nick goes to bed early. In his dreams, visions of his tawdry life flow through his intestines like water through a pipe carrying sediments of his old self into a sewer. He wakes up startled, with a new destination in mind. He zips up his brown leather jacket, tilts his fedora, and with an umbrella in hand, he tells Hal to take the day off. Taking the elevator down to the lobby, he sees a father holding the hands of two young children. He wonders how old his child would have been.

The streets are flooded, and the wind and the rain tear at his back. He holds onto his hat with one hand and with the other, grips the umbrella as it veers away from him. Out of habit, he peers into the window of *Taylor and Taylor*. The mannequins appear stuck in time. He walks on.

Stopping at the corner, he waits for the light to change and gets splashed by a passing cab. It is a substantial splash. His clothes are soaked, but giving that no heed he crosses the street and heads toward his destination. He walks up a dozen or more steps, and then through a doorway. He is accustomed to people looking at him, admiring him, and calling his name, but here in the library he goes unnoticed.

With so many books and categories to choose from, where should he start? With a serious expression and unquestionable intent, he decides to begin with the first letter of the alphabet. He walks over to a shelf looking for books that begin with A. He has no luck—too many books. He speaks to the librarian sitting behind her desk, wearing thick glasses that remind him of the ones Harry wore. She gives him a brief lesson on the Dewy Decimal system. Numbers are his thing and in no time he's looking at the spines of books for call numbers and quickly has all the books he can carry. He lugs the books to the nearest table, where a mature woman, about fifty, smiles and points to the coatroom.

Her light brown hair is styled in finger waves, so flat that they appear to be pasted to her scalp. The severe look exposes her oval face that is pretty with her slightly turned up nose and large brown eyes. Nick thinks she must have been a babe in her day. She must sense his ineptitude, because she gets up from her seat, buttons her blue cardigan, and escorts him. Struggling to fit his coat on the rack between a green jacket and a brown one, he looks around for a place to hang his hat. The woman points to the shelf above the rack. She takes his umbrella and places it in a corner with the others. Such a fuss just to rid himself of his coat, hat and umbrella. At the club, there's a coat check girl to do all that.

Looking down at his stack of books, he contemplates which one to open first. The same woman asks him, "Anyone ever tell you that you look like Howard Hughes?" Her voice has a deep tone, almost velvety.

"I've heard Rudolph Valentino, but maybe it's better to look like Howard Hughes. He won an academy award and he hangs out with women like Katherine Hepburn."

The woman laughs. "Actually, I think you look quite okay looking like yourself."

Nick skims through the first aviation book about Major Gilory "Pappy" Boyington. Fascinated by the man's life, he reads more attentively. He learns that Boyington participated in high school wrestling, his own favorite sport, and that the man was a risk taker. He enlisted in the Marine Corps and went to flight training in Pensacola.

The next book is about Charles Lindberg. This man graduated from flight training school as the best pilot in his class. He made the first solo non-stop flight from New York to Paris. The best and the first. Nick likes that. Something begins to click in his mind. He reads about Ira Biffle, the man who taught Colonel Charles A. Lindberg to fly. When he reads about Amelia Earhart, the first woman to fly across the Atlantic, he's convinced that if a woman can be a pilot, it will be a snap for him. He stays in the library until his eyes burn, and he barely put a dent in the books. He feels that old fire in his veins returning.

Leaving the library, he feels lighter, yet something has been added to his life. He imagines what it would be like in the cockpit of a plane:

the thrill of takeoff, the kick of the landing. And if any plane needed repair, he could just fix it himself.

The pelting rain is no more than a drizzle now. He stops in at *Taylor and Taylor*. Richard is folding shirts and placing them neatly in a pile. When he looks up and sees Nick, his face brightens with a huge smile and a surprised look. Nick grins, showing the dimple in his left cheek and the two men walk toward each other for a handshake, a slap on the back, and some time to catch up on the past few years.

"Suppose you need a new wardrobe, Nick. Let me take you around and show you our new arrivals."

"Richard, you won't find me shopping in here anytime soon," he says. "I'm ready for a complete wardrobe style change."

"I always thought you liked the stuff we have."

Nick laughs. "I'm joining the Marines."

Hal breaks down and cries when he hears the news.

"Don't do that, Hal," Nick tells him. "You'll be busy. Remember, keep track of Lucille."

"I'll be busy all right. I'm signing up, too."

At six o'clock on Monday morning, Nick and Hal are first in line at the Recruiting Office. Nick reads the sign on the wall, "Uncle Sam Wants You."

"Not as much as I want you," he answers.

Marine training is brutal. When the drill officer tells the men to do something, they do it. And he's not very nice about it. Nick is not accustomed to that. Swallowing his pride, he does what he is told, but longs for the days when he gave the orders. He passes elimination training without any trouble. He contacts Hal, who is stationed in Virginia, to tell him the news.

"I'm having a tough time getting through boot camp," Hal jokes. "My job working for you was too cushy. I wasn't prepared for this."

Nick is placed alongside a crew of ten men to restructure aircrafts. With his ingenuity, the new planes become faster as he designs lighter engines and less cumbersome armament. But this is not the job he wants to do. He wants to be in the cockpit, with his hands on the artillery, ready for combat.

He attends officer candidate school and becomes a marine officer. He joins a small unit of marine fighter pilots. He's an instant hit with the men. Something about him is captivating. When he tells them he owned a car repair shop before entering the service, one fellow marine, Andy, says, "If you owned a car repair shop in the Catskills, like you say you did, how come you're so classy?"

Nick laughs. "Because that kind of work can make a class guy out of anybody."

When Japan attacks Pearl Harbor, leading to the United States entry into World War II, Nick gets his chance at military combat. After fifty missions, his fellow marines dub him "The High Flier." On Nick's fiftieth mission over Germany he and his crew knock out an enclave stocked with weapons, completely destroying the ammunition facility. In the process, a German fighter pilot maneuvering alongside him opens fire, damaging Nick's aircraft engine. With the adeptness that earned him the name "High Flier," he manages to make his way back to the base. But on his next mission he isn't as lucky. Targeting The Ludendorff Bridge over the Rhine River, his fighter plane, a B-17F, is hit. A section of his right wing breaks loose and he plunges from the sky.

Nick Martin Sr.

Nick Martin Sr.'s office walls are filled with pictures of his son. They create a topic of conversation with his clients. "My kid, a chip off the old block," he says. He gravitates toward Jerry's General Store and meets with the men, telling stories that keep them listening for hours. The men no longer refer to Nick Jr. as the kid who speeds through town looking for trouble, but as a courageous American who volunteered to fight for his country. Mr. Martin is a proud man.

On an Iowa morning when the snow comes down in thick flakes and piles up in high mounds, the men get themselves over to the store early to have their coffee and crowd around the Philco and listen to the news. With the bad weather interfering with the sound, coffee cups in hand, they press their ears to the radio. But soon they lift their heads in unison.

Paul says, "Listen, they're repeating it."

Jerry and Howie look at each other for confirmation. Hutch might just pass out. "Nick Martin Jr. from Harvest Iowa, missing in action," the voice on the radio says.

Mr. Martin pales and excuses himself from the store. From his office, he calls the Defense Department to make sure that the Nick Martin Jr. reported missing in action is his son. He wants to know who is looking for him, and what intelligence they are using to find him. Nick Sr. tells the representative to call him any time, night or day, if they learn anything.

Although he and Anita barely speak, they now seek each other out for comfort. Neither one of them can sleep well, so they stay up nights talking in the kitchen. Sometimes Mr. Martin's head drops onto the table. When he awakens, the pain starts all over again. Never an avid churchgoer, he now sits among the empty pews from early morning on, praying. On Sunday mornings, members of the congregation greet him with a nod. He aches too much to respond.

NICK

After grueling questioning by the Gestapo followed by a night of beatings, Nick is thrown into a cell. To pass the time, he ruminates about his life as the big cheese at Harvest High, as the Kingpin at the clubs, as the High Flier in the Marines. That will all be part of his eulogy. He'll never see his way out of here. He'd like to give his dad his red Model T, his Model A, and his limousine. He could never part with any car he owned. When he sold the Model T. to pay for Lucille's doctor bills, he bought it back as soon as he could. Or was that the Model A.? He never would have had trouble remembering something like that, but having his head pounded for so many hours, he's confused. He wonders if Lucille heard of his capture. He sure hopes Hal didn't. He'd never be able to cope with it.

The guard, a heavy muscular woman, paces the dirt in front of his cell. Walking back and forth, she swears at him and spits. He watches silently, but when he sees her drag Cal, a member of his crew, in from the outside by his hair and kick him into the cell next to his, he yells an obscenity he didn't think he knew. The guard's mood suddenly changes, as if his language titillated her. She becomes jovial. She hums, and her steps become lively. When she looks at him, she holds his gaze. He turns away, but when he turns back, she's still looking at him. He never questioned his sexual prowess before, but now, bloody, weak, and dirty, he questions whether he still possesses that power. He brushes his filthy hair with his fingers and tries to wipe the grime off his face with his sleeve. His eyelids bend partially over his eyes, and he returns her gaze. Slowly, his eyes travel up and down her body. He smiles at her, showing the dimple in his left cheek.

Looking from side to side, she puts her finger to her lips, signaling him to be silent, and then gives him a nod. The key moves toward the lock and Nick watches his cell door swing open.

"Ssh." The guard puts her finger to her lips again. The club falls from her hand. She pushes him down on the floor and pulls his pants below his knees. She fondles him with such a strong grip that Nick calls out in pain.

Her arousal propels her into a frenzy and she rips the sleeves from his shirt as she tries to remove it. Nick, seeing an opportunity, wraps one sleeve around her mouth and ties it at the back of her head. She moans in ecstasy. He removes her pants and then her shirt. Wired to work systematically, he takes her hands and ties them behind her back with his other sleeve. She moans for more. "Close your eyes," he says.

"Fick mich," she screams.

"Beg," he says. "Don't open your eyes. I have a big surprise for you."

He pulls her shirt over his head and her pants over his legs. He needs her thick leather belt to hold up the pants, but before putting it on he raises the strap and lands a whack on her back.

He grabs the keys dangling from her shirt pocket and leaves the cell to the muffled music of her moans. He stops once to open the cell next to him to release Cal.

Nick receives an honorable discharge when the war ends and he ponders the next stage of his life. After devoting his time to his country it's time to do something for himself. And the four years at Highland University taught him that he has what it takes to be a good student. He applies to the University of California, determined to earn an advanced degree in aeronautical engineering.

ℒUCILLE

Gifts have been arriving all week for Paco's thirteenth birthday. Although Paco planned to open them after his Bar Mitzvah, he tells his mother he can't resist opening at least one before then. When Lucille sees the model airplane he unwraps, she asks, "Who is that from?"

"This *is* a surprise," Paco answers. "The man kept his word."

"But who is it from?"

"He's one of Mr. Taylor's customers. A groovy guy. Joel introduced me to him."

"But who is he? A stranger doesn't just send you a gift."

"He never told me his name. Joel and I were just hanging around the store, and this really nice man was talking to Mr. Taylor and then he started talking to us. He said he would have had a kid around my age or maybe a little older, but he never had a chance in life. When he found out about my birthday, he said he didn't know a thing about Bar Mitzvahs, but he does know about aeronautics and that he'd like to send me a model plane as a gift."

"You gave a stranger your address?"

"Ma, he said he knew it."

The model plane is a replica of a B-17F, and Paco is impressed. He reads the note aloud to her. "The real thing can carry 8,000 pounds of bombs. I hope you and your Dad enjoy putting it together. Your mother might find it fun, too."

Lucille looks at the card. It is a business card. It reads N.I.C. Inc. Aircraft Co.

On the day of the celebration, Paco Whitefeather sits in the front row of the synagogue with a little round skullcap propped on the back of his head and his black ponytail swinging down his back. Lucille and Charlie sit down beside him. They scoot over to make room for Rose and Bill who arrived from Harvest yesterday afternoon. Bill picks up a prayer book and turns the pages filled with Hebrew words. Looking perplexed, he closes it and holds it on his lap.

Lucille whispers to Whitefeather, "When we lived in Minnesota we learned about your culture. Now you will learn about ours."

When his namesake chants from the Torah and Haftora, Whitefeather leans forward to hear every word.

"God casts a ladder between heaven and earth," young Paco says, "and when a person climbs the ladder, he reaches closer to God. He can do that by performing kind deeds. This is the way I choose to live my life."

Whitefeather nods his head in affirmation. "That is a universal truth," he whispers to Lucille. "You've done a good job with that boy. He is wise for his age."

The evening festivities are held in the banquet room of the 21 Club on West 49th Street. Lucille wonders what Whitefeather might be thinking. There are vases of roses on each table, blue and white balloons floating across the ceiling with small scrolls attached to each string, heaps of halvah, strudels, cakes and tarts on the "sweet table," and of course, the Bar Mitzvah cake. Will Whitefeather believe that her family has become snobbish? This is a far cry from the simple life of the reservation. When they lock eyes, she tries to read his thoughts. She walks toward him. "Look at us, Whitefeather," she says, gathering her family around her. "We've come a long way since we were kids in Riverview."

"And that brings me great joy. I would like my wife to learn from you. You are a fine example of how a woman should lead her life. Perhaps the two of you will have a chance to spend some time together in Riverview."

"Charlie and I are thinking about a trip there soon. We want our children to see the life we once lived."

Under the Red Ribbon

Whitefeather reaches into the hand-woven basket he is carrying and presents each of the four Rosen's with a gift as he explains each one. "New York City is a busy place where harmony and balance is difficult to find," he says, "so I present you, Charlie, my dearest friend, with a bronze sculpture of a deer, a symbol of power, love and gentleness. To you, Paco, this silver medallion. This is called the *Man in the Maze*, depicting life's cycles and the choices we are asked to make. Let your choices lead you to overcome difficult challenges. Always take care of our earth."

Lucille nudges Paco to stop staring at Whitefeather's leather boots. He stops, but his eyes land on the strands of yellow, turquoise, and red beads hanging around Whitefeather's neck, and then on his long ponytail.

"I hope Paco's staring isn't bothering you," Lucille apologizes. "You know kids."

"It's good to notice everything. Then you will never be fooled." He presents Kimimela with a little ceramic frog. "For you, my precious one, named for my beloved sister. This frog represents renewal, fertility, and the advent of spring. Like your mama, your ideas will become fertile, helping you make life better for all." Finally, his voice quivering, he presents Lucille with her gift. "Remember when I pronounced you my new sister here on earth? Our tears ran together as one. I give you this painting of Father Sky and Mother Earth. They show the duality of life that is so pronounced in you. Opposites exist within us all, but more in some than others. When we try to overturn one in favor of the other, we suffer along the way. We must embrace all of who we are and all that life is."

"You know me well, Whitefeather, as only good friends do. Please, tell my son how your people celebrate when a boy turns thirteen."

"We have what we call an Indian Rite of Passage Ceremony. When a young boy passes into young adulthood, he sits in the wilderness, without food or drink, getting in touch with his inner spirit. We call this ritual the Hablacia. We have lavish traditions, too, when our tables overflow with salmon, wild mushrooms, squash, and blueberry pie. That's our way of giving thanks for a good crop, or the renewal of the spirit. But we are getting too serious. Let's enjoy the rest of the evening. And now, how do we say congratulations?"

"Mazel Tov," the family sings out in unison.

"Mazel Tov," he repeats.

Bill's ears are alert to every word coming out of Whitefeather's mouth. "My grandson got his smarts from his parents, but his wisdom from you, Whitefeather. We'll talk later. Let's do that Jewish dance. Charlie tells me they call it the Hora."

"The what?"

"The Hora. You know, that circle dance."

Whitefeather takes Bill's hand and the circle continues to grow until all of the guests have joined in. "Just like our Ghost Dance," Whitefeather says.

As Lucille looks on, Whitefeather introduces the other guests to the art of Indian dancing. He says that there are as many different Indian dances as there are shapes of snowflakes. He demonstrates with a slow side-to-side movement, like flowers swaying in the breeze. The guests follow, and when he asks them to take on the persona of an animal, the real fun begins. The guests seem to be reluctant to leave when the evening draws to a close. While the waiters clear the tables and the floral arrangements are dismantled, Paco, Kimimela, Charlie, and Lucille walk into the lobby for some private time with Whitefeather.

"Young Paco's like you," Charlie says. "Did you watch him tonight, how he picked up the Indian dances so quickly?"

"He told me he wants to try the pipe," Whitefeather says. "I laughed. I told him it is not an excuse to smoke but a very sacred ritual."

When the conversation turns to Indian affairs, Whitefeather clasps his hands in front of him and speaks in a soft, agonizing voice. He tells them that the young boys who helped search for his sister all served their country. His friend Dakota lost an arm when a grenade hit him. After his discharge, he worked in a defense plant. "We answered the call. We never thought of it as the white man's war. The war touched us deeply, too. Even Mama Nadie sewed uniforms. Adrien and Yakekan won Medals of Honor for bravery. Eighty-five percent of the men in our tribe alone were in the military.

I started English classes on the reservation so that more of us could be qualified to fight, but then I left for the war, too. There is a reason we are called warriors. Our marksmanship is so accurate, our good friend the sun is happy to have us on its side." Shaking his head, he tells them of other effects of the war. "For the first time, our Indian people have been exposed to the white world and many of them are forgetting about our culture. Making more money has spoiled them. But what of our native dances, our clothing our chants? Slowly our ways are losing ground. That's why I hold onto my ponytail, my beads, and boots. People see me and they remember."

"Education, not Assimilation. I remember that slogan," Lucille says. "Does it have to be one way or the other? American Indians can assimilate in ways that are good for them, and still keep their culture, can't they? Hanson and Ellie are doing it. Hasn't the war changed things?"

"Changed things? People still ridicule our powwows, walking sticks, dream catchers, animal totems, and so many of our traditions, simply because they don't know what they symbolize, and don't care to know."

It's getting late. It's time for Whitefeather to return to Minnesota. He wraps his arms around Charlie and Lucille. "You are my family, all of you." He hugs Kimimela. Taking his red beads from his neck, he turns to young Paco. "I saw you looking at these. Take them. They will ensure that you are a success."

With the celebration behind her, Lucille realizes how much of her time was spent on the preparations. Finally, she finds time to talk to Ellie about one of her students, Alyana. They agree to meet at the small restaurant, "The Meeting Place" that recently opened just down the street from Lucille's apartment. It's about ten o'clock in the morning and the breakfast crowd has faded. A few mothers and their children fill some of the tables. Otherwise the place is relatively quiet. The waitress has a little down time and pours their coffee as soon as they are seated and shortly after, asks if they want a refill.

Lucille gets straight to the point. She explains to Ellie that her class is studying *The Canterbury Tales* and one of her students, Alyana, had a tale of her own to tell that involved a murder at Riverview.

Ellie put her fingers to her lips, looks rather serious, and then says, "Alyana? I remember that name. There was a young Indian girl who used to work for Mr. Baran. You may have seen her. She became pregnant at a tender age. Mr. Baran, of course, was responsible for that. The baby lived on the reservation under her grandmother's care. We all knew who she was. Then Mr. Baran sent the child to live with his sister in New York City. He was afraid he might lose his job, if the higher ups got wind of it. The government liked their school workers to be squeaky clean. He paid his sister a lot of money. Alyana's mother stayed in touch with her. She must have told her about Kimimela's murder. And by the way, Alyana's mother married Whitefeather's good friend, Dakota."

Lucille remembers seeing the mother, who was nothing but a child herself then, walking into Mr. Baran's office. Charlie had even pointed her out. She'll tell Charlie as soon as he comes home from work.

Charlie arrives home late, after a long meeting at the school. Her story can wait for another day. The following morning, a cold rain and a dark sky leaves Lucille wishing that she could stay in bed all day. But, she doesn't have that luxury. When Lucille thinks of the day ahead, she throws her feet over the side of the bed, then sits there awhile, deciding what to do first. Charlie is still asleep, lying beside her. Today is Kimimela's eleventh birthday and she's having five girls over for a sleepover. Lucille and Charlie bought Kimimela a locket, and Paco thought that she would like some beads. Lucille will pick up the cake on her way home from work.

Getting dressed, she remembers that tomorrow night she and Charlie will be attending a concert and that she'd better stop and pick up his suit at the dry cleaner. Still buttoning her skirt, she tiptoes out of the bedroom. She'll give Charlie an extra few minutes to sleep.

Turning the kitchen radio on, she hears that a motorcade will be traveling down the very route Charlie takes to work. It's best that she alert him.

"Charlie, time to get up," she says, standing in their bedroom doorway, in a melodic voice. She leans over the bed to give him a kiss. She pulls back. Something isn't right. He's too still. He isn't breathing. "My God," she screams, throwing herself on top of his body. She shakes him and pleads with him to move. She stumbles to the telephone and calls emergency. The children are up now. They hear her on the phone and rush to wake their father. Kimimela shrieks and Paco yells, "Oh, no!"

When the ambulance arrives, Lucille begs the medics to revive her husband. She stands back while a young man, beads of sweat forming on his brow, works to revive Charlie's unresponsive body. Lucille clasps and unclasps her hands, praying, hoping. Then she hears the medic say, "I did the best I could, Ma'am. I'm so sorry."

Lucille's body turns to ice. She squeezes Charlie's cold hands. They don't squeeze back. "Charlie, tell me, how will I live without you?" She kisses his hands, his mouth, and his cheeks. "Charlie, do you know how much I love you?" The paramedics hear her ask that question again and again. Only she hears Charlie's reply.

I know. That's why we met on your first day at the Little River Indian Residential School. I waited a long time for you to come along. Lucille, you were able to do what no other woman could. Your love took my sadness away.

She shouts, "Charlie, who's going to take *my* sadness away?" Her head drops onto the bed. One of the men pulls her away, while two other men lift Charlie onto a gurney and carry him into the ambulance.

Lucille requests a simple pine casket, although Bill tells her to get one that he feels better befits a professor at Columbia. "Charlie would want it simple," she explains. "People equal in death. No opulence. No pretense."

Charlie was well known at the school and throughout the science community, and news of his death spreads like wildfire. At the time of his death, Lucille tells her children, he was researching heart medicines to reduce artery plaques. She explains that Charlie's arteries were clogged with plaque.

When friends and relatives visit the Abraham Funeral Home on Ludlow Street two days after Charlie's death, they extend their condolences to the family secluded in a small room in the back of the chapel. Some are choked up, others teary, and some cry outwardly. Lucille's tears have already dried. She feels like a pool sucked of its water. Wearing a black dress and small velvet hat with a veil falling just past her eyes, she appears diminutive and frail, shaking hands with people whose faces pass in a haze.

"I'm so sorry, Lucille. I never had the pleasure of getting to know Charlie, but I understand he was a man of character," says a gentleman waiting in line to offer his condolences. Glancing up, she notices his lowered eyelids and the dimple that appears in his left cheek and acknowledges that her mind is playing tricks on her. He takes her hand into his, and she almost smiles. He touches her arm. "I'm in town for a few days. When Richard Taylor told me, I had to come."

"How nice of you. Thank you," she says, extending her hand to the next visitor.

Whitefeather, one of the pallbearers, stares straight ahead as he helps carry the casket from the chapel. He lets the tears flow. He was the first to offer his condolences to Lucille and the children in the small receiving room. He told her at that time that he plans to stay in New York for the entire seven days of the mourning ritual. "I have lost a brother," he explains.

When the week of the traditional observance draws to an end, people stop visiting the house. Lucille sits in the quiet of the dead. The hardest time is six o'clock, when Charlie used to walk through the door and call her name. Now there are no open arms for her to leap into.

She makes dinner for the children every evening, but their talk is minimal. She can't stomach breakfast, she has only coffee, which she buys from the school cafeteria. She sees the horror in her face when she stares into her bedroom mirror. Her eyes are sunken; her cheeks are pale and hollow. In an effort to look better, she has her hair cut and styled. Without Charlie there to comment, it makes little difference. *Women lose their husbands every day*, Lucille thinks. *How do they go on?*

On school days, Kimimela goes straight to her room when she returns. She does her homework and says very little to Paco or her mother. On Saturday afternoon, when most kids are with their friends, Lucille finds her sobbing on her bed. "Mama," she asks, lifting her head, "how will I ever have another happy birthday?" Lucille wonders if she herself will ever have another happy day.

Paco comes into Kimimela's bedroom from Charlie's office "Kimimela," he yells, "why are you worrying about a happy birthday at a time like this?"

Kimimela continues sobbing. Lucille tries at once to calm her and to explain to Paco that he has misunderstood, but her own grief is all consuming. After that, when Lucille and the children's eyes meet, they close them in unison, unable to tolerate the pain in each other's faces.

After a few weeks of mourning, Lucille encourages the children to socialize with their friends. But young Paco is steadfast. He wants to avoid parties for eleven months. Kimimela does the same. Lucille would rather be home alone, where she can look through her husband's belongings and cry over them without upsetting the children, but Charlie meant too much to her children and they aren't ready to move on.

Carrying on with her job at Columbia, Lucille pretends to move forth with dignity, but at home her pain is obvious. She isn't at all cheerful when she speaks to the children, picks at her food when she eats, and retires early, only to be up all night. The dreary monotony of the weeks and months following Charlie's death blend into each other, and soon a year passes. Lucille lights the twenty-four-hour memorial candle on the one-year anniversary of her husband's death. Paco, who has been saying a prayer for his father every day since he died, tells Lucille that he has been saving his money so that they can buy a plaque to place on the synagogue wall in Charlie's memory. "When I told the Rabbi, he said someone had set up a fund for us."

"I know. The Rabbi notified me."

"I asked the rabbi who the man was," Paco says, "but he said the man wouldn't give his name."

Later that evening, Lucille carries a birthday cake for Kimimela to the dinner table. After blowing out the candles, Kimimela says she has a present from her father.

Lucille is startled. "You have a present from your father?"

Her daughter walks into her room and returns with a trophy. "I won first prize at the Science Fair. Daddy gave me a gift. The love of science."

Kimimela and Paco's friends visit, rarely at first and then with more and more frequency. Soon, Lucille can hear them laughing again. But for her, life without Charlie is just empty. So familiar with waking up lying next to him in bed, her anguish begins early in the morning. After dinner, the sight of his empty chair plagues her for the rest of the evening. So accustomed to buying tickets for two, she refuses to buy just one. Her social agenda becomes non-existent

Ellie calls often, asking her to come to dinner or have lunch, but Lucille refuses. Sheila keeps in touch, but even she is unable to cheer up Lucille. At night, Lucille pulls the covers up to her neck, checks the clock, and counts the hours until morning. She, who helped Charlie overcome his sadness, cannot overcome her own.

Every day she feels worse. It becomes more difficult to accomplish everyday things like cooking, dressing, and teaching her classes. Terrible thoughts fill her mind. Her life is in disarray, and she can't get a handle on it. She straightens her drawers, trying to control what she can. Taking a few weeks off from work to pull herself together, she stays at home and doesn't even bother to dress. Wearing the same pink nightgown day and night, she retreats to her bedroom as soon as the children leave for school. She knows that she needs to get back to her old self for the sake of her children, but her old self has run off and left her. At two o'clock in the morning one day she awakes with her heart pounding. She can't catch her breath. She runs to the window for air, and collapses on the floor. It is evident that her emotional life has taken its toll.

Dan will help her. He always has. She relied on him the day her mother died. She relied on him after her high school graduation, when she trudged along the dark road afraid to face her father. She relied on him when she needed help adjusting to city life. He'll come now, even at this hour. He'll clear the heavy fog she has been living through.

Under the Red Ribbon

He does come. Looking doleful, his arms outstretched, he embraces her and together they sit at the edge of the bed. He holds her close as she sobs.

"Sometimes we need more than a helping hand from someone like me," he says. He takes a card from his pocket." Here, take this. You need to see a professional."

Finally, a month after having the conversation with Dan, she gets an appointment with a psychiatrist. On a warm fall morning, she hails a cab and notices the bright sunshine of early afternoon, and wonders why she can't feel its warmth or brightness. She enters the psychiatrist's office with trepidation. This is new for her. When the doctor arrives to meet her, he appears to be roughly fifty years old. He looks nothing like Freud; no goatee. Just a man like any other. Seated in his office, she glances around the room, avoiding his eyes. The doctor's eyes stay fixed on hers, and though she is reluctant, she finally looks directly at him. She learns the first rule of therapy: there is no turning away. She tells him her reason for coming, and he simply nods. She repeats the words over and over. "My husband is dead. He'd still be alive, if I stopped him from working such long hours." Then she tries to reason away his death. "He's still alive to me." If she came for answers, she didn't get any.

Dan said that if anyone could help her, Dr. Hartfeld could. So she continues her sessions, although the thought of stopping occurs to her many times. *What's the sense in going,* she thinks, *he can't bring Charlie back.* Gradually, her thinking changes. Maybe the doctor can't bring Charlie back, but is it possible that he can bring her back to what she once was?

After her Friday night appointment she plans on spending another night glancing through a magazine before falling asleep on the couch. On her way home in a cab, the traffic uptown is stop and go. Men and women hurry home from work, looking forward to the weekend. Some have begun their evening engagements and walk in couples down the sidewalk.

The restaurants lining Third Avenue are busy with a steady flow of people coming and going. They don't call it rush hour for nothing,

Lucille thinks. When the cab passes *Taylor and Taylor*, she sees the lights go out in the clothing store. Richard and his wife will probably share a nice dinner together. For a moment she thought that perhaps her sadness was lifting, but now it returns, landing on her like a heavy hammer. She feels hopeless; she'll never be able to repair the destruction that losing Charlie has wreaked on her life.

The cab stops for a red light, and a woman crossing the street catches her attention. *Is that Sheila,* Lucile wonders? It isn't possible. In that crowd, how could Lucille possibly spot her? Surely Sheila would call if she were in New York. Still, this woman in her beautiful tailored gray jacket and pleated plaid skirt has a striking resemblance to her friend.

The phone rings as Lucille enters her apartment. It's her daughter. Kimimela tells Lucille that she is going out to dinner with her friend Robert. *Kimimela misses her father, and must always have a male around,* Lucile thinks, but catches herself before she continues the thought. She must remember to leave the analyzing to Dr. Hartfeld. After she hangs up, she showers and changes into a fresh nightgown. She has been wearing the old pink one for so long that it has become frayed. About to open the refrigerator, she hears the phone ring again.

"This is Sheila. I've been trying to get you all day," Sheila says, when Lucille answers.

"Sheila, you won't believe it! On my way home, looking out the cab window, I spotted you. In all that crowd, I spotted you."

"You didn't!"

"Yes, I did."

They set a luncheon date. Twelve o'clock on Sunday at La Silas. Lucille has one day to get herself together. She feels like a house that has been hit by a tornado. She makes a list of the things she must get before seeing Sheila: a haircut, a manicure, and a new dress. She doesn't want her friend to see her looking frumpy.

Getting her hair done makes all the difference. She giggles, looking at herself in the mirror. With her blonde hair covering one eye, she looks like the actress, Veronica Lake. She sees a glimpse of her younger self.

Under the Red Ribbon

Conveniently located two doors down from Richard Taylor's store is a small boutique where the fashions are elegant, unique, and affordable. Instead of purchasing a tailored suit, she opts for an emerald green silk dress with a sweetheart neckline, cap sleeves, and gathers under the bodice. Since Charlie died she's gotten quite thin, and this dress emphasizes her curves. She also buys a pair of black pumps and some short black gloves. Looking in the mirror, she sees a woman who is definitely overdressed for lunch. But she likes the way she looks.

On Sunday afternoon promptly at twelve o'clock, Lucille and Sheila wrap their arms around each other at the quaint Italian restaurant. Stepping back, they take a long look at each other and begin to laugh. They are both sporting the same hairstyle. "Together, we have one set of eyes to see through," Sheila says.

Requesting a table toward the rear of the restaurant, they talk all the way to their seats. Lucille clasps her hands on the red-and-white checkered tablecloth and basks in the energy she hears in Sheila's voice. It's hard to imagine anything bad happening in her presence. Reed thin and wearing a gunmetal grey wool dress topped with a silver fox stole trailing down her back, Sheila has undeniable star quality. Lucille still has the stole Nick gave her hidden in the back of her closet. She's wearing a black jacket with a Persian lamb collar, a gift from Charlie. Lucille is having fun. Being with Sheila reminds her that she is alive, after all.

The waiter arrives with a basket of rolls and places it in the center of the small table. He appears to be about thirty years old with dark curly hair. Wearing black pants, a white shirt and a buttoned black vest, he makes a handsome figure. Both ladies glance up to look at him. "Now, he's something to look at, isn't he Lucille? But you know me, I go for a man with maturity. You won't believe this, Lucille, but I bumped into Nick Sr. a few nights back."

Lucille opens her mouth about to say something, but changes her mind.

"He's here in New York. He was walking down the street with—yes, his son, when we almost collided. What are the chances of something like that happening? Then the three of us went down to the Jazz club to say hello to Dan. Mr. Charmer wanted some alone time with me and we went back to my hotel. I know Gil would be so hurt if he knew."

"Sheila, Gil would be devastated."

"You're not married anymore. Did you ever give any thought to rekindling your romance with . . ."

"Of course not," Lucille says, before Sheila has a chance to finish her sentence. "Anyway, why the visit to New York?"

"Just a shopping trip. I will say, Gil spoils me and gives me the best of everything. Always wants me looking smashing. Oh, Lucille, why do I still yearn for that old charmer?"

"Stop talking like that. I thought you gave up on him when you married Gil."

"Well I didn't," she says, taking her hands off the table to make room for the salad the waiter sets before her. "I'm hopeless, but I can give you some advice. It's time for you to meet someone."

Someone? She doesn't want someone. She wants Charlie. "I'm just not ready."

The women grow quiet, nibbling on rolls, commenting about the lights strung around the room that give the space an evening atmosphere. "We're both are at crossroads, aren't we, Sheila?"

"Seems I'm at a roadblock," she answers.

"Dan once told me that when we reach a roadblock, we take a detour. One day the roadblock goes away, and we move on."

"Dan has his own roadblock to contend with."

"What do you mean?"

"You don't know? He let the cat out of the bag when I last saw him. I guess he'll tell you soon enough."

The women barely taste their food; they are so busy catching up on things. When the waiter begins clearing the table, they pay their bill and promise to meet again soon. Sheila hands Lucille an envelope, telling her that she has been designated carrier pigeon. Looking at the typewritten address, it appears to be a business letter. Lucille glances at it and drops it in her pocketbook, thinking she'll read it when she gets home.

Under the Red Ribbon

Two notes hang from the empty coat rack when Lucille arrives home, one from Kimimela, the other from Paco. Whenever the children take their coats, they leave a note behind telling Lucille where they are going. They have been doing this since they were old enough to go out by themselves. Now fifteen and thirteen, they continue the ritual. Lucille once thought of having a spot there for herself, but she really doesn't go out much.

She has the urge to leave the house again, but where will she go? Sheila sparked her curiosity. What roadblock is Dan facing? She decides to find out.

⁓

The dark room with only the glow of table lamps and flickering cigarettes casts a soft light on Dan's face. He is playing "Body and Soul" at the Jazz Club. Lucille studies his intense expression. His body vibrates with the music. Standing at the entrance, she watches him finish the piece and walk towards a tall blonde cigarette girl with a red flower in her hair. She's wearing a black halter-top showing lots of cleavage and a short skirt showing lots of leg. He swings his arm around her shoulder. Lucille thinks that maybe she should have notified him before coming,

Why shouldn't Dan have a girlfriend? Come to think of it, he's probably had quite a few by now. The cigarette girl moves on, but not before blowing Dan a kiss. Lucille takes a good look at her and realizes that she is very young, probably not even twenty years old.

When Dan catches sight of Lucille, his face breaks into a huge smile. He motions her to a table set against the wall, away from any noise.

"You came by at just the right time," he says. "I want to introduce you to someone. For the longest time, I've wanted you two to meet." Lucille's eyes wander over to the cigarette girl. She appears to be no older than eighteen. *This is what Sheila was talking about*, she thinks. *Dan is infatuated with a much too young woman.* Her eyes still on the cigarette girl, she says, "Is she the one you want to introduce me to?"

He laughs.

"You can tell me, Dan."

"Oh, no. She's just a kid, but I give her credit. She's working here to pay her way through college." Lucille sighs in relief.

A man wearing a pastel blue long-sleeved shirt with a navy blue blazer tossed over his shoulder walks toward them.

"Andrew, I want to introduce you to someone very dear to me," says Dan.

"Well, this is a pleasure," the man answers. "Maybe I will sit for a moment, or longer."

Andrew asks Lucille about her line of work and where she lives. She finds him engaging. Their conversation flows easily. They talk about New York, and what a great city it is, about the galleries, concerts, and museums.

"I knew you two would get along. I just knew it."

Is Dan playing matchmaker? Although the gentleman is engaging, she is not ready for a new relationship. She'll thank Dan later for his effort. He'll understand. He always does. Dan's expression changes, as if he's agonizing over something. "I've been like a man hiding from the cops all these years. I'm not doing that anymore. I can't live that way. When Sheila and Nick Sr. were here, I decided I'd just come out with it. So, I am going to tell you. Andrew and I are...how should I put it? I suppose I could say, like you and Charlie were."

"What are you saying?"

Andrew looks over at him. "Tell her, Dan."

"We live together. You know, we shop for food, we work, we eat together, and we complete each other's lives." Dan's voice is soft but his face is tense. "This isn't easy for me or for Andrew. People like us are not accepted as a couple, you know that. We can't openly hold hands, kiss, or do any of that. We're scoffed at. Maybe in years to come, things will change. But that change will be a long time in coming."

Andrew puts his hand on top of Dan's and then pulls it back. "We love each other."

Lucille knew only one person in all of Harvest like that. People joked about frail Jamie Dolson. But Dan is anything but frail. He's tall and muscular. So is Andrew. This will take a while to sink in.

"Yes Lucille, I'm all those names you've heard: a fag, a queer, an oddball. But really, I'm just Dan, the man you have known all your life."

Does Bill know? And how about Paul? Did her mother know? Is she the only one who didn't suspect?

"I guess that puts you in a special category," she says. "According to Pausanias from Plato's Symposium, heavenly love and men loving other men have a connection."

"Leave it to Lucille to insert a bit of literature into this," Dan jokes.

◦◦◦

Lucille's therapy sessions become painful as her past catches up with her. She begins to learn things about herself. When she discovered who her true father was, did she gloss over that too quickly? Did she take enough time to grasp the situation? Her tears flow. Who does she consider her father to be? She talks about Charlie and Nick. One resided in her house and one resided in her mind. Which resided in her heart? Was there room for both? The complexity of her relationship with both men would take years to tackle. There's more. Why didn't she hold Nick responsible for their baby? Why did she make excuses for him? And what about Bill? Why does he carry so much hate for the Martin men?

"There are more questions than answers," Dr. Hartfeld says. "My job is to help you find those answers."

It isn't until after many therapy sessions that Lucille mentions Dan's sexual orientation. Dr. Hartfeld's slight smile tells her that he knew all along she wasn't telling him everything. "When you first started coming here," he says, "you talked about him incessantly, and suddenly, not so much."

"I guess…well, I guess you can say I was embarrassed. After all, he's not just anybody. He's my father. All those years in Harvest, Dan shared Bill's life: his wife, me. Finally he can live his own life. I wonder if he'll ever tell Bill how I came into this world?" She realizes that withholding information from her therapist is not in her best interest. Still, it is tough to say some things. She musters her courage and says, "I'm thinking of contacting Nick. I know so much time has passed and we would have little to say to each other, but just the same, it would give whatever we had together finality."

She waits for his reply, but there is none. As she gets ready to leave, he says, "Lucille, is that what you are really thinking? Finality? Or do you hope that it ends like a fairy tale, with the prince and the princess living happily ever after?"

She doesn't know how to answer.

⁓

Sitting with her bowl of cereal and coffee in front of her on a sunny Saturday morning while the kids are out with their friends, Lucille suddenly remembers the letter Sheila gave her. She finds it mixed in with her comb and makeup at the bottom of her pocketbook. She finds her reading glasses, and rips open the envelope.

Dear Lucille,

I have written to you many times since your husband's death. Each time I crumpled the letter and threw it away. Sometimes I carried it around in my pocket for so long, hoping I'd find the courage to stop by and leave it at your doorstep. I often wonder if you ever think of me, or if you do, just let my image flash through your mind before you go on to another thought. At your husband's funeral, I held your hand longer than I should have and the feel of you is still with me.

I heard wonderful things about Charlie, and of course he was the kind of man you deserved. I met him briefly on your porch that day in Harvest. So many years ago. Remember? I acted like a jerk. I'm surprised he didn't punch me out for what I said. But to be honest, I always felt that you belonged with me. Guess you didn't think so. You married the guy.

That is the past. Now for the future. I will be in New York City on June 26. I would like to drop by and say hello. No need to tell me how to get to your house. Like I always said, I'll find you. I'll always find you. If I don't hear from you, I'll assume we have a date. I hope sometime around 3:00 is fine with you. If you are wondering about the formality of a typewritten letter, blame it on Hal, who now thinks I should dictate my letters to him. Yes, helpful Hal is still with me.

Nick

Under the Red Ribbon

Glancing at the calendar, Lucille realizes she has only two weeks to prepare before seeing him. She circles the date. She doesn't tear off the page and put it under the red ribbon yet; she doesn't know how memorable it will be. She paces back and forth from the kitchen to the bedroom. She rereads the letter. She notices that he didn't sign the letter with the word *love*. But then she reads *the feel of you is still with me*.

Did he ever marry? Is he married now? Has he changed much? She searches through her drawers, through all the mementos she has hidden away: the diamond bracelet he sent her when she received her PhD, the barrette he gave her the night they made love in his apartment. She even kept the replica of the Model T that he sent for Paco's first birthday. Then she sees the poem she wrote at Dan's kitchen table, when she saw Nick again for the first time since that afternoon at the creek.

The leaves are turning green again,
I still remember the first time when
I saw your face, so heaven sent,
And fell in love with you.

She calls Dan and tells him about the letter. His reply surprises her. "It's been a while since you two were together. Life changes all of us."

As June 26 moves closer, minor decisions become major ones. Should her children be home to meet Nick? What should she wear? Should she have her hair and nails done on the day of his arrival, or the day before? Charlie's picture is on the kitchen counter. She moves it into the bedroom. Feeling a surge of guilt, she moves the picture to the living room and places it on the coffee table.

Of course the children should spend the afternoon at a friend's house. She should be alone when she meets him. She'll have her hair and nails done the morning of June 26th so that she'll look fresh and well groomed, and she will buy a new dress. Everything is falling into place.

With an excitement she hasn't felt in years, Lucille gives the salesgirl at *Silk and Chiffon* a short version of the saga of Nick and Lucille.

She's noticed that it always seems to inspire a salesperson when he or she hears of possible romance. Agnes is no exception. The woman is about fifty-five years old, slim, and attired impeccably, making a fashion statement of her own. Although she's wearing a black suit and black shoes, she sparkles. The crystal buttons on her jacket, the crystal necklace around her neck, and the crystal earrings enhance the twinkle in her eyes. Her red lipstick has a sheen and her skin is moist. Lucille likes looking at her.

Agnes propels into ecstasy as she listens to Lucille's story. She cups her hand around her chin, as if contemplating the most serious of matters. When Lucille has finished, Agnes disappears into a secluded corner of the store, returning with a huge smile on her face. She's carrying a pale pink cotton dress with a peplum. "This is it. This will accentuate your tiny waist. And look, the neckline plunges ever so slightly. You want to look elegantly casual, but, my dear, still alluring."

Lucille remembers that Nick likes her in blue, but studying herself in the mirror and noticing the way the color reflects on her cheeks, she thinks he just might change his mind.

At close to three o'clock in the afternoon on June 26, Lucille is ready. Her hair is coiffed in a pompadour with the back rolled and off her shoulders, giving her an elegant look, but she remembers that Nick likes her hair down. Lucille unrolls her hair and lets it fall over her shoulders. She has been rolling and unrolling her hair for the past half hour.

Noticing the bright sunrays coming through the kitchen window, Lucille ponders for a moment. Would a darker room be more intimate for them to have their tea? She places a bouquet of tulips on the kitchen table and positions another small empty vase in the living room. Perhaps Nick will bring her flowers, and nothing would be more awkward than to leave him holding them while she goes looking for a vase. She turns on the radio and searches for just the right music. When she hears Frank Sinatra in his new 1950 hit sing, "It Had To Be You," she turns the radio off. Too staged.

Last night, she spent hours studying her high school pictures to see just how much she has changed. Certainly she's aged, but living in New

York City has given her sophistication, which is more enticing than youth. He won't think she's a "stale piece of bread." She's still pretty. Not pretty like her daughter, but men still admire her.

When the doorbell rings, she glances in the mirror one more time. Yes, the blonde rinse has given her hair sparkle and brightness. She slaps her cheeks, in case her nervousness has drained her color. She takes a deep breath and opens the door.

In front of her, wearing a navy blue blazer, white shirt, gray pants and hair still dark with a smattering of gray, stands Nick Martin Jr. She doesn't speak. She can't. Extending her hand and hoping that it isn't too cold or too hot, or worse yet perspiring, she moves toward him. He is unmoved by the gesture.

She drops her hand to her side. He must be shocked to see her. That's it. When his face shows no emotion, she starts to fear the worst. He's disappointed. After Charlie died, she let herself go for too long. She looks like a mature woman. She's no longer the young Lucille. After all, her own daughter is about the age she was when Nick told her that he would never love anyone else. Nick always liked beautiful young women. Is this why Dan warned her? What did she really expect, anyway? Was Dr. Hartfeld right? Was she anticipating the prince to return to the princess, and that they would live happily ever after?

"Come in, Nick. Come in and sit down." She recognizes Hal with the cherub face. Did Nick bring him along so that he could make a quick getaway if he had to? She remembers Max, the teacher at Little River Indian Residential School, saying that Hal fawns all over Nick like he's aristocracy. Lucille thinks he's still fawning over him, or at the very least, hovering.

Well, of course this meeting would be awkward. The whole thing is a big mistake. Better to live in illusions, her mind filling in the blank spaces, then go through this. She automatically repeats the same mundane words. "Come in, have a seat. Let's sit in the living room." Good thing she put Charlie's picture there. Let Nick see that someone else fills her heart.

She thought she looked good. She looks down at her dress. It really isn't as pretty as she imagined. Maybe she imagined too many things.

What difference does it make? He's nothing but an old classmate. She had her love with Charlie. Why did Charlie leave her, and leave her to this humiliation? She'll tell him she has an appointment in ten minutes and so he'll leave. Oh, she hopes he doesn't see her eyes welling up. She wishes her kids were home, and then he'd see that she is much too busy for him.

Then she notices: Nick is carrying a white cane. She watches him tap his way into the living room with Hal at his side.

Her hands automatically spring to her mouth. She wants to say something, but what can she say?

"Surprised, Lucille? It's startling, isn't it?"

She has to be careful. "Nick, you look...you look like the same Nick I remember."

"And you, Lucille? Tell me Hal, how does she look? The same, huh? The same gorgeous Lucille? You and Hal met in Minnesota. Do you remember?"

"Oh, yes, I haven't forgotten him."

"So tell me, Hal, how does she look?"

"Still a gorgeous woman, Nick."

Finally she stammers, "Did you...did you find it here alright? Some people have a little trouble." She stops herself from picking the polish off her fresh manicure.

"Oh, no problem. Hal has a good sense of direction, always has."

She wants to show him pictures of her children, but she immediately nixes that idea. She's so nervous, she can't think. If she were prepared for this, she would know what to say. She feels a chill on this warm summer day. "Nick, if you'll excuse me, I have to run to the bathroom, I'll be right back."

Slamming the bathroom door behind her, she holds onto the sink. She's shaking. He is dazzling with gray hair around his temples, and his face shows a deep, rich quality he didn't have years ago. She looks in the mirror. The irony of having her makeup done professionally, her hair styled, and her nails painted! None of that matters now. She reaches for the bottle of *Evening in Paris*. She continued buying it all these years, although she has trouble finding it in the stores. She sprays herself with the perfume.

When she walks back into the living room, she announces her entrance. "I'm back."

"I know. Nothing wrong with my olfactory bulb."

She laughs. He still has that Martin charm. She sits down on the small leg stool in front of his chair. She takes both his hands in hers. "Nick, what happened?"

"An accident during an air show. Made an outlandish dive and ended up hitting a mountain. I did something too daring for even Nick Martin Jr. I had a few broken bones, too. They healed, but my eyes are another story."

Her smile is controlled, her insides tangled in knots.

He reaches into his pocket and takes out a tissue-wrapped object. When she removes the paper, she whispers, "Nick, where did you get this?"

"Found it in my car. It must have fallen from your neck that day you told me you were pregnant. Remember how we held on to each other?"

"I'll never forget that day."

"I was a kid. What did I know?"

She doesn't want to talk about that yet, so she looks at the necklace and asks, "Did you read the engraving on the locket? Nick, it's not what you think."

"Few things are," he says.

She doesn't want him thinking that her mother had an affair with Dan. "The thing is..." *Oh no*, she thinks. *It's too complicated. He won't understand.*

Maybe he hears the change in her breathing, now magnified. He laughs. "I never gave it any serious thought. I always knew Dan wasn't like the rest of the guys. It's obvious. Who knows why he gave your mother the locket? But he's a good fella. Last week he dedicated a song to me at the club, 'Don't Fence Me In.' He said that song fit me to a 'T.'" He fumbles with the chain but manages to circle it around her neck. "Why do you wear this, anyway?"

She doesn't answer.

Hal is trying to keep himself busy in the kitchen by turning the pages of a newspaper, but he never takes his eyes off of the boss.

Nick outlines her face with his fingertips, stopping at her lips. "May I, Lucille?" When he kisses her, she remembers the day at the creek when the Eastern Goldfinch flew across the sky and she asked, "Will he ever come back?" Nick said, "Only if he had a darn good reason to." She has so many things to ask him, but she has time. He's only been here fifteen minutes.

She walks into the kitchen to make Nick and Hal a cup of tea. She carries a cup into the living room and helps Nick with the hot liquid, and their hands meet around the cup.

She gazes at him, and the young Nick emerges: the fearless Nick who sped around the curves of gravel roads, the envy of all the boys, the love of all the girls. In the lines around his eyes she sees the courage of John Milton. She sees Homer and a myriad of inventors, artists, and attorneys, all blind and miraculous in their undertakings. Her Nick is one of them.

She takes his face in her hands and kisses his eyelids. She whispers, "Nick, how are you getting through this?"

"You were the only thing I ever saw. The rest was just background. And your face is still here before me. So, I haven't lost anything." He stands to hold her close and whispers, "I have to go now."

Nick

Nick owns a red car again. No need for the white limousine. Hal drives him to a large office building about four blocks from Lucille's apartment. A woman and two children move out of the way when Nick enters the elevator, as if a blind man takes up more space than a sighted one. Hal and Nick walk into a wood-paneled office, and then Hal retreats into the hall.

The Colonel is waiting. Sitting in full uniform behind a carved mahogany desk, he welcomes Nick with a handshake. He gets right to the point. "The strategic intelligence information you collected is invaluable for our National Security, but your work is not done. We are sending you out of the country next week. Get your business in order. Here, take these papers with you."

Back in the car, Nick knows exactly what he has to do, and with any luck he'll get through his mission quickly. He's been in this line of work since Truman created the agency, and he's found himself doing the oddest things in remote places. His name has been changed so many times, some days he has to think hard to remember who he really is. There are stacks of papers in the backseat, ready to be burned. He picks up a sheet and scribbles on the back; the writing zigzags over the page. "Hal, write this down for me and send it to Lucille. *If you but knew, how all my days seemed filled with dreams of you . . .*"

"Stop, Nick. You've been reciting that poem for at least twenty years. I know it by heart."

From Sunday through Friday, Nick mulls over the plans for his new mission. Thanks to Hal, the paperwork goes faster. Hal doesn't ask questions and if he suspects anything, he doesn't let on. When Arnold died, Nick never thought he could have a good, loyal friend like him again, but he's been lucky. Hal comes pretty darn close. He fixed him up with a babe years ago, but Hal won't marry her. "I don't want anyone taking time away from you, boss."

On Saturday evening, he arrives at Lucille's apartment carrying a bouquet of red roses. He knocks on the door expecting Lucille to answer, but when the door opens, he hears a young girl's voice. "Sir, are you lost?" the girl asks him.

Nick lets it go. "I'm here to see your mother," he says. "Lucille Rosen." His voice trips over the last word.

Kimimela calls out to her mother. "Ma, are you expecting anyone?" When she hears the "yes" coming from her mother's bedroom, she invites them in. Hal escorts Nick into the living room and makes sure that he's comfortably seated. Nick is not accustomed to waiting for a woman, and he wonders if he is losing his touch. He might be out of practice; the past few years, his mind has been strictly on his work.

"I know you," Paco says, when he sees Nick. "We met at my friend's father's store, *Taylor and Taylor*. You sent me the model airplane for my thirteenth birthday. I didn't know you and my father were friends."

"I'm a friend of your mother's."

"A friend of my mother's? She's never mentioned you."

Feeling a bit slighted, Nick says, "I guess she wouldn't mention me. But let's take a look at that plane I sent you."

"A look?"

Nick can sense the boy's discomfort. "You don't see only through your eyes. We have other senses, you know. We just don't use them enough."

Paco leads Nick to his bedroom, where he keeps the plane. "There it is, on the bottom shelf." He guides Nick's hand over to it.

Feeling each part of the model with his fingers Nick says, "You did a great job putting this together. So, are you interested in planes?"

"Well, when you told me that the real version of this plane carries 8,000 pounds of bombs, I wanted to find out more about it. I started reading airplane magazines, and then I saw your picture and read an article about you."

"I'm impressed," Nick says, with a chuckle.

"I read that you flew your plane over an enclave of enemy ammunition and flattened it. It said all kinds of great stuff about you. I told my friends, 'Hey, I know this guy.'"

For Nick, the incident is still raw. That was the mission right before his last. He wants to talk about something else. "Hey, I have a brand new red car. How about Hal taking you and your sister for a ride? I've always owned a red car, except when I had the limo."

"We have a family friend who says that red stands for power and success."

"Smart fella. Red happens to be my favorite color. And he's right; it does stand for power. Take it from me. I know."

"I like cars, too. Just got my license."

"Don't tell anybody, but I drove way before I got mine."

Nick's father taught him how to drive when he was only eleven years old. The two of them drove down the back roads of Harvest where they wouldn't get caught. When he got his first car, his Dad told him, "If you don't know the mechanics of a car, you're not ready to drive one." When he was much younger than this kid, he knew about keeping the spark plugs clean and the carburetor adjusted, and what he didn't know he picked up in a hurry. Now he can service cars better than guys with full vision.

"Boy, my old jalopy can really use some work," Paco says.

"Where is this car of yours?" Nick asks. "I can come down and teach you a few things."

"You would do that?"

"Sure. I remember this guy Izzy. We called him Izzy with the Tin Lizzy. He had a real old car, from the early 1900's, and my Dad and I helped him restore it, made it drive smooth as...as smooth as your mother's blue satin dress."

"When did you see my mother wear that?"

When did he see her wear that? Every day since that party at Sheila's house. "Before you were born. I'm a lucky man. I love the work I do. Not everybody is that lucky."

"How can a blind man be lucky?"

Nick understands that the kid doesn't know that a loss can sometimes be a gain. Because of his loss, he designed an airplane a blind man will be able to pilot. Actually, he came up with that idea while still in high school. Seeing Harry in those thick glasses got him thinking. Although getting it perfected is still years away, he's confident his design will become a reality.

"Of course I'm lucky," he says. "About three o'clock in the morning, when the road is still empty, Hal here puts the car in full throttle and we speed down the road, just so I have the sensation of the wind blowing through my hair, and the thrill of my heart thumping right through my shirt. I need speed, like your mom needs poetry."

"You know a lot about my mother. But do you know about my Dad? He would think all that speed is reckless. And he would know. He was a top-notch scientist. He was smart."

"Speed isn't reckless. One time, right after World War I, Ralph de Palma drove his car faster than an airplane. Doing something like that isn't reckless. It builds a man's fortitude right from his core. A man who can do that isn't afraid to do anything."

"My Dad did great things before he died. Did you know he was trying to cure heart disease? But I guess none of that stuff helped him."

Nick finds his way over to Paco and puts his arms around his shoulders. He knows about loss. It's like letting air out of tires. You have to plug it up somehow before it flattens you.

They walk back into the living room, and Nick is running out of conversation. Hal speaks up from the kitchen and asks the kids if they want a ride in the new red car. They can't get their coats on fast enough. Paco runs back to his mother's bedroom to tell her they are taking a ride with Hal. Nick sits on the couch wondering where Lucille is.

Lucille makes her entrance from her bedroom and sits beside him on the couch. "I heard you speaking to the kids," she says, "and I stayed out of the way, so you could get to know them and they could get to know you."

How he ever shared Lucille with another man, he'll never know. The frivolous, arrogant boy at the creek trying to make out with a sweet young girl was the boy of his youth, but he has no excuse for behaving like a coward when Lucille told him she was pregnant. "Was our baby a boy or a girl?"

"I named him Arnold."

His son would have been old enough now for them to tinker in a garage together. They would have been buddies. They'd live in a house with a huge workspace and they'd spend hours restoring engines and adjusting wires. They would streamline planes to make them go faster, fly smoother. They would come home at the end of the day with their arms slung around each other's shoulders like real pals, and they would . . . But what's the sense of making up stories? That's for writers.

"Nick, do you think it was a mistake for you to come back to me?"

"Have we ever really been away from each other?"

LUCILLE

The next morning at breakfast, before Lucille is able to take a bite of toast, her daughter bubbles over with enthusiasm. "Mom, how did you keep that man a secret? He's the cat's meow."

"I knew you'd like him."

Paco looks at his sister with annoyance. "A guy comes to visit mom, and you get all gushy. She's not interested in getting married again, so don't give her any ideas."

Lucille laughs. It's been awhile since the three of them had a lively discussion. She feels lighthearted, even optimistic.

Returning home from work on a Friday afternoon, she spots Nick's red car outside her apartment. With a spring in her step, she runs toward it. *How long has Nick been waiting*, she wonders? She finds Hal standing beside the car with a message from Nick. "He said to tell you he had some business out of town. Came up suddenly. He'll be away for a short time."

"How long?" Lucille asks, but Hal doesn't know.

Lucille didn't think that a short time meant six months. She's worried. She lost Charlie; she can't bear another loss. She remembers her conversation with Hal. *Business out of town. He'll be away for a short time.*

On a Sunday morning in June, Lucille is reading the New York Herald at the kitchen table when she spots a picture of Nick in the travel section. She's not sure at first and takes the newspaper to the window to see the picture in a brighter light. She's never seen him in a tennis outfit, and she studies his face. He looks tan and fit. He's seated in a lounge chair near the tennis court of the famous Hoberg Hotel in northern California. A woman sits across from him, attired in a white sundress, donning large sunglasses, and sipping a drink. She appears not to have a care in the world.

Sitting in her apartment at her kitchen table, sipping a glass of milk and nibbling on an Oreo cookie, she almost laughs at the contrast. That woman doesn't have a care in the world and she, Lucille Rosen, spent the last six months worrying herself sick wondering what happened to the man that woman is sitting with.

Paco, having his share of cookies, looks over her shoulder and sees the picture. "I knew he wasn't going to help me fix up my car. Who cares? I didn't want him hanging around anyway, hemming in on Daddy."

"Paco," Lucille says, staying calm. "My life with your dad was like one of these Oreo cookies. Nick was there at the beginning, and then came back at the end. But, see that delicious creamy part in the middle? That's where Daddy and I had our life together. So don't worry about anyone hemming in on Daddy."

After Charlie died, Lucille found comfort in her friendship with Richard Taylor. One afternoon over coffee, she told him all about her relationship with Nick. He didn't seem surprised. Nick had been giving him clues that were easy to connect. She wants to see him now, and talk to him.

Taylor and Taylor is bustling with customers when she arrives. Mulling around the store waiting for business to slow, she recalls the dream she had the night before. It was about the Oenikika, the Indian purification ceremony. Nick was there, and when he offered tobacco to the sacred fire, the smoke carried his request to the Great Spirit. "I want to see again," Nick said. The medicine man smudged him with the smoke of burning sweet grass, cedar, and sage, enabling the spirits to do their work. She kneeled at Nick's side, holding his hands.

Richard Taylor sees Lucille and comes right over. "What brings you here?"

"I wanted to ask you if Nick said anything to you before leaving town."

"No. It's like he dropped off the earth."

"I know where he is." She shows him the copy of *The New York Herald* and the picture of Nick and the woman.

"Oh, that picture. That's an advertisement for our special sports collection. Didn't you notice the words under the picture? 'Men's clothing from *Taylor and Taylor*.' That's Lola in the picture. She dyed her hair black for the photograph. The ad was done last year."

She was so disturbed seeing the picture, her mind became a blur. She couldn't think straight. She didn't read anything under the picture. She could only see Nick with another woman. Lucille sits down on the nearest chair. "Thank you, Richard. Thank you."

"For what?" he asks.

Whitefeather told her to pay close attention to dreams; they are messages. The dream about the *Oenikika* was telling her to return to Riverview, she is sure of that. After making arrangements at work and leaving Dan to look after the children, she leaves for Riverview to visit Whitefeather. And then she plans to visit Harvest; her mother's memorial service will be coming up.

Stepping off the train, she notices immediately the quietness and ease of this small town; there's no fuss, and a cab driver is waiting at the curb for her to hop in. In New York City, nothing is this simple, not even hailing a cab.

Sitting close to the window, she watches for familiar landmarks. The farms are flourishing, unlike when the dust storms ruled the land, and she breathes in the wonderful scent. Nearing town, she searches for the library, post office, movie house, and dress shop. When she asks the cabbie where they are, he tells her that the dress shop was torn down a long time ago and replaced with a department store. The movie house was moved in order to accommodate a larger audience and a parking lot. The post office goes unnoticed, because the large brick structure they drive past doesn't look anything like the insignificant building she remembers. Finally, they pull up close to a store she remembers. Nothing about it seems to have changed. "Stop, right here," she says. "I want to surprise Mr. Johnson."

The driver points to the name on the canopy. "It's P.T. Grocers now," he says.

She wants to go in anyway. There are so many memories right here in this store. This is where she met Whitefeather who became her lifelong friend. This is where she got directions to the residential school. This place marked the beginning of a new life. She stands with her suitcases at her side and studies the façade of the General Store. Her mind fills with memories. It was her first time away from home.

She examines every detail of the store before entering: the Coca-Cola sign hanging from a chain, the wooden flowerboxes along the porch rail filled with forsythia blossoms. They are just the way Mr. Johnson had them. The only difference she sees is the advertisements for wine, beer, and cigarettes taped to the window.

She carries her suitcases into the store, her heart palpitating. The shelves are stacked with everyday staples like Cheerios, Cream of Wheat, Aunt Jemima Pancake mixes, and Campbell's soups. On the counter are boxes of Tootsie Rolls, Juicy Fruit, M&M's, and Life Savers. Much the same as Mr. Johnson had it, and much the same as Jerry Sloane arranged his store in Harvest. But, now two large refrigerators stand in the corner, one labeled "Dairy" and the other "Meat." The floor is covered with bright yellow linoleum.

An elderly man is engaged in an argument with a dark-haired woman behind the counter. No long apron for this woman, like Mr. Johnson wore. She's wearing a bright green blouse dipping low in the front and a much too tight skirt, outlining her buttocks. The man, dirty and exuding a foul odor, insists on speaking to the woman's husband, and he won't take no for an answer. Watching the man point his finger at the woman, Lucille becomes anxious and wants to help, but the woman is relaxed and firm. She says, "No, you cannot see my husband. He is out of town." The man exits the store in a huff, but not before he snatches a box of crayons off the shelf and races across the street. He reaches the bookstore, scribbles on the window, and runs further down the street in the direction of the Little River Indian Residential School.

The woman looks up at Lucille. "I hope that man didn't frighten you. He does this all the time. It's just a part of his day now. Can I help you? You must be a visitor. I know almost everyone who comes in here to shop."

"Not really a visitor. I used to live here."

"Well, you must have changed an awful lot. I only see people like you in magazines: skinny women in pretty blouses and long skirts. Where do you live now?"

"New York City."

"Ah, New York City." The woman says those words with so much dreaminess in her eyes, Lucille can't help but wonder what she is thinking. "I lived there for a few years," she goes on to say, "and when I came back to Riverview, it was hard for me to adjust, even though I was born and raised here. I had a beautiful shape like you and long black hair. Now I cut it short. It is easier that way." She touches her hair when she says this and smoothes it into place. "And my skin was as smooth as yours. Now I have lines around my eyes, and look here, around my mouth." She looks away now and closes her eyes. "When I strutted around in my high heels, the men went wild. But now I eat too much," she says, patting her hips. "The beautiful Tara is gone."

"Tara? I know that name." Taking a closer look at the woman's face, Lucille sees remnants of the Tara she remembers: the way she tosses her head, the self-assured smile and the white teeth. The years have changed her, but still, this could be the woman she met at the Street Fair years ago, the woman who toyed with Charlie's heart. She could be the woman who posed with Nick in that photograph she saw on Ellie's desk.

"People call me Whitefeather's wife now."

Whitefeather? Paco Whitefeather is her husband? Lucille tries not to look flabbergasted, but she must not be doing a very good job of it.

"You look shocked. Do you know my husband?"

"That's the reason for my visit."

"A pretty woman like you coming all this way to see my Paco Whitefeather? I guess he's attractive enough."

"He's my good friend. I'm his sister here on earth, he likes to say."

"That's as good an excuse as any. But he's not in town. He'll be back in a day or two. We bought this store from Mr. Johnson before Whitefeather left for the war. I run the place."

Lucille introduces herself. "You do remember my husband, Charlie. Charlie Rosen?"

"Now I'm shocked," Tara stammers. "Remember? How could I forget him?" She gives a hint of a laugh, just enough to make Lucille pick up her suitcases and head for the exit. "Please," Tara says, stopping her at the door. "Spend the night at our house. If you're Whitefeather's friend, then you're a friend of mine. You must be tired. It's time to close the store for the day anyway. I'll drive you." She leads Lucille to the truck.

"Oh, just put your feet on top of the cartons," Tara says, when she notices Lucille trying to find a place for her feet on the floor of the vehicle. "Whitefeather is the liaison between the federal government and our tribal government and that's all of his paperwork. He should be back in the morning."

Lucille is familiar with the drive to the reservation and she's quiet along the way, observing everything. When they arrive at the house, Tara asks, "Do you know who used to live here?" Before Lucille has a chance to answer, she says, "Miss Halliday's sister." Showing Lucille through the house, she chatters on. "It's only a small house, but we have a nice parlor to sit in, and a large kitchen. Miss Holliday's sister liked to cook. And I like to sew so I made all new red and yellow slipcovers, and the striped drapes to match. I love color.

"Anyway, Miss Halliday's sister, her name is Aldina, she left in a hurry. She couldn't take the shame after Whitefeather's sister was murdered. She told us we could have this place. That was her way of making it up to my husband. She thought everyone knew and cared about Kimimela's death. To tell the truth, only we on the reservation cared. I overheard the white people say, 'one less.'"

For Lucille, reliving those memories is to be expected. Riverview is full of memories, some joyous and others painful.

Tara reaches for two glasses from a cabinet over her kitchen sink and fills them with wine. Lucille takes only a sip and puts down her glass. She's so tired, she's afraid the wine will put her to sleep. She watches Tara pull out a bowl from a drawer and start chopping vegetables.

"You like the way I chop? Chopping vegetables is like chopping up your life in little pieces. You digest it better." She laughs, and refills her wine glass. Gulping and chopping, she surprises Lucille when she says, "So you married Charlie Rosen. Did you ever believe those orphanage stories?"

"I don't know what you mean?"

"He lived in an orphanage, and a couple from New York adopted him. That part is true. But those people he went to live with coddled him too much. When he sneezed, they said it was pneumonia. When he coughed, it was whooping cough. They didn't let him become strong. I met the Rosens only once when they came for a visit. They didn't like me much. That problem he had, it was really strange. But men like different things, you know. No big deal. It was fun for both of us." She pours herself another drink.

Tara's words hit, straight and pointed, like an arrow to Lucille's heart. She lashes back. "Why are you insulting my husband? Why are you telling me?"

Tara interrupts. "Why am I telling you what you already know?"

Lucille thinks the woman's arrogance is appalling. She should never have accepted her offer to sleep here. Tara was wicked long ago, and she is wicked now. She exhales deeply and shakes her head.

Ignoring Lucille's anger, Tara continues. "Beautiful Tara did things no one else could get away with. She could snap her fingers and get any man. Was I honorable? Who cares. When I was young, I wanted to play. But Whitefeather changed all that. When he caught me selling dope to the people on the reservation, he threw me in his truck and forced me to sit in the woods for three days without food or drink or a change of clothes. Emptied of earthly needs, I filled with the goodness of the Creator."

"You really think you filled with the goodness of the Creator?" Lucille's voice is filled with sarcasm as her eyes stare deeply into Tara's.

"Yes, after three days, Whitefeather joined me and we sat under the big sky and chanted together. He gave me a rose-red stone that belonged to his great-great-grandmother because he said that it opened the heart and brought forth pure love. As I held the stone, our lovemaking was so full, the sky opened and sprinkled us with stars. Oh, yes. That night changed me."

Lucille has never met anyone quite like this woman. After dinner, she helps Tara clear the dishes and places them in the sink. Tara fills the sink with sudsy water, and washes each dish as if it were a sacred artifact.

"You're angry because I spoke the truth about your husband," Tara says, lifting the wine bottle and refilling her glass. "I won't ask for your forgiveness. The truth is the truth. If you wish to believe otherwise or if you wish to live a lie, that's up to you."

If Lucille could leave and sleep elsewhere, she would. She'll wait until morning and then she'll go.

"This is healing soap," Tara says, showing Lucille the soap in her palm. "It is made with ground sagebrush. Notice how slowly I wash each dish. I am kind to the dish, and at the same time I heal my sore bones."

"What else can it heal?"

"What do you want it to heal?"

"My friend. He lost his eyesight."

"Our customs and rituals don't help everyone. You have to have strong intent. What kind of person is this man?"

"Smart, unpredictable, intelligent, loveable, and often irritating."

Tara delivers a raucous laugh. "That's my kind of man. Do you love him?"

Lucille is silent.

"Well?"

"I can't answer that."

"Why not?" Tara wipes her hands with a dishtowel and pulls Lucille over to the couch. "Tell me."

"Charlie is pulling me in one direction, this man in another."

"Charlie is dead. He would not want you to bury your heart with him." Tara finishes the bottle of wine. She is beginning to slur her words. "By the way, you really haven't changed very much."

"You remember me?"

"Only from the picture Nick carried in his wallet."

When Lucille is ready to retire for the night, Tara offers her fluffy white towels, crisp white sheets, and embroidered pillowcases. "From my wedding night. A gift from Whitefeather's mother, Nadie," she says as she makes up the bed in the spare room.

Watching Tara make the room comfortable for her, she is struck by the haunting fragrance in the room. It is a scent she has never forgotten. Hesitating a moment, she asks, "Are you the woman who wrapped Charlie and me in the white blanket at our wedding? The scent in this room, I remember it. It was there in the cottage on our wedding night. And the woman who ran from the cottage, was that you?"

"I am not that woman. I am the new Tara."

The night passes quickly; Lucille falls asleep as soon as her head hits the pillow. In the morning, she hears Tara's truck pull away and wrapping the robe Tara left for her around her body, she walks into the kitchen.

To her surprise, she sees Whitefeather sitting at the kitchen table mulling over a stack of papers. His hair hangs down the back of his red shirt, and his forehead is wrinkled as though he is reading something difficult to understand.

"My wife told me you were here," he says, standing to embrace Lucille. He tells her about the conference he attended that didn't go very well. "The problem is that the Indian people want more autonomy, but we still need aid from the Federal Government."

"Dualities are difficult to come to grips with. I know something about that."

"So you spent some time getting acquainted with my wife? You're probably wondering how we ever became a couple. I never excused Tara for the way she treated Charlie."

"I don't want to get into that, Whitefeather. It's too painful."

"When our people break the circle, a little of all of us fall. So I married Tara to help her become one who delivers kindness to all people. And when I mend Tara, I mend the circle. But enough talk about problems. Enjoy a walk after breakfast, and see what's become of the residential school." Pointing to the papers on the table, he says, "You can see I have lots of work to do. I'll meet up with you soon."

Lucille strolls around the reservation thinking back to when she and Charlie played an integral part in these people's lives. She sees the men sitting on porch steps smoking cigarettes, women planting in their gardens. It is quiet. The older children are in school. Babies sleep in their carriages.

She knows most of the federal government programs have terminated and without them, Indian education, infrastructure, and health care have gone by the wayside. For the Indians, daily life is still a struggle. Whitefeather told her that he has watched U.S. policy toward the Indians change so many times, he is never sure from day to day where they stand.

She continues down the road leading to the Little River Indian Residential School where Whitefeather said he would meet her. Reaching the familiar landmarks, she stops and walks into the church. It has been a long time since she visited a church. Sitting in a pew, she prays for her family and friends, for Charlie and Nick. She prays for all the people on the reservation.

Walking out into the sunlight, she sees that a bank has replaced the Tanker. She mutters a prayer of thanks. The landscape looks so different without the Advisory Building, the cottage, and the school. She hardly believes it is the same place. But she'll always remember Riverview the way it was. She thinks about Miss Wilson, Mr. Baran, the matrons, and most of all, the children. Ellie told Lucille that she ran into Max at an off-Broadway play. He told Ellie that he owns a dance studio in Manhattan, and he gave her his card. "We were a confused bunch of kids ourselves back then," he said, "and we were supposed to be changing the lives of those little Indian kids. A pity, really." He was sad to hear that Charlie died. "He was a great guy. I was a fool."

She walks up a blacktop driveway toward a large building with a sign that reads, "Welcome to the Riverview Hotel." She pauses for a moment and realizes that this building has replaced the Residential School. She walks around the back and sees a parking area, but also a familiar bench under a maple tree. It's situated close to the back of the hotel. She smiles when she sees the bench. That's where Charlie carved a heart containing the initials CR and LR. "One day," he said, "we'll come back and show it to our children." *We'll* come back. It took years of hard work for their marriage to evolve into a strong, loving relationship, but it happened. Here in Riverview, Charlie's presence touches the air she breathes.

Whitefeather's truck, with P.T. Groceries printed across the driver's door, pulls into view and he parks on the street. He spots her. When he jumps out of the truck, Lucille visualizes the young Paco Whitefeather, old for his years, a leader among his people. She juxtapositions that boy with the man he is today. He's still striving to make an Indian's life better: a life where each one of them can live with honor and dignity. He sprints towards her and she gestures for him to meet her at the bench.

When she turns, she sees a man heading in that direction. He's carrying a large bag and his hair is disheveled. He mumbles nonsense to himself and has difficulty getting seated. When he glances up and sees Lucille, he calls out, "Hey you, come over here!"

When Whitefeather reaches the place where Lucille is standing on the grass, she grabs a hold of his arm. "I think that man needs help."

The man's long gray hair falls over his face and his limp hand fumbles as he reaches into the bag. Walking closer to him, the stench of sour milk and sweat causes Lucille to step back.

"So, here he is," Whitefeather says.

"You know him?"

"Yes, I know him. He's the wanderer. He wanders from bench to bench, store to store, street to street. Wanders through town like he was struck by the devil. Always makes sure to stop at our store. Tells the same story over and over again, about how he innocently walked out of his office one day to take a breath of fresh air, and the chauffeur of a white limousine grabbed his arm and cracked it at the wrist and elbow. Then the man in the limousine, called out, 'what about his shoulder?' So the limousine driver cracked his shoulder.

"I heard about it when it happened. Everybody in town heard about it. He didn't have many friends so no one seemed to care. But when we heard the news on the reservation, we prayed for him to come to his senses. But just the opposite happened. Take a good look. You know him, too."

"He looks like the man I saw pestering Tara in the store yesterday," Lucille says.

The man sneers at her. "So, it's the farm girl, Miss Kramer, and a hussy at that. I heard you were in town. Word gets around."

Lucille hasn't been called "Miss Kramer," for a long time. Scrutinizing the man, she moves closer to Whitefeather.

"You know, Miss Kramer, you caused me to lose my job. The school was investigated after you stirred up that trouble. I even heard that you were pregnant with my child."

Lucille knows him now. She lifts her hand, ready to strike him, but Whitefeather holds her back.

"I have never forgiven you for it. You and that Charlie Rosen. Those were bad years; it was hard to land another job. But you didn't care; you were an Indian lover. I see you still are." Looking at Whitefeather, he forces a grotesque laugh. He puts his bag down on the bench and his hand trembles as he pulls out a yellowed newspaper. Blinking rapidly, he asks, "Whitefeather, recognize your kin? She didn't like the name Wilma—not Indian enough. It's all here in the paper, the way she died. Tried to pin it on Miss Halliday, you and those other injuns on the reservation."

Whitefeather's eyes bulge. He clenches his jaw.

"The whole mess started because of your uncivilized little sister. Because of her, my life has come to this. Now God has forgotten me."

Whitefeather crosses the yard of grass in between them with one stride, and grabs Mr. Baran by the collar. "Do you want your other arm broken?"

The man jeers at him. "I used to put dollar bills in your wife's panties when she danced on tables. Tara would do anything for a buck."

Lucille remembers that the Ghost Dance frightened Mr. Baran. She grabs Whitefeather's hand, and leading him, she starts to sway from side to side. "More Indians will be joining us soon," she says.

Mr. Baran's legs buckle. He falls to the ground. He tears at his hair and howls at the sky.

Whitefeather says, "The Ghost Dance is his weak spot. Large numbers of Indians frighten him. The story goes that he was walking toward the reservation one night, on the rare occasion that he took a walk, and a group of Indian men, maybe ten or fifteen, who were drinking too much, started heckling him. He ran like hell. But they caught up with him, and yelled, 'stay out of our territory if you know what's good for you.' He didn't need any more reason to hate Indians or fear them."

Whitefeather and Lucille walk back to the truck. When Lucille looks back at the pitiful man, she sees him writhing on the ground and kicking his feet.

Lucille is silent on the way back to the house.

Whitefeather continues to speak. "Mr. Baran really started going crazy after his arm was broken. It never set right and it became useless. After you left your job, he started harassing Miss Wilson. He actually accused her of stealing money from the school. When the inspector came to investigate, they learned that Mr. Baran was stealing the money.

"Anyway, the story has a good ending. Miss Wilson and the inspector struck up a romance, and they ended up getting married. They took in three foster children, all from the residential school, and did a damn good job raising them. The kids all graduated high school. Got educated in an all-white school, in the town of Harwick, just ten miles from here. All three eventually became teachers and work at that school now. Had they continued in the residential school, they'd be cleaning rich people's homes."

Tara greets them at the door carrying a bundle of papers and letters from the federal government. She places them on the kitchen table. She's wearing a snug green sweater, heavy makeup and perfume. Lucille sees more of the Tara she remembers.

Lucille and Whitefeather sit down at the table while Tara boils water for tea. "We know we can speak honestly to you, Lucille," Tara says. "Whitefeather has an appointment with the tribal leaders on Tuesday. They want him to represent them in the National Congress of American Indians. But Whitefeather thinks maybe someone else can get better results."

Whitefeather doodles on a pad of paper, stopping to push his hair back and rub his eyes.

"If anyone is capable of filling that position, Whitefeather is," Lucille says.

"That's what I tell him, but sometimes I speak to him and his mind is far away."

Whitefeather lifts his head and looks at Lucille. "Right now I'm working with the Indian Claims Commission and I'm urging the government to make restitutions for the loss of our land. I'm having trouble. A lone Indian voice is just a ripple, and it takes many voices to at least make a wave." He draws on the pad again. "See all these white men sitting around the table, and here I am: one Paco Whitefeather.

"I argue, 'the land is not a lone entity. Everything is connected: the air that gives us breath, the sky that gives us rain and sun, and the river that gives us food.' That's the message from Chief Seattle and I abide by it."

Tara nods. "And when you tell them that, they scoff. And they scoff at your long hair and beads, don't they?"

Whitefeather shrugs. "Let them scoff. The message of Chief Seattle was true yesterday, and it is true today. It will always be true. And I will not give up who I am or who my people are."

Lucille knows of Chief Seattle, the deceased tribal leader. He held the most stringent views on Indian tradition. "Didn't he believe that earth doesn't belong to man, but man belongs to the earth?"

"Yes, and I believe the same."

"It's a tough battle, even for a warrior like you," Lucille says. If you want support, you must get your message out to the general public. How about contacting Ellie's husband, Hanson? He's living in New York now, working as a journalist. He might be the one to help you create a wave."

"Ahhh, you truly are so intelligent. I knew what I was doing when I selected you as our Meda Minda at the residential school."

"My time is your time, Lucille," Whitefeather says the next morning over coffee. "Any place you want to go, we'll go together." And so their first stop is at the cemetery located just down the road from Elu and Nadie's house, close enough for them to walk.

After prayers and chants at his sister's grave, Paco walks Lucille to her baby's grave. Seeing a small bouquet of red roses near the tiny memorial stone, Lucille asks Whitefeather if he knows who put them there.

"Two men come by this area every year around this time. They always visit this grave. The taller gentleman places some flowers, and then they leave."

"The flowers are still fresh," Lucille says.

They arrive at Nadie's house just in time. Summer is on its way, and the people of the reservation are preparing for the Sun Dance Ceremony. The ceremony was outlawed by the United States for many years because of its ritual of self-inflicted suffering. Although it has been modified, Nadie forbids Whitefeather and Elu from participating. "My men have always made great sacrifices, giving of themselves in return for what the Creator has given us. But offering their flesh through piercing in return for healing or wisdom is not something I believe in anymore. I have grown wiser through the years."

Lucille bends to embrace Nadie, who is sitting in a chair embroidering a scarf. She studies the woman: the lines that crisscross her face like thin ropes, her thin fingers, her small body, delicate as a bird. Her hair is white and soft falling over her shoulders. This woman of wisdom has lived a full life and experienced many things, Lucille thinks.

"I will be with Kimimela soon," she says. "I see her in my dreams every night now. And it is time. It is time for me to leave this earth, and be with her again."

Lucille smoothes Nadie's hair. "Your image, your words, and your wisdom will remain here with us, Nadie."

"So Lucille, where has your path taken you since I saw you last?"

Lucille is silent for a moment. "You know about Charlie, my dear husband. And now this man that I have known for a long time has come back into my life. He made me happy. But he has gone away. I don't know what to do."

"Be careful of what you do. What you decide will affect you and others." Nadie reaches into a jar and pulls out a totem spider. She drops it into Lucille's hand. "Keep it close to you. It brings the wisdom of Chief Seattle. 'Humankind has not woven the web of life; we are but one thread within it. Whatever we do to the web, we do to ourselves. All things are bound together. All things connect.'"

Lucille grips Nadie's hand. "Thank you for your wisdom."

Dakota walks through the doorway with his wife. He embraces Lucille with his one arm, and she's disheartened to see the void beneath his short sleeve. "I stopped by to see Nadie," he says, "and I get an added treat. I get to see you again. What a nice surprise." He introduces Lucille to his wife. In conversation, Lucille tells her that she is a professor at Columbia University.

"My daughter, Alyana, attends that school," Dakota's wife says. "She's planning on returning to Riverview after she graduates. I wonder if she knows what it will be like, living here. She left when she was a baby."

"I wouldn't be concerned she says, with a glint in her eye. "I think she knows."

───※───

Lucille has her suitcases packed and she's ready to leave for Harvest. Her father is having his annual tribute for Evelyn. Dan will be there, too; he has never missed a tribute. The children will be going to overnight camp at Racket Lake for the next month and he made sure they were packed and ready to go. Lucille thinks Dan is turning into a heck of a grandfather. The children adore him.

Whitefeather is setting out the dishes and placing them on the table. A friend for all these years," she thinks. Working here in Riverview brought her pain and pleasure. She remembers the old saying, "We'd never see the stars if it weren't for the darkness." She can't remember who said that, but she knows those are true words. Offering to help prepare breakfast, she is told by Tara to sit down, she is a guest. Watching Tara prepare breakfast, Lucille finds it strange that she has actually befriended this woman. Charlie would be aghast.

"Why are you watching me?" Tara asks.

"Knowing you and knowing *about* you are quite different."

"What you know *about* me is nothing like what I'm really like. Whitefeather thinks I'm a better person now, but the old Tara shows up from time to time." The telephone rings. Still holding the spatula in one hand, Tara lifts the receiver. "Hello? Who? Why are you calling me after all these years?" She fixes her hair with her hand, as if the person on the other end can see her. "Yes, it has been a long time. Oh, I see," she stammers. "How did you know you would find her here?" Tara laughs and hands the phone to Lucille. "He said to tell you that magnets attract."

Lucille takes the receiver. Her hands shake. "Where have you been, Nick? I've been worried."

Nick raises his voice so that his words echo through Tara's kitchen. "It doesn't matter where I've been; it's where I am going. And I'm going to marry you."

Lucille laughs. "I think we should take a little time to think about this."

"I'm almost half a century old and walking with a cane. Too much time has gone by already."

Lucille pauses to think. Why is she hesitating? Hasn't Nick been the one she always wanted? Since she's been here, she's seen Charlie at every turn. The image of the young man she met on her first day in Riverview, with red hair and freckles and wearing that yellow sweater, is still deeply embedded within her.

"Lucille? Lucille, are you still there?"

Nick is still unpredictable. Waking up to him in the morning and never knowing for certain if he'll come home to her at the end of the day, knowing he'll never think to give her an explanation for his whereabouts. Is this what she wants? "I...I'm not sure."

"What do you mean, you're not sure? Is this one of those 'I see my Daddy's face' deals? We belong together."

She remembers the feel of Charlie's arms around her, his desperate need for her when they made love, their long talks, and the children they had together. "It's too late for us, Nick."

"You sound like you mean that."

"I do." She puts the receiver back in its cradle and turns to Whitefeather, who has been listening to the conversation. Tara continues stirring the eggs, frying potatoes, and preparing toast as if she hasn't heard a thing. Extending his hand, Whitefeather rises from his seat at the kitchen table. Lucille allows him to lead her down a path at the back of the house, which meets a wooden bridge. They cross over it and sit beneath a willow tree, watching the water flow over the rocks. "Now tell me, tell me what causes you such anguish."

Perspiration trickles down her body. Her hands are clammy. She always thought the final good-bye would come from Nick. Realizing that she made the final decision astonishes her. She tells Whitefeather about Nick, and the story is long. Whitefeather's words cut through the jargon like a machete. "I don't know this man Nick, but I know my dearest friend Charlie. One lives among us, the other lives in another realm. Charlie will still be with you, watching over you as you live your life here on earth. The totem spider is bringing Nick back from the past. He is your future."

Lucille takes Charlie's picture from her pocketbook and looks at it. She brushes his face with her fingertips. Her heart feels heavy. She hears his voice as clearly as if he is right next to her. *Nick taught you how to love a man and I will always be grateful to him for that.*

They return to the house, where Tara has breakfast on the table. When they are finished eating, Whitefeather offers to drive Lucille to the train station. Lifting her suitcases, he takes them outside to his truck. A red car is car parked in front of the house.

"Need a ride, Princess?"

"Nick?"

He behaves as though they've seen each other as recently as last night; as though it hasn't been six months since she's seen his face. Lucille admits that this might be exactly what she loves about him.

"Just got into town a few hours ago. Visited our boy. I told him I'm marrying his mother. He said not to take no for an answer."

"And who makes the rules, Nick?"

Nick grins, showing the deep dimple in his left cheek. "I guess you do, Princess."

"Then yes. I say yes." Lucille runs into the house, turning around once to make sure that life is not playing a trick on her. She calls home and tells her children that she's getting married. Kimimela is giddy. She shouts with excitement.

"What about Dad?" Paco asks.

"He'll still be with us. We're just adding a mix of sunshine and a hurricane to our family."

"Well then, let that Speed King get back here. My car broke down again, and I have to get it fixed before prom."

⌒○

Bill is standing directly in front of Lucille when she steps off the train in Harvest, but she sees him searching for her in the crowd.

"Looking for someone?" she asks, and he finally spots her. He picks her up and twirls her around like he did when she was a child. When he walks her over to his new Dodge, she's surprised. "What happened to the truck?"

"Nothing but the best for my daughter's homecoming," he answers.

"I miss the truck."

"Tell you the truth, so do I."

Sitting next to Bill in his new car is comforting, and coming home with good news makes everything better. Lucille contemplates telling him about the upcoming wedding. After all, he ought to be the first to know. But before she has the chance, he stops the car in front of the animal hospital.

"Did you get a dog while I was away?" she asks.

"No, but I do have a surprise for you."

They enter the building, Bill pushing her along as though he can't wait to get her inside. After he talks to the receptionist, they wait a short while before the veterinarian joins them. Lucille looks at the young man with the wavy brown hair, and her hand automatically moves to her heart. *No it can't be,* she thinks.

'Skip Mosley, meet my daughter Lucille. A dear friend of your father's."

She sees Arnold in front of her. He's even wearing a white knee-length jacket over his dungarees, just like Arnold did when he helped Dr. Mutsfeld.

"Dr. Skip...I mean Dr. Mosley..." Oh, how she wants to call him Arnold!

"Just call me Skip. That's what most people in town call me."

You are where your father dreamed to be. "Your father would be so proud of you."

He laughs. "I hear that all the time. People think I went into this profession because of my Dad. It had nothing to do with him."

"Really?"

"Really. As a kid, I owned a German shepherd. I called him T-Bone. One day he ran out into the road and got hit by a car. Somehow he returned to the house, and hid under the porch. By the time I found him and got him to the Vet, his heart almost gave out. I wanted to save him so badly. But I was helpless. All my tears couldn't do a thing. But the Vet knew what to do. Weeks later, T-Bone was back to his old self. That incident planted the seed. From then on, I was determined to become a vet. My way of making it up to T-Bone. And you can be sure, every dog owner who comes into my office learns how to keep their pet safe."

"Skip, one day I'd like to introduce you to your father's best friend. They went to high school together. He can tell you a lot about your father."

"I think I've heard about him. He turned out to be a genius in his field."

"Who graduated from Harvest High and became a genius in his field? Harry? That's the only person I can think of offhand," Bill says.

On the way home, Bill fills her in on what he knows about Skip's mother. "Millie finally had the good sense to leave the murderer, Dr. Derik. Imagine, performing Dottie's abortion in the back room of the dry good store and then getting Millie and Skip to leave town with him. Millie came back to Harvest a few months later. I will say one thing for her; she worked her butt off getting that kid through college and veterinarian school. But Hutch still clings to his 'guardian angel' bull. Says some guardian angel kept sending money for his grandson's education.

Lucille realizes that although so many years have gone by, her father has stayed relatively the same. Yes, she is glad to be home. If Bill had changed too much, coming home just wouldn't be the same. She looks at him lovingly and throws her arm around his shoulder as he drives. He glances at her and smiles.

"So good to have you home, Lucille. Too bad your mother couldn't be around to see how nice you turned out. And wouldn't it have been nice if she could have known her grandchildren. Yup, life can't be perfect. We have to be grateful for what the Good Lord gives us."

BILL

Driving up to the house, Bill sees Dan sitting on the porch steps. He chuckles. "Just like old times, huh, Lucille? Look at him, happy to be back home. And this is his home, Lucille. Harvest is his home. Don't forget that." *Why did he have to move away*, Bill wonders? *He didn't just take himself away; he took all the good times, too. All the laughs, the tears, and the dreams. Drinking a beer was never the same when he couldn't share one with Dan.*

Dan rises from the step as soon as he sees the car and rushes over to greet Bill. The men wrap their arms around each other. "Let's go inside," says Bill.

Dan kisses Lucille on the cheek and tells her the children were just fine while she was away and they couldn't wait to leave for camp.

"I knew you'd never miss Evelyn's tribute," Bill says.

"Never. And besides, it gives me another chance to see you." Dan takes a deep breath. "Did it rain this afternoon? Can't buy perfume that smells this good."

That's a good sign. Seeing him all dressed up in his white silk shirt and gold cuff links caused Bill some worry. Perhaps Dan may have outgrown Harvest.

"I came here straight from the club. You'll have to lend me a pair of overalls and one of your old shirts. Don't feel comfortable dressed like this when I'm in Harvest. Paul said he'd run home and get me some clothes, but yours will fit me better. He's a little skinny since he got married."

"I know Pauline doesn't cook any more. She says she has better things to do. What a joke."

The screen door slams behind them and they head for Bill's bedroom. "What do you say we sneak down to the tavern tonight and have ourselves a few beers," Bill says, as he opens his closet door to search for a shirt and overalls for Dan.

"Sounds great. Is Beerkill still open?"

"Nah. Shut down a long time ago. I know a better place off the main road. Little place, hardly a soul knows it's there. We'll go right after the tribute for Evelyn."

"Count me in," Dan says, pulling off his pants and removing his shirt.

Bill looks at his friend's bare chest and says, joking, "Hey, you need more of a work out than playing the piano. Get'n a little flabby."

"Who are you call'n flabby? I can still take you on." He pushes Bill down on the bed, leans over him, and holds his arms above his head. He teases, "Get up if you can." The men pretend to struggle and laugh like they haven't laughed since they were kids.

"I miss you, Dan," Bill says. "I really miss you."

Rose takes them by surprise when she walks into the room. Dan releases Bill's arms and grabs the shirt. "Wonder what Rose was thinking," he says, after she leaves.

"Wouldn't enter her mind. She doesn't know about things like that."

"Nice looking cake Rose baked," Lucille says, motioning to the chocolate cake on the kitchen counter when Bill and Dan exit his bedroom.

"Hogwash. I baked it. It's a Betty Crocker mix. Jerry can't keep enough of them in stock. This was the last one on the shelf. Just open the box, pour the contents in a bowl, and stir in water, Crisco, and eggs. Bingo, it's ready for the oven. Pauline can't say women are over worked in the kitchen anymore. But she'll never be satisfied until a woman has her turn in the White House."

Pauline, sitting at the kitchen table, frowns. "Bill would be quite satisfied with you as our president, Lucille, but as for the rest of us women, he thinks we should walk around in aprons."

"I think you'd make a good president too, honey," Paul says, pulling a chair out next to her. He sits down and swings his arm around her shoulders. "But what would the women's movement do without you?"

Lucille laughs. "It's good to be home."

Bill makes a toast. "To my wonderful family. Let's raise our glasses to my daughter and my best friend, who came all the way from New York City to be here. Dan knows if anything ever happens to me, he is Lucille's guardian."

"I'm a grown woman," Lucille says. "Why do I need a guardian?"

"Because the years may pass, but you are always my little girl."

Good cheer hangs over his household, and Bill is so filled with happiness that he can't stop smiling. All the people he loves most are here, and because it's the night of Evelyn's tribute, that makes her almost here. Rose serves dinner, and soon the men are reaching for second servings of chicken and potatoes.

"Have a good flight, Dan?" Bill asks, scraping his dish.

"Nothing to it. I wasn't exactly Captain Odor or Milton Reynold trying to break Howard Hughes record on the around the world flight. Just a passenger, closing my eyes and praying for the best."

"Those two guys cut twelve hours and fifty-five minutes off the record set by Hughes. Some men are sticklers for speed."

Dan, puffing on his cigarette, says, "You know, that Nick Martin Jr. became a hot shot in the sky, too."

"Yeah, but he'll do anything for show."

It's time for Evelyn's memorial tribute. Rose exits the room as she always does at this event, but Pauline sticks around.

"Pauline, the husband of the deceased requests you to leave," Bill says firmly. "This tribute is for immediate family only."

Throwing her napkin down on the table, she leaves. Good thing he didn't marry someone like Pauline. That frown on her face would drive him crazy. Going to all those women's suffrage meetings sunk into her like ink into a blotter. But this is his house, and he has his rules.

Paul pulls three candles out of a drawer and hands one to Dan and another to Bill, keeping one for himself. Bill watches to see that everything is done in order. There can't be any changes from year to year, or the tradition will disappear. He remembers the first tribute for Evelyn and it gives him chills. Madeline showed up, then Nick Sr., and Lucille wasn't even there. After each candle is lit, the men stand very still, and

Lucille recites the poem she wrote when she was a teenager. Dan plays the song, "Always," on the piano, and they all sing along, ending the tribute with "Blue Skies."

Evelyn's picture is on a small table by the front door. He kisses her photograph. Unable to place it back into the drawer, he carries it into his bedroom. With no one watching, he is free to sob into his handkerchief. Why would the Good Lord take her away from him at such a young age? She should be at the table with her family.

Dan suggests that he and Bill take a walk into town to digest their food before having their dessert. Bill couldn't agree more. They trek down the gravel road until they arrive at the new restaurant in town. Bill points to the fancy sign hanging out front and explains that the restaurant's main attractions is their five course meals and live music. "They'd hire you in a minute. Want to go in and talk to the owner?" When Dan doesn't answer, he asks, "Have a woman in New York?"

"A woman? Heck no. And I haven't ruled out coming back."

"Ever think of coming back and the three of us becoming farmers again?"

"With all the new equipment, it would be a lot safer," Dan says. "Last time my tractor tipped, I thought I'd never play the piano again. But I don't know if I want to spend my time on a tractor anymore."

"I've been toying with the idea of getting back into it. It's the only thing I know, really."

"What about the volunteer work you're doing to help the blind veterans?"

"I'd never give that up."

They cut through the field and start heading back towards the house. When they come to a log jutting into their path, they stop and Dan plops down on it, stretching his feet out in front of him. Bill sits by his side plucking on the grass. The air is still, and in the serenity of the woods, his voice resonates with sweetness. "Dan, ever wonder why we stayed so close?"

"I know why I have. You saved my life at the river. And then we made that vow. 'Friends forever.' I'll never forget that." Putting his arm around his friend, Dan says, "It's you, me, and Paul. New people come into our lives, but it's always the three of us."

"I appreciate you saying that, Dan."

"And you, why have you stuck so close?"

"Because I never met anyone I could trust the way I trust you."

Dan looks away. "Where has the time gone?"

Seeing a glimpse of sorrow in his friend's eyes, Bill playfully tackles him and throws him to the ground. Then he runs behind a tree. "Try to find me," he yells. Dan never liked that game, because losing Bill even for a moment scared him. But they're grown men now, and just having fun. Bill stays hidden for a few minutes. Finally Dan, on the verge of panic, says in a trembling voice, "Bill, where are you? It's getting dark. We have to get back."

"Just went to take a piss," Bill says, emerging from behind the trees, still pulling up his zipper. "Don't tell me you're still afraid of losing me?"

"But it's getting dark."

"Are you still afraid of the dark? You're kidding me. Even I outgrew my asthma." Throwing his arm around Dan, they walk back to the house.

"My, this *is* a real party," Bill says, when he sees the table set with dessert dishes, coffee cups, and the chocolate cake set in the center. Clanking a spoon against his glass, he says, "You're on, Lucille. You said you were going to make an announcement. But remember, he has to pass my inspection first."

"How did you know, Daddy?"

"You look smitten. A father knows things like that."

"Tell us, Lucille," Rose says, "tell us who he is."

"Oh, you all know him. He's so special, always has been. And we're going to get married."

Bill sits with his hands clasped on the table and looks into his daughter's face. "Enough suspense, tell us who the gentleman is!"

Rose suggests they make a game of it. "Lucille, give us a hint and we'll take turns guessing."

"I'll play along. Let me see," she says, squinting and scrunching up her face. "He's a great patriot."

"Not the President of the United States, he's already married," Rose says.

Lucille giggles. "He's very smart."

"Did Harry leave his wife to marry you?" Paul asks.

"I only wish," Bill says. "I think he's one of the professors you teach with at the university."

"Daddy, I'll give you another hint. The man I'm going to marry is from Harvest. He used to live here."

"It's my turn," Dan says. "From Harvest. Let me see. Could it be one of your old classmates, like Tommy Brown? He went on to be a big shot surgeon in New York."

"Stop all this nonsense," Pauline says. "It's Nick Martin Jr."

"You win," Lucille says. "Teachers always know the correct answers. You get the first piece of Daddy's Betty Crocker cake."

The women clap, Paul whistles, and Dan blows her a kiss from across the table. Rose moves the dessert dishes and stacks them in front of her husband. "Cut the cake, Bill, and pass the dishes around. The first one goes to Pauline."

"Yes," Pauline says. "I guessed right because Nick is a good match for Lucille's intelligence. He used to sit in my classroom and design engines and spacecrafts. He couldn't care less about poetry, but I knew with his mind, he would accomplish great things. He left some of his sketches behind, and I marveled at all he knew. And now we're reading about him in newspapers. I'm proud to say I was his teacher."

Bill doesn't say anything. His face turns white.

"Daddy, are you happy for me?"

He'd prepared for this, for if the time ever came, he would be ready. He'd memorized the words he would say. When Lucille married Charlie, he thanked the Lord that he would never have to say them. But suddenly he's not prepared at all.

"Well, Daddy?"

"Lucille, you cannot marry Nick."

Lucille looks at him. "What are you saying?"

"You heard me."

"Nick and I *are* getting married. And soon."

Pauline shakes her head. "Do women still need their father's approval before they get married?"

Bill ignores Pauline. "You cannot marry Nick. That is final."

Rose stands, accidently spilling her glass of water. No one moves to help her wipe the puddle that has formed on the floor. With unexpected aggressiveness, she says, "Bill, don't interfere in Lucille's life."

"Daddy, I'm not a child any more. I have grown children of my own. You can't tell me who to marry."

Bill stands and clears his throat. He holds onto the edge of the table. His face isn't just drained of color; it is as white as the freshly painted kitchen wall. "Listen closely to what I have to say. You see, when your mother died, people said I took care of you like I was both your mother and your father. But I was neither."

Paul and Pauline drop their forks in unison.

"You're overly excited, Bill," Rose says. "Just wish Lucille well."

Bill waves his hand, dismissing her words. "Please, be quiet. I guess I'll just come out with it. Lucille's father and Nick's father are the same person."

The room is so silent that Bill can hear the frosting on the chocolate cake drip onto the dish beneath it. Pauline turns to Paul, and he shrugs his shoulders. Rose moves toward Lucille and places a cold cloth on the back of her neck. She stares at Bill as if he has gone mad. Dan pulls out a cigarette.

'Daddy, are you okay? You're talking crazy."

"I know this is a blow to you. I never wanted to tell you. Never thought I had to. Lucille, I could not give your mother a child. Do you understand me? The doctor told me that. So you are probably wondering how you got here. When your mother was alive, I traveled out of town a lot, to farm meetings. But I always left Dan to look after her. The winter before you were born, I went away during a terrible snowstorm. I almost canceled my trip, but I didn't. When I came back, I went shopping over at Jerry's and he told me something that irritated me at first."

Rubbing his temples, his shoulders slumped, he continues. "The storm hit Harvest hard. Jerry rode around delivering food to some of the folks for several days. That's how he came to see Nick Martin Sr.'s car in front of our house. A bright red car, just like Nick Jr.'s. So bright, you couldn't miss it. Anyway, the attorney always had a thing for your mother, so it didn't take me by surprise. She was attracted to him, too, like all the women. At church dances I'd catch them looking at each other.

"A few months after the storm, your mother started showing that little bump, and I knew. I knew the man responsible for that. Evelyn glowed with happiness, that's all I cared about. Marrying Nick Jr. would be...I forget the name for it...incest, or something or other. It wouldn't be right. It would be a sin in God's eyes." He shakes his head and closes his eyes. He said what he had to say. "Now you know why I tried to keep the two of you away from each other all these years. You would be marrying your...I can't even say it."

"No, Daddy, it's not a sin," Lucille says. "I am not Mr. Martin's daughter. Why do you believe everything Jerry says? Why don't you think for yourself? His store is not a place to shop. It's a place to drink from the cup that poisons. It turns people against each other. Dan, tell him it's not true. Dan, tell him."

Bill rubs his lower back. He looks up, but he can't look anyone in the eye. "Dan, you know. Tell Lucille I couldn't have children."

Dan, standing close to Bill now, attempts to light his cigarette, but his hand shakes and he shoves it back in the pack. "Guess this is confession day. Only there is one truth here. I am Lucille's father."

"This isn't a time for jokes," Bill says, waving his hand, as if to wipe away Dan's words.

"I'm not joking," Dan says. "Look at the shape of Lucille's lips, look at her curly blonde hair, her long tapered fingers. Look at me."

Bill examines Dan's face. He's never studied his friend's lips, hair, and fingers before. Whenever he looked at him in the past, he just saw his good friend.

"You are looking at Lucille's Daddy," Dan says, emphasizing each word.

Bill takes out a cigarette, lights it, and takes a long drag. "I don't understand what you're saying."

"You must understand, Bill. You've been living with a story Jerry concocted," Dan says.

"Concocted? But the red car. Jerry saw it."

"I had a red truck at that time. Jerry couldn't tell a car from a truck with all that snow coming down. Bill, I thought I was doing the right thing."

The women drop back, sinking into the shadows. Paul stares at his brother. Lucille, sweating profusely, reaches for a glass of water. Bill lumbers toward the door, moving as though his legs are shackled with weights. His new blue striped shirt that he bought especially for Lucille's homecoming hangs rumpled, like a used hankie on the bones of a tired man. His body bends forward. He stumbles toward the porch, and then he stops. He leans against the wall.

"Doing the right thing, Dan? You thought you were doing the right thing? Good friend Dan, were you doing the right thing when you were again going to give Evelyn what I couldn't? I knew she wanted to have another child when Lucille talked about going off to college. She thought she would be lonely with her daughter away. You hungered for my wife and took advantage of the situation. Should I forgive you for not knowing Evelyn's body was too fragile, and could not withstand another childbirth? You killed Evelyn."

Dan's head falls to the table. "No," he screams.

"Dan," Lucille says, "tell him what you told me. He'll understand. Best friends understand. Daddy, go to the tavern with Dan. Go together like the good friends you are, and let him explain."

Bill continues out the door. Dan starts to follow him out.

"No," Rose says. "Let him be."

Bill shuffles toward the road. He drops his harmonica. Dan runs out after him, yelling after Bill to stop.

Bill continues to trudge forward. With the inveterate gesture of a farmer, he studies the sky. "Looks like a storm brewing," he says, to no one in particular. "Better get the cattle into the barn." A grain truck lurches from behind the hill. Bill hears the screech of the wheels before he feels the impact of the truck. His panoramic view of the world sifts through a kaleidoscope of corn, rye, and oats. From where he lies ravaged under its weight, Bill sees the driver jump from his truck, his face ashen. Blood from a gash on his forehead dribbles down his face. He dabs at it with one hand and wipes the cut with his shirtsleeve.

"I tried to stop, honest. I was on my way to the market. A truck full of vegetables. Just kissed my wife and baby son goodbye. They were waving to me when I drove off. Now this," he babbles, as if his words could change things.

$\mathcal{D}$ A N

For days, Dan stares aimlessly at the dull green hospital walls. He loses the slight potbelly he acquired from too many rich meals at the club. His blonde hair turns white. "Sink or swim, friends forever," he mumbles, again and again. He stays at the hospital long after visiting hours. All of Lucille's coaxing can't persuade him to leave. It's only when Andrew arrives that he is finally convinced that he is in need of a good night's sleep.

After a fitful night of tossing and turning, he makes it into the kitchen holding onto Andrew. Groggy and with swollen eyes, he sits down in a chair and drops his head onto the table. Can it really be that Bill, his very best friend, is lying in intensive care at the hospital? Worse yet, can it be his fault?

Lucille, distraught herself, places a cup of coffee in front of him. She reaches for a bowl in the cupboard, fills it with cold water, and urges Dan to wash his face. "Pull yourself together, Dan. Go see Bill and tell him the truth."

The hospital is quiet this time of morning, and Dan and Andrew receive permission to visit the intensive care unit. "Only five minutes," the nurse on duty says.

Once again seeing Bill's head wound in bandages and his neck secured in a brace, Dan sobs into a handkerchief. Just a few days ago, they were walking through town together and returning home with their arms around each other. Now he prays for his friend's life. He stands at his bedside, unable to say anything. Andrew nudges him. "Tell him, Dan."

"Can you hear me, Bill?" When he receives no response, he turns to Andrew.

"Go on, Dan."

"That day at the river we made a pledge. 'Sink or swim, friends forever.' I believed those words then and I believe them now. I didn't want you to lose Evelyn. She said you both wanted a baby, and I could help with that. I had a hard time doing what she asked me to do. I didn't love her the way you do. That wasn't possible. I live with Andrew now. He's here with me."

Taking Andrew's hand, he places it on Bill's. "Can you feel his hand? Remember when we went hunting and the sheriff found us with our arms around each other, trying to keep warm? He said we looked like two queers. People can call me what they want, but I too am God's child. He just made me different from other men. All these years, I tried to hide that part of me. That's why I jumped into the rapids: to show you I was brave. But I'm not brave. The dark scared me. It still does. Only you and Paul know that. And this, this is too dark for me. I can't see my way without you. You saved me from the rapids. It's like the rapids pulling me again. Without your help, I won't make it." Andrew rubs Dan's shoulders to relieve some of his tension, and Dan continues. "Lucille *is* your daughter. I made her for you and Evelyn. And now I want to tell you something.

"When Evelyn became pregnant again, *you* made that possible. I told Evelyn I couldn't go through with that again. Once was enough. The medicine the doctor gave you worked. Evelyn was pregnant with your baby. I'm so sorry you lost them both." The nurse wraps a curtain around Bill's bed. Dan has only a few more minutes. "Bill, me losing you is like you losing Evelyn. No one ever took her place. No one will ever take yours. Andrew knows that. Before you meet the good Lord, tell me you understand."

Bill's body remains motionless.

Dan falls to his knees. His head drops on the bed. He slowly lifts his head and leans toward Bill. Then he hears something.

My best friend Dan. Since that day at the river we were always there for each other. Lucille is our daughter, yours and mine. And Dan, you could never kill anybody. I said that because anger got the best of me. Take care of Lucille. And Dan, I love you, too.

"Andrew, did you hear what Bill said?"

"I, uh...I guess I did. I heard whatever you heard."

At the funeral home, one day later, Dan stands close to the casket. "What's the date, Paul?"

"Doesn't matter, we'll do Bill's memorial tribute on June 26, combine it with Evelyn's. That's what Bill would want."

"This accident opened my eyes to a few things. I'm ready to come back to Harvest for good. Andrew says this town needs an art gallery."

"Problem is, Harvest isn't ready for either one of you."

LUCILLE

Mourners crowd the small wooden church in Harvest. Lucille is seated in the front row with her children and Rose and Dan. Rose weeps, as though she is unaware that her husband always considered Evelyn his one and only wife. Pauline sits upright, her eyes searching the room. She would have made Bill proud, the way she handled things. She called the ambulance and made the funeral arrangements. She spent hours with the Reverend, talking about the Bill she knew. Everyone else succumbed to grief, even Lucille.

Jerry and Lily are among the first of Bill's friends to arrive. "Just can't imagine going into my store and not having Bill drop in," Lucille overhears Jerry say. "He called me his personal newspaper. I'm closing down the store for the remainder of the week. Left a sign in the window, *death in the family*. That's just how it feels."

Hutch, Brenda, Millie, and Skip follow close behind. "Like they say, accidents usually happen close to home. Just not like Bill to cross the road without looking out for trucks. Reminds me of my Arnold," Hutch says. "Never knew how that accident could have happened either."

Lucille remembers the young children who sat in the circle of chairs at the Little River Indian Residential School after Whitefeather's little sister died, trying to make sense of a senseless death. She remembers the death of her mother, and how as a young teen, she ran to find solace under the weeping willow, asking the Lord *why?* She thinks of Charlie. How ironic that Bill would still be alive today if Charlie were. The organ music begins, and Lucille hears muffled sniffling and sobbing from behind her. After the prayers, Dan walks to the front of the church to eulogize his friend.

"We will always remember Bill," he begins. "He is the story of a small town—the touch, the sound, the face of Harvest. His farm, his friends, and his family were the nucleus of his life, the small town chitchat his truths. He trusted that chitchat, but never got around to hearing the real thing. But I loved him, and will always love him. My best buddy is gone, and I am blessed to have known him. He saved my life when I was twelve years old, and at the end, when it comes right down to it, I couldn't save his."

But only Lucille hears his words. He is too grief-stricken to speak into the microphone.

Except for Rose, who rides in the hearse with her deceased husband, Bill's friends, family, and relatives form a procession and walk the quarter mile down the newly paved road to the burial site.

Just before the burial service begins, Lucille sees Nick approaching from the parking lot. He made it just in time. He stops to talk to Harry. The antagonism the two men harbored for each other flashes through Lucille's mind. Tragedy finally brought them together. Dan, leaning on Andrew's shoulder, causes a chain reaction in the crowd: Mr. Olson nudges his wife, the former Anita Martin, who in turn taps Brenda on the arm. Brenda opens her mouth in a huge O and then whispers to Hutch before going on to nudge Lily. Lily then points her finger not so discretely in Dan's direction. She didn't have to nudge her husband. Jerry already knew.

Hutch doesn't concern himself with any of that. His eyes remain fixed on the man gliding through the crowd in a glow of light, his black ponytail swinging down his back. The woman he is with shows her bright white teeth when she speaks, and her shiny black hair fans out in the breeze. Lucille hears him tell Brenda that he thinks that must be Charlie Rosen's friend, Whitefeather, "the one who taught me how to live again."

"I thought Charlie did that?"

"No, Charlie was the messenger," Hutch says.

After the final prayers, people Lucille has never met before greet her and shake her hand. Many farmers traveled great distances to show their respect. When her father went to the agricultural meetings out of town, he wasn't known as Bill, but Mr. Kramer. They learned from the expert, they say, and they are here to show their gratitude.

A woman, nervously tucking gray strands of hair behind her white cap, approaches Lucille. With everyone in black attire, this woman dressed in white stands out like the moon against a black sky. It isn't until Lucille hears her say, "I'm sorry the man we loved is gone," that she recognizes her as Madeline.

"Can't blame you for not recognizing me," Madeline says to Lucille. "Probably should have changed out of my nurse's uniform before coming here." Madeline's fingers linger on the raised scars on her face, and she wipes her watery eyes. "This is what I look like after three operations. If it weren't for the Madeline Fund you set up for me, I'd be dead. And I'm sorry for how I treated you. I sure had my head messed up in those years. I remember the poem you wrote for your mother. I couldn't imagine having a daughter who could write a poem like that about me. And Lucille..." Madeline looks around to see if anyone is listening. "Bill talked in his sleep, you know. He used to shout something all the time about Nick Martin Sr. being your. . ."

Lucille stops her mid-sentence. "Thank you, Madeline. Erase that from your memory. He uttered nonsense. As a nurse, you probably know that people often mumble nonsense in their sleep."

"Of course," she says. "Being a nurse, I see and hear lots of things, and I just keep it to myself. I never mentioned before what I heard Bill say, and I never will again."

Lucille knows that the woman had a reputation for many things, but spreading gossip isn't among them.

"Bill must have been born under a lucky star," she hears. Lucille turns her head and sees Nick Martin Sr. "He had a wife he adored, and Evelyn adored him." She watches him inch over to Rose's side and take her hand. "Don't worry about this woman," he says, to anyone in earshot. "I'll make sure she gets home safely."

Paul and Dan, standing close by, roll their eyes, and then walk toward Paul's truck.

$\mathcal{D}$ AN

"Take me down to that river," Andrew says. "I want to see the place where Bill saved your life, and it might do you good to see it again."

The two brothers and Andrew wedge into the front seat of the Hillsdale truck, which now belongs to Paul, ready to take a journey into the past. They drive by what was once Izzy's house. Pneumonia and old age got to him, but not before he found a home for that old Tin Lizzy at the Harvest Historical Museum. Dan searches on the way for the little store that sold beach balls, beach hats, and lotions, but it's gone. As kids, they spent time there reading the postcards with the funny sayings, doubling over in laughter at the ones that showed an outhouse with the words, "The Pause that Refreshes."

Approaching the river, Dan looks around for the boardwalk and the steps leading down to the water. Not a trace of it ever being there remains, or of the warning sign. Paul parks and Dan climbs out of the truck first. He loosens his tie and beckons for Paul and Andrew to follow him. Together, they jump over the huge rocks lining the river to get to the bottom. When Dan sees the clump of trees off to the side, he scans the area for the rock where they made their pledge of friendship.

"Found it," Paul says, pointing.

"No, that's not it. The *big* rock, the one the three of us stood on," Dan says, with indignation.

"This is the rock," Paul insists. "Don't you remember? It still has the moss growing over it."

"But that rock reached up beyond my waist. I remember."

"Dan, get up here," Paul orders, climbing to the top of the rock. "What's the matter with you? We were smaller then."

Andrew leans against a tree and watches.

The rock is hardly wide enough for the two of them. Dan is still not convinced. He feels silly. What must Andrew be thinking? He remembers back to that hot summer day when Bill saved him from the rapids. They stood on a *big* rock. "This is not the rock," he says, emphatically. Then he hears rumbling in the sky. "I hear thunder."

"Yup, it's thunder alright," Paul says.

The rain pours down in large drops at first, and then a torrent of rain crashes down upon them. "I hear a voice," says Dan. "It's Bill. Do you hear him?"

"Hard to hear in this pouring rain."

Dan's face grows somber. "He says it's time for a new member in our men's club. Andrew, you're one of us now."

"You mean, I take Bill's place?" asks Andrew.

"That's the way Bill would want it."

Lucille

Parked in the empty field adjacent to the river, Hal exits the car. "Think I'll leave you two alone," he says.

Lucille rolls down the window to catch the breeze coming off the water. Watching the men jump over the rocks, she is reminded of her father's death. She puts her head on Nick's shoulder and weeps. He smoothes her hair with his palm and kisses her. She wants him to hold her this way forever and never let go. They sit with their arms around each other until she says, "Let's talk about the wedding. A small wedding would be nice, don't you think?"

Nick is silent. Cars speed down the road beside them. She thinks that perhaps he didn't hear her. "Nick, what do you think of having a small wedding?"

"I think the cars are making too much noise. That's what I think."

She remembers when he liked hearing the sound of screeching tires.

"Don't know why they drive so damn fast. No wonder there are so many accidents on this road."

She detects a crack in his veneer. *Of course, he longs to be behind the wheel again.* She moves closer to him. "Forget the cars. Let's talk about us."

"Not now."

"Okay, then later."

"I won't be here later. I'm leaving town tonight."

"Now I think I'm having trouble hearing. Did you say you're leaving tonight?"

"That's what I said."

He seemed preoccupied at the funeral; cemeteries sometimes have strange effects on people. But now he seems to be distancing himself from her. "No explanation, you are just leaving?"

"No explanation."

"I don't like being shut out of your life like this."

"This is how it has to be for now."

"It's always for now, and look how many years have gone by." She pulls on the door handle and leaves the car.

He calls after her, but she continues walking. She walks past the old run down diner on the corner, and she crosses over the busy road to a parade of honking horns. A man yells from his car window, "Get off the road, lady. You wanna get killed?"

Right now, the answer might be yes. She walks until she sees Izzy's old house. She walks behind the fence and sits down on the ground. She's at her wits end. She is angry with herself for allowing Nick to hurt her again.

Maybe her first reaction was the correct one. When he contacted her at Whitefeather's house, she turned him down. Yes, way down deep she always knew marrying Nick was never possible. With so many women adoring him, why would he want to settle down?

She remembers Bill saying that in life we must be grateful for what the good Lord gives us. She still has her work, her children and her friends. She'll pick herself up, dust herself off, put one foot in front of the other and move on.

But she's not ready to move on. Her heart aches too much. She turns over on her stomach and dozes off. When she awakens, she stands and looks around the property and remembers Izzy with the Tin Lizzy. He was grateful for what he had. His car was everything to him, and when he drove it, he smiled and waved and kept on driving. She continues her walk home.

NICK

Driving in a cab to the Ryan Airport, thirty miles outside of Harvest, is alien to Nick. For years he has depended on Hal. But for him, this is the way it must be. He has one last job to tackle in New York. It is for the C.I A., and it has to be done in the wee hours of the night. This is one adventure that Hal knows nothing about. A man who will introduce himself as John will meet Nick at the airport, and the Colonel will be waiting for them when they land in New York City. The job should only take a few hours, and then he'll meet Harry at the hospital for the eye operation.

After his accident, the loss of his eyesight gained lots of attention. When Harry got wind of it, he tracked him down. Not long afterwards, the two men met in his prestigious office on Madison Avenue. After determining that he was a good candidate for cornea implants, all Harry needed was a donor. As one of the top eye surgeons in the country, Harry had already performed nearly ten of those operations. "In years to come," he said, "this operation won't be a big deal at all."

Thinking back to his high school years, Nick acknowledges that his behavior toward his classmate was abysmal, but he did make it up to him in the only way he knew. Harry struggled to pay for his schooling, while he, Nick Martin Jr., churned out big money. So Nick left a box stuffed with hundred dollar bills at his doorstep at his shabby New York apartment. He included a note with only one line, and it read: "Yes Sir, She's my Baby." Nick knew that Harry would never forget that that was the song he and Lucille danced to at Sheila's party when Harry drained the whisky bottle and stormed out of the house. He knew Harry didn't want to be reminded of that night, but heck, he didn't want him thinking Nick Martin Jr. had a magnanimous heart, either.

Dan got the ball rolling on his eye operation. He'd found Bill's eye bank pledge card on the kitchen floor the night Bill died. As soon as he sent it over to the hospital, the eye bank was notified, and Harry received the news.

"See you at the hospital at six o'clock tomorrow morning," Harry said at the funeral. "We just got our donor."

Nick couldn't tell Lucille about the operation. He didn't want to get her hopes up in case the operation failed. She would be disappointed to her core. He'd rather let her be mad at him. She'd been mad at him before.

"Traffic's heavy," the cab driver says. "See that guy? What the heck is he doing? He looks like he's coming straight at us. Why doesn't he stay in his own lane?"

Nick doesn't know what's going on. As a driver, Hal would never put him under this much stress. He'd just move along like he was driving a country road with no one on it but him. With the cabby unnerving him, Nick has a strong urge to take the wheel. Some nights he dreams he's driving again and awakens with his fingers bent and beads of sweat running down his face.

Thinking of Bill as an eye bank cardholder, he can't help but chuckle. *I promise him one thing,* Nick thinks. *If his eyes end up in my head, he's in for one hell of a ride.*

LUCILLE

Throwing off her shoes, Lucille goes directly to the bedroom to shower. She scrubs each part of her body with care, as if she can wash off the losses of the day. Opening the window to allow some fresh air in, she sees Hal sitting behind the wheel of Nick's car. The passenger seat is vacant. She calls to him and he jumps out as if he were waiting for the invitation.

Sitting at the kitchen table, Hal's cherub look is replaced with one much more serious.

"Why are you here?" Lucille asks him.

"Because I'm lonely, same as you. Nick left town without me, without an explanation. This has never happened before."

"It's happened to me more times than I can count. Fortunately, I always found a way to keep myself busy. Isn't there some part of your life that doesn't include Nick?"

"We've been a team since the day we crashed into each other in a parking lot." He smiles now, and the cherub look seeps back into his face. "We were both backing out of a parking space, and wham! We slammed right into each other. We blamed each other but settled the dispute by flipping a coin. I lost. I thought for sure he'd make a fuss, because his beautiful red car had a dent in it. I told him I knew a place to get it fixed cheap, but he said he always did his own work. We started talking cars and before we knew it, we were having dinner at the diner. The only money I had happened to be the coin I flipped, so Nick picked up the bill. He's been paying my way ever since. For most people, that friendship would never have started."

"Friendship is one thing. Why do you jump at his every whim?"

Hal gets up from his seat and paces the kitchen floor. For the first time, she notices his slight limp. "What are you thinking, that Nick has taken advantage of me?" He rolls up his pants and shows her his prosthesis. "I lost my leg in the war. Nick wanted something better than the prosthesis they gave me at the veteran's hospital, and so he had one customized for me by a world famous doctor. I have a high school diploma, too. The boss studied with me until I passed all my exams. I could talk all day, telling you things about Nick."

"Hal, he's full of himself. He doesn't know when to stop. An airplane exhibition cost him his eyesight."

Hal's eyes draw down at the corners. "Is that what you heard? Nick never did like being thought of as a hero, but I can tell you the real story. After his capture, he escaped by luring a woman guard into his cell."

"I didn't know he was captured. He never told me. Actually, he hasn't told me much."

"He was captured alright. He ended up wearing a German woman guard's uniform and making a getaway. He was with one of his crew, a guy named Cal, but they separated. Nick scrounged around in the woods for weeks. He was so desperate, he ate weeds and insects and drank water from dirty swamps. On a day when his spirits were the lowest, he found himself standing in front of a farmhouse watching a young girl eat a sandwich. When she saw him, she threw her food away and ran into the house. He was so hungry that he grabbed the sandwich from the garbage and gobbled it up. The house was a hideaway for the Gestapo. They saw him and dragged him into the house. Beating him wasn't enough. They turned the dogs loose."

Lucille gasps. "Oh, Hal, I can't listen to this."

Now Hal swears under his breath. "Lucky for him, the allies started bombing the area and the bastards ran for cover. The next thing Nick remembers is someone telling him the wonderful words: 'You're in an American hospital.' But Nick couldn't see. After his discharge, he worried more about my leg than his eyes. But I've said enough." He hands Lucille a white envelope. "I had a hard time helping Nick with his little project, but he wanted me to come over and give this to you."

Under the Red Ribbon

After Hal drives away, Lucille lies down on her bed. The story he told has left her remorseful. All these years Nick has stood by him, and she always thought it was the other way around. Or, maybe they stood by each other, like good friends do. Nick never stayed around long enough for her to peer under his slick exterior, but Hal pierced that exterior a long time ago. He didn't need a PhD to do it, either.

⁓∂

For a month, Lucille stays in Harvest, helping Rose get her papers in order. Her children were eager to go home, so she decided to let them leave with Dan. He said he'd stay at the house with them until she returned home. A bird chirping outside her window reminds her of life outside the house. She sees a deer nibbling on the lilies and the rabbits scurrying through the shrubs. She decides that a walk will do her good. She remembers the envelope Hal gave her, and she brings it with her when she leaves the house.

Taking the back road, still unpaved and unaltered, she walks beneath the full-leaved trees that form a canopy over the road. She smells the subtle fragrance of the wild roses. It brings back memories of the young, studious, and very innocent Lucille Kramer. She makes her way across the woods and finds the pathway leading to the creek. Finding a circle of shade under a tree, she sits down on the ground and leans her back against the trunk. She tears the envelope open. She pulls out a sheet of paper with lines on it, the kind students use in school. On top of the page, she sees three words written in pencil: *Girls to Marry*. Women's names reach down to the bottom line, each one crossed out, except for one. Her name has two stars next to it. She is engrossed in thought about the ebb and flow of their relationship. She understands that sometimes it's best to give up someone you love. She closes her eyes, remembering, and is distracted by a noise coming from behind her. She turns and sees a red car parked behind the tree.

"I had to come all the way to the creek to find you," she hears Nick say.

Startled by his presence and still dazzled by his beautiful blue eyes and his silken voice, Lucille feels the magnetic pull that draws her to him. It won't be easy giving up the wonder of Nick Martin Jr.

"Nick, I don't want you to change. Be who you are. Cross my name off your list. You will be happier without me."

"Have you lost your mind? Catch." He throws a set of keys on a chain into the palm of her hand.

"Keys? You've given me diamonds, furs, and the loveliest poem, but never keys."

"That gold key is for the new house I bought for us, so your son and I can tinker in the garage. The smaller one there is for the car. From now on, you're in the driver's seat." He picks her up, spins her around, and carries her behind the tree where he places her on the leather seat of his new red car.

"You mean Hal is out of a job?" Lucille asks.

"You must have told him something when he came over to see you, something to cause him to run off and get married." He's smiling and the dimple in his left cheek appears deeper than ever.

When she starts the car, she is delighted by the sound of the revving motor. Driving along the unpaved back road, she honks the horn as they pass the farmhouses and waves to the men working in the fields.

"Hold it now, you're going too fast," Nick says, with a grin.

She looks over at him and giggles like a young girl. And then she notices that he doesn't have his cane. She was so excited to see him again, she didn't notice before. She stops the car, throws her arms around him, and screams, "Oh, Nick you can see."

"And what I see is our wonderful life together."

She starts the car again, but slows down to chat with two children playing on tire swings, and to wink at their fathers.

"Lucille, I hope you didn't pick up my bad habits. We're getting married. None of that winking."

Passing Scoops, Lucille remembers the day her father threw an ice cream cone at Nick's father, and the ice cream got all over the attorney's pinstripe. "I wish Daddy could see us now."

"I'm certain he can," Nick says, with a wink.

They travel down the country road, the past following closely behind. With one hand securely on the wheel and the other holding Nick's, Lucille presses down on the gas pedal, and they move forward.

Made in the USA
Lexington, KY
23 October 2014